CLOUD GAMING

by Mark Fouty

Cover Illustration by Christine Fouty

Inspired by many experiences, places, people, and above all, a great family

ISBN: 9781520441788

TABLE OF CONTENTS

PROLOGUE 1

CHAPTER 1 4

CHAPTER 2 13

CHAPTER 3 19

CHAPTER 4 25

CHAPTER 5 29

CHAPTER 6 35

CHAPTER 7 37

CHAPTER 8 41

CHAPTER 9 47

CHAPTER 10 50

CHAPTER 11 54

CHAPTER 12 57

CHAPTER 13 60

CHAPTER 14 64

CHAPTER 15 69

CHAPTER 16 75

CHAPTER 17 77

CHAPTER 18 82

CHAPTER 19 87

CHAPTER 20 92

CHAPTER 21 97

CHAPTER 22 101

CHAPTER 23 106

CHAPTER 24 111

CHAPTER 25 118

CHAPTER 26 121

CHAPTER 27 131

CHAPTER 28 137

CHAPTER 29 139

CHAPTER 30 143

CHAPTER 31 147

CHAPTER 32 150

CHAPTER 33 157

CHAPTER 34 165

CHAPTER 35 169

CHAPTER 36 174

CHAPTER 37 180

CHAPTER 38 184

CHAPTER 39 190

CHAPTER 40 192

CHAPTER 41 199

CHAPTER 42 203

CHAPTER 43 207

CHAPTER 44 212

CHAPTER 45 216

CHAPTER 46 220

CHAPTER 47 224

CHAPTER 48 230

CHAPTER 49 236

CHAPTER 50 241

CHAPTER 51 252

CHAPTER 52 256

CHAPTER 53 259

CHAPTER 54 265

CHAPTER 55 270

CHAPTER 56 275

CHAPTER 57 281

CHAPTER 58 287

CHAPTER 59 291

CHAPTER 60 296

CHAPTER 61 298

CHAPTER 62 300

CHAPTER 63 302

EPILOGUE..304

PROLOGUE

"Well, how about that. He did it."

Greg Galkin stared at the TV in his Georgetown brownstone as his boyhood chum, Billy Wilson, rang the opening bell at the New York Stock Exchange. Billy's start-up, Cloud Gaming Co., had been the darling of the venture community ever since it burst onto the scene with a high speed, cloud-based gaming system, and after a few short years of exponential growth, the company was going public.

Greg felt he should have been there, too. The two of them had been inseparable growing up in suburban Washington, DC, fooling around with computer games before they could even walk. Once they discovered their toys were run by computers, they spent hours dissecting them to make them run faster on the inside, rather than getting their thumbs to go faster on the outside, like all the other kids did. As they grew older, they realized their programming skills were remarkably complementary—Billy was great at writing simple, elegant code, Greg at building security within the code to prevent unwanted intruders from stealing it. Together they were going to build the "next, big thing."

But all that changed in an instant, when Billy's dad was crushed between a guard rail and the grille of a speeding, white, pick-up truck. Both boys' lives would never be the same, with Billy losing the man he idolized, and Greg ultimately losing his best and only real friend, Billy. Contributing to the nightmare was that Greg's father was behind the wheel, drunk to the point of unconsciousness. Why he was on that particular bridge over the Potomac River when it added 45 minutes to his commute was anybody's guess, but there was no disputing that Alexander Galkin was sitting in the driver's seat, slumped over in a drunken stupor.

However, none of that mattered to Billy's mom when her cell phone rang with the dreadful news. She had just pulled up to Greg's house, dropping him off after a sleepover where the two boys had finished a spirited night of video games. They had been chattering away on how to amp up the processing speed by tweaking this thing or that, and while none of their computer jargon ever made sense to her, she was just thankful they had each other: two extraordinarily gifted—but idiosyncratic—boys that shared a passion for computers. As she listened to the caller, she knew that was about to change.

Billy immediately sensed something was wrong. "What's up mom?"

"There's been an accident..." was all Billy heard, fearing the worst, but believing that somehow the outcome would be different if he managed to shut it all out. At that moment, neither boy could have imagined they might never see each other again, but watching Billy ring the bell to commence trading in CGC stock was the first time in ten years that Greg had actually seen the friend he used to call "3".

"Damn, he actually did it," he muttered, "...without me."

#

CIA headquarters, some months earlier

Jeremy Thomas was only six-months into his career at the CIA, but was already an integral part of the Russian and European team because of his computer science expertise. As sharp as he was, though, he was still low man on the totem pole when it came to hours. That usually meant graveyard, and tonight was no exception. The only good thing was that the midnight-9am, Langley-time shift corresponded to mid-day in Russia, so if anything was going on, he got a first-hand look at the satellite images as they were happening. His team had plenty of eyes on the volatile Ukrainian region, so Jeremy spent his time focusing on the rest of the country. It was usually pretty boring, but at least he had access to the best high-tech equipment money could buy, and for a gearhead like him, it was about as good as it got.

"What the—" Jeremy's voice trailed off, his eyes glued to the monitor focused on the northern Siberia region, where nothing usually ever happened. It showed significant electromagnetic activity, like a grid of cell phone towers going active. Not that odd for someplace like Moscow or New York, but no one lived in Siberia—at least by choice.

"Hey Chief, take a look at this!" Jeremy exclaimed while waving excitedly at the Siberian monitor, thinking he had stumbled on to something meaningful.

"Humph. Maybe the Russkies are giving their prisoners free Wi-Fi," Jeremy's boss snickered. "It's probably nothing, but keep an eye on it anyway. Hey, you want anything from the cafeteria?"

"A Diet Pepsi would be great, please."

2

"Hah, you kids are all the same—diet drinks and greasy pizza!" his boss bellowed as he walked out of the room.

"Wi-Fi for the prisoners, ha-ha, that's a good one," Jeremy mumbled under his breath, gratified that his superior had affirmed that he had found something worth noting. He looked at the monitor again, scratching his head. *Strange,* he thought.

CHAPTER 1

Billy Wilson turned to head out to his waiting limousine after ringing the opening bell and a series of obligatory pictures on the New York Stock Exchange floor. He lingered momentarily to watch the beehive of activity that was the trading floor of the world's greatest stock market. It was beautiful, really, as perfect an interface between man and machine as probably existed. Buyers and sellers were matched by market makers, sometimes humans jostling for position and screaming at the top of their lungs, but more often than not, computers. The human element was fascinating—almost humorous—but computers were what made it all go, systematically processing billions of bytes of information in the blink of an eye to determine the price of a stock, only to repeat the cycle in the next nanosecond.

If anyone understood the power of computers, it was William Walker Wilson, III, who couldn't remember a day when tinkering with the programs that ran them wasn't a part of his life. He had written and re-written millions of lines of code to get it just right—driving his programming team crazy—but in some ways, it had all culminated in today. As Billy watched the price of CGC tick higher, he had become the latest tech wizard from Seattle to crack the *Forbes 400* list of wealthiest people in the world.

"I did it Dad," he whispered to himself, looking upward in homage to the man who had given him his passion for simplifying how things worked on the inside. It was the genesis of the company's advertising tag line: "Simple. Fast. Strong." Billy missed him terribly.

"Time to go, Mr. Wilson." The voice of CGC's Marketing VP, Susan Green, snapped him out of his reverie. "We've got to get to Midtown for the *Tech Movers* interview."

He quickly turned, briskly striding out, leaving the entourage in his wake. He hated crowds like this, but unlike the typical computer geek, he towered over most everyone. It took people who had never met him by surprise, expecting a scrawny, bespectacled, ordinary-looking man and not the imposing, athletic figure that was Billy Wilson. Looking over the crowd, he saw his driver waiting curbside, holding the limousine's door open with one arm while keeping the hordes of cameras and gawkers at bay with the other.

"Well done, sir," his driver stated, "you were smashing." They exchanged a quick fist-bump as Billy ducked into the limo, his Marketing VP just ahead of him. The chauffeur deftly maneuvered his way through the crowd to the driver's side, got in and quickly pulled away from the curb.

"That wasn't so bad, was it?" Susan said, in a voice that had a slight, "I-told-you-so" ring to it.

"No, it wasn't," Billy retorted, "but I still hated it. And now we have to do this damn interview. I can't wait to get back on the plane and head home."

As the car navigated its way through lower Manhattan, Billy's phone buzzed.

"Perry Mason calls!" he sarcastically answered, his lawyer on the other end.

"Shut up and listen..." came the retort as Billy shifted the phone to his other ear, away from his Marketing VP. There was a break in the one-sided conversation.

"Oh, c'mon, that's BS and you know it. We answered all those questions during our last round of venture financing. You told me the SEC doesn't even think about letting this stuff go through unless it is squeaky clean and I just rang the freakin' opening bell at the New York Stock Exchange for crying out loud!"

There was another pause as Billy listened to his lawyer.

"I tell you, it is total BS!"

Another pause.

"Right now we are headed to that interview Susan set up," Billy continued, "I'll be careful. Yeah, yeah, I'll be fine. Don't worry." After a few more moments, Billy pulled the phone away from his ear and punched the hang-up icon.

"What was that all about?" Susan queried, already nervous about Billy's upcoming interview with Maria Incandella, host of the widely watched *Tech Movers*.

"Oh, nothing," Billy sighed, processing what he had just heard. He knew it was more than nothing, but he also knew he had a good lawyer. "You go on TV and it brings out the crazies. It's all good."

"I guess now that you're famous, everyone wants a piece of you," Susan murmured, ever so slightly licking her lips in the process. Billy didn't notice, but his driver did, glancing in the rear view mirror as he switched lanes on 6th Avenue.

#

As Billy sat in the Green Room, Susan could see he was growing impatient with both the make-up crew and her decision to put him on this show.

"Dammit, Susan, I know what to say. This has been my baby for the past five years, I'll be fine. If she asks me a question I don't know, I'll hire her to find the answer!"

But it wasn't the geek-speak questions Susan was worried about, rather the political and social ones. She feared that the host of *Tech Movers* would make Billy look foolish on national TV and undo all the groundwork on CGC's corporate image Susan had so painstakingly worked to craft since leaving the investment bank, McDonough & Partners. She saw CGC as an "once-in-a-lifetime opportunity," but as the Marketing VP sat in front of her increasingly agitated boss, she fumed. This was her moment, too, but as Susan was seeing all too clearly, her boss hated crowds, hated public speaking and, as she was discovering, hated having anyone put make-up on his face.

"I know that Mr. Wilson," Susan responded in the professional, clinical manner that was on display whenever she was in the public eye, "this is just like a final walk through before a game—think of the make-up as eye-black."

Billy chuckled at the analogy.

"Eye black, huh? That's funny. But honestly, Susan," Billy leaned closer, looked her right in the eyes and calmly said, "I got this." It made her relax, if only a bit.

At that moment, Maria walked in, sucking all the air out of the room. Susan had met her once before, but she had been around a dozen or so of her fawning, male colleagues at McDonough, and was sure she had been all but invisible.

"William Wilson! Welcome to New York. What a pleasure to meet you! My nephew will be insanely jealous—he's a big fan of *Battle for Babylon* and already made it to the Master 1-Star level!"

"Glad to hear that Maria, thank you for having me on your show. Give me his address later and I'll send him a copy of our newest game, *Armageddon and Beyond.* We're in beta testing now and it's always good to get feedback from the experts!"

"Marvelous!" Maria was beaming like a schoolgirl at her first dance after having been asked out by the best looking boy. "I'll hold you to that."

"Maria," Susan coolly stated, extending her hand, "Susan Green, Marketing VP." The two women eyed each other suspiciously. Susan was more attractive, but after an hour's worth of pampering by her make-up crew, Maria had an air of glamour that was stunning. She also got to wear the best wardrobe that money could rent.

Maria was dangerous, as well. She had already disarmed Billy with her cute nephew shtick; it was only a matter of time before she went in for the kill. *Damn,* Susan thought to herself, *what a mistake this is.*

"Suzanne, of course, it is so good to see you again," Maria oozed of insincerity; Susan grit her teeth.

Maria had already moved on, putting her hand firmly on Billy's back, guiding him to the interview set, making small talk all the way.

"It's 'Susan', bitch," she muttered to herself, sitting back down in the Green Room. She said a silent prayer for Billy.

#

Jeremy finished his graveyard shift and hurried into the employee lounge, flipping on the large, flat screen TV on the wall. He tried never to miss *Tech Movers* and if he could watch it on some of Uncle Sam's finest equipment, all the better. Today was a two-fer—not only was he going to get 60-inches of Super HD resolution of the hot, Maria Incandella, she was going to be interviewing the founder and CEO of Cloud Gaming Co., William Wilson, III. Jeremy, like most of his classmates at MIT, was an ardent gamer and an intensely loyal CGC fan. He knew how hard it was to be "simple, fast, and strong" in the code world, and so was particularly interested in this interview.

He sat down and popped open a Diet Pepsi.

"Whoa!" he exclaimed, to no one in particular, spitting out his drink in the process. Maria was known for her clingy sweaters and tight skirts, but today's were ridiculous.

"Hey, Jeremy, you got the fashion channel on or what?" hooted Beth Hopkins, a young analyst in Jeremy's class at Langley who worked on the Asian Pacific team.

"Naw, it's a tech show," Jeremy sheepishly replied, feeling his neck turn bright crimson. "I watch it all the time to hear what's going on in tech. There's a guy on from a Seattle company that just went public." It didn't sound convincing.

"Oh?" Beth replied, sounding interested, "you mean Billy Wilson, the founder of Cloud Gaming?"

Jeremy's head spun around and he looked at Beth quizzically. "You know who he is?"

"I'm a Master 3-Star General in *Battle for Babylon*. You think only guys are into video games?" Beth shot back derisively.

"Sorry. I just never knew any girls at MIT who were," Jeremy said apologetically, filing away the information. Beth pulled up a chair next to Jeremy.

"That's OK, I never knew any guys at Stanford who drank Diet Pepsi, so we're even," she chirped, winking at him. Jeremy's face turned red again.

"Touché."

They both looked up at the TV at the sound of Maria's Brooklyn accent.

"Hi, I'm Maria Incandella and today on Tech Movers, William Wilson, III, founder and CEO of Cloud Gaming Co., joins us fresh from the floor at the New York Stock Exchange after ringing the opening bell. William, thanks for joining me today."

The camera panned out to capture Billy.

"Wow. He's cute," Beth said matter-of-factly.

"You're welcome, Maria, thanks for having me. I've always been a big fan of the show. And please call me 'Billy'."

"All right, 'Billy' it is," Maria countered, turning to face him and ever so subtly throwing her chest out. *"So tell me how CGC came to be, as you put it: 'simple, fast and strong'."*

#

Susan squirmed in her chair off-camera. "C'mon, Billy, don't be distracted by the glitz."

#

"She's hitting on him, right on the set!" Beth was incredulous. "What a bimbo!"

Jeremy immediately liked this girl.

#

"I've been fiddling with the insides of computers all my life, it's always been my passion..." Billy started, walking through the talking points that he and Susan had worked on the last three months. He seemed to be mentally ticking them off, one-by-one, like he was playing a recording in his head, only doing it with feeling.

Remarkable, Susan mused to herself, gaining new found respect for the 24-year-old. She'd seen 50-year-old partners at McDonough struggle with the circus that was the media environment.

"...and today I got to ring the opening bell at the NYSE, so it has been quite a ride!"

#

"Wow, eye candy with brains and passion," Beth blurted out, "what a rare treat!"

"Gee, thanks," Jeremy retorted glumly.

"You know what I mean!" Beth teased, but upset at herself for speaking her thoughts so bluntly.

#

The interview was winding down and Susan was beginning to relax. Maria had tried to set Billy up to step in it at least half a dozen times, but he was having none of it. *Only five more minutes,* Susan thought, *and then we're home free.* There was a brief lull in the conversation, as though Maria were listening to one of her off-camera assistants. Maria's countenance changed, almost imperceptibly, but Susan saw it and knew right away what it meant. *Uh oh,* she thought, *here it comes.*

#

"So Billy, we're hearing reports that some of the key components of Cloud Gaming's code were stolen from competitors, that you and your crackerjack programmers hacked into their computers, stole their best ideas and left behind malicious code to set them back months. In fact, we're hearing right now that one of them has just filed suit with the Manhattan District Attorney to enjoin you from selling *Battle for Babylon* until the suit can be heard. Can you comment on these allegations?"

#

"Ooh, this is getting good," Beth murmured, engrossed in the suddenly uncomfortable scene that was unfolding right before their eyes.

#

The blood was draining from Susan's face. She gripped the side of her chair, fighting an intense bout of nausea and immediately realized what Billy had been talking about on the phone in the car only moments before. Her young boss, who could be as naïve as they came when dealing with someone as manipulative as Maria, was about to be ripped to shreds and there was nothing Susan could do about it. *Why did I quit McDonough?* she screamed in her thoughts.

#

The question hung in the air for what seemed like an eternity. The moment Maria uttered it, the stock started to nosedive, crashing through the IPO price in a flash. Billy's eyes narrowed and a smirk came over his face, as he calmly began.

"You know, Maria, you know what is great about America? What's great about America is that an awkward guy like me can follow his passion and create something so complex that hardly anyone understands it, yet is simple enough to give joy and pleasure to people all across this great country. And you know what? I get paid for it! Then I get invited to New York City, the seat of capitalism for the Free World, and get to ring the opening bell at the greatest stock market in the world, to signify the start of trading of the stock of a company that positively impacts the lives of..."

#

"...*millions of people across the US.*"

Susan sat in stunned silence. *Who is this guy?* she thought, temporarily arresting the thousand horrible narratives exploding in her mind of how she would be the laughingstock of the colleagues she left behind at McDonough, never to get another job on Wall

Street after stupidly putting her boss in a chair opposite Maria Incandella.

"These are people who get up every day, work hard to put food on the table and come home to spend time with their family. They're the ones who are buying Battle for Babylon, *and they're buying because video games are fun, they foster competition, and they help stimulate imagination in people's lives, help people solve complex problems, gives them confidence…"*

#

"Preach it, Billy! Preach it!" Jeremy shouted, on his feet, arms high and fists clenched in a victory pose.

#

Billy was on a roll. Very few people had seen this side of him and it was clear that Maria had no idea what she had just unleashed. He leaned closer to her, lowering his voice, but not his passion.

"And you know what else, Maria? Do you know how many people benefit from what we do? How many people earn a living working for CGC, or for the companies that supply CGC? Or how many retirement accounts of families in Middle America will be a little—heck, maybe even a lot—better off because they will own stock of Cloud Gaming? Government…"

#

"…didn't create those jobs, didn't do any of that—we did— Americans like me and you! And I am proud of that and you should be, too!"

Susan was struggling to come to terms with what she was seeing and hearing. She had gone from a state of abject fear to breathless euphoria in a few short moments. The Marketing VP had come into the Green Room with a feeling of trepidation, wondering if Billy Wilson could handle the bright lights and yet here he was, absolutely killing it.

"But you know what the downside of this hyper-competitive technology market is? It's that some companies just don't make it. They are too slow, or too bureaucratic, or too political. They're not smart enough, or run out of money, or are just plain jealous that someone else is more successful. But rather than admit they are

beaten, you know what they do? They complain to the government. They try to smear you in the media. They file meritless lawsuits. And that's what this lawsuit is—meritless—and we will fight it tooth and nail."

Billy had been masterful. Maria was fumbling through her sign off. During the three minutes of Billy's impassioned soliloquy, the stock had erased all its intraday losses and then some, touching a new high.

#

The cameras went dark and Billy stood up, towering over Maria. She grabbed both of his hands.

"I must say, that was some kind of speech you just gave Billy. If you ever decide to run for office, please give me the honor of announcing on my show."

"Speech? That was no speech," Billy responded, irritated at the implication. "Maria, I have the greatest job in the world. I can't imagine doing anything else."

"Perhaps than just dinner, tonight?"

"Dinner? Tonight?" Billy was confused, not sure how to respond. Susan walked out and rescued him.

"I'm sorry, Maria, but we are headed directly out to Teeterboro. We have to be back in Seattle tonight."

"Perhaps the next time you are on the show, then. I'd love to have you back out."

"We'll see," was all that Billy could muster, yanking off his microphone and handing it to the technical assistant.

And with that, they were done. In moments they were out the back door of the studio, cruising through the Lincoln Tunnel. Susan's smart phone vibrated incessantly as one after another of her McDonough colleagues congratulated her on her brilliant attack strategy. *If they only knew,* she thought, *if they only knew.* They were wheels up in the Gulfstream before the hour.

CHAPTER 2

Mikhail Yikovich watched the *Tech Movers'* interview from his luxurious flat in Moscow, a glass of sherry in hand to dull the senses of another day in the Russian bureaucracy. He had a keen interest in American technology for both public and personal reasons. By day, he was General Mikhail Yikovich, Chief Researcher of the secretive Department T, where he was charged with obtaining—by any means necessary—the latest technology developed outside Russia. His directive was to determine if the new technology either posed a threat *to* Russia, or more provocatively, could be used to pose one itself *by* Russia.

But General Yikovich's interest in Cloud Gaming Co. was more than just how to keep his homeland safe. Privately, he was also interested in the stock, having used his secret Swiss account to acquire 100,000 shares at the IPO price of $20 a share. Billy Wilson's impassioned defense of Cloud Gaming Co. that ended the interview had helped drive the price up to $50; Yikovich had made $3 million in one day alone! That could buy a nice *dachau* anywhere.

He swirled his snifter and took another sip. He had never met Billy Wilson, but could see why he was successful—he had a single-minded determination that was slightly unnerving. The General smiled at his good fortune, before noticing the blinking light of his Alienware X51 gaming computer. He had a message.

"Da!" Yikovich shrieked like a school-boy. He had recently ramped up his gaming and was now a Master 2-Star General on *Battle for Babylon,* under the name of *Polar Bear.* General Yikovich forgot all about the *dachau* and in moments was engrossed in *Battle for Babylon* with more than ten million other gamers on-line, all seamlessly battling one another using CGC's technology platform.

#

The Russians had made great strides in their use of technology once General Yikovich had been elevated to the head of Department T. Despite his age and rank, he was young at heart and willing to try almost anything involving technology. It was a side benefit of the General's secret passion for video games, an addiction he did his best to hide. Fortunately, since he was the chief technologist within the Russian military, he had unfettered on-line access to anything he wanted and he spent much of his free time playing video games, his mind working on a novel military strategy in the process. However lately, the increasing demands of integrating that strategy into the Russian military command structure had kept the General at work most of the day.

The Russians were close to going live with their first test of it, and General Yikovich wasn't about to let any of his programming colleagues screw things up. That had almost happened a few months earlier when one had stupidly turned on all the network towers simultaneously, sending out a surge of electromagnetic energy that might have scrambled Western warplanes if it had happened near the Ukrainian border. Fortunately, nobody really cared about what happened in Siberia.

#

But Jeremy had noticed—at least he had noticed something. He had no idea what had caused the electro-magnetic pulse to show up on his monitor a few months earlier. The electronic signature was not that unusual, common in almost any city in America where mobile phone towers were constantly emitting pulses of information as they handled phone calls and wireless internet connections. But Siberia was a remote wasteland, known more for its *gulag* during the Cold War years, than a place where wireless technology was needed. Jeremy knew the electronic pulse could be anything, but one thing he knew for sure was that it was something.

Frustratingly, he hadn't noticed any other unusual activity in Siberia since that day. The young CIA analyst had been monitoring it carefully and there wasn't much going on. There were a lot more vehicles than normal, but they weren't doing anything unusual—no missile launchers or heavy trucks. He also noticed a few old tanks, but they weren't using that model in battle any more.

"Hey, Tony," Jeremy hesitantly asked his boss, "can I pick your brain a little bit here?" Tony Smith, the Director of his team, was as old as Jeremy's dad, but worked graveyard to get to his kids' ballgames.

"Just a sec," Tony responded without looking up, "I'm finishing up the last line of the daily intelligence report." Three taps of the keyboard later, Tony swiveled his chair around to face Jeremy.

"What's up?"

Tony was rapidly gaining respect for his charge. Despite Jeremy's youth, he clearly had the technology chops—he went to MIT, after all—but also wasn't so caught up in the jargon that he couldn't simply explain something to someone who didn't. He also asked good questions.

"I've been watching that area in Siberia where we had the electronic spike a few months ago. There hasn't been anything really major since then, just a lot of little things," Jeremy responded.

"For instance?" Tony volleyed back.

"Well," Jeremy began, choosing his words carefully, "there have been a lot of regular, low-grade electronic pulses, similar to the one that caught my attention, but much weaker, like someone turning a switch on and off."

"And?" Tony looked down as his android phone vibrated, indicating the brass had received his report.

"Well, the signals are all more or less the same, and as best as I can tell, they are cell tower transmitters—it looks like they are building a wireless grid in the middle of nowhere." Jeremy reached down to the controls on his monitor and focused on one specific area.

"These look like trees," he continued, slowly zooming in for emphasis, "until you get to here." Jeremy pointed at what looked like an evergreen tree, but to the trained eye, it was unmistakably an artificial tower with electronic gear on it.

"And here and here," he quickly panned out and zoomed in to reveal another tree-like tower, and then another. "There are a lot of them around here and my guess is they are testing them to make sure they work."

"Hmmm. Seems like a lot of effort for maybe a few phones," Tony replied. "Is there someone important there that needs to be in constant contact?"

It was a good question. Jeremy could see why Tony was such an asset—he didn't just think in terms of what and why, but more importantly, who.

"Huh? Oh, I see, what you mean. I haven't thought that far along yet," Jeremy countered without a hint of embarrassment in his voice, "but I don't think they are for phones, because after a few miles out, there aren't any more towers and so the phone signal would just die."

Of course, Tony thought, though it wasn't such an obvious conclusion. *This kid is smart.*

"I actually think it's a Wi-Fi network, but why here and for what reason, doesn't make sense to me. Any ideas?"

Tony looked at the monitor, panned it out a bit and queried, "Have you seen any weapons?"

"There are some tanks, armored troop carriers, and jeeps, but they are all vintage WWII as far as I can tell. Can't imagine they are using those for training, but maybe the Russians are worse off financially than we think and have been relegated to antiques for training," Jeremy replied. "But I doubt it—particularly next to all those cell towers."

"Well, you never know with those bastards, they like to throw a lot of brute strength at things," Tony cackled. "What else would a Wi-Fi network run?"

"We use them for mobile communications, video games, wireless computers, local area intra-nets, stuff like that," Jeremy countered expectantly.

Tony continued to move the mouse, stopping suddenly, "Hey! What's that?"

Jeremy peered at the screen, enhancing the resolution. The image was blurry, but it was unmistakably a drone, hovering above one of the tanks.

"Humph, it's a drone," Jeremy replied, slightly embarrassed he had missed it.

"A drone? Have you seen any explosions? It looks like it's set-up for target practice, which would explain all of Stalin's old crap," a now curious Tony queried.

"None I've seen. But there wouldn't have to be explosions to test an electronic warfare system. You could accomplish the same thing by lighting them up with a laser," Jeremy replied.

"Can you find that?" Tony asked. It was less of a question and more of an order.

"I can," Jeremy responded, drawing out the "I" for emphasis. MIT had taught him a few tricks.

#

General Yikovich was getting impatient with the testing phase of *Operation Oblaka*. He realized that each tower had to be calibrated and tested individually, and that their remote location made it harder to accomplish than would be the case in Moscow. For someone like him who spent much of his life in the virtual world, the time it took to test, adjust, then test again—only to go through the whole process multiple times—was maddening.

"Sergey, why does it take so long? Is there no way to test this using a computer simulation?"

"*Nyet,* Comrade General. This is the real world, not the virtual one. Your strategy is revolutionary," the Sergeant said, "and because of it, we are getting ready to do something no one has ever done before. Yet, we will only get one chance to set it up on our terms. We must be patient."

#

Sergey Kachinko was not only politically savvy; he was also an excellent video gamer. He had been playing since he was seven, the youngest in a family of three. Under the *nom de guerre* of *Pinball*, he planned on participating in the Gaming Olympics. Kachinko had been spending as much of his free time as he could playing *Battle for Babylon,* and because he was neither married nor a drinker, his activity of choice to decompress from a day at work was playing video games.

The Sergeant was a skilled video game tactician, and when he went in for the kill, was brutal and efficient. Yet, he found himself in an uncomfortable spot battling in the *Corridor of the Hanging Gardens* against an aggressive gamer called *Blunt Instrument.* His attacker had achieved a high enough rank to have air cover and was attempting to lure him out from the *Corridor* by dashing between the virtual pillars and shooting, hoping to elicit counter-fire to identify precisely where to send air power. This would force *Pinball* to simultaneously defend against both air and ground attack, an almost certain losing proposition.

But *Pinball* had managed to maneuver nearly the complete length of the *Corridor* without having to fire a shot and was getting close to *Blunt Instrument.* When *Pinball* finally positioned himself to attack, he was close enough to see that the avatar was female.

"*Die suka!*" Kachinko snarled in a mix of English and Russian as he pulled the trigger at nearly point blank range. But his surprise that someone with such a crude avatar name was a curvaceous blonde, warrior princess, caused him to hesitate. *Blunt Instrument* was gone before *Pinball's* weapon fired its first round and all its second did was give *Blunt Instrument's* air force a clear fix on where to fire. As the jets screamed in for the kill, *Pinball* dove back into the shadows and hit EXIT. Kachinko had had enough. His avatar faded from view.

#

"You bastard!" screamed *Blunt Instrument's* master, disgusted both at herself that she had almost been killed, and at the coward named *Pinball,* whom she was certain she would have vaporized if he had stayed and fought like a true soldier.

"More like 'no balls', you effing wimp!" She had not expected anyone would have had the stealth to be able to sneak up on her without having to fire a shot. But to run away rather than fight? What kind of warrior did that? She filed both the style of play and the avatar away in her memory. Next time *Pinball* was lurking she would destroy him with overwhelming force.

CHAPTER 3

"Good work accomplishing your programming goal, Mitchell, but your code has a lot of extra lines in it. That doesn't really matter if you are writing a simple program, but when it is part of a larger one and you lose precious nanoseconds, it could be the difference between winning and losing—or worse. What were you trying to accomplish?"

Dr. Mikel Johnson was everyone's favorite teacher at Queen's High School in Seattle. He always tried to see the good in people and usually doled out both praise and constructive criticism when reviewing a student's work. He genuinely took an interest in kids that didn't seem to have a lot of structure in their lives and Mitchell Patkanim was such a kid.

A Native American kid from north of Seattle, Mitchell was the fifth boy of parents who demanded each child strive for excellence in something; for Mitchell, it was in computers. At first, it was just the normal infatuation most boys his age had with video games. As the youngest, he was always last in line for the computer "hand-me-downs" and so spent hours fixing what his brothers had broken. Initially it was out of necessity, but it soon became a labor of love, his way of giving back to the land by not wasting things that still had value, a lesson learned from his great-grandfather while fishing the Stillaguamish River. Before long Mitchell was resurrecting long-since-dead computers back to life with his programming ability.

That skill had drawn the attention of Dr. Johnson in the computer science competition Queen's held for precocious junior high kids in the state of Washington. The judges had unanimously awarded Mitchell first place for programming a 1980s-vintage, *Macintosh Performa 575* to run as fast as a three-year-old *Dell*. It was one thing to get a brand-new computer to fly with the right programming, it was something altogether different to do it with a relic that wasn't designed for it. It was like putting a Ferrari engine in a Model T chassis, hitting the gas, and going from zero-to-60 in three seconds; it shouldn't have worked, but somehow it did.

The prize was a full scholarship to Queen's—including room-and-board—and he was accepted despite not having the kind of educational background of most students. Yet in short order, he'd become one of Dr. Johnson's favorite students.

"Um, I was trying to create a feedback loop that could learn from its mistakes and write its own code to prevent the same mistake from happening again. The extra lines directed the program to automatically generate new code so I could see where my mistake was," Mitchell replied. "Is that bad?"

"No, no, not at all, I just didn't understand it, but now I see what you are trying to do. That's very clever. Do you do that in all your programming?"

"Naw, I just got tired of rewriting stuff all the time and it seemed like a cool way to get things done quicker. I'm trying to figure out how to do it in my other programming, but haven't spent too much time on it because I have so much homework. It really sucks, man!"

It was a remarkable insight for someone so young. Most programmers tried to think of all possible outcomes and write elaborate code to deal with each of them. It was one of the reasons most software required so much computer memory and worked so slowly when performing complicated functions.

But Mitchell was trying to figure out how to let the computer do the heavy lifting; it was a rudimentary form of artificial intelligence. It relied on learning from unsatisfactory outcomes to reduce lines in the code, rather than trying to cover every possible outcome in a decision tree and then adding lines. *Brilliant,* thought Dr. Johnson.

"Well this is very interesting work you're doing Mitchell. Very interesting, indeed. Keep me posted on your progress."

"Yeah, cool, Dr. J, will do…hey, I gotta run!" the sophomore yelled as he dashed out the door.

Dr. Johnson sat down and reviewed the lines of programming that Mitchell had laid down. *Ah, I see it now,* he thought to himself. He hadn't had a kid like this since Billy Wilson.

#

Mitchell was running behind schedule. He was flattered by Dr. Johnson's attention, but he had his campus movements timed to avoid a group of upper classmen. They were elite gamers on Queen's varsity gaming team, and Dr. Johnson worshipped them because they had brought home a seventh-place trophy in the previous year's Gaming Olympics. It was the first time the school had finished in the top 50, and since the Olympics weren't just for high schoolers, it was quite an accomplishment. Seventh-place was also worth $100,000 in prize money for the Computer Sciences Department. The varsity gamers were the toast of the school and were prepping to win it all this year—and the $1 million first prize.

Mitchell grudgingly acknowledged they were a clever group of kids, though for someone like him, a little different than most of the entitled student body at Queen's, they were also remarkably mean-spirited. He found this out when the ring leader sent embarrassing texts to Marjorie Jeffries, a girl Mitchell secretly had a crush on, and made it appear as though they were from Mitchell. Even though he protested and had proof of his innocence, Mitchell got suspended from school for three days. *I'll get those bastards back somehow,* he thought.

"What's up Pocahontas?" Marjorie's older brother, Brad, derisively called from the bottom of the stairs.

Damn, Mitchell thought, as he raced down the stairs, only to find his tormentors waiting.

"C'mon, guys, give it a rest! Don't you have to train for the Olympics?" he queried, hoping to appeal to their egos. He was still at full speed when he reached the bottom, and one of the kids stuck his foot out and tripped him, sending Mitchell's books flying and his cell phone skidding across the floor, shattering as it hit the wall. The three bullies guffawed heartily, until they noticed the Principal coming down the otherwise empty hall.

"Are you all right, Mitchell?" they said in unison, feigning concern. "Here, let us help you."

The Principal beamed: "Way to set a good example, boys. Mitchell, you're lucky to have such fine young gentlemen as classmates, particularly after that little episode with Brad's sister."

"Yes sir," Mitchell stammered, rushing to gather his things while the grown-up was still around. "I'm really lucky." He felt like throwing up.

He rushed out of the building, and sprinted across campus to get to his dorm room. He ran up the stairs and down the hall to the last room on the left. It took him a few seconds to locate his keys, but Mitchell was in his room in no time, finally safe in one of his sanctuaries at Queen's.

Mitchell put down his stuff, fighting back tears as he sat on his bed. He looked across the room to the picture of his great-grandfather, Chief Running Stream. The sunlight beaming through the old leaded-glass windows of the dormitory refracted an array of brilliant colors onto the face of the Chief, making him seem alive. It both startled and reassured Mitchell.

A sign not to give up, he thought. The Chief had told him always to be proud of his heritage, no matter who made fun of it. Mitchell was proud, but sometimes just wanted to blend in, particularly at this school with so many entitled phonies; yet a desire for revenge boiled just beneath the surface.

He got up and sat down at his desk, reaching for his backpack.

"Dammit," he mumbled, as he pulled out the pieces of his phone—or at least what was left of it. It had broken into half-a-dozen pieces when it hit the wall, and though Mitchell was a whiz at fixing old and broken hardware, the glass screen had shattered into tiny little fragments, still hanging onto his phone by a thread, but completely useless. He sighed.

At least I know where I can find a replacement, he thought, putting his jacket back on to go over to the Computer Science Building.

#

"Hey, Mitchell, where ya' goin?" came a sweet, female voice behind him that caused his heart to skip a beat—it was Marjorie.

"I'm...I'm going to see Dr. Johnson," Mitchell stammered nervously, looking around to see if he was being set up.

"Boys and their toys!" she giggled.

"Um, Marjorie?"

"Yeah?"

"You know those texts I got in trouble for? I never sent them, I promise you."

"I know you didn't. Look, my brother can be a jerk sometimes," Marjorie replied, her tone changing to one of seriousness.

"So you don't hate me?" Mitchell asked hopefully.

22

"What? You? No, silly," Marjorie bantered back, smiling. "I think you're nice...kind of a breath of fresh air, ya' know?"

"Yes, I do...wait...no...um well, I think I know what you mean. I'll take it as a compliment." Mitchell stumbled on his reply.

"You should, silly," she retorted, playfully punching him in the shoulder. "Well, I gotta go now, so see you tomorrow! Oh, wait...I have a phone my brother doesn't know about. Lemme text you now so you have it on your phone, OK?"

Mitchell loved her confident boldness.

"OK, but I won't be able to respond right away," he replied, pulling out the pieces of the phone from his pocket, "my phone had a little accident this afternoon."

"Ohhh...that stinks," Marjorie whimpered sympathetically.

"But please send it anyway, I'll reply as soon as I get another phone, OK?" Mitchell asked hopefully.

"OK, sure," came the cheery response, as she furiously tapped away with her thumbs.

"Oh, hey wait!" Mitchell said, gaining confidence, "can I take a picture of you with your phone and ask you to send the picture with the message?" Mitchell wasn't sure he'd ever have this girl's undivided attention like he did now and didn't want to waste the opportunity.

Three clicks later, he handed the phone back to his pretty classmate.

She hit SEND. "See you tomorrow, Mitchell!"

"Okay, yeah, see you tomorrow, Marjorie!" He waved as she walked away, his mood considerably brighter. The campus was deserted now, and with none of the students around, it was truly beautiful.

Mitchell stood in front of the Computer Science Building. *Why did I come here again?* He reached into his pocket and fumbled with what was left of his phone. *Oh yeah,* he thought, recalling the humiliation earlier in the day. *I'll get those bastards back.*

#

"Hey, Dr. J," Mitchell waved as he entered Dr. Johnson's classroom, empty of everyone but the teacher. "Can I have one of the old cell phones in the storage room downstairs? I dropped mine today and it's busted."

"Of course, Mitchell. No one will ever use them anyway. Oh, can you take these old books down there while you're at it?"

"Sure. Where do you want 'em?"

"If you can find room on the top shelf that would be great, but anywhere's OK. Just let me know where you put them."

"Will do."

Mitchell carried the box of books down three flights of stairs to the storage room in the basement. The room had countless books, old computers and other gadgets, and dozens of old phones. They weren't the latest models, but they were better than Mitchell had ever had. He put the box down and reached into the drawer with all the phones in it. He grabbed a Samsung still in its shrink-wrap packaging.

"Sweet!" he gleefully said, carefully putting it in his backpack, "not even used!" He then grabbed the old books, clambering up the stepladder and sliding them into the space he created. As he put the last book up on the shelf, it knocked one off the other end.

"Oops!" he said to no one in particular as he climbed down to retrieve the book. *Advanced Programming & Troubleshooting* was the title, long since relegated to the dustbin of computer books—most of which were obsolete before they were published. A cloud of dust had exploded from the book when it hit the floor and the front cover was open.

"Whoa!" Mitchell exclaimed, eyes wide in disbelief at his good fortune. The book was ten years old, ancient by computer industry standards, but its value was in to whom it had last been issued: then sophomore, William Wilson, III. He quickly flipped through the book—there were all kinds of notes written in the margins by the man himself.

Jackpot baby! the 15-year-old thought as he put the book into his backpack.

CHAPTER 4

As 9am approached, Jeremy was getting ready to call it a day. He focused the satellite video feed on the Wi-Fi network he had discovered, but there wasn't much going on, though there seemed to be more electromagnetic pulses than he had seen in recent weeks.

Jeremy was looking forward to flipping on *Tech Movers*— and hoping that Beth would be there to watch, as well. She was cute, but more importantly, she was smart. Tony had told him of the importance of building alliances within the Agency and he figured his blonde colleague was a good start.

A sudden surge of activity on the monitor snapped him out of his daydream.

"Whoa, look at that!" he exclaimed out loud. Jeremy had programmed the equipment to track both actual and electronic activity and suddenly the screen was a blur of motion and color.

Tony saw the action and scurried over. "What the hell is going on down there, Thomas?!" It seemed a full-scale battle was being waged, albeit only in Siberia, but Jeremy knew the official Tony Smith voice when he heard it.

"It's like a video game, sir!" Jeremy replied.

"What?! A damn video game?! What the hell are you doing playing video games on US Government-issued equipment?!" Tony couldn't believe his ears. He thought the kid was solid.

"I beg your pardon, sir?" Jeremy looked at his boss quizzically, unsure if they were in the same conversation.

"You said you're playing a video game, didn't you?" Tony queried back, most of the intensity drained from his voice.

Jeremy suppressed a laugh.

"No sir, I said it's *like* a video game. I adjusted the monitoring equipment to track electromagnetic signals as well as physical movement. Right now, there is a lot of both going on, so it looks like a video game."

"Oh, I see." But Tony had no idea what Jeremy was talking about. The kid's mastery of technology made him feel old and stupid. He was starting to wonder if he should hang it up. Jeremy could see that his superior was struggling.

"Electromagnetic and kinetic mapping, sir. It was the emphasis of my senior thesis," Jeremy replied. "Creating a heat map to reveal speed, direction and intensity in both time and space for physical and electromagnetic movement."

Tony was getting impatient.

"English, please," he snapped, though gratified to hear it was cutting edge technology and not some ten-year-old stuff.

"Sorry sir," Jeremy responded, "the drones are using lasers to find and lock onto targets—those are the red lines. The return color is graded from yellow to orange, depending on how fast and in what direction the target is moving—kind of like a Doppler effect. The green lines are counter-signals, using the laser lock to attempt to send a deadly payload back to the attacker. The blue is the drone's response to being lit up on the counter-signal return message, changing hue as it takes evasive maneuvers," Jeremy excitedly replied, as his boss nodded.

"It looks like a video game or at least it does to me, but the amazing thing is that it isn't virtual, it's real! It is really damn impressive! Uh, sir..." Jeremy quickly added. This was the first real, all business interaction the two of them had had and he didn't want to step over the line of professionalism.

"What are the white lines?" Tony asked. Jeremy hadn't noticed them. Maybe his boss had been following him.

"What white lines?" Jeremy believed he had only thought it, but Tony's response made it clear he hadn't.

"The ones connecting the drones," his boss curtly responded.

Jeremy looked at the screen. *How did I miss that?* he wondered. Sure enough, there was a web of electromagnetic white lines connecting each drone to a communications hub. It looked like a spider web, shifting as the drones moved through the air.

"Humph. I didn't notice those, but I think the white lines are friendly communication," Jeremy replied, clearly perplexed. "I guess when I programmed the monitor, I adjusted the settings to include more than just weapons-driven applications. It looks like the drones are communicating with each other. Fascinating."

"Is it dangerous?" Tony worriedly queried.

"What, the communications?" Jeremy and Tony were reading off a different page again.

"No, no. The whole damn thing!" Tony barked.

"Oh, umm. Not in and of itself. Those drones don't have enough power to have any real weaponry on them, but I guess you could amp them up and put on something nasty. However, nobody is using lasers as weapons yet, as far as I know," Jeremy definitively responded.

The activity was over as soon as it started. Jeremy marveled at what he had seen, though troubled that he couldn't explain it all. Tony just worried that they were missing something.

The Russians wouldn't be playing video games in Siberia for the hell of it, he thought.

#

General Yikovich sat in the Strategic War Room and breathed a sigh of relief. The first major test of the clandestine project on which he had been working for the last 18-months was a success. The drones they had secretly built had worked exactly as expected, even though they hadn't fully deployed their stealth capabilities. Nevertheless, Yikovich was certain that the composites used to build the drones and the Russians' ability to jam enemy signals would make it difficult for an opposing army to assess the real threat the drones posed until it was too late. The politicians watching on the screen with the General were just pleased that the group of young men sitting in front of them controlling the drones had "destroyed" the opponent, all while evading any serious counter-attack.

"The first stage is complete," General Yikovich asserted. Premier Vladimir Buskin, his childhood friend, shook his hand.

"Well done, Mikhail. Well done. We are on schedule, but there is still much work to do, no?"

"*Da,* Comrade Premier," General Yikovich professionally responded. Buskin was a friend, but there were jealous men with them as well. "We will be ready."

He was confident in his statement, as they were actually much farther along than he let on.

#

The two Russian military officers were the last to leave the building; they were a good team, having worked closely for the last five years. General Yikovich needed like-minded scientists to realize his vision of using the virtual world to create a strategic and tactical military plan in the real one. He had specifically selected Sergeant

Kachinko because of his keen mind, attention to detail, and youthful exuberance. The General convinced Kachinko to switch allegiances from Yikovich's chief rival within the Russian military by promising a major role in developing and beta testing the new strategy. The Sergeant was also smart enough to see the future involved the use of the technology of tomorrow, not the brute force of yesterday. Their first real test was on the horizon; they could barely wait.

CHAPTER 5

Billy Wilson gazed out the window of his top floor, corner office in one of Seattle's best business addresses. The space was more than they needed, but the all-or-nothing deal was too attractive to pass up. The previous tenant, an investment firm, had suffered an ignominious end when the co-founders were led out of the building in handcuffs after perpetrating a Ponzi scheme on the public and their own employees. Just like that, 200 people were out of a job, their retirement accounts drained, and their office space now empty and vacant. Cloud Gaming Co. was next in line and grabbed the space; business could be brutal that way.

Billy stood motionless, reflecting on how quickly his life had gone from high-school whiz kid to a spot on the *Forbes 400*. Puget Sound shimmered below, and the snow-capped Olympic Mountains cut a jagged edge across the horizon. When it wasn't overcast and raining, there were very few places as picturesque as Seattle.

Billy remembered the palpable excitement he had had after a robust discussion in Dr. Johnson's class on an entertaining piece of research called *The Wisdom of Crowds*. The concept was simple, summed up in the axiom: two heads are better than one. CGC's founder already knew from first-hand experience that multiple gamers in the same environment created an unpredictable and entertaining element. Human-against-human, rather than just human-against-machine, enhanced the game immeasurably, and the cloud allowed potentially an unlimited number of players to simultaneously play the same game.

The genius of Billy Wilson and CGC was that its gaming system was condensed into so few lines of code, that it could easily be paired with a robust security infrastructure and still leave significant bandwidth for gaming. Cloud Gaming Co.'s software opened up the worldwide gaming environment to virtually anyone, regardless of hardware.

Ping! An instant message from his Marketing VP knocked him from his state of reminiscing.

Sorry but I'll be a few minutes late for our Weekly 10:30, just finishing up a call with the Financial Times *regarding our trip to London next month.*

Billy met with Susan Green for at least thirty minutes every Tuesday to go over marketing initiatives and public relations. While he never held the idea of marketing and spin in much regard, he did admit that Susan Green had been a good hire. Other than CGC's Chief Counsel, she was the only Wall Streeter on the payroll.

But the events in New York convinced him she had been worth it. He got high marks from the media pundits for his interview on *Tech Movers,* and it was Susan who crafted that message. She also knew how to play the game in the rough-and-tumble media spotlight.

"Ms. Green to see you, Mr. Wilson," his executive assistant announced.

"Send her in," he curtly responded.

He tapped the last few key strokes of an e-mail to Dr. Johnson, hit SEND and swiveled his chair around.

Wow, he thought, as Susan walked in wearing a perfectly tailored outfit, her pastel pink blouse matching the faint pinstripes of her designer suit. Susan Green had spent the money on a professional Wall Street wardrobe and figured she might as well use it, even though it was a stark contrast to the casual "uniform" of the computer programming world.

"So what's on the agenda for today?" Billy inquired. Susan was still learning the business and these sessions were designed to educate her on the more arcane aspects of it, so she could spin it in a way that people outside the industry could digest.

"In the interview you touched on aspects of the cloud, crowd psychology, simple code and video games. Maybe you can walk me through the connections in more detail," Susan matter-of-factly replied.

"OK, let's start with the cloud," Billy began. "In the 'old days', every computer had to have the software for any program it wanted to run, loaded onto its hard drive."

"You mean like Microsoft Excel or Word?" Susan interjected.

"Exactly, and as updates and newer versions became available, you kept needing to add more and more computer horsepower just to have enough memory for the updates. And if you had fifty computers, every single one had to have the software on the machine. It was all very inefficient, but it made some people very wealthy," he waved in the direction of Microsoft across Lake Washington.

Susan smiled.

"The cloud essentially moved much of the software off the individual computer to a place—the so-called cloud—where any computer could access it."

"So where is this cloud?" Susan queried. "I mean, you still need to have software running somewhere, don't you?"

"Of course, it just doesn't all need to be on your computer anymore. Instead, most cloud-based applications and software are housed remotely on servers all around the world, and can be accessed simultaneously by multiple users. So the software is not 'in here'," Billy stated, gently tapping his tablet for emphasis, "but somewhere 'out there', up in the cloud!" Billy waved his left hand toward the window, where appropriately enough, white, billowy clouds provided a sharp contrast to the azure sky.

"Any downside?" Susan knew the answer, but it was good to hear it directly from Billy—he was the one that would be talking after all, and it made it easier to craft the message in his style.

"A few, like having to share programs in the cloud, generally making everyone less efficient—there's only so much bandwidth, after all. There are also 'dead zones' where you can't access the cloud because there's no Wi-Fi signal, or it is too weak," Billy continued, in command of his material. After his performance on *Tech Movers* in New York, she knew not to underestimate him again.

"So is there any need for laptops or desktops?" Susan inquired.

"Sure there is. Software on your own computer usually runs faster, has more horsepower and of course, is more private, so it's a tradeoff."

"So, how does crowd psychology play into this?" Susan asked, genuinely curious.

"It comes from a book, *The Wisdom of Crowds*, which says that collectively, groups of people make better decisions than anyone does individually. Most of the time when you hear somebody say 'crowd psychology', it's about brainwashed idiots following some crazy leader in suicide, or getting sucked into the latest fad." Billy stood up and started to pace; he was warming up. "It's the herd instinct at its worst. But there's another side to the 'crowd' coin and the research is pretty interesting stuff," Billy looked at Susan, making sure she was following; she was.

"Basically, if people make intelligent decisions with good information, the average of everyone's answer is usually better than anyone's by themselves, making it a 'wise' crowd decision."

"Can you give me an example?" Susan asked.

"Sure. If you fill a jar with 20,000 pennies and ask a hundred people how many there are, you'll probably get a hundred different answers. Everyone will use some kind of logic to come up with their own guess."

Billy hadn't really ever had to explain it to someone like this before, but it was a good exercise. He had been surrounded by computer geeks most of his life and found Susan's perspective surprisingly refreshing. Conversations between coders almost always devolved into excruciating minutiae; he and Greg had been like that, their communication almost telepathic at times. He missed that kind of camaraderie, but was finding something similar with Susan.

"Some might try to count a row, some look at how tall or wide the jar is. Some will remember their own penny jar when they were a kid that was about 1/20th the size and extrapolate, etc. Some will be way over, some way under, and some close. But when you average all those guesses that used a million different assumptions, the average answer is frequently very close to the correct one. And it happens in all sorts of situations."

"Interesting," Susan murmured, listening intently as she watched Billy walk back-and-forth.

"Competitive situations like our video games, are particularly good forums for 'crowd wisdom' because decisions are either rewarded with success or punished with failure, and by analyzing these decisions, it helps us build better software and better games in the future." Billy stopped for a few moments, watching the TV. Half the screen was showing the stock market moving sharply lower, the other half what looked like the buildup to a military engagement somewhere.

Susan could see the unmistakable, jagged, downward sloping line indicating that someone's equity wealth was evaporating. She wondered how much he might be worth. She would have died to have a client like this at McDonough.

"Humph," Billy grunted, "I didn't think the Russians were serious about going after the Ukraine. It looks like they mean business." Billy was also a history buff and knew how quickly conflagrations in that area could escalate. He seemed genuinely worried.

Susan was surprised at his response. "Why don't we finish the other two things some other time," Susan suggested to her now clearly distracted boss. His head snapped around, catching her staring at him.

"Huh? What did you say?" He was momentarily lost in the world of real warfare.

"It's not important," Susan quietly replied, slightly on edge. "Just a couple more things, Mr. Wilson. Your interview with the *Financial Times* is all set..." After his *Tech Movers* appearance, he was suddenly in great demand by the world media.

"...and also one with *Le Monde* and *Der Spiegel.*"

Billy raised his eyebrows. "Is that really our audience?"

"I think we need to explore it, Mr. Wilson. Our gaming platform is becoming the *de facto* world standard in the industry, which is not just teenage boys anymore. There is genuine interest across the cultural spectrum in what you have created."

"I see," he countered, unconvinced and smirking. "I just thought that only the elite read those magazines—not actually your video gamer profile."

"Well, the elite *does* read *Le Monde* and *Der Spiegel,* but sometimes they are the ones that are the first to accept—or reject—new ideas and technology," Susan started, simultaneously defensive and professorial. "If you can capture their imagination somehow, you don't have them outwardly fighting what you are doing and it ultimately lowers the cultural resistance to adoption."

"Makes sense."

"Think of the World Cup or the Olympics," she continued, the enthusiasm in her voice rising, "and how people around the world are glued to their TVs rooting for the 'home team' partly because of national pride in the 'French-ness' or 'German-ness' of the athletes. The genius of CGC is that it lets the French or the German play video games in their own way and the outcome is very much French or German."

"Really?" Billy got the analogy, and while he still wasn't totally sold on the idea, her explanation did have an intriguing appeal to it. He felt her passion and enthusiasm for something he didn't understand at all, yet it was clear that she had been spot on about how a favorable TV interview would help his company.

"Trust me, Mr. Wilson, they will eat it up," she confidently asserted.

"OK," he replied, his intonation rising to reveal lingering doubt. "This is your world, I suppose. I can't say it makes a lot of sense to me, but it is logical…and, by the way, you don't need to call me 'Mr. Wilson'. We're practically the same age—'Billy' is just fine."

She flushed ever so slightly, though she hoped he didn't notice. They continued to chat on the initiatives she was developing: the ad campaign, the upcoming investor call, and the European tour that was fast approaching. Susan knew she was good at what she did, but Billy picked it up more quickly than she ever imagined he would. When her mentor was describing the job, he had warned Billy could be slow and quirky, but he was neither. Instead, she found him intellectually stimulating and surprisingly refreshing. She was used to the Wall Street types—both male and female—that always seemed threatened by your ideas, knowledge, and analysis. But Billy Wilson not only listened to advice, he absorbed it, and was willing to be persuaded by it as well. As she found her ideas being relied upon in real and meaningful ways by someone who was not threatened by them, it was exhilarating. Her young boss was actually quite remarkable; the meeting was coming to a close.

"Excellent. Just give me time to go over everything," Billy clinically replied, before softening, "you know, Susan, I wasn't really sure we needed someone with your background here, but I am glad we have you. You're damn good at what you do."

Susan blushed. "Thank you, Mr. Wil— I mean Billy!" she smiled as she corrected herself.

"I also don't think I ever thanked you for rescuing me from Maria," he smiled. "Thanks for having my back."

"Anytime, sir."

He laughed as Susan slowly got up, turned and left. Billy's eyes followed her every step.

CHAPTER 6

Mitchell made his way back to the dorm, sneaking through the secret passage that he had accidentally discovered shortly after he had moved in. He had seen his tormentors staked out near the front door, no doubt wanting to add to the misery of what had occurred a few hours before. He knew he risked being seen walking into the long ivy that densely cascaded down from the old, English Tudor-style building that housed the few boarders, but it was getting dark, and if Mitchell had learned anything from his Native American heritage, it was stealth. Queen's had once been a tuberculosis asylum and when patients died, they were usually quietly transported off the campus through a series of tunnels that connected the patient rooms to the basement. Most of the passageways had been boarded up when the school was remodeled many years ago, but not all of them. Mitchell was thankful for that now.

He put his backpack onto the desk and pulled out his new treasures. Though it was past dusk, he kept the lights off in his room. *If those fools want to stand outside in the cold waiting for me, so be it!* he laughed to himself. The Samsung phone was a clear upgrade, though it would be time-consuming to transfer all the data, making him wait for a certain text.

"Oh, well," he sighed, "at least I have a new phone."

And what would turn out to be a very, very valuable book. He gently pulled it from his backpack, reverently holding it as though it were the Holy Grail; it was more like the Rosetta Stone. The title, *Advanced Programming & Troubleshooting,* suggested a daunting book of turgid, technical prose written by a committee of computer geeks, indecipherable to almost everyone but the most hard-core nerds. But instead, its chapters were brief and well written, with examples that would make sense to most laymen. Better still, Billy Wilson himself had made significant notations in the margins of almost every page, revealing a remarkable clarity of thinking and a deep understanding of computer programming.

Mitchell was hooked, oblivious to the passage of time until his phone beeped; it was past midnight. *Yikes!* Mitchell thought, fatigue rearing its head, *I have to go to bed. I have that Geometry test tomorrow.*

He flipped off the light and rolled into bed, but not before sneaking a peak at the picture of Marjorie she had sent earlier in the day.

CHAPTER 7

Russia's Premier, Vladimir Buskin, had ruthlessly consolidated political power by cleverly rewarding two groups with the fruits of capitalism. The disenfranchised old guard was put in charge of the country's past—oil, steel, and other basic industries, while the increasingly sophisticated young elite were running the technology sector. Buskin's goal was to blend the two and create an unrivaled economic and military superpower.

The grand plan required a solid financial base, and petroleum was at the heart of it. Black gold had supported those countries blessed with reserves for decades, but everyone seemed to be supplying it now—even the US had become an exporter because of its shale oil fields in the Midwest—and the price had collapsed. Yet the changing structure of the oil market in the United States was also a blessing for Russia as it diminished the Middle East as a focus of US strategic interest.

That the US President, Jackson Cahill, had also unknowingly been so accommodating to Buskin's plan was a stroke of luck that emboldened the Premier even more. Supported by radical environmentalists, Cahill railed against fracking and seemed to believe that falling oil prices were a function of his green technology platform and not simple economics. Buskin did not completely understand the US political system, but his intelligence was clear about the math: the US military had been dangerously scaled back by Cahill's so-called "green dividend" to where it could only effectively fight in one theater at a time.

Buskin planned to probe that weakness by sending a small, specialized force to attack the Ukraine. The pretext was an explosion in Crimea that allegedly killed ten Russian soldiers, but the real aims were to test a radical, new military strategy and gauge the United States' reaction.

The Russian incursion was over almost as soon as it started. While the Ukrainian military was well-positioned, having entrenched itself over weeks of Russian saber rattling, they were overrun in remarkably short order. Every counterattack was immediately and forcefully repelled. Video images suggested that the Russians had lost very little—if any—equipment or lives, and even the more sophisticated equipment the Ukrainians had gotten from Western allies seemed to be of little use. It was as though the Russians had managed to steal the Ukrainian war playbook. For Jeremy and the West, it was unnerving, for General Yikovich and his team, it was glorious.

#

Jeremy couldn't believe his good fortune when the Russians went "live" with their invasion of the Ukraine. He intellectually knew people were being killed miles below the CIA's satellites monitoring the area, yet it just seemed like he was watching a crude video game. He found himself morbidly fascinated by the surgical precision of the attack, rather than being repulsed at the death and destruction below.

Because it happened at the beginning of his shift, he had the opportunity to watch it unfold over the following eight hours. Thinking his recent discovery in Siberia and this Ukrainian battle could be related, he also kept a close eye on Siberia.

#

Premier Buskin and his Cabinet incredulously watched their HD video monitors at what they were seeing in the Ukraine.

"General Yikovich," the Premier started in a somber and threatening tone, "I hope for your sake, and the sake of your team, that this is not some technological, smoke-and-mirrors trick you are playing on us." The mood in the room bristling with the latest in home-grown and stolen technology instantly went from one of pride and disbelief to icy frigidity. Every man, including those in the Cabinet, knew that making Premier Vladimir Buskin look foolish was a one way trip to—well, no one really knew where. But they had all heard the rumors and no one ever returned.

"Comrade Premier," Yikovich warily replied, "we have known each other since childhood. Have I ever been able to hide anything from you?"

Premier Buskin smiled, ever so slightly. General Yikovich had a point. He was as close as the Premier had to a real friend, and was always an open book. They had grown up together in Moscow as part of the aristocracy, but vowed they would make their own mark on the world. They both had embraced technology early on, and it had enabled them to climb over more senior, but less ambitious men.

The Premier also did not really believe that Mikhail Yikovich was trying to pull the wool over his eyes—the General was too much of a pragmatist for that. But Premier Buskin felt the growing tension in the room, and he approved. *Fear is a good thing*, he thought, *it makes people work harder and more desperately.*

"Perhaps not, Mikhail," softening a bit in his reply, before dropping the hammer: "but there is a first time for everything, no?"

General Yikovich stiffened. "I assure you what you are seeing is real. Perhaps you could ask General Petrov to confirm what his ground intelligence is telling him this very moment."

Besides Mikhail Yikovich, Oleg Petrov was the only four-star general in the Russian military and as head of the ground forces and artillery, was perhaps the second most powerful man in the Russian hierarchy after Premier Buskin, himself. He had been Buskin's most dangerous competitor as they fought for the top spot in the Russian government, but had been leapfrogged because he lacked Buskin's understanding of technology.

"I am checking now," General Petrov snapped in a gruff voice. He did not see this coming. How could his allies on the ground and in the government not know about this new technology-based battleground strategy? *There will be hell to pay,* he thought. After a five-minute interregnum that seemed like hours, General Petrov spoke again.

"While we cannot yet confirm all the details, it does appear to be as we have witnessed. You and your team are to be commended, Comrade Mikhail. I would like to see more of how this is being accomplished. I can see many uses."

"Spasibo, Comrade Oleg," General Yikovich smugly preened. "We are still working on some important details, but you will be briefed at our next Intelligence Meeting."

Bastards, General Petrov seethed.

He was an archetypical Russian warrior, making his way to the top by boldly carrying out missions that others were unwilling—or unable—to do. Seemingly devoid of conscience, Petrov could be disarmingly charming one moment and sadistically murderous the next. No one knew how many "enemies of the State" he had killed, but enough senior party members knew or heard of someone who had gotten on his wrong side and were never heard from again. Yet despite his notorious reputation, he had an intensely loyal group of subordinates that had their fingerprints on virtually every aspect of Russian society.

Except the technology one.

General Petrov was old enough to have survived and climbed in the Russian government without a mastery of technology, but still young enough to be limited by that very same lack of mastery. While he had engendered a grudging respect among his peers for his strength, courage, and cunning in the field, he was a bull, not a geek, and under the calculating hand of Premier Buskin, the geeks were running the show. His one technology expert, Sergey Kachinko, had been recruited by General Yikovich some time ago, convinced that the future of the military was in technology. At the time, General Petrov believed his young friend had made a foolish choice, but based on what Petrov had just witnessed, it was now clear the Sergeant had not. The General was both secretly awestruck by what he had seen, and equally terrified by what it meant for old warriors like him.

CHAPTER 8

While the Gaming Olympics were still weeks away, it was predicted to be the most competitive and far-reaching to date. It was open to anyone, anywhere, all on-line. It lasted six-months or until there was a winner, whichever came first, and no one was completely eliminated until then. The rapid rise of professional gaming leagues globally had created a huge fan following of the best individual and team gamers in the world, many of them with corporate sponsors. As a result, though the competition would literally be open to anyone, there would be a significant shakeout in the early stages as the best gamers quickly separated themselves from the rest of the field, something critical to the success of General Yikovich's novel strategy.

Because of *Battle for Babylon's* software efficiency, there was very little advantage to be gained by harnessing it to high-powered hardware. It was more about quick thinking and manual dexterity, leveling the playing field to more players around the world. The fact that Cloud Gaming Co. had just gone public and its founder had suddenly become a high-profile tech maven, only added fuel to the fire.

#

The Metro pulled into Jeremy's station in suburban Virginia, coming to a creaking halt. He stepped off the train, swimming upstream against the hordes headed into Washington for another day. He hadn't realized how easy the reverse commute would be when he agreed to work the graveyard shift, but was reminded of it every time he stepped off the train.

He had just experienced his most stressful day since joining the CIA directly from MIT, and had loved every minute of it. He was too young to fully comprehend how crushing war could be on the societies it engulfed and the soldiers who gave their lives—some experiencing a slow agonizing death from shrapnel wounds while lying unattended on the battlefield. Jeremy saw it clinically: hundreds dead were just nameless and faceless numbers.

He hustled across the street, just barely beating the light and scampered into the local Starbucks and ordered his usual—double-tall, sugar-free, vanilla latte. He chuckled to himself; *Tony would love my "diet" coffee.*

As he waited in line, he was drawn to the television monitor. The talking heads were yammering on about the brief skirmish in the Ukraine. The expert testimony of some retired Army general was that *"...while it was a provocative move by the Russians, it was nothing to be concerned about, because it didn't involve any of the Russian battalions or major weapons."*

Jeremy slightly shook his head from side-to-side and snickered—*that was precisely why we should be concerned about it,* he thought. He had just witnessed what appeared to be a fascinating real-life, video game and people had actually died. Judging from the body language of the senior US government officials he saw who had spent the better part of their night watching and analyzing what the Russians were doing, they weren't concerned, they were terrified.

"Coffee for Jeremy!" the barista called out. He grabbed it, nodded his thanks, and headed out.

He was in his apartment in two minutes. Both of his roommates worked day jobs and so he had the place all to himself. While he missed the camaraderie some of the time, he was happy they were gone today because Jeremy needed to work on his game. He thought he had a real chance to finish in the top 100 of *Battle for Babylon*, but his recent work schedule had prevented him from playing as much as he had needed in order to stay sharp. He planned to spend the next three hours playing and then crash.

Jeremy turned on his Alienware X51 and pulled up the *Battle for Babylon* login page, typing in his user name and password, and dialing up his favorite playlist on his iPod. As the opening rifts of the guitar solo from AC/DC's *Thunderstruck* filled his headphones, his computer came to life: *Welcome Thunderstruck! Are you ready for battle?*

"Hell, yeah!" Jeremy shouted in his empty apartment, as both his head and his leg bobbed up and down to the beat of the mesmerizing rock classic. Jeremy's adrenaline high from the day's proceedings had yet to subside, and he slashed and shot his way through the initial three levels with nary a close call. *Thunderstruck doing work, baby!* he thought, as he hit PAUSE to take a swig of his now tepid latte.

Meanwhile, half a world away, *Polar Bear* was also logged into *Battle for Babylon;* General Yikovich was equally as fired up. The first live stage of a new kind of tactical warfare that he had been instrumental in developing was a major success and he needed an outlet for his own adrenaline rush. He had taken a brief break to check his stock portfolio; CGC was up again. He pumped his fist.

As he re-engaged in *Battle for Babylon,* he suddenly found himself in the middle of a major firefight. Usually during the day when US high school and college kids were in class, there was very little competition. But here he was, under heavy attack from some avatar called *Thunderstruck.* He tried the evasive maneuvers that had recently saved him in a similar attack a few weeks ago, vaulting him to Master 2-Star General status. Nothing worked.

Who the hell is this Thunderstruck? he fumed as he considered his options. *He's not even a Master!*

#

What's this?! Jeremy excitedly thought, eyes widening. *An M2?!*

His fingers adeptly raced over the keyboard as he fired, repositioned, fired again and advanced through the strewn and bombed-out armored vehicles and tanks left on the virtual streets of Fallujah.

"I've got the poor sap," Jeremy roared with delight, "I've got him!"

#

Not so quick my friend, Yikovich steeled himself. He was rapidly running out of options, but saw an escape route across the narrow alley. He knew where *Thunderstruck* was and also where he was likely to go, so he carefully pulled the pin from a grenade and reached out to throw it to where his attacker was most certainly heading. But at that very moment, Jeremy's avatar was rolling out from behind the tank and blasted the grenade before it could gain any elevation from *Polar Bear's* hand. The instant that *Polar Bear* was making a run across the alley, the grenade exploded, sending shrapnel everywhere and the Russian six feet under—at least virtually.

"Master 2-Star, my ass, *Polar Bear!* You've been *Thunderstruck!*" Jeremy gloated as he quickly moved on, looking for another hapless foe. He was on fire.

General Yikovich sat stunned, resisting the urge to smash his computer to bits. He had failed in one of the basic tenets of gaming: focus. He vowed it would not happen again. He would find this *Thunderstruck* and annihilate him. He switched his computer to view mode, put it on the big screen, and got up to pour a glass of sherry. *Let's see what this Thunderstruck can do.* After a few minutes, the General begrudgingly acknowledged *Thunderstruck* was a good gamer, perhaps very good. Yet he was not a Master like Mikhail was. *I have to be better in the Olympics,* he thought.

The General had seen enough. As he logged off, his computer flashed:

You have been terminated and relegated to Master 1-Star General. EXIT?

His blood pressure rose again, as he replayed in his mind what had just happened, pausing briefly before hitting EXIT.

Death claims us all, came the message. *Be strong and courageous. Babylon awaits!*

Jeremy Thomas' work phone pinged once, then twice, and finally a third time, before he noticed, so engrossed was he in his best engagement yet of *Battle for Babylon.* He hit PAUSE and quickly picked up.

"Jeremy Thomas speaking," he answered in a flat monotone, his mind still engaged in the video game.

"Jeremy?" It was his boss. *"Did I wake you up?"*

"No, why?" Jeremy replied, this time more naturally.

"Nothing, you just sounded zoned out for a minute. No big deal," Tony moved on. *"Hey, I want you in here today at 5pm."*

Jeremy looked at his watch. Five and a half hours from now. He was wired from the game, but knew he needed to get some sleep or he would be a zombie by the time his shift rolled around.

"Yeah, sure. What's up?" Jeremy queried, curious at the first non-scheduled request for his time.

"The brass is having a meeting at 7pm to try to make sense of what just happened in the Ukraine and I need your take on it."

Sweet! Jeremy thought, though he was nervous about what he didn't know.

"Sure, Chief," he responded, hoping his excitement didn't show too much. It was a potentially serious national security situation, after all, not a game. "Anything specific you want me to focus on?"

"No, we are just getting intel from assets on the ground and it seems it was as one-sided a battle as anyone had seen in some time. Lots of damage and deaths for the Ukrainians, yet hardly a blemish for the Russians. Given what you have been working on, I need your insight."

"Yes sir. I'm going to crash for a couple of hours, but I will be there." He would set three alarms—phone, clock, and computer. One of them would surely roust him in time.

"Roger," Tony replied in his staccato Marines' voice, *"1700 hours."*

Jeremy hung up, his mind whirring, but his body crashing. He wished he hadn't spent so much time on the video game, and he knew he would pay for it. Nevertheless, he considered going another five minutes because he was so close to the next stage. But he was out of the "zone" and he knew it. *Stay focused and live to fight another day* was his mantra. He clicked on EXIT, his eyelids already feeling like they had weights on them.

He was out like a light.

#

The link to the servers that were connected to CGC's data center back in Washington State was also terminated, a nanosecond after the last bit of information had been transferred via the Cloud from Jeremy's computer in Washington, DC. A moment later a message was sent to *Thunderstruck's* account at CGC:

Congratulations! You are now a Master 1-Star warrior. Be brave and courageous! Babylon still awaits.

Jeremy would have to wait to learn this. He was already dead to the world, hoping his body would recover during the next few hours of sleep.

CHAPTER 9

Greg Galkin's aunt called from Moscow and left a brief message on his voice mail: *call me now.* He had been deep in thought and hadn't noticed his phone vibrating when the call had come in three hours ago. He was ready to call it a day, collecting his things when he picked up his phone.

"Shoot," he mumbled, looking at his watch. It was already 11pm in Russia, "Aunt Lydia will kill me if I wake her up."

Lydia was his mom's younger sister, the only real sane one in the family. She was the lone relative willing to help Greg and his mom when they suddenly had to move back to Moscow two days after the accident that had killed Billy Wilson's father. Greg's dad, Alexander, had been sent home the day before, after disgracing the Russian diplomatic corps investigating the accident. He had vehemently denied driving his pick-up truck the day of the accident, making a scene at the DC Police Department when shown pictures of him in the wrecked truck in a clearly inebriated state.

"You have the wrong man!" he screamed, "I was not driving!"

"Then who's this crazy bastard!" the detective smirked, pointing at the picture, "your evil twin?"

In a feral rage, knowing his life was collapsing around him, Greg's father cold-cocked the man, stepping in to the punch with such force that he knocked the detective out, smashing his nose and jaw beyond recognition, and breaking his own knuckles in the process. It took four police officers to subdue and drag him out of the station and into the waiting Russian diplomatic SUV, which took him straight to the airport for the next plane back to Russia. He was never the same man and committed suicide three years later. Greg winced at the memory.

But Lydia was still awake, tending to her ailing sister, Natasha Galkin, Greg's mom. His phone lit up at that moment and he put it to his ear.

"Alexander, you no use your phone?" came the unmistakably Russian voice of his aunt. Very few people called him by his given name, preferring instead to use the Americanized version of his middle name, Gregor. It was the easiest way to distinguish between father and son.

"*Prostite,*" Greg replied, "I was working and just got your message. I thought it too late to call."

"*Is not too late if mother is dying, no? You need come home right now.*"

It was a gut punch. He knew his mom wasn't feeling well when he spoke to her last month, but did not know she was really ill until Lydia's call.

"I will leave tomorrow. *Spasibo.*"

#

Though Greg was Russian, in many ways he was American, too, having lived more of his life in the US. Nevertheless, he had a Russian passport he used when he traveled home, and showed it to the gruff customs' agent; he was immediately waved through. He handed the address of his old home to the cab driver and 500 rubles later, they were there. Lydia was crying.

"Too late, her heart no work."

"*Proshu proshcheniya,*" Greg said, hugging his aunt. After a few moments, they went inside.

"Tasha leave stuff up in bedroom," Lydia stated, using the nickname by which most people knew Greg's mom.

He disappeared down the hall and up the stairs; it was strange being back. He sat down on the bed, looking at the few boxes of stuff that his mom must have thought he wanted. *She was a good mom,* he thought. *She deserved better.* Two of the boxes still bore the marks of the company that had moved them back to Moscow; they were unopened.

He grabbed the first one and gently pulled at the packaging tape, raising a cloud of dust as it came off. Inside there were some pictures of Greg with his dad, some of him and Billy Wilson, too, in a happier time, and a bunch of folders with papers; he would look at them later. There was also one of his dad's old business cards. He gently picked it up and stared at it: *Alexander G. Galkin, Glavnyy Nauchnyy Sotrudnik* was all it said. He turned it over to see the English translation: *Chief Researcher.* There was something else, as well, a note written in his father's hand. It had faded over time, so it was faint, but Greg could see it was part of an e-mail address.

He immediately knew what was missing, the second part of a mnemonic his dad had taught him long ago when he was learning about computers. It would have been meaningless to anyone but Greg. He put the card in his wallet, grabbed the pictures and the miscellaneous papers his father had left him, and closed the boxes back up. He went downstairs to help Lydia prepare for the wake. There would be a lot of guests. His mother was loved by many people here.

CHAPTER 10

The Russian attack had been the first major test of the Cahill Doctrine, the platform on which US President, Jackson Cahill, had been swept into power. He had persuasively argued that the United States had no real national interest in either religious disputes or historical regional conflicts on the other side of the globe, viewing them both as irrational and unwinnable. He demanded countries most affected by those conflicts be more responsible in resolving them.

Yet, the President also emphasized that US support would only be gradually withdrawn, and so as other countries initially shouldered the burden, it led to a brief period of global stability. However, for an opportunist like Buskin, the Cahill Doctrine also provided a roadmap to where he could strike with impunity and so he chose Russia's historical conflict with the Ukraine as the first live testing ground for its new strategy.

As the CIA processed the intelligence and military information gathered on the one-sided battle that had just occurred in the Ukraine, there was an anxious, but growing fascination at what had happened both on the ground and in the air. The phrases that came to mind were "surgical precision," "economy of ordnance," "effective and immediate counterattack." The 7pm meeting was the first time that senior military and intelligence officials were gathering to try to sort out fact from fiction, and determine what steps to take next.

Jeremy placed his personal items on the metal detector's conveyor belt at the entrance to the CIA office, showing his ID badge to the guard. The beehive of activity around him made it clear this would be no ordinary meeting. He had arrived at 4pm so as to prepare, but as he walked into the Russian and European team's wing, he could already feel the oppressive atmosphere hanging over the room.

He sat down at his desk and got to work. He wasn't sure what Tony might ask, but Jeremy already had an idea what was important and started cataloging his intelligence. He could feel the room's tension increase every time a new senior civilian, military or intelligence official entered the room. It was hard not to be distracted.

"Jeremy," Tony half-whispered, shortly before 5pm. "Thanks for coming in. We are going to be overrun by brass the next few hours. You know the equipment and technology we have in here better than anyone…"

Jeremy gulped.

"…so know where all the important clips are on our video feed because I am going to ask you to cue them up as we get the inevitable, 'what the hell is going on down there?' questions."

"Yes sir," Jeremy replied unemotionally, without so much as a tremor in his voice, though his heart was beating wildly. "I assumed you might be asking me that and so I have already begun logging them. I'm sure you have seen the drones down there like I have," Jeremy continued, though he wasn't so sure that was the case.

"Drones?" Tony replied raising his voice in surprise. "You mean like we saw in Siberia?"

"Similar, but I can't really say if they are doing the same thing, you know, lighting up the targets and taking evasive action because the monitors weren't always focused to track electro-kinetic activity," Jeremy clinically continued, his mind racing as he processed the line of discussion he was having with his boss. He wanted to make sure he wasn't getting too far out over his skis in case Tony asked for his opinion in front of everyone.

"So what do they look like and what do you think they are doing?" Tony's years as an analyst were on display, dispassionately clicking through a list of "who, what, why, where, when, and how" to come to a conclusion. He trusted Jeremy's instincts and analysis, but his charge had only been there a short time. It made Tony nervous to think he might have to rely on some young twenty-something for substantive answers—MIT grad or not.

"I've tracked at least three kinds. There might be more, I don't know. There was so much going on down there it was hard to make sense of it all," Jeremy began, "but there are some that are clearly weapons."

He clicked on the folder with screen shots of unmanned aircraft outfitted with small rockets and machine guns.

Damn, Tony was blown away by how thorough Jeremy already was after less than a year on the job, *this kid is light years beyond where I was at his age. A keeper for sure.*

"These," Jeremy continued, clicking on another folder, "are probably just recording the proceedings or maybe communications links. You can see the sensors and cameras on them. They seem to have jamming capabilities as well, though I am not really sure."

"Uh huh," Tony murmured. He *could* see it. "They don't seem that sturdy, do they?"

"No, they're built for speed and agility," Jeremy countered, enjoying the back-and-forth and appreciating Tony's genuine reliance on his analysis, "but I'm guessing that given the history of Russian technology, they probably have way more than they really need, so if they lose a bunch, they still have enough."

"I see. Anything else?" Tony looked ready to disengage as his android phone buzzed again, heralding the arrival of another message from someone above him in pay-grade.

Jeremy hesitated, unsure how far he should go with so little concrete evidence to support what was rattling around in his brain.

"Um. There are two things that seem a bit strange…"

"Oh?"

"There do not seem to be many soldiers anywhere on the Russian side. The terrain is rugged and there are a lot of trees, so perhaps they are just hidden," Jeremy was thinking on the fly, "but bodies have always been Russia's comparative advantage. It seems unusual not to be able to spot a large number of them."

Tony scratched his head. It was a good observation and it was curious, but he challenged Jeremy, nonetheless.

"But based on what we have seen, it looks like an aerial assault only—a damn good one—but just death from above," Tony shot back. "Maybe there just aren't any."

"Perhaps," Jeremy countered, unconvinced, "but there seems to be a lot of close-range damage down there, suggesting ground troops. I dunno, maybe it's nothing, I'm still new to this after all."

"Don't go all rookie on me Thomas," Tony forcefully countered, wanting to arrest whatever seeds of doubt Jeremy might have. He knew he had a star on his staff.

"What is the other thing?"

"What?" Jeremy momentarily lost his train of thought, "Oh, yeah. The other thing is how the drones and some of the weaponry are acting. It's not as seamless as I would have imagined it would be."

"What do you mean by 'seamless'?"

"There is a jerkiness about how they move sometime, like they are waiting for something."

"I'm sorry, Jeremy, I still don't get it," Tony was perplexed.

"Well, you know when you have a bad Wi-Fi connection and you get a bit of your video stream, then it freezes, then streams again, then freezes?" Jeremy replied.

"Yeah, yeah, yeah. That's annoying as hell."

"It happens because either the Wi-Fi signal is weak and can't quickly deliver all the data, or there is just too much data trying to go through a system not designed to handle it," Jeremy had grown up in the wireless age, but had tinkered enough with dial-up modems to know how slow internet speeds affected data transmission.

"So you're saying that they have a bad Wi-Fi connection and some of their weapons are momentarily freezing up, waiting to be told what to do next?"

"That's what I *think* is happening, but it is hard to know for sure. It isn't that perceptible, but the buffering is happening, so I'd be inclined to say they are still early in the development."

"Good stuff, man. Be ready if the teacher calls on you today!" Tony cackled and slapped Jeremy on the back.

What?! Jeremy mentally pissed in his pants.

CHAPTER 11

Billy was always in the office before dawn and today was no different. As the first faint streaks of light illuminated Mt. Rainier in a brilliant alpenglow, he sat at this desk, reading through management reports and news from around the world. The room was lit only by the screens of his computer and the muted monitor tuned to the news. The solitude and quiet helped him think.

The information from the Ukraine was both curious and concerning. Billy had always been fascinated by history and wars were often turning points in that history; he wondered if this battle might be such a turning point. Though he probably had as much information on what had happened as everyone else did, he always filtered the news through the prism of technology. As he put the fragments of light from that prism together, it seemed that technology was not only part of the success of the Russians in the Ukraine, it was integral to it.

What are they up to? he thought to himself. He had always respected the Russian brute force approach to technology. It showed there was more than one way to tackle a problem. But if the reports were accurate, this was different. It was elegant, efficient, and clean. *Who's running the technology show over there?* he wondered. The only two Russian computer scientists he had ever known—Greg and his dad—were both smart and creative, so he figured there must be others.

He also wondered what was next. The move into Eastern Ukraine had been quick and easy; he doubted it was the end. Were they just testing some new technology? Did they have their sights on Europe again? The Middle East? Troops seemed to be congregated in both places, though that always seemed to be the case. It was intriguing to a history buff whose programming team wrote software for video games about war.

Maybe there is some good material there for one of our new games, he thought to himself.

#

During his long flight back home across the Atlantic, Greg had time to reflect on all that had happened in just a few short days. His mother was dead, the Russians had successfully overrun the

Ukraine using tactics that seemed revolutionary, and he was in possession of information that might fill in the gaps of what had happened to his father a decade ago, changing the lives of so many people close to him. He opened his wallet and pulled out his dad's old business card.

Oh, what secrets will you reveal? he thought as he re-read the partial e-mail address, the sound of the jet engines causing his mind to drift off into his painful past. As he closed his eyes, he could see the events of his childhood as though they had occurred yesterday. When he and Billy were boys, they had hacked into networks and computers all the time. It was a rite of passage for programmers everywhere and the two of them never left anything malicious behind. Mostly it was about seeing if they could get inside, and then "borrowing" any code they found they thought they could use. Greg was the mastermind at cracking the security, the code breaker who managed to find whatever backdoor might exist.

As he struggled to come to terms with what his dad had done to his friend, his friend's family, and ultimately to himself, the thrill of breaking in and eluding people and systems designed to catch him was one of the few things that had sustained him through the pain. Over time, breaking into systems had become such an integral part of Greg's consulting success that his conscience rarely bothered him. But he initially rejected the request from a Russian technology start-up to "research" Cloud Gaming Co. because he worried it would scar the only good memory he had about growing up, and he wasn't ready to go down that dark alley.

However, the Russians were insistent, ultimately agreeing to pay Greg a ridiculous sum that he threw out just to get them to leave him alone. They did not, saying only he would be paid the other half on delivery. *Billy would have wanted me to enjoy in the success of his company,* Greg rationalized in his mind. He knew the way his old friend thought like the back of his own hand and was inside CGC's backdoor in less than an hour. He snooped around a bit, to make sure he wasn't setting off any intruder alarms. He immediately recognized the clean, crisp code writing, surprised so much of it was Billy's. He logged off after thirty-minutes, satisfied there were no landmines waiting for his client. He summarized his findings in a report and hit SEND; he instantly regretted it.

Greg's mind was jolted back to the present as the flight attendant gently tapped him on the shoulder and asked him to put his seat back up.

"Oh, sorry," he replied, putting the card back into his wallet. The plane was at the gate within minutes and before long, Greg was home.

#

Billy reviewed the daily reports from his now public company. There were so many new things he had to worry about since the listing. Many of them seemed ridiculous and intrusive, but his Chief Counsel and his Marketing VP had spent more than a little time educating him about why they were important. It still seemed like overkill and he left most of it to his Investor Relations staff, but he at least understood that as the CEO, he had to be aware of that side of the business.

But the activity reports on the product side of the business, the gaming side, were always more interesting. They showed where CGC's games were being played, player rankings, new customers signing up, and of course, how the system was being stressed. Billy knew security was as important as anything they did and CGC was known as having as impenetrable a system as any in the world—video game company or not. He had implemented a lot of the concepts he had learned from his dad and Dr. Johnson, as well as what he absorbed from his childhood buddy, Greg.

Billy had always wondered what had happened to Greg. One minute they were two peas-in-a-pod, spending almost every waking moment together playing games or in school; the next, he was gone, leaving without even saying "good-bye." When he learned that Greg's dad had been behind the wheel of the truck that killed his dad, he never wanted to speak to either of them again. By the time he had softened, years had passed and as different as his own life had become, he could only imagine that Greg's had been even more tumultuous. Billy only moved across the country, not across the world. *That must have been tough,* he thought. Yet it still hurt, a lingering wound.

CHAPTER 12

Greg held his dad's business card reverently. Though the ink was faded and the e-mail address was missing some critical information, his dad had taught him a number of mnemonic devices growing up, and he confidently filled in the gaps. He was immediately logged into his father's old e-mail account, finding a handful of messages left in the "Drafts" folder. He clicked on the most recent one: its last entry was a few days before Billy's dad was killed.

Greg slowly read through the e-mail. It was long and detailed, reflecting the thoughts of a man who clearly distrusted the system in which he had been given so much privilege and power, but equally trusted his son enough to be totally open about that system. The first part was about his father's work in the Russian technology field, lastly as *Chief Researcher* of something called Department T. Greg had heard bits and pieces of information in his consulting work about some secret Russian government group of technology experts that was always prowling for information and was willing to pay handsomely for it. Now he knew who they were and what they did; he suspected they were the client to whom he had sold the information about Billy's company and chuckled at the irony. It also explained why he and Billy always had such cool stuff to play with while they were growing up.

It was also fascinating to see that even though he didn't spend a whole lot of time with his dad, they were into the same kind of high-tech, cloak-and-dagger stuff. Greg approved. *The apple doesn't fall far from the tree,* he thought, laughing to himself.

But as he read on, the content and meaning of his dad's e-mail became overwhelming. Greg had experienced pain and suffering—the death of his friend's dad, being ripped out of the only place he had known to be dragged back to Russia, his own father's suicide, most recently his mother's death—but none of those events required him to make a choice. They had just happened to him.

His father, on the other hand, had to choose his poison, and even now, more than ten years later, it was crushing to think how anguished by it he must have been. It was no wonder he drank. That his father was a spy was not that surprising, though he probably wouldn't have believed it then, even if his father had told him so face-to-face. But he and Billy had been friends and their families had also socialized. It was hard to believe that anyone would be asked to kill a friend who had done nothing to him and was also the father of his own son's best friend. He was immediately ashamed of his Russian heritage. He was numb that the world could be so cruel and cold-hearted. He was proud that his father had so wrestled with the decision, yet perplexed that he seemed to have carried it out anyway.

As Greg continued to read, he felt as though he was inside his father's head and heart, being granted an unedited look into Alexander Gregor Galkin's life by the man himself, speaking in the present even though he had been dead for many years. Much of the narrative had been well thought out and written long before the accident, but as the date of Billy's father's death drew nearer, the words became more urgent, more rambling, more blunt. Greg could feel the growing tension in his father's words.

Greg occasionally had to stop reading, the words and thoughts so unvarnished, so jarring, so painful. But like a compelling horror flick, he couldn't avert his eyes for long and continued reading. In a strange way, Greg was strengthened by his father's words—words clearly meant for him. And Greg felt pride that his father would struggle with the immorality of an order by the system that had given him so much privilege.

The last posting occurred a few days before the accident, though his father clearly had an inkling that his time was running out. As Greg read it, his heart stopped.

"What the—!!" Greg exclaimed. He re-read the sentence:

"*I have installed a hidden wireless video cam in the cab of my truck to record my driving movements. Remember it's the journey, not the destination.*"

Blood rushed to Greg's head as he processed this piece of information. *There might be evidence about the crash that no one knows!* It suddenly became clear. His father had been speaking to him in code during many of the lessons he had learned from him while growing up: how to use mnemonics to hide information in plain sight, and the importance of stealth in both collecting and storing information.

Damn! Greg was overcome with emotion, crying as he realized how much his father wanted him to know the truth about his secret life, but afraid that he might be drawn into it like he was, and be forced to decide between life and death. He could read no more.

CHAPTER 13

General Mikhail Yikovich grew up in an aristocratic family and had lived a privileged life. His father was a true scientist and the Russian equivalent of a computer nerd. He loved the whole idea of computers and technology, and would likely have been a Paul Allen to someone else's Bill Gates, if he had grown up in the West. As one of the most senior and trusted technology scientists for the Soviet Union, his father was allowed to travel outside the country to technology conferences. He always brought back whatever computer parts he could jam into his suitcase, and his standing within Soviet society also meant the intimidating Russian customs officials never asked him any questions.

General Yikovich's father would spend hours in his work room at home, tinkering with the parts and gadgets he had purchased abroad, educating his young son about what he was doing and why. It was fascinating for the young boy and by the time he was ready for school, he was so far ahead of his peers that he easily qualified for the nation's elite educational program for precocious kids.

The young boy was also a legend at the new video games that were slowly becoming available in Russia, a side benefit of having a dad with privilege and the freedom to travel. Mikhail was always mindful not to be showy with his electronic stuff, even as he got older and proud of how good he had become. But he was also not averse to selling on the thriving black market the equipment for which he no longer had any use.

Video games were still his main, secret indulgence, and the internet and wireless technology allowed him to test his mettle against gamers anywhere in the world. Using the moniker *Polar Bear*, Mikhail Yikovich was known as a formidable virtual warrior. His addiction to the virtual world was also the genesis of his novel idea to succeed in the real one. Acquiring both the gaming system and artificial intelligence programs that would be the foundation for his master plan had been remarkably easy and it rapidly vaulted him to the top of the Russian science community. He was now tantalizing close to achieving success.

It had been two years since then-Colonel Yikovich had bought illicit access to CGC's gaming system. The first time he had logged on and realized he was completely inside what was arguably the most secure network on the planet, he had fallen back in his chair like he had just punched the afterburners of a fighter plane and been slammed into his seat by G-forces. He could hardly breathe, he was so excited. It had allowed him to speed up his artificial intelligence military research by years, and had led to his promotion to General. Though he had paid a king's ransom to a mysterious consultant by the name of "2", it had been worth it.

#

Jeremy booted up his computer and logged into *Battle for Babylon*. He would not be fighting this session, but rather watching; he was looking for a particular Master 3-Star General. Although he knew neither the avatar's name, nor what it might look like, he could guess. He had played enough video games to know that avid gamers' avatars often said something about them: what or whom they liked, or what they looked like—or at least wished they did.

Beth had already scolded him for his surprise that girls played video games. But as he surveyed the various battlefields, he was surprised again. He couldn't believe how many there actually were. *Wow,* he thought to himself, *I guess I really haven't been paying attention.* He had seen them as warriors only, never really thinking that girls might put as much time and effort into constructing a virtual alter-ego as they did in constructing their real one. But at least he had a profile: blonde, bold, confident, outspoken, and in charge.

"Of course she chose to be a General!" Jeremy chuckled to himself. At least it would be easier than finding a solitary *samurai,* the other category of Masters in the game. As he surveyed the battlefields, he came across a few that might fit the bill, but there was always something missing—not aggressive enough, wrong hair color, too calculating. But when he saw the avatar, *Blunt Instrument,* he knew it immediately. Everything fit: the look, the dress, the tactics. He laughed out loud at the name.

"Absolutely perfect!"

#

General Yikovich and Sergeant Kachinko, the two architects of the short, but devastating, military battle in the Ukraine huddled together over a map of southern Russia and the Middle East. The just concluded offensive was an integral step in the overall military strategy with which Premier Buskin had tasked them, but just a step nonetheless. Yet it had accomplished two main objectives.

It had shown that their technology-centered approach was not just a pipe dream. It was a viable, new strategy that had been successful from a military perspective: it had vanquished an entrenched opponent, secured ground, and lost very few assets in the process. It also made the intelligence community in the West nervous as hell.

It had also accomplished a tactical goal by focusing the attention of the rest of the world on the Ukrainian front, rather than where the Russians were planning on striking next. In fact, the world's diplomats were already up in arms about the increasing adventurism of the hard-line Buskin, as the invasion brought Russia one step closer to Europe's door. This Western hand wringing would allow the Russian army to feel justified in bolstering forces on all their exposed fronts. Both men acknowledged that Vladimir Buskin was a shrewd man; the West took the bait, just as he expected. The table was being set.

#

Jeremy watched in fascination as his colleague, Beth Hopkins, aka *Blunt Instrument,* methodically and surgically dispatched a variety of foes, using a host of clever moves. She obviously had spent a lot of time playing video games, but there was also a purpose in how she played. She had a tactical efficiency about her that reflected something Jeremy had not noticed in the CIA building, though they hadn't really spent that much time together. *Perhaps she was military,* Jeremy wondered to himself, *she probably would have made an equally formidable* samurai. But he had also seen enough of the real Beth to fully understand her desire to be in control.

As he logged off, he wasn't sure if he had a crush on Beth or her avatar. *Maybe both,* he chuckled to himself. Yet as strange as this thought was, it was a testament to how effective Beth's video game avatar was in reflecting her own character. Jeremy had seen enough of her personality in the real world to see all those qualities at play in *Blunt Instrument* in the virtual one. He could easily see why she was a Master 3-Star General, and how her aggressive battlefield tactics made her a formidable opponent.

The avatar figure was also beautiful in a way he hadn't fully appreciated in real life. When they had first met, he had noticed her physical attractiveness immediately, but as he watched *Blunt Instrument* attack and dispatch her foes on the *Battle for Babylon* battlefield, he became enamored with the avatar's striking features. He'd have to pay better attention to the real thing.

CHAPTER 14

Mitchell slept right through his alarm, and if it hadn't been for the ping that awakened him to a text from Marjorie, he risked missing the Geometry test altogether. He bolted out of bed, threw on a wrinkled sweatshirt and a pair of jeans, and sprinted out of the dorm, sliding into his seat fifteen seconds before the bell. He looked over at Marjorie and mouthed the words "thank you." She smiled. Fortunately, math was one of the things in which he excelled, so it helped keep his GPA up and his scholarship intact. He finished the test well before anyone else.

As he sat in class, waiting for the bell to ring, he mentally reviewed what he had read the previous night in the computer textbook he had discovered. Although the margin notes were at least eight years old, it was clear that Billy Wilson had a brilliant mind; he could only imagine what he was like now.

Mitchell put away his things and grabbed his backpack at the sound of the bell. He started to walk over to where Marjorie was standing to thank her in person, but she was surrounded by her clique, most of whom didn't seem to care much for Mitchell. He slipped out the backdoor and headed across campus to the Computer Science Building for what was both his most—and least—favorite class, *Advanced Programming.*

He loved the class, his classmates, not so much. Dr. Johnson was a great teacher and the class was intellectually stimulating because only students who could handle the rigor of ninety minutes of technical computer science were in it. Unfortunately, that included the three bullies he did his best to avoid: Brad Jeffries, Jerry Anderson, and Nate Brackman.

"Obviously, the issue of security is probably as critical to writing successful programs as anything," Dr. Johnson began the day's class. "All of us have already embraced this idea by creating user names and passwords that hopefully only you know so as to prevent unwanted intruders from ruining your programs, stealing your ideas or controlling your devices in such a way as to create mischief."

Brad and Nate looked at each other and snickered. They had managed to create their share of grief for classmates by sending embarrassing texts that appeared to come from some unsuspecting student's phone. Mitchell knew this first-hand, as it had gotten him sent to the Principal's office and suspended for three days as a freshman. He resisted the urge to turn around and glare.

"Some of the best security programming is team written," Dr. Johnson continued, "because having a number of people involved blends the strengths of all of the programmers, creating a composite that is different from any one of them. It creates a randomness that makes it much more difficult to break into using normal hacking methods. Of course, programmers sometimes defeat their own security by creating so-called 'backdoors' that only they know and which gives them unfettered access to the program, but that is more the exception than the rule."

Backdoors? Mitchell was hanging on every word. Programmers were artists as much as anything and so it was logical that the best wished to maintain control over their creation, but he hadn't thought of the backdoor as a means to defeat the security of a program. He had spent most of his time trying to break into one of his tormentor's front doors, maybe there was a backdoor somewhere. He wondered if Billy Wilson's old textbook had anything in it on backdoors. He would check tonight.

#

Dr. Johnson watched his students file out after the bell rang, signifying the end of his day in class. He had devoted his life to teaching, but in particular he loved his advanced class. Though his students were only teenagers, their ability to absorb technical information that was PhD level stuff a generation ago was astonishing. The questions and new concepts they came up with stretched him daily.

But as much as he enjoyed teaching high school, he also loved being a part of the tech community in Seattle. Billy Wilson was the most famous and wealthiest of his protégés, but Dr. Johnson was connected in some way to almost every new technology venture in the area, making him both influential and extremely wealthy. While he never charged for any of his advice, he did take a small ownership stake in every venture on which he provided advice, and even though only a few had paid off, he had made a bundle.

Yet there was a downside to his 24/7 obsession with technology and teaching: it had driven his wife to drinking and ultimately, away. It was his biggest failure, one he kept closely guarded, though he was reminded of it every month when his financial adviser wrote her a five-figure alimony check.

#

The day Billy Wilson's company went public, its cross-town rival, StormClouds, had sued CGC for allegedly hacking into their system. The complaint had been strong enough to be heard by a judge, but it had a lot of holes in it, and CGC was clearly winning the day in court. Yet StormClouds was effectively countering with a public relations campaign, and its executive team was preparing their CEO for an upcoming interview on *Tech Movers*. The host of the show, Maria Incandella, knew great theater when she saw it and pitting the two Seattle tech CEOs against each other was juicy. She also hoped to parlay it into another sit-down with Billy Wilson.

#

Mitchell opened the small closet in his dorm room and pulled out the *Advanced Programming & Troubleshooting* book that he hid under his shirts. He doubted anyone would find the book even remotely interesting and worth stealing, but he hid it nonetheless, an old habit from living with four older brothers. He turned on the light and sat down, leafing through the index.

"Yes!" He pumped his fist as he found a citation for "Backdoors" and quickly flipped to the page. The text was not particularly insightful, discussing the dangers of rogue programmers who created backdoors that left entire companies vulnerable to hackers or the disaffected programmers, themselves. But it also included a cryptic passage about how backdoors could be used to take back control of a hacked program or affect the workings of a program without anyone knowing about it. Mitchell was intrigued by the possibilities.

Mitchell flipped the page to reveal some of Billy's doodles in the margins: "WorldWideWebthreeatmark...0728140901391207410625500807640802900320003XX12XX". He wrote the numbers down in his notebook, thinking how odd it was for someone to write down "WorldWideWeb" rather than just www. Even though the string of numbers seemed endless and random, Mitchell knew he was probably missing something. This was Billy Wilson, after all.

He looked for a pattern in the numbers—*Fibonacci perhaps?* he thought, though it was immediately clear that was wrong. He started adding, subtracting, multiplying, dividing, looking for something to connect the numbers. Some sequencing seemed promising, then petered out into nothingness. *Maybe a different base?* Mitchell's mind was deep in thought, mentally crunching the numbers, tracing lines between some of them, looking for relationships. He got zip.

Ping! went his phone, snapping him from his reverie. Marjorie's face lit up the screen and he was immediately disengaged from his task.

"Don't forget that paragraph on The Great Gatsby *is due tomorrow!!!"*

Mitchell's thumbs sprang into action. He hated English, but he would talk about anything if it meant having a conversation with Marjorie.

"Yeah, I know. I was trying to put it off...don't get any of what that dude is writing about, do you?"

He waited thirty seconds for the answer.

"Just think of him being a guy out of place in the middle of all sorts of people with money who do crazy things."

That's actually a great way to look at it, he thought to himself. He was the guy—Mitchell Patkanim—and Queen's High was where all the money was. Marjorie was both pretty and smart.

#

Mitchell looked out his window across the quad to the Computer Science Building where the light in Dr. Johnson's office always seemed to be on. "Dr. J," as his students affectionately called him, was available to anyone for help on projects, writing code or just shooting the breeze. The students loved this about him and his fellow teachers felt lucky to have such a devoted and influential teacher on the staff, even if his accessibility set a high bar for the other teachers at Queen's.

Of course, he spent plenty of time doing what his colleagues did—grading homework, preparing lessons, and planning tests. But as a teacher in a field where history was literally being made every day, he also had to keep up on new technology developments as they were happening around the world. Part of that was his one secret obsession: video games, and ever since he wife had left him, it filled his empty spaces. It was one of the reasons the light was always on.

CHAPTER 15

Greg woke up at 6am, after a fitful night of sleep. What he had recently learned about his father's past troubled him deeply. He had always wondered what had caused his dad to spiral down so far, so fast. He now knew, and it enraged him. He wanted to know more, but there was no one to ask, now that his mother was gone. He also doubted she would have much to add, but he would never know. It was up to him to find out and clear his father's name, at least in his own mind and perhaps in Billy Wilson's, as well.

Greg shuffled out the door of his brownstone. His body was fatigued, but his mind was sharp. He walked into the corner Starbucks to order as strong a coffee as they made—he would need the extra caffeine. He sat down at one of the tables, reflecting on the task at hand.

He had always been slightly paranoid about the people around him, a trait he no doubt picked up from both his parents. However, now that he was armed with new knowledge about his father, he had become even more so. He had his own car, but decided it made more sense not to use it for this trip, just in case someone might be tailing him in some way.

He would take a train to Newark Airport, where he would rent a car and make his way down the Garden State Parkway to the Princeton exit. He had purposely left his phone in his apartment and had withdrawn $200 from his bank account for incidentals and gas. He knew he had to use a credit card to rent a car, but that would be far from Princeton. If everything went according to plan, he would be back home by nightfall. The stealth was overkill, but it made him feel better.

The train ride from Washington to New York was one he frequently made. He enjoyed the countryside, particularly once the train got out of the suburban Washington area. It was especially beautiful today, with the mix of the cold, crisp fall air and the brilliance of the leaves creating a burnt golden hue as they reflected the morning sun. It was a great day for hunting.

#

"I don't have a reservation, but would like to rent a car for the day," Greg said to the clerk at the car rental counter.

"Certainly, sir!" came the cheery response from a uniformed woman, "it is a gorgeous day for the leaves, that's for sure. What kind of car would you like?"

"I'd like a Suburban if you have one," he replied. He *was* hunting after all. "Preferably a dark one," he added, playing the part of the spy.

"Hmmm," the clerk responded after tapping on a few keys and surveying her computer screen, "we don't have any Suburban's left, but we do have some pick-up trucks that are nice. I can set you up with a new Ford F-150 in midnight blue. Would that be OK?"

"That would be fine," Greg said, handing the clerk his ID.

"'Galkin' is an unusual name," the clerk inquired, looking at Greg in the eyes, "is that Russian?" She was just making small talk, but it made him nervous, nonetheless.

"Yes it is, but I've lived here all my life." It was mostly true, but Greg just wanted to be moving on and was not interested in chit-chat.

#

Mitchell's first class of the day, English, was winding down. He had turned in what he thought was a great paper, and the teacher always gave them the last ten minutes of class to work on homework. Instead, he pulled out his notebook. Ever since looking at the section on backdoors in Billy's old textbook, his mind had been working on the series of words and numbers on the page, trying to make heads or tails of it. They still didn't make any sense and it was driving him crazy. He looked at them again, hoping for a flash of insight. Nothing.

#

As Greg motored down one of New Jersey's two main toll roads, he wondered what the Princeton area now looked like. He could hear his father's words: *"It's the journey, not the destination"* although in this case, it *was* about the destination. Greg exited the Parkway and made his way through the backroads to where the duck club had been.

His heart sank. There were houses everywhere, the result of a rapid influx of population into Princeton housing New York commuters, University researchers, and employees of financial institutions who worked in one of the large number of back offices that had gobbled up most of the free land. He was amazed that the countryside had changed so much in such a short period of time. Then he spotted it: an old, ramshackle garage.

#

Mitchell tried a different approach, using technology to solve the puzzle. He pulled out his tablet computer and opened up its Excel program. He voiced the words softly as he typed:

"World wide web three at mark dot dot dot" he whispered aloud, inadvertently hitting @ itself, rather than the words "at mark". He typed in the rest of the numbers exactly as written and hit ENTER.

"Whoa!" he gasped, forgetting class hadn't ended yet.

"Yes, Mr. Patkanim? Something you'd like to share with us?" remonstrated the teacher.

"Huh?" Mitchell responded, not realizing he had verbalized his surprise at what was staring back at him on his computer. "No, I'm sorry, ma'am."

She held her glare at him, but Mitchell had already tuned her out. Blinking back at him was exactly what he typed, only in light blue and underlined, the Excel program having auto-formatted the long string of letters and numbers.

Of course! Mitchell's mind was racing now, *it's an e-mail address!* He looked at the letters again: *worldwidewebthree@... @ where?* The web had so many addresses; a thousand possibilities battled for his brain's bandwidth. *And what about the numbers?* As he pondered what his new revelations meant, he felt a nudge.

#

As Greg pulled up to the house with the large field and the old garage, he could not believe his good fortune. It was obviously on someone's property and there were dogs around, but it was no doubt the old duck blind where he had spent many hours with his dad. He rang the doorbell and an older gentleman answered.

"May I help you?" he inquired in a faint Russian accent.

Damn! Greg thought, *a Russian.* He hadn't thought that the reason they were hunting at *this* duck club might have been because it was owned by the Russian government. He stayed calm.

"Hi, I am in town for business for the day and just enjoying the countryside between meetings. My dad and I used to hunt out here when I was boy and I noticed the old duck blind is still standing," Greg stated, convincingly. "Mind if I go out and reminisce?"

"Sure, sure, be my guest," came the enthusiastic reply. "We had heard that this used to be a duck hunting ground when we bought the property. Kind of a shame you can't do that anymore. The gate is open." Greg felt momentarily relived when he heard they were new owners. *Just a coincidence he is Russian,* he thought.

"Thank you, sir," Greg warmly replied, "I won't be long— maybe ten minutes, just wanna get a feel for the place."

"Take as long as you need. I remember my hunting days when I was kid in Russia. Good memories, for sure," the man volunteered. Greg resisted the urge to engage in banter.

"Well, thanks a lot," Greg said as he turned to go down the stairs, "I'll make sure I close the gate when I leave."

#

"Earth to Mitchell!" Marjorie said in a silly voice. He looked up at her, then around to find the class empty, so engrossed was he in his discovery.

"Hey, where did everyone go?" Mitchell queried, totally clueless that the bell had rung and the students had already left for the next class.

Marjorie tilted her head and looked at him like he was the oddest person in the world.

"Is that a serious question? Class has been over for five minutes, silly."

"Wow, I must have been totally zoned out. You must think I'm really weird!" Mitchell said, shaking his head side-to-side.

"Not one bit," Marjorie shot back, "my brother gets just like that sometimes, so I kind of know the look, but you were really out there!" She playfully punched him in the shoulder.

"Owww!" Mitchell whined in a pretend voice, "that hurt!"

Marjorie smiled and reached down to rub his shoulder, "Ahh, the poor baby!" she was so close that Mitchell could smell her perfume—it was exciting and dangerous at the same time. He wasn't sure what to do. This wasn't his turf and he didn't know the rules.

Mitchell put his tablet into his back-pack and tried to stand up; Marjorie didn't move an inch.

"Um, excuse me?" he stammered, his voice rising in confusion. He couldn't get up and had expected her to move, but she stood her ground, just inches away. His heart was racing and his mind and body were swirling with a thousand emotions. The two of them were alone, but the halls outside were jammed with students between classes and someone could walk in at any moment.

Just then the warning bell rang and students for the next class started flooding in, eyeing them both suspiciously. Marjorie quickly turned to leave. Mitchell waited half a second, then grabbed his back-pack to follow her out, getting caught in the incoming tide of students. She was gone.

#

Greg slowly walked up to the gate, lifted the latch and pulled it to him; it squeaked as though it hadn't been opened in years. *Ten years,* Greg hoped to himself. He walked out into the field, breathing in the cold air. He actually felt nostalgic, as the smell of dead leaves and burning fire wood brought back memories of this place when he was a kid. He realized that he had enjoyed it more than he let on, remembering how patient his father had been in educating him about things a man should know when out in the wilderness all on his own. Like now.

He bent down and grabbed a handful of leaves, throwing them in the air. He noticed the older man watching from the window, smiling while talking on the phone. *Yeah, just a coincidence,* Greg thought again, trying to reassure himself. Just then a flock of ducks flew overhead. Greg looked up, pretending to fire at them. *Might as well put on a show,* he mused to himself, but it did bring back memories. He turned towards the old garage that had served as a more than capable duck blind. It had been much farther away from all the houses then, but it still had an isolated feel to it. *What are the odds?* he thought to himself. This had to be the "destination" to which his dad had cryptically referred in the e-mail—someplace they would both know, even after a long passage of time.

He surveyed the inside, looking for potential hiding places, using a rickety ladder to climb up to the loft area. He gingerly felt around in the eaves with his hand. A part of the beam had been cut out and replaced by a hollowed-out, 4x4 piece of wood ten inches long. A plastic bag with what looked like a small electronic device was in it.

Bingo! His heart was beating a hundred miles-an-hour. He put the plastic bag inside his chest pocket before carefully placing the piece of wood back in the corner of the building. *No sense leaving any obvious traces,* he thought.

Greg walked back to the gate—neither suspiciously fast nor invitingly slow—waving his appreciation to the man in the window. Though he could see the man coming to the door, Greg quickly hopped into his truck and pulled away—he was in no mood to linger. There was no telling to whom he was talking on the phone and the sooner he was clear of the house, the better.

He was back at the airport in no time, dropping off the truck and rushing up the stairs—he could make the 15:08 if the monorail was there. It was! He managed to jump into the last car as the doors were closing, the last person on. He patted his chest pocket. It was still there, but more importantly, he was alone.

CHAPTER 16

Mitchell slid into his seat in Dr. Johnson's class just before the bell rang. The last class of the day was usually his favorite, though today Brad Jeffries was being particularly annoying, glaring at him and mumbling just loudly enough for Mitchell to hear.

"Stay away from my sister," he warned, "I mean it."

Jerry and Nate both chimed in a half-beat later, "he means it Pocahontas!"

"Whatever," Mitchell replied dismissively, waving his hand in Brad's direction. One thing he knew for sure was that he could easily handle any of his classmates in a fight—maybe even all of them at the same time. But it was best not to fuel their bullying tendencies, so he kept his eyes forward and just stayed engaged as Dr. Johnson spun his favorite stories about the start-ups on which he had consulted. This intersection of the real world and the academic one made it clear to Mitchell how toiling away in class had a direct link to his future.

As the bell rang to end class, Mitchell grabbed his things and made a beeline to the front of the class, so as to avoid needless confrontation. He had some questions for Dr. Johnson and wanted to make an appointment.

"Dr. Johnson?"

"Yes, Mitchell. What can I do for you?" Dr. Johnson was growing in respect for the young sophomore and his unusual programming skills. "How's the AI stuff coming along?"

"OK, I guess. I haven't really spent a lot of time lately on it, but I am running some programs where it is coming in handy, and it's definitely saving me some time." If Dr. Johnson knew that Mitchell was using it to try to hack into the social media accounts of his three star pupils, he might not be so thrilled about it, so he quickly changed the subject.

"I'd like to meet with you when you are free after classes today to ask you some questions about Billy Wilson," Mitchell asked as innocently as possible.

"Oh? Are you doing a research project on him?" Dr. Johnson's question was completely without ulterior suspicion, but Mitchell felt defensive nonetheless.

"Uh, no. You just talk about him a lot and obviously he's a successful alum of the school. I'm just curious, that's all." This was all true, though not the main reason for his curiosity.

"Yeah, sure. I'm done at 4. Come by my office then."

"OK, see you then, Dr. J." Mitchell turned around to see Brad Jeffries lurking, still glaring at him. He turned back around. "Hey, Dr. Johnson? Can you call Brad up here so I can get out of here without having to talk to him? He's kind of being a pain right now."

Dr. Johnson glanced over Mitchell's shoulder at Brad in the background, scowling at no one in particular. He knew Brad could be a jerk, even though he had a great computer mind and was the school's top gun in the upcoming Gaming Olympics. Dr. Johnson chuckled and smiled.

"Sure, Mitch. See you at 4." He was done talking to Mitchell, though not finished talking. "Hey Brad, can you come up here a minute?"

The two boys glared at each other as they passed in the classroom.

CHAPTER 17

Though William Wilson, III was remarkably gifted as a young boy, he wasn't particularly interested in anything but fiddling with computer code, and even that had no grand purpose. It started off as nothing more than a young boy mimicking his father, though the elder Wilson recognized that Billy had a special talent. William Jr. fostered and encouraged the simplicity and clarity in code writing that would become the hallmark of his son's programs, and ultimately the foundation and competitive advantage of Cloud Gaming Co. To his dad, Billy was like one of the great classical composers who heard music in their heads and then just wrote it down from memory. But as far as Billy was concerned, he was only hanging out with his dad, soaking up every detail of the instruction of the man he idolized.

However, it was his growing friendship with Alexander Gregor Galkin, Jr., that quickly morphed into full-blown—though remarkably friendly—competition. Billy and his boyhood pal drew out each other's passion for the inner workings of computer toys and video games, albeit in starkly different ways. They were exactly the kind of computer prodigies that might be expected from two strong, but in many ways, diametrically opposed societies.

Both were only-children, raised in traditional households. Each had a mother who, despite education and intelligence, had chosen to put her own intellectual pursuits on hold to support a husband and raise a family. And both boys were pushed to strive for excellence in all their endeavors, though loved regardless of the outcome. Yet there was one critical difference in each boy's worldview that affected how they programmed: the issue of trust.

Billy trusted almost everyone he met, a certain naiveté which was charming as a boy, but left him increasingly vulnerable to mischief makers as he grew older. He believed that people said what they meant, meant what they said, and usually wanted the best for everyone. It was why he was such a perfectionist in programming, simplifying his code to the nth degree because each change made things faster—even if only by nanoseconds—and faster was better and fastest was best. It was that simple and would ultimately make him a wealthy man.

Greg knew trust in his family life, but from his father he also learned that most of the world was not trustworthy. As a consequence, it was absolutely critical to protect what was important—yourself, your reputation, your family, and your work. Because Alexander Sr. taught these lessons in a matter-of-fact way, stripped of their moral undertones, Greg also learned them that way. They were facts, not judgments: people weren't trustworthy and you had to protect yourself, and in programming, that meant protecting your code.

This philosophy was so ingrained in Greg from a young age that every time he looked at software code, he instinctively thought first about how it was protected and secondly, how quickly he could circumvent whatever protection was there. It was never about maliciousness, but rather a skill to be honed on the shortcomings of other programmers. In time, he became skilled at the defensive and offensive elements of security: how to keep people out of your code, and how to break into theirs.

These radically different viewpoints of trust, when married to the remarkable programming talent each boy had, created a dynamic that made everyone in the coding world sit up and take notice. They were two incredibly creative and gifted boys who had almost perfectly complementary skills, and actually enjoyed hanging out together. They also lived in supportive homes where excellence was modeled at every turn, and were genuinely nice kids. It was only a matter of time before they would be doing great things—together.

But that was before that gray, winter day, ten long years ago. Greg had never heard what had actually happened, only that there had been an accident involving his father and Billy's dad, and William Wilson, Jr. had been killed. A day later, his dad was gone—back to Russia—followed by Greg and his mom less than a week later. He wasn't even allowed to say "good-bye" to his best friend.

Even now, it was gut-wrenching for him to think about. Yet here he was, in possession of some device that might possibly shed light on what had happened that night. He wrestled incessantly about going down that road in his past.

#

"Hi Mitchell. Please sit down."
"Thanks Dr. J. I appreciate the time."

"My pleasure. Hopefully we can get you on the team next year," Dr. Johnson replied, half pleading. Although Mitchell was not on the gaming varsity, it wasn't because he wasn't good enough. He just couldn't stand the thought of spending any more time than necessary with his smug, entitled classmates.

"Yeah, maybe next year," Mitchell half-heartedly replied. But he wasn't there to chat about video games; he was hopefully going to find out something to unlock the code scribbled in the margins of Billy Wilson's old textbook.

"So, you want to know about the founder of the world famous Cloud Gaming Co.?" Mikel Johnson started by asking his own rhetorical question. He commenced with "where shall we begin…" and for the next thirty-minutes, barely came up for air. He was obviously proud of Billy's accomplishments, and in some ways felt that he was the father that Billy no longer had. It was fascinating to learn about someone so famous and wealthy, yet who had sat in the same classroom under the same teacher with whom he was now talking.

"Wow. That is a great story. What a shame about his dad. I can't imagine."

"Yeah, he was pretty broken when he came here," Dr. Johnson replied, "but he managed to grind through and is doing great things now."

"Do you mind if I ask some questions?" Mitchell queried.

"Not at all. As you can tell, I have a real fondness for Billy and what he's done."

"What other classes did he like here? I mean, I'm sure he didn't just take computer classes, as cool as that might be," Mitchell asked expectantly.

"Hmmm. You know, no one has ever asked me that before. You definitely walk your own path, Mitchell," Dr. Johnson replied pensively.

"No one here knows that path, Dr. J, but it's who I am." Mitchell was proud of his Native American heritage and his strong family.

"Indeed. Well, you know Billy liked to talk about history, past and future," the teacher started.

"Huh, 'future history'? That's heavy Dr. J. What does it mean?"

"Prophecy. Bible stuff, Revelation, Nostradamus, those kinds of things. My guess is you have your own Native American stories about prophecy or 'future history'."

"Oh, I see. Yeah, that stuff is really cool. I loved listening to my great-grandfather before he died," Mitchell's face went sad momentarily as he remembered him. "Was there anything specific he liked about history?"

Dr. Johnson looked at his young pupil, wondering what was eliciting such an unusual line of questioning. Mitchell Patkanim didn't think like a programmer and he certainly wasn't like any of the other kids at the school.

"Another interesting one, Mitchell. Well, Billy seemed particularly fascinated with the history of warfare, both past and future. When and why they started and ended, where they took place, what kind of tactics were most successful."

Bingo! Mitchell thought. *When they started means dates!* He was bursting with excitement, thinking that could be the key to unlocking the code in the Backdoors' section.

"That explains why his best video games are about war, I guess," Mitchell replied. "Sounds like the dude was totally into it. Babylon, Armageddon, Thermopylae are all famous battles—some in the past, some in the future."

"Very perceptive of you, Mitchell." Dr. Johnson doubted Brad Jeffries had this kind of depth of thinking. "Very perceptive, indeed."

Mitchell's phone pinged; it was Marjorie.

"Well, thanks a lot Dr. J. That was really interesting. Wow, that dude has come a long way. I guess there's hope for us all, isn't there?"

"Yes, there is Mitchell. Yes, there is," Dr. Johnson replied. "Before you leave, do you mind if I ask what's up with you and Brad?"

"He doesn't seem to like me very much, Dr. J. Indian name-calling, bullying, that kind of stuff. I don't know why, but I can deal with it," he wasn't totally sure he could, but put on a brave face.

"Well, Brad said that you are harassing his sister and she wants you to stop, and you won't," the computer science teacher stated in somber tones, "that's serious stuff, Mitchell. People get expelled for that."

Mitchell was enraged.

"That's bulls—oops! I mean that's baloney, Dr. Johnson!" Mitchell fired back, his face flush with rage. "Ask her yourself if it's true. Not with those clowns around, but you and her, one-on-one. I swear that if she says I'm harassing her, I will never talk to her again. But it's a lie. Just like the phony text messages I got accused of sending. Brad's a smart guy, Dr. J, and maybe he can do magic playing video games, but he is the biggest a-hole I have ever met in my life!"

Mitchell's vehemence startled Dr. Johnson. It also had the ring of truth to it.

"Calm down, son. I'll talk to her and sort it out. In the meantime, just be careful around her."

"It's hard to calm down when people are spreading lies about you, Dr. J!" Mitchell was near tears, but fought them back.

"I know, Mitchell, I know. Frankly, I wouldn't turn my back on them either. But I can't have my best students at each other's throats in the buildup to the Olympics now, can I?"

"I hear ya' Dr. J, I hear ya'."

CHAPTER 18

The latest and most advanced game in Cloud Gaming's "War Series," *Battle for Babylon* was designed for hard core gamers who understood military tactics. Master-level players could call in air, artillery, and naval power, depending on their rank. CGC's software catalogued and analyzed the military effectiveness of each action, and after enough data points, was able to create a personalized, virtual military signature of every player. Masters could then choose an integrated military force that reflected their own style of play and aggressiveness.

But having the additional firepower had downsides, as well, the major one being the loss of flexibility caused by running a large-scale military operation. Generals became increasingly critical to the success of their own military engagement. If they failed to exercise caution in their individual endeavors, they risked being terminated—along with their military—creating a vacuum to be filled by some competing General.

However, the biggest threat to Generals was the other group of Masters, the *Samurais*. These warriors chose not to acquire the military hardware to which their rank entitled them, and instead traveled alone. Unencumbered by the logistical and tactical aspects of running a complex military, the *Samurais* could easily move across battlefields, skillfully warding off most opponents. More importantly, their mastery of stealth and elusiveness made them deadly threats to unsuspecting Generals and other combatants, adding a layer of complexity to an already chaotic battlefield. It was the first major strategic decision any aspiring player had to make when they reached the Master level.

Beth Hopkins, aka *Blunt Instrument,* had chosen to become a General and was now a Master 3-Star, commanding an air force and army that reflected her aggressive tactics. She settled into her gaming chair and fired up her computer.

She enjoyed working at the CIA and was gratified to be making friends with her colleagues. She had always been the smartest in every class, and most boys felt threatened by that. However, that didn't seem to be the case in the real world; or at least in her world at the CIA. Perhaps it was because the boys were now men, perhaps because it truly was an egalitarian field whose collective goal was to protect the United States from threats. In any event, it had created a sense of non-virtual purpose in her work life, and as she found herself increasingly attracted to Jeremy Thomas, in her personal life, as well. He was good looking, smart, *and* tech-savvy, a trifecta in her book.

Yet her passion was video games and she loved the CGC games with their high-speed interface. In the cyber world, nobody really knew with whom they were battling, and people created avatars for all kinds of reasons. But Beth made sure it was known she was a girl and delighted in giving the gamer alpha males a beat down whenever she could. The avatar she created was a reasonable reflection of how she saw herself—a feminine, warrior princess with shoulder-length, blonde hair. She typed in her login information and as her alter-ego, *Blunt Instrument,* Beth was immediately at her command bunker of Level 5 in *Battle for Babylon.*

After a spirited battle where her aggressiveness had allowed her to dispatch a Master 2-Star General called *Hunker Down,* she now had control over a large battlefield. Beth decided to go looking for one particular avatar: *Pinball,* the coward that had eluded her by fleeing, rather than fighting. Her previous encounter with him had almost resulted in disaster, and while she had maintained her Master 3-Star status, the near miss had cost her points.

Beth panned out on the battlefield, using her air force to survey the territory two levels below and intently scanning for any sign of *Pinball.* Her intensity and focus were two reasons she was a fearsome warrior and a Master 3-Star, but today was more about revenge. It would be her undoing.

As the brains behind *Blunt Instrument's* military, Beth Hopkins' job was to make sure her avatar was protected from attacks. Although her bunker was out in the open to minimize the threat of a land invasion, it would usually be well fortified and guarded by both her air and ground forces. Yet with her air force engaged far from home, the aerial surveillance and ordnance that would normally protect her from advancing ground threats was virtually non-existent. Instead, it was two levels below, looking for revenge and not for danger.

Suddenly, a stranger was in her compound, quickly and effortlessly subduing half a dozen of her ground forces, who were tactically stretched thin by Beth's focus on finding *Pinball* and not defending her fortress. *Blunt Instrument* sprang into action, calling her air force back and screaming for her soldiers to assist, but the few moments spent attempting to organize her forces, rather than defending herself, were deadly. She had never seen a Master 4-Star anything, but here was a Master 5-Star *Samurai,* obviously having dispatched all of her bodyguards without her even being aware, and now he had her in his sights. The attack was swift and violent, and then he was gone—almost vanishing into thin air.

#

The servers at Cloud Gaming Co. processed the events as they unfolded. *Blunt Instrument* was dead, lying in a pool of remarkably realistic blood.

You have been terminated and relegated to Master 2-Star General. Continue playing two levels lower or EXIT? flickered in bold on her screen.

Beth seethed with rage. She knew she had broken every rule in the book by chasing down *Pinball,* and probably deserved her fate, but she still couldn't believe *she* had been eliminated. She never lost at anything related to technology. Her blood was boiling.

"How dare you!…you!…" she screamed at the screen, realizing that she never even got a glimpse of who—or what—eliminated her.

"CONTINUE!!!" she screamed, an octave higher, slamming the return key that immediately deposited *Blunt Instrument* two levels lower. She landed on an open plain, a sitting duck to whatever might be waiting.

"WHAT THE…!!!" Beth shrieked, once she realized how exposed she now was, "THIS IS NOT FAIR!!!" But war—even the virtual kind—rarely was.

#

Pinball was waiting in the shadows, more than happy to engage such a spirited, feminine avatar.

"*DA!* I have you now!" Sergey Kachinko squealed in delight, recognizing *Blunt Instrument* as the female avatar that had almost terminated him in a previous fight before he managed to sneak away. "Who's your *comrade* tonight?" he cackled.

Though disoriented at the sudden turn of events, *Blunt Instrument* put up a valiant fight. Her ground troops were gone, stripped from her when she lost her third star, and air power was two levels higher and at least two-minutes away. Recalling her air force to Level 5 was the last thing she did before the Master 5-Star *Samurai* had ended her life—at least electronically—and now she desperately needed them on Level 3, exactly where she suspected the coward, *Pinball,* had been all along.

But her fighting skills were rusty, a casualty of choosing to be a general instead of a warrior, and *Pinball* was more skilled at the hand-to-hand combat the battle had become. He had her in a choke hold from behind, and despite *Blunt Instrument's* frantic attempt to claw and scratch her way to freedom, she was doomed. *Pinball* pulled a knife out of his sheath, and with one sharp motion, slit *Blunt Instrument's* neck, slowly dropping her limp body to the floor, watching what had been searing blue eyes flicker to gray as the last few moments of life left the avatar's body. He stood over her, the pitiless conqueror who had just brutally vanquished a woman. It touched some primordial taboo in *Pinball's* psyche. He loved every minute of it.

#

Beth gasped at the grisliness of it all, her own blue eyes watering as she instinctively reached for her throat to make sure it wasn't real. Yet it *was* real to her. She was passionate about her gaming and she had just committed two foolish blunders to undo six-months of intense gaming that made her a Master 3-Star General. All gone in a flash. She stared at the lifeless body of the avatar on the screen below, a work of beauty she had worked so hard to create and felt…nothing.

Her computer flashed: *you have been terminated and relegated. Continue or EXIT?*

Beth sighed and pushed EXIT.

Death claims us all, came the message. *Be strong and courageous. Babylon still awaits!*

The screen went dark. It was almost too much for Beth to digest. Yet, rather than stew about it, she took stock of the lessons she had learned, cataloguing the series of emotional blunders into which she had rushed headlong, vowing she would not repeat them.

She would also rethink her military strategy, realizing she had been stretched far too thinly to deal with the one-on-one ambushes she had only moments before faced. Beth would also spend some time watching various battlefields to try to find out anything she could about this mysterious Master 5-Star *Samurai* who had managed to elude her defenses—thinly stretched or not—and skip in and out almost without a trace.

#

The CGC servers in central Washington State tabulated the scores, the actions, and the outcome. *Blunt Instrument* had been relegated to Master 1-Star General, and *Pinball* had been promoted, also to Master 1-Star warrior. One a crushing blow, the other a moment of euphoria.

#

Sergey Kachinko got one more message: *General or Samurai?* He highlighted the cursor over *Samurai,* and hit ENTER. *Battle for Babylon* had a new Master 1-Star *Samurai.*

"Da!" Sergey Kachinko said to himself as he logged off the computer. It had been a good day.

CHAPTER 19

Security Central was a vast room of flickering, multi-colored lights that monitored and processed every byte of information flowing through CGC's system of electronic devices around the globe. The collective soft hum of each piece of equipment, and the HVAC system that ran night and day to keep the room manageably cool, created a roar of white noise that rivaled that of a small jet. It would have deafened the technicians who worked there had they not sat in a room of floor-to-ceiling, triple-paned glass situated high above the rows and rows of equipment.

Sebastiano DiCarlo headed the department, a graduate of New York's Rensselaer Polytechnic Institute. He had joined right out of college, landing in the security area when the firm was still a fledgling operation. He had been surprised at how well constructed the security systems of CGC's platform had been. They were light years beyond anything he had seen or heard about at one of America's premier tech schools, but he was a quick study and before long, the now 28-year-old was leading a team of ten.

"Are you sure these reports are accurate?" he asked one of the technicians working for him. Seb had noticed an increasing yellowish hue of the ocean of equipment on the floor, signifying stress on the system.

"I believe so," the tech replied, looking up from his monitor. "Why do you ask?"

"I dunno. When I look out there," Seb said, waving his hand towards the window, "I get the sense I am seeing more yellow than I remember recently, and yet your report doesn't seem to register any unusual activity."

His subordinate looked through the window at the blinking lights. Despite all the electronic security in which CGC had invested, part of the beauty of the security system was that it also relied on the intuition and observations of humans. The floor was arranged by geographic region and the various shades of lights reflected the existence of actual or possible threats—red, orange, yellow, blue, and green in descending order of concern. When seen together, it was possible to quickly identify how the system was being stressed, and from where. The monitoring lights were mostly green or blue, with increasing, but moderate, shades of yellow in the big metropolitan areas around the world, the occasional orange, and fortunately, hardly ever any red.

"Hmm, I think I see what you mean." The young tech's eyes were locked onto equipment banks that represented Eastern Europe and Russia. "Russia seems to be much more active than usual."

"Exactly," replied Seb. "It's something I have been noticing the last few months, yet it doesn't seem to show up on our reports. Please do some diagnostics and check it out."

"Will do," the tech blandly responded, seemingly oblivious to his boss' concern.

But Seb was concerned. Part of the reason that CGC had been so rapidly adopted as the *de facto* gaming protocol was that its blend of simple code and perceived impenetrability made its legion of fans comfortable they were playing on a level field. Cloud Gaming Co. also did not desire to rule the cyber world like some of its peers in the industry, so gamers who jealously guarded their privacy when in the virtual realm, felt comfortable that their information was secure and not for sale.

Seb walked into his office and shut his door, pulling out his phone in the process and hitting the speed dial for Billy Wilson. One of the things he enjoyed about working at CGC was that its flat management structure meant he was one call from the top. He also loved that he could talk shop in all its complexity with his boss and not have to dumb it down. Billy picked up on the first ring.

"Sebastiano, how are things over there?" Billy answered, referencing the location of his nerve center near Quincy, in the center of Washington State.

"Busy as ever, man," came the usual reply. But he quickly got down to business. "Look Billy, I have noticed increasing Yellow Stress in Russia and Eastern Europe."

"Oh?" Seb immediately had Billy's attention. He knew what a whiz Seb was and he had never been wrong about his concerns in the past.

"Yeah, over the last few months it seems the Stress from those places has gone from Blue to Yellow, with the occasional Orange," Seb began.

"Really? What do the reports say is going on?" Billy replied inquisitively.

"That's just it. The reports say everything is fine, no material deviations from the norm. I'm having one of my guys run diagnostics on it now," Seb responded.

"I see. Care to speculate?" Billy trusted his lieutenants and expected them to think and analyze information, no matter how it was derived or far out their suppositions might be.

"Well, we have gotten some probing from Washington, DC—mainly Georgetown—a few times. Not exactly where the geeks hang out but I know there are a lot spooks that live there, so it could be CIA or NSA nosing around."

"Um huh," Billy intoned, pulling up the cameras monitoring Security Central for his own view of the visual light map; he could see what Seb was seeing.

"The Russian stuff is a bit more than normal, though we know they have been trying to crack us for years," Seb continued. "It could be nothing, but the fact that it is not showing up in our reports has me perplexed and…" Seb's voice trailed off.

"And what?" Billy immediately shot back.

"Well, I know that the Gaming Olympics is coming up soon, so the system's going to be stressed in ways we haven't had to deal with before—"

"Do we need more equipment?" Billy interrupted. *"The Games are huge for us so we have to stay ahead of the curve. The IPO has given us plenty of money to upgrade if necessary."*

"More equipment?" Seb queried. "No, what I was going to say is that—"

"More techs then?" Billy interrupted again; it was a bad habit that few people corrected him on given his position. But Seb had been hired as one of the first employees and they were friends as well as colleagues, even if Billy Wilson was the CEO.

"Dammit Billy!" he yelled into the phone, "shut up and lemme talk!"

"Oh, sorry, man," Billy was genuinely apologetic. *"You know me!"*

Seb *did* know Billy, and he felt badly about jumping down his throat. Billy was truly a good dude.

"Sorry about that." Now it was Seb's turn to apologize.

"It's all good, man, don't sweat it. I deserved it," Billy replied. *"Now what were you saying?"*

Seb returned to his train of thought.

"There is big money in the Gaming Olympics, not to mention the street cred the top performers will garner. I also trust my eyes more than what I see on any report." Seb was being cryptic, carefully choosing his words.

"And?"

"And I just wonder if someone is somehow hacking into the system, and affecting what we see as managers. To make us think everything is fine in the system, when in fact, everything is not fine and someone is working to game the system and win fraudulently."

Billy went silent. He knew that security was as critical a function of a company like his as anything and the possibility that there was a traitor on the inside made his mind race.

"Billy?" Seb queried, wondering if he had lost his boss.

"I'm still here," he replied vacantly, staring out his window at the tugboats maneuvering massive cargo ships in the harbor. *"I trust your instincts, Seb, but what you are suggesting strikes at the very core of CGC. Dig around, but be discreet. If someone is doing what you suggest—and that is a big 'if'—they are probably being super careful in how they cover their tracks. And if the media gets a hold of this before the Olympics start, we will be worried about a lot more than who wins."*

"Understood."

Seb had never heard such—what was it? Fear? Sadness? Pain?—in Billy's voice before. And it scared him more than a little bit.

"Hey man, is everything OK? I am not sure about this, you know, just something doesn't add up."

Billy snapped out of his momentary bout of nostalgia and how the old friend he used to call "2" probably would have had an answer and a solution already.

"Sebastiano," Billy's tone went from friend to boss, just like that, *"I trust your instincts and you have your marching orders. We are where we are today because of people like you. I hope it is nothing, but if it is something and we can shut it down before it becomes a mess, we will have all done the job millions of people around the world expect from us."*

"Got it," Seb replied in a relieved voice, "I promise I will find out what is wrong."

"I know you will, Seb, I know you will. Thanks for calling."
Billy pushed the red phone icon.

CHAPTER 20

It had already been two weeks since Greg discovered the receiver his father had hidden in the duck blind, yet could not bring himself to watch it. He knew the information might clear his father's name in the death of Billy's dad, but what if it didn't? He sat in front of his computer, paralyzed by ten years of not really knowing what had happened that day. He had always been willing to give his dad the benefit of the doubt and after reading the e-mail, was even more certain that his father—whatever he might have done in the end—was not a cold-blooded killer.

Yet the alternative, particularly if it played out in living color in front of his very own eyes, was too horrible for Greg to contemplate. He couldn't bring himself to connect the small device to his computer. *I'll do it tomorrow,* he thought, a line he would repeat for longer than he wished.

#

Midterms were looming and Mitchell was behind in his reading, particularly in US History. The perspective was different from what he had learned growing up, but it was one of the hoops he needed to jump through to maintain his scholarship; the book was open to the chapter on World War I:

"...the war officially started on July 28, 1914, when the Austro-Hungarians declared war on Serbia..."

It hit Mitchell like a bolt of lightning—07-28-14! Those were the first six numbers of the sequence Billy wrote down in the section on Backdoors! Could it be?

"YES!!!" Mitchell screamed at the top of his lungs. He had been looking at the formatting of the numbers as the key, rather than the numbers themselves. He grabbed his notebook, frantically opening it to the long string of numbers he had written in it, reading the second set of six numbers out loud.

"090139...September 1, 1939..." he excitedly blurted out to no one, flipping forward to the next chapter in the history book:

"...World War II started on September 1, 1939 when Hitler invaded Poland ..."

"120741...December 7, 1941..." Pearl Harbor Day—he knew this one without even looking in the book.

"YES!! YES!!!" he clenched his fists and danced around. He had unlocked part of the key to Billy's backdoor, he was sure of it.

But to what? He sat down and took a deep breath, wondering if he might be playing with fire.

#

Susan Green was in her office when she got an IM from her boss. It was brief and blunt:

"Get down here right away!"

Susan could feel the intensity in the message, wondering if she had done anything to upset Billy. She picked up her notebook, straightened her scarf and started walking down the hall to the other side of the building, doing a mental checklist of everything that was going on at the firm that might create such a sense of urgency. Nothing came to mind. She had heard he had a temper, but had never seen it before.

"There's a first time for everything," she mumbled under her breath as she walked by the elevator banks, a pit growing in her stomach with each passing step.

The Marketing VP gingerly approached Claire, Billy's Executive Assistant.

"Oh, hi Susan. Nice to see you today. That's a lovely color on you by the way." Claire was a kind, middle-aged woman, totally professional in her dealings with everyone. Susan was momentarily flummoxed by the compliment, so preoccupied about the reason she had been called to Billy's office.

"Um, yes it is…I mean thank you," she turned red at the *faux pas. Nobody compliments themselves, stupid,* she thought, almost out loud.

"What can I do for you?" Claire asked inquisitively.

"I'm here to see Mr. Wilson. He asked me to come down here," Susan replied, even more confused than before.

"Oh? He didn't say anything to me."

Now both of the women were perplexed. Billy liked everything to be planned out and while this was just a simple meeting request, it wasn't on the schedule. And everyone knew if you wanted to get on Billy's schedule, you had to go through the guardian of William Wilson's office, and that was Claire Rothberg.

Just then Billy looked up from his desk.

"Susan, come on in," Billy asserted, sharply motioning her with the wave of his hand. Both women glanced at each other as Susan slowly walked into Billy's corner office.

"Please close the door and sit down, I'll be just a sec," he continued, sounding slightly ominous. His Marketing VP did as she was told. After a few moments, Billy got up and walked over to the desk and sat down.

"You've been over to the Quincy facility, right?" he began.

"Yes. I toured the place during the interview and we had one of our quarterly meetings there," Susan replied, still totally in the dark about why she was sitting in Billy's office. "It's pretty impressive." She knew it never hurt to stroke the male ego.

Billy slightly smiled, then looked at his VP for a few moments, as though he were mulling over what to say next. A few more moments passed, then a few more; Susan could stand it no longer.

"Look, I don't think you asked me in here to see if I've been to Quincy. What's up? The suspense is killing me!" Her comments brought another smile to his face.

Billy opened his mouth, measuring every word that came out.

"You know we have a Threat Board over there, right?"

"I've never seen it, but yes, I know about it."

Billy got up from his chair and motioned for Susan to follow him to his computer, where the camera feed from Security Central showing the geographic "heat" map was still on his screen. He briefly explained what it all meant, Susan nodding in understanding. Billy was having a hard time concentrating, standing this close to his attractive Marketing VP. He had always wondered how executives were foolish enough to risk their position by getting involved with someone at work, but as he stood inches from Susan, he now knew. The scent of her faint perfume only compounded the problem. He motioned her back to his conference table in the center of his office and their discussion continued.

"So, here's the issue. We run a series of reports every hour to monitor changes in those threats and there seems to be some disconnect between the Threat Board and the reports."

Susan immediately understood the gravity of the situation, and it made her heart skip, though she maintained her composure.

"Are you saying that Seb thinks someone is hacking into the system?" Her question was more of a statement. "How certain is he?"

Billy was impressed not only how quickly Susan was connecting the dots, but that she also seemed unfazed by the revelation, as though it was a normal part of the business. *Damn, she's good,* he thought to himself.

"Not really, but the reports he gets are different than the eye test on the Threat Board and he's usually spot on when it comes to stuff like this."

"I see," Susan replied, her mind clearly chewing on the implications. "What does Joe think about this?" Susan continued, knowing how much Billy trusted the firm's chief counsel.

"I haven't told him. I wanted to get your take on it before setting off alarm bells with the lawyers. If it's true and it gets out to the media, you'll be the one defending us, so I wanted you to know before anyone else."

Wow! she thought to herself, *I walked down here thinking 'worst case scenarios' and he basically just told me that he trusts me more than his lawyer. Did I ever get that one wrong!*

"So what is Seb doing about it?" Susan was now thinking in damage control mode. "Does he have any suspects in mind? Is it internal? External?"

"We don't know anything at all yet, just suspicions. But that's the kind of thinking we need to get to the bottom of this. Do we tell the shareholders anything?" It was a good question.

"Not yet. Right now we don't know anything and it could be nothing, so jumping the gun with any kind of announcement would be counterproductive," Susan clinically replied, "so no, we are good with the SEC—for now at least. Just don't sell any of your stock." This applied to her as well, now that she knew.

The thought of selling his stock had never occurred to Billy, but with insider trading rules being what they were, it had to be mentioned. Billy breathed a sigh of relief. "So no lawyers, then, until we get more information, okay? I'll tell Seb to expect your call."

Susan wasn't totally sure it was such a great idea to keep the Chief Counsel out of the loop, but because Joe was busy working on the defense to the StormClouds' lawsuit, she agreed anyway. She knew Wall Street well enough to have earned Billy's trust, and that made her feel good, even if it clouded her judgment.

"Is that all, Mr. Wilson?" Susan queried, in her cool investment banker voice.

"Yeah, thanks so much, Ms. Green," Billy winked at her as she realized she had sounded like his advisor instead of his employee.

She smiled. "Sorry, Billy, old habits die hard."

She collected her notebook and got up to leave when Billy interjected:

"Hey, this is way off topic, but I have Seahawks' tickets for the game next week. Would you like to go with me?" His stomach was churning as he completely ignored the advice his Chief Counsel had given him about dating one of his subordinates.

Susan's heart skipped another beat. *Did he just ask me out on a date?*

"I'd love to!" The words were out of her mouth before she realized it. *It's just a football game,* she rationalized.

"Awesome! I'll get back to you later next week with details," Billy responded back, enthusiastically grinning.

Susan opened his door and walked back to her office. She had an extra spring in her step.

She had a date with Billy Wilson.

CHAPTER 21

Greg awoke with a start from a recurring nightmare. In it, the Russians—mob or military, he couldn't tell—were after him and his new found electronic treasure. How they discovered he had it, he could not guess. Perhaps the owner of the duck blind had been retired KGB and he was expected, or he was still being tailed after all these years, though he hadn't noticed anything out of the ordinary for some time. In any event, each time the dream occurred, his pursuers inched closer, and as his weariness increased daily, it was only a matter of time before they would have him and his device. Or at least that is how he interpreted the nightmare.

He looked at the clock: 2:55am. He rubbed his eyes, got up and went to get a cold glass of water. Greg hadn't really slept since getting back from Princeton and he was sure he was being hounded by his father speaking from the grave, now that he had what had been left for him to find. He sat down at his desk and booted up his computer.

He carefully pulled out the old device and gently inserted the cable into the female slot on it. A bubble popped up from his task bar; his computer was searching for a driver to run the video. *So far, so good,* he thought, his heart beating faster by the second.

Your driver has been installed was the only message, but it was exactly what he hoped to see. He double clicked on the icon to open his newly attached device.

The software slowly loaded the files—there were ten of them. Except for the last one, they were all relatively short, five or ten minutes in length, or about the time it took his father to commute to and from work. Greg hadn't expected so many. In fact, he was so focused on what might be on the last video, he hadn't even thought there might be others. He surveyed the files arranged in chronological order, beginning in early October 2002, and resisted the temptation to click on the last one, the day Billy's dad died. Instead, he clicked on the first one.

His father came to life in living color and it took his breath away. It wasn't HD quality, but it was in remarkably good condition given where it had spent the last ten years. There was even sound. Greg was riveted, a flood of emotions rushing back as he saw his father in his truck, just driving to work, listening to Rush Limbaugh on the local news channel. Greg chuckled to himself at the thought that his dad, a Russian spy, was listening to America's leading, conservative talk show host.

In five minutes, it was over. It was clear that the camera was activated when his key fob unlocked the truck, and then stayed on for thirty-seconds after the door was locked at the end of the journey. It was a remarkable device for its time; it had three cameras—one filming the inside of the cab, one monitoring the rear traffic, and one facing forward, capturing the road ahead. Greg grimaced, realizing that would include William Wilson, Jr., himself. He felt nauseous.

He watched the next video, this one a ten-minute clip of his dad driving home, listening to a local sports channel after another Redskins' loss and arguing with the host. It was amusing. And it ripped his heart out. His father was a good man and a good father. Greg could not—would not—countenance the thought that his dad had deliberately killed William Wilson, Jr.

#

Jeremy had more than enough information to analyze, even though not all the cameras could interpret the battle using his electro-kinetic program. He had spent hours poring over the videos and had identified hundreds of drones, some for communicating, some for aerial attack, some designed for ground combat, yet many with an unknown purpose.

They were all simple, but well designed, and it was clear these very two characteristics were *what* made them so effective in the face of the sophisticated weapons the Ukrainian forces had. Despite this, though, Jeremy still wasn't able to determine *why* they were so effective. Controlling so many electronic devices moving in three-dimensions was a Herculean task and though they certainly had their share of failures and glitches, on the whole, the drones were deadly.

#

Greg took a deep breath. He couldn't bear it any longer. There was only one file that was longer than eleven minutes and it was the last one, logging in at fifty minutes. It seemed odd that it was so long, but given how far from work the accident had occurred, it was only logical.

He double clicked on the file and it came to life. The truck was parked in the garage, where it always was. But there was something else. There was another person, a burly man, hiding next to the truck on the passenger side. Greg stopped the video stream and shifted camera views and replayed the section in slow motion. The man looked up, the camera catching his face; he was clearly Russian. Greg paused and took a screen shot, then hit PLAY again.

"*Nyet, papa, nyet*!" Greg screamed at the video on the screen. "Please don't get in the truck!"

Greg could hardly look. It was like watching a horror flick and seeing the psycho before the actors did, yet this was real. It was *his* dad, he could see what was coming and it made him sick. Despite it being 3:25am, he was now fully awake and enraged. He hadn't even seen the whole video but had a new mission in life: hunt this piece of scum down and destroy him every way possible.

The moment his dad opened the door to his truck, the other man ripped open the passenger door, bull-rushed into the cab and caught Alexander Galkin completely by surprise. There was a struggle, but his father was no match for his attacker. The other man had his dad in a headlock, pulled out a syringe and jabbed it into his father's thigh. In a matter of moments, his body went limp.

His father's attacker quickly pulled Alexander to the passenger side, put on his seatbelt, and hopped into the driver's side. He pulled out a whisky flask, took a swig himself and then doused his father's clothes with the stuff. He had heard his father was drunk, now he knew why. It was despicable. The whole sequence took less than a minute and they were on the road.

As Greg watched the screen for the next forty minutes, the image of this big, Russian bully castigating his father for being an "enemy of the State" was seared into his brain. The only positive was that Greg now knew, beyond any shadow of doubt, that whatever happened to Billy's dad had nothing to do with his own father; it was a major burden off his shoulders.

As they approached the bridge where Billy's father was walking, Greg could see his own father trying to roust himself into action, to prevent whatever nefarious act his attacker had in mind. But he was no match for the Russian thug. With the front-facing camera occupying his full screen, Greg could see William Wilson walking along the bridge, a cup of coffee in his hand. As the truck accelerated, he seemed to sense danger, turning around in time to look with horror at the fate that was to befall him.

The thud and scream that followed stunned Greg. He had seen accidents in the movies before, but this was real and involved two people he knew and loved. He was shaking with rage. The assassin quickly got out of the truck, pulled Greg's father into the driver's seat, and momentarily ducked out of sight, heading to the front of the truck where Billy's father writhed in pain, pinned against the guard rail, but not dead. The thug rectified that with a quick snap of the neck of the defenseless man, and then scampered towards a black SUV that had arrived on the scene. The side door quickly opened and the murderer hopped in as the SUV sped away, but not before another face appeared on the screen.

"Target #2," Greg growled, taking a screen shot of the second face, a younger, Russian man, as well. The video ran for another thirty seconds before automatically shutting off. His father stirred but no doubt had no idea what had just happened.

What Greg had seen was both crushing and liberating. As horrifying as the cold-blooded hit on Billy's father had been, Alexander Galkin had had absolutely no part in it. Greg was relieved beyond words. At some point, he knew he would have to show this to his old friend, Billy Wilson. But he would exact revenge first. He laid his head down on the pillow and succumbed to the exhaustion of the previous weeks. The nightmare was gone.

CHAPTER 22

The entire tech world was abuzz with the imminent commencement of the Gaming Olympics. As many as fifteen million gamers from more than fifty countries were expected to be competing in *Battle for Babylon*. Most had no chance of even making the top 1000, but the thought that everyone was in the same arena as the world's best gamers had an incredibly egalitarian feel to it. It was like playing in the US Open and being paired with Tiger Woods in his prime. Enthusiasm was so high that Cloud Gaming Co. had signed a deal with ESPN to run daily highlights across the world in twenty languages, a testament to the growing popularity of video games globally.

Susan Green's marketing plan had worked brilliantly. The campaign had two main prongs, the first being to get Billy Wilson as many interviews as was practical. She had stumbled upon this part of the strategy after Billy's rock star performance on *Tech Movers* the day the company went public. That interview was unavoidable, as much of an opening-day-of-trading tradition as was ringing the bell at the NYSE. The host, Maria Incandella, had been particularly insistent about getting Billy on her show, and it turned out to be her most watched segment ever, as the head of Cloud Gaming Co. gave a spirited defense of free enterprise in response to a loaded question about a lawsuit. The clip immediately went viral, pushing both the price of the stock higher, as well as Billy's CEO star power.

His performance on the show and the rapid rise to prominence in the gaming world of *Battle for Babylon* had led to inquiries not just from traditional magazines aimed at video gamers, but also from a number of leading cultural magazines whose readers wanted to know what all the fuss was about. As she married those two concepts together, interest in *Battle for Babylon* took off, with the two of them crisscrossing the globe getting the message out. The interviews in the UK, Germany, China and Japan in particular had been very well received, leading to a sharp upsurge in new revenues, as well as increasing stress on the system.

But just as important as the interviews were, was the clever advertising strategy she had devised. It chronicled the history of Babylon, the ancient city in modern day Iraq, after which Billy had named his game. Over the course of weekly briefings with her boss, she had realized that his fascination with history and war could be leveraged into an ad campaign to both stimulate interest in the game and create hype for the upcoming Olympics.

She had directed the programmers at CGC to work with the ad agency, Ezell & Cambrea, on recreating the city and its surrounding area as described at different times by historians over the ages. Depictions of it as the "Gate of the Gods," a major city on the Euphrates River, the home of impressive architectural structures including the Tower of Babel and the magnificent Hanging Gardens, the seat of the vast empires of Kings Hammurabi and Nebuchadnezzar, and the place of a future major battle alluded to in the Bible, all came to life using the same vivid graphics that made the game realistic.

Brad Jeffries, aka *BetterThanYou,* was an experienced gamer, a steady tactician with deadly aim. He didn't have the extraordinarily quick reflexes or keyboard dexterity that elite gamers had, but because of his calm under pressure, Dr. Johnson made him the star of the Queen's team. He was a Master 3-Star General, the highest ranking Master in the school—at least as far as anyone knew. However, it wasn't all him.

He was good, exceptional, in fact, but part of the reason he had ascended so high was that he, Jerry, and Nate worked as a team. Dr. Johnson had stressed that each of them had to be willing to play a role and Brad's was as the lead dog, which meant he was more or less always protected. Nate as *MVP* and Jerry as *Slasher,* both had bailed him out with their quick thinking and reflexes on more than one occasion. Both had also taken bullets for him. Nate's creativity and speed, in particular, would have made him a star on most gaming teams, but he took too many risks in Dr. Johnson's eyes, so he was *BetterThanYou's* wingman, instead of the other way around.

They were all at Brad's house for a gaming session and *BetterThanYou* was logging on for the first time since witnessing *Blunt Instrument's* throat being slit a few days before. The fallen Master 2-Star General had obviously just been relegated, materializing as she did a short distance from him on a desert plain in the Middle East. The savagery and brutality of the victor, *Pinball,* and the fact that *Blunt Instrument,* the vanquished, looked a lot like his sister had unnerved him. He and his buddies at Queen's were playing mostly for fun and while the money and glory of winning the Olympics would give them bragging rights forever, some of these Masters seemed like they were playing for real. He wasn't sure if he really had *that* kind of killer instinct, though he would never admit it to Nate or Jerry.

#

Beth Hopkins logged onto her three-year old Dell. Though it was relatively slow compared to newer models in almost every way, the high-powered CGC gaming system running the game made that irrelevant. Despite recently taking a beating and getting relegated twice in the span of one minute, she had learned some valuable lessons.

She was ready to test her mettle again, down on the third level, relatively low in the *Battle for Babylon* environment. Because it was the final buildup before the Olympics, there were a lot of high-level players there working on their fighting skills. Master Generals could not call in air, ground or naval power below the fourth level, so it was all one-on-one fighting—or at least it was supposed to be.

#

"Look Brad! There's that Master General you saw get iced," Nate cracked, "let's gang up on her!" The glee in his voice was evident and Brad felt he had no choice.

"Nate, we are supposed to working on team tactics, not bullying!" Brad retorted, half-heartedly.

"Come on man, it'll be fun!"

Brad quickly gave in to Nate's badgering. His avatar, *BetterThanYou,* skulked forward through the shadows. It wasn't clear if *Blunt Instrument* saw him, but judging by how she parried his first blow, it was apparent that at least she had great reflexes. Brad went skittering away like a June bug.

#

"Get off me little boy!" she thundered at her screen, before realizing it was a Master 3-Star General that had attacked her.

"Whoa! What do we have here?" She didn't attack though, sensing other threats. She had learned.

#

"Dude!" badgered Nate. "That was so lame. Give me a crack at the blonde bimbo!" Just then Marjorie walked by the gaming room.

"Hey, Nate! I am not a bimbo!"

The boys all laughed at Marjorie's impeccable timing as Nate rushed in to engage *Blunt Instrument.* He was a much faster and dexterous gamer than was Brad…

#

…and as soon as he attacked, *Blunt Instrument* knew it. But she was also up to the task, neutralizing *MVP's* quick thrust-and-parrying with artful footwork. *BetterThanYou* and *Slasher* were circling as well. She sprang to higher ground, but they all followed.

Be who you are, she thought, *you are a "Blunt Instrument!"* She feinted left at Nate, causing him to step away and then attacked Jerry, slicing him down with swift and sudden force.

"Relegate *THAT!*" she screamed, as *Slasher* faded from view, deposited somewhere two stages lower. *MVP* was upon her again, *BetterThanYou* had seen her only escape and blocked it.

"Damn good tactics, boys," Beth was talking and thinking at the same time.

#

"Hey man, we got her surrounded!" Nate squealed in delight, closing in for the kill. "I got her man!! She's dead meat!" Marjorie doubled back to watch the finale. It disturbed her that her brother and his friends seemed to delight in bullying avatars as much as they enjoyed doing it to their classmates. She secretly hoped someone would knock them down a peg or two. It happened sooner than she thought.

"WHAT THE—!?" Nate was whining, this time in anger.

#

"Take that you losers!" Jeremy Thomas roared, his avatar, *Thunderstruck,* seemingly materializing out of thin air and eliminating *MVP* with one, sharp blow.

#

As *MVP* faded from view to join *Slasher* somewhere below, *BetterThanYou* started a fast retreat.

"What are you doin' man?" screamed Nate. "You're running from a *GIRL,* you big wuss! What's wrong with you?? Be a man!"

#

"Oh no, you don't!" Beth screamed, as *BetterThanYou* darted away. "I'm faster than you!" she laughed at her play on words as she swung her sword. He crumbled to the ground moments before *Blunt Instrument* finished him off.

#

Marjorie laughed. "You guys got slammed by a *girl?* A blonde bimbo no less? What studs!" The boys hissed at her.

#

Blunt Instrument wheeled, assuming *Thunderstruck* was lurking, but he was gone. *A gallant soul, disappearing into the night as quickly as he had arrived on the scene,* she thought. Beth felt a romantic twinge.

#

CGC's servers were working overtime, the flickering lights monitoring threats and calculating scores. *Thunderstruck* and *Blunt Instrument* both were elevated to Master 2-Star. Brad Jeffries was relegated, also to Master 2-Star status as well, though his cowardly attempt at running away had nearly pushed him to Master 1-Star. Nate and Jerry were licking their wounds, skilled, but unrated. The Queen's team had work to do.

CHAPTER 23

Mitchell raced through the sequence of numbers scribbled in the margins of Billy's old textbook—they had all been a match to the start date of one of the major wars in which the US was a combatant; he pumped his fist at every hit. But as he reached the last sequence, he was stumped. He wasn't even sure what the final set of figures were. A date from history? The future? A sequence of random numbers, meaningless to anyone but the author? It would be virtually impossible to remember a long string of numbers without some kind of memory device, but cleverly fashioned, a history book might be all that was needed to create a very complex password. Mitchell had already figured out the easy part, though; he faced a daunting task and sighed. *At least I have all weekend.*

He started systematically: "XX twelve XX" he said aloud, writing it in his notebook, as well. Perhaps it was as simple as the Roman numeral equivalent, 20-12-20, but there was no twentieth month, so that made no sense at all. *Maybe the order is different?* he thought, thinking it might be written the way Europeans wrote dates: day-month-year. He typed December 20, 1920 in his search engine and hit GO. Nothing.

"1820?" he asked to no one in particular, his voice rising in a combination of uncertainty, speculation and hope. Zip. The process continued: 1720? Nope. 1620? Excluding an interesting factual tidbit that December 20, 1620 was when the Mayflower Compact was signed and the passengers first set foot in North America, this, too, was a dead end.

It also didn't make sense. All the dates had been month-day-year and they had been in chronological order. Each date had also been the start of a significant US military engagement. Mitchell knew enough history to know that after the Iraq War, there weren't any of the latter. He was stumped.

"Damn," Mitchell's frustrations spewed out, resignation in his voice. He was stuck—for now. "Time to move on."

#

CGC's Chief Counsel, Joe Williams, had been reviewing the lawsuit brought by StormClouds, a firm that developed artificial intelligence applications for military logistics and transportation. On the surface the suit appeared meritless, but Joe had to take it seriously. At some level, it seemed ridiculous that a company working on military applications and a video game developer were legal adversaries, but it was a real business threat and it was his job to make it go away as quickly and quietly as possible.

The essence of the suit was the alleged similarity between the two companies' operating systems, which StormClouds believed was more than a coincidence. They both reacted to battlefield threats such as enemy position, strength of force, incoming fire, temperature, weather, terrain, time of day, and a host of other variables, and StormClouds' lawyers focused on this aspect of it as evidence they had been ripped off.

But Joe and his legal team focused on how that data was actually used. StormClouds' AI software was utilized on a real battlefield and had multiple redundancies built in to prevent failure mid-mission. CGC's, on the other hand, powered a video game—a sophisticated one perhaps—but a video game, nonetheless. One was machine-to-machine, interacted with the real world, and had to be very precise, the other was machine-to-human, interacted with the virtual world and just needed to be useful. The difference seemed pretty self-evident to CGC's lawyers, and they were confident the case would be thrown out.

Joe didn't know if it was jealousy driving the lawsuit, or the fact that StormClouds had indeed been hacked and was lashing out at all possible—even if not probable—suspects, but the fact remained that StormClouds had incurred considerable damage, so someone had done something. He just had to show that no one at Cloud Gaming Co. had been that someone.

#

Department T was now in a constant state of activity. After the success of the Ukrainian battle, politics had been quickly inserted into the fray and depending on alliances, the new direction of the Russian military was seen as either visionary or threatening. General Yikovich had always been good in the political realm, having been brought up in a privileged household and identified as a potential leader at an early age. But this was different. While he—and to a lesser extent—his Department, were always in the mix when jockeying for power, they were now at the center of the storm. It was a constant distraction.

"Comrade Mikhail," Oleg Petrov's gravelly voice immediately grabbed the attention of the room, "everyone can see that you and your department achieved a stunning victory using a revolutionary approach and new technology. I am the first to congratulate you. But what is the long range goal of this military strategy? Are ground forces not part of the plan, as was the case in the Ukraine?" The Intelligence Briefing had barely begun and General Petrov was already stirring the pot.

"Comrade Oleg," General Yikovich patiently began, "as we both know, our country is strong and feared because of our military forces. The main pillar of this strength is, and always has been, our ground forces, you, of course, being the latest in a long procession of brave and bold heroes to lead those forces." He paused momentarily, allowing General Petrov to both bathe in the compliment, and squirm in its spotlight. A wry smile came across Premier Buskin's face; his old friend was skilled in this arena. "So to answer your second question first, 'no' that is not, nor has ever been part of the plan," General Yikovich ended his assertion by raising his voice for emphasis.

A chill filled the room. Everyone present knew that Mikhail Yikovich had Premier Buskin's backing and so could afford to be bold. Yet the men in this room also knew that Oleg Petrov was the ruthless leader of the old guard, and many had likely met a premature death by crossing him. To do it in such a public forum was bold indeed.

"As for your first question, the long range objective of this new, technology-based strategic prong is to protect the Motherland from new threats that emerge from our enemies. These threats have increasingly taken on the form of technology, an area where we do not have such a decided advantage as we do in other branches of the military." Another veiled barb.

The ball was now in General Petrov's court.

"I am gratified to hear that," Petrov gruffly replied, on the defensive. "Your answer is what I expected out of a patriot such as you have always shown yourself to be." All eyes shifted to General Yikovich, who remained expressionless. "Tell us please, then, Comrade Mikhail, how is it that your Department has managed to achieve this progress so quickly? These strides are monumental, even for a team as superior as yours, are they not?" Two could play at this game and Oleg Petrov had not risen to Four-Star General on brass knuckles alone. A bead of sweat formed on General Yikovich's forehead; the Premier was enjoying this.

"They indeed are monumental, but your suggestion that Department T's team is solely responsible is off the mark." Now it was Mikhail Yikovich who was on the hot seat. "Many areas have supported our endeavors, including yours, of course. We do have some brilliant technology minds working to defend Mother Russia," Yikovich winced at his boast, even though he believed it to be true, "and they have created some novel strategic and tactical approaches. But it is also true that the walls guarding the fortresses of technology are not nearly as daunting—or dangerous—as the ones our brave ground troops face in every battle, and so when necessary, we attack in our own way." It was as close as General Yikovich would get to acknowledging some of his technology was not home grown.

"But how will this new reliance on technology affect our ground troops? I have heard nothing about it!" General Petrov was getting impatient with General Yikovich's artful dodging.

General Yikovich wasn't really that sure himself. He believed that technology could run the entire military strategy—indeed, that is what he had been hoping for all along—but he was not yet ready to stake that ground. But before he could reply, Premier Buskin interjected.

"Gentlemen, we have all been part of this new strategy, and we all will continue to be so. Comrade Oleg, your questions are, as always, excellent and reflect genuine and proper concern about how we defend our national interests going forward. The Ukrainian exercise was designed to show what might be possible in this new area of strategy and tactics. It would be foolish to eliminate any of our strategic advantages, don't you agree, Comrade Mikhail?" The question was rhetorical, but demanded an answer.

"Of course, Comrade Premier." Mikhail Yikovich nodded for emphasis.

The meeting was drawing to a close. General Petrov had not really gotten any of his questions answered, but he had raised them and knew there were others—perhaps many others—in the room that shared his uncertainty and concern. Yet, he was also careful not to overplay his hand. This strategy was uncharted territory and its novelty alone might be enough to derail it, regardless of how supportive Premier Buskin might be. The truth was, technology was clearly *not* a Russian strength, no matter how successful it had just seemed to be in a battle against an overmatched foe. He had also lived long enough to know that technology moved at lightning speed and today's decided advantage could change in the blink of an eye.

CHAPTER 24

Dr. Johnson reviewed the most recent training session of his team of warriors. It was disappointing to say the least. Brad had seemed indifferent at best. Nate had been his bullying worst and Jerry showed none of the aggressiveness that made him a feared, one-on-one fighter. He knew these boys were better than this, but the Olympics were almost upon them and they seemed to be going backward, not forward.

"Class, apologies to those of you not on the gaming varsity, but today is going to be a film study session for our Gaming Olympics' team. The competition is not far off, and frankly, we seem to be in a funk."

Mitchell's head snapped up; his tormentors stiffened. They were not used to being called out anywhere, much less in front of their classmates. Dr. Johnson continued.

"We are going to watch a few recent theaters in *Battle for Babylon,* to see if we can get our rhythm back. I've picked a few that I think we can learn from. Those of you not on the gaming team may study in the library, if you wish." Half the class filed out. Mitchell was the only one not on the team who chose to stay.

"Hey, Pocahontas," Brad whispered, "big dogs only. Beat it."

"I dunno," Mitchell snickered back, "I think I might learn something. Who knows, maybe Dr. J will show you guys getting whupped by that girl. Sounds like three against one weren't favorable enough odds."

Brad slouched in his chair. *Word travels fast,* he thought, never thinking his own sister had provided the damning intel.

#

After the Intelligence Briefing, General Yikovich and Sergeant Kachinko met with their team in Department T. Though the leader of the department had accorded himself at the Briefing better than many were expecting, it was also clear there were opponents as well. Until now, the team the General had assembled had been working under the radar, but they no longer were. He wanted to make sure there were no squeamish souls in the mix, and he also wanted to observe each of them very closely, to see if any of them betrayed the look of a political officer. General Yikovich had been around long enough to know there had to be at least one.

"Gentlemen, through our efforts, we have reached a point where we are now the envy of the country's leaders. But as we have seen, not everyone shares our vision, sees our objectives, understands our strategy." As the General began, he searched the faces of his men for telltale signs of a traitor among them. "We are the future, the hope for our generation and those to come, and we must redouble our efforts to push beyond the petty jealousies of those less visionary than we are!"

Mikhail Yikovich had always been persuasive. It was part of having a privileged upbringing, but it was also a gift. His men were on the edge of their seats, hanging on every word. Yikovich was well-liked by his men and through the combination of his intelligence, influence and connections, had elevated them to a place none of them could have imagined when they started work on *Operation Oblaka* in earnest nearly two years ago.

#

"OK, this first battle involves a Master 3-Star General called *Blunt Instrument,*" started Dr. Johnson. Brad, Nate and Jerry all simultaneously cringed, though it was clear their teacher had chosen a different encounter than their recent humiliation.

"You're familiar with her aren't you, Brad?" It cut like a knife. This was very un-Dr. Johnson-like.

"Um…yes," he stammered, "she is an aggressive warrior." His neck turned red.

"Indeed," Dr. Johnson stated flatly. "We will look at that aggressiveness in this clip." The large video screen came to life, showing her leading a battalion of ground forces up a plain towards the Euphrates River, an air force circling overhead.

"As you can see here, *Blunt Instrument* is almost in the first wave of the attack, very close to the front line. This is unusual for someone with such a high rank, but as we will soon see, because of the way CGC's system analyzes data, her ground battalion and air force have a similar edge to them, making her a fearsome, if occasionally reckless, opponent." The opponent was a Master 2-Star General called *Hunker Down,* fortified in a bunker with a well-camouflaged ground force spread out in the hills overlooking the plain.

Brad and his teammates seemed to be over their embarrassment and were focused intently on the battle set to take place before them. Mitchell was fascinated, too, as it appealed to his warrior heritage.

"Mr. Jeffries, how might you attack *Hunker Down* if you were a 3-Star?"

"Well, as you noted, she is an aggressive warrior and she seems to be inviting them to attack her first wave with artillery in the hopes of finding out where the firepower is, so maybe go after them with the air force first to smoke them out," Brad replied, as the screen showed a war plane diving to engage a surface-to-air missile battery that seemed to have fired pre-maturely. Part of *Blunt Instrument's* left flank broke off and scurried to where the missile had been fired and after a few moments of chaos, a large explosion could be seen where the surface-to-air battery had once been. Dr. Johnson paused the video.

"Excellent assessment, Brad. You can see here that as the ground forces break off to attack, *Blunt Instrument* is momentarily exposed, but it appears that *Hunker Down,* as the name suggests, is a defensive general and hesitates, then BOOM!" Dr. Johnson spread his fingers in an imaginary explosion. "Her aggressiveness could have exposed her, but when paired with ground and air support, the enemy has to pick a poison. It is too late in this instance."

The video continued playing, with *Blunt Instrument's* forces resuming their march. Dr. Johnson continued, focusing on the defensive side of the mix.

"So Nate, what would you have done in this case, knowing you had an aggressive warrior on the other side?" Dr. Johnson was stretching the boys.

"I would fake an attack with my weakest flank, then when she responded, send in my artillery and air force and go right at her. Kill the head and the snake dies!"

"Excellent, excellent," Dr. Johnson replied. "Fight fire with fire."

The battle was over in relatively short order. As *Blunt Instrument's* army made its inexorable march, *Hunker Down* got rattled and soon was hiding in a poorly defended bunker. *Blunt*

Instrument's ground forces quickly overran the fortress and he was done; *Hunker Down's* avatar quickly faded from view, a victim of relegation.

#

Operation Oblaka, was the military vision of Mikhail Yikovich when he had ascended to Chief Researcher of Department T nearly ten years ago, and over time had managed to get buy in from his childhood friend, Vladimir Buskin. Yikovich knew where technology was headed and believed that Russia could leapfrog the West by relying on better tactics, rather than just on better weaponry. By using a blend of real battlefield data and artificial intelligence to analyze it, he believed it was possible to be two steps ahead of the adversary, defeating it with superior tactics and execution, no matter the deficiencies in weaponry.

It is why he found Billy Wilson's embrace of crowd wisdom so intriguing. It recognized that well-informed, but independent thinking in a military environment was more powerful than just superior hardware. General Yikovich believed that from a soldier's perspective, the collective wisdom of strategy and tactics in a well-designed video game like *Battle for Babylon* had the ability to provide meaningful and critical insight into real battlefield situations. But for most people, it was just a game—a violent one perhaps, but a game nonetheless. Except to a visionary like General Yikovich.

#

Dr. Johnson clicked on the next clip; it was also *Blunt Instrument.*

"We will see the same aggressive warrior on this clip, but for some unknown reason, she sends her air force to another battlefield, while she takes a more defensive strategy. Thoughts Mr. Anderson?"

"Perhaps she is supporting a teammate," the senior replied, "or after some particular avatar?"

"Quite possibly. But look what happens. A normally aggressive, offensive minded warrior switches to defense, believing she and her charge are safe since they have just vanquished an army controlling the region. Yet by holing up in a bunker without air cover, she is exposed to *samurais*, who are now free to roam."

Ronin, a Master 5-star *Samurai,* slides in virtually unnoticed and decapitates *Blunt Instrument* with a quick flash of a sword and then disappears into the hills.

"Whoa! What was that??" the class exclaimed, almost in unison at the sight of the camouflaged, but seemingly invisible, Master 5-Star *Samurai.*

"She deserved to die," Dr. Johnson said matter-of-factly. "Generals who don't secure their territory after vanquishing another general invite rogues into the vacuum. *Samurais* love that. Don't forget it." If it weren't Dr. Mikel Johnson saying it, it would have sounded creepy. Still, most of the class looked at him funny.

#

"So despite the distractions and the jealousies of those around us," the Chief Researcher continued, "we must soldier on to make sure that when our new system is needed, it will not just be fully operational, but unstoppable. We are close, comrades, we are so very close!"

As the Russians wrestled with the integration of the two systems, General Yikovich and Sergeant Kachinko had decided it best to split the group into two teams, so each could devote undivided attention to their specific task. Kachinko had the easier job, though it was by no means simple. His team had to write the code that would allow the program they had stolen from StormClouds to interface with the command structures of the Air Force, the Navy and the Army. They were close to achieving that, though the interface had a hard time keeping up with the data feed.

General Yikovich's job was much more delicate. This was because the live data being generated by CGC's software could only interface with the StormClouds' AI program if they could continue to access the CGC servers. It caused General Yikovich to hold his breath every time he logged on, believing it only a matter of time before he was discovered and the backdoor closed. He had been careful to make sure he didn't open it either too often or for too long. Although he was confident that he had not been detected, he was unwilling to push his luck until they were sure the AI program was fully operational and debugged. He knew how strong the security system at CGC was, and all he needed was some programming mistake on his side that alerted CGC that someone had hacked their way inside to have the backdoor closed forever. He had come too far to let that happen.

#

Part of General Yikovich's increasingly busy schedule included a weekly briefing with Premier Buskin on *Operation Oblaka*. The two of them met late Friday afternoon, and while it was serious business, it was often a discussion over a glass of sherry. Today was one of those days.

"Mikhail," the Premier began, pouring both men a glass, "are we going to be ready by spring?" It was less than six months away.

"Vladimir, my friend," the General replied, "we are right on schedule, in fact we might even be operational three weeks before spring, at the end of February." He was feeling particularly confident given how well both teams had taken to their respective tasks, and every day he managed to breach CGC's security system undetected made him increasingly confident that he would not be discovered.

"I am counting on you, old friend," the Premier retorted with a slight edge that only the General would pick up. "Is there anything we should be concerned about? You and I both know we have developed a bold strategy and while I believe we will be successful, there are risks, no?"

General Yikovich took a sip, savoring the sherry for a few seconds before swallowing. "My only concern at this point is how quickly we can attack once our troops and weapons have been inevitably discovered. In addition, if the desert winds come early, our communication tanks may struggle, and while the airborne and satellite communications' links can handle the job on their own, their Wi-Fi signals are not quite as effective as our tank-based ones."

Unlike the test in Siberia where the Russian military command could rely on their own stationary wireless towers to communicate with the drones and the weapons, the Middle Eastern desert included a fair amount of desolate terrain, so they would have to rely on their air and ground mobile Wi-Fi grid to direct the attack. Given the events of the past weeks and the fact that the Western allies were still focused on the Ukraine, General Yikovich was confident they still had the element of stealth on their side. While he doubted the enemy could stop what the Russians were planning, he knew that the weather and geography could, so any advantage they had on timing they might have to use.

"We have already negotiated a secret agreement with Iran, they will be waiting for us with open arms and they have promised us ease of passage!" Premier Buskin said with a flourish. "As long as we continue to make noise in Eastern Europe, we will be virtually unopposed, and by the time our enemies figure out they have been deceived, it will be too late! And if you are ready three weeks early, that will give us some leeway to pick an opportune time."

General Yikovich loved his friend's enthusiasm, though he thought the Premier might have started early on the sherry, so it could have been the alcohol talking. But he didn't like the fact that Premier Buskin was already eating into the three-week cushion he had built into his plan to be fully operational; he regretted mentioning their excellent progress.

"Perhaps, Comrade Vladimir," the General replied, "but remember the timing of the Gaming Olympics is also important to our plan. I am confident that the most intense competition will be during March and April, and we will gain critical tactical and strategic intelligence when the best gamers will be converging on the Middle East. Only the best will survive and we will only follow the best." He believed that *Polar Bear,* his avatar, might be one of those "best" battling it out in the Middle East.

CHAPTER 25

Despite the worrying series of events during the prior two weeks at Cloud Gaming Co., Billy was looking forward to Sunday and the Seahawks' football game. He was not only excited about the game, but also because he had managed to summon the courage to ask his Marketing VP, Susan Green, to join him. Susan had not only become a trusted member of his management team, he enjoyed being around her, too. He didn't know if she was a football fan, though growing up with four brothers, she probably had no choice.

Billy and his driver engaged in chitchat on his way to the Laurelhurst neighborhood where Susan lived. Although the driver was English, he was also a fan of American football and the two of them carried on about what was going on around the NFL. As they got closer to Susan's home, Billy grew increasingly quiet.

"Is everything all right, sir?" the driver queried in a genuinely inquisitive manner. He felt it partly his duty to look out for his young boss.

"Just nervous. It has always been hard for me to ask a girl out. Hell, I don't even know if she likes football."

"Well, far be it for me to assume sir," the driver replied, in a reassuring tone, "but based on what I have observed, that girl fancies you. I wouldn't worry about it, though. Worst case scenario? You have a miserable time and the Hawks lose, but I think we are safe on that second one, now aren't we?" The driver smiled as he saw his boss' face brighten.

"Got that right. Go Hawks, baby!" Billy punched the air with his fist. Sometimes his driver forgot that Billy Wilson was still just a kid trying to figure it out. A rich kid, perhaps, but just a kid, nonetheless. They pulled into the driveway of Susan's home, a modest, but well-manicured house in a *cul de sac*. Billy took a deep breath.

"Well, here goes," he said nervously.

#

Susan Green discretely looked out her window as Billy's car pulled up. Her heart was thumping. She was wearing a jersey and jeans, Seahawk blue and green ribbons in her brunette hair; her nails were also blue and green. It was feminine, but not frilly. It was a football game, after all.

Damn, he is good looking, she thought. She practically jumped at the sound of the doorbell. "It's just a football game…" she reminded herself, opening the door.

Billy was wearing the jersey of Russell Wilson, Seattle's quarterback.

"They even put your name on it!" Susan said, eyeing Billy's jersey and nodding affirmatively,

"Right down to the #3!" he exclaimed, explaining to Susan how he was the third William Walker Wilson in his family.

"I'd love to hear about your dad some day!" Susan offered, as they walked to the car, not noticing the sudden change in his demeanor at the mention of his father. The driver had emerged from the car to open the door.

"Thank you," Susan graciously said, sliding in to the car.

"My pleasure, Ms. Green."

In a moment, they were off, heading down Interstate 5 towards the stadium.

#

The game was spectacular, Billy's date even better. She didn't just like football, she loved it, and better still, understood it, too, questioning coverages, blocking schemes and route patterns. It was as much fun as Billy had ever had at a football game.

Yet after the game, as they waded through the crowd to their waiting car, Billy was in a state of deep emotional turmoil. Susan had asked about his father, a subject he thought about often, but never talked about. He hadn't ever really come to terms with it, not even with his mother. Yet here he was with a work colleague— maybe more, he wasn't sure yet—who probably knew nothing about his past, asking about the one thing he never talked about with anyone and he wanted to unburden his soul to her. He felt like a dam ready to burst.

Billy had bought his driver a season ticket in another section of the stadium as a sign of his appreciation to his driver, but he was always at the car before Billy. He cheerily greeted the two, holding the door open for them both; Susan entered first. Billy hesitated before entering the vehicle.

"Is everything all right, sir?" the driver queried, wondering if perhaps the "date" had been less than he had hoped.

"Huh? Yeah, just thinking, that's all." Billy's mind was someplace ten years earlier.

As the car inched forward out of the crowded VIP parking lot, Billy looked at Susan.

"So you want to know about my dad, do you?"

Susan was momentarily caught off guard, forgetting her innocuous comment when Billy came to pick her up. His driver's ears perked up, too. He had never heard anything about William Wilson, Jr.

Susan could see it was a serious question and quickly shifted gears.

"I do," she said, looking at his face intently. "Tell me about him."

For the next hour, while the car slowly moved through the post-game traffic on the drive back to Susan's home, Billy didn't come up for air. It started with a torrent, his thoughts and emotions cascading out after ten long years of being shut in. It was raw and it was jagged. It was at once endearingly special and jarringly crushing. He spoke about his dad, about his mom, about his boyhood friend, Greg, about the accident, about being ripped from everything he knew to move to Seattle. It was heartbreaking to hear, and more than once Susan reached out to put her hand on his arm in sympathy. As the car pulled to a stop outside of Susan's house, Billy suddenly realized he had been talking non-stop for the better part of an hour.

"Wow, I am really, really sorry. I never let you get a word in edgewise—." Susan cut him off.

"Don't be ridiculous. I loved every second of it. What a bond you two had. Remarkable." The driver nodded in agreement. *It takes a woman sometimes,* he thought. He had a new found appreciation for both his boss and the Marketing VP. *They look good together,* he mused.

CHAPTER 26

Mikhail Yikovich rolled out of bed at 0400 hours, and logged into his *Battle for Babylon* account for the first time in two days. The General followed this routine three times a week, getting up early enough to compete with gamers in the US. It was one of the few times in the day when he had a clear enough head to focus on video games, and with the Olympics approaching, he needed every opportunity to practice.

He had set his status to autoplay when he had last logged off, knowing he wouldn't have time to engage in any meaningful play for a few days and wanting to see how his avatar, *Polar Bear*, would fare without him at the actual commands. As a Master, he had logged enough game action to enable his avatar and its army to automatically perform as though General Yikovich were fighting himself. He had a message from CGC:

Congratulations! You have been promoted to Master 2-Star General. Do you wish to command an air force or a navy?

"Da! I'm back," General Yikovich whispered to himself as he pumped his fist. He covered "air force" with his cursor and hit ENTER. He checked his battle record, wanting to see whom he had beaten and why. The system instantly loaded a video replay of the action. He had surprised a Master 2-Star General, *Desert Nomad,* by racing across the Middle Eastern desert at night, attacking from the east at sunrise and routing the blinded *Desert Nomad's* army before it had a chance to call in air support from its navy in the Persian Gulf.

Speed and surprise is almost always a lethal combination, the General thought to himself. The additional tactic of using the sun on the horizon was something he had learned a number of months before when he had been beaten by a lone *Samurai* that he never was able to identify.

The autoplay feature Cloud Gaming Co. integrated into their *Battle for Babylon* software was extraordinary. It was designed to reflect the reality that real battles continued even when the generals were sleeping. Like real war, the autoplay's effectiveness degraded over time without additional input from military command and Mikhail Yikovich's two days on automatic tested the limits. Still, he was extremely pleased.

Beth was slightly envious of her CIA colleague. All of the intelligence action was happening in the Russian theater and judging from the constant stream of senior military and intelligence officials the past week, there seemed to be no sign of it abating. She had only seen Jeremy in passing, and while he looked tired, he also seemed to be having the time of his life. She ran into him getting a Diet Pepsi from the cafeteria at 0500, four hours before their shifts were to end.

"Hi Jeremy. Still doing the diet thing I see," she said with a twinkle in her eye.

"You know me," he nodded as he raised the can in salute. "How have you been? I've missed catching up on *Tech Movers.* What's Maria up to these days?"

"Things are good, though not quite as busy as they seem to be on your side of the building. You look like you haven't slept in days!" *That wasn't very nice, stupid,* she thought to herself.

"That bad, huh?" he grimaced in feigned distress. "But I'm loving every minute of it—at least so far."

"Hey, the head of StormClouds is on *Tech Movers* this morning to talk about their lawsuit against CGC. Wanna join me at 9?" Beth asked hopefully.

"If Tony lets me out of there on time, I'll be there...Diet Pepsi in hand!" He smiled at her. "Thanks for asking."

#

At the end of the work day, General Yikovich's short ten-minute walk from the office to his Moscow flat was both mind-clearing and physically refreshing, particularly as the Russian weather turned colder. Once inside, he poured himself the usual glass of sherry to warm up and logged onto his personal computer. It had been another fourteen-hour day in the bowels of the stately building that housed Department T, as he and his staff worked overtime crunching code to make sure the critical elements of *Operation Oblaka* were ready.

Getting the stolen artificial intelligence program to seamlessly work with the CGC gaming system was proving tricky. As a military application, the StormClouds' AI protocol was designed to integrate with slower executing, secure military systems that had redundancies built into them to prevent failure in extreme battlefield conditions. Because CGC's system was not designed as a military application, it didn't need the same redundancies and so it was always two- or three-steps ahead of the artificial intelligence program's ability to interpret the data. To the naked eye, the slightly jerky interaction of the two programs wasn't that noticeable, but in computer time, it was significant. More importantly, because the CGC program kept running ahead of the AI program, any potential tactical benefit was delayed, potentially to the point of uselessness.

To make matters worse, General Yikovich had bungled part of the program transfer from StormClouds when he had hacked into their system and inadvertently overtyped some code on the company's hard drive, causing it to crash and kicking him out of the system. Yikovich had been unable to get back in because StormClouds security was on high alert. Consequently, he and Sergeant Kachinko had been trying to develop a work around, but it had been a challenge. He was hoping to learn some piece of information from the founder of StormClouds during his interview on *Tech Movers* that would help push them forward.

The familiar New York staccato of Maria Incandella's voice heralded the beginning of her show and as she worked through her monologue about the two companies from Seattle that were locked in an increasingly contentious lawsuit, the General chuckled to himself. He was probably the only person who knew the real truth behind what had caused StormClouds' server to crash, ruining a chunk of its software in the process. He had seen the code of both systems and knew how different they were—it was partly the reason the Russians were having such a hard time integrating the two.

The fact that he, General Yikovich, was an unknown character in this drama made the interview all the more interesting for him and as he studied Maria in all her glitz and glamour, he wondered what she would be willing to do to obtain information that only he knew. He was tempted to find out, as foolish as it might be professionally.

#

Though the *Tech Movers* interview with the CEO of StormClouds was at 6:30am on the West Coast, Susan had suggested that she, Billy, and Joe all gather in the main conference room to watch. Joe grumbled at the hour, being a night owl like most lawyers, and he doubted there would be anything worth hearing, much less noteworthy from a legal perspective. But Susan had seen Maria in action enough times to not underestimate her ability to trip up even the most prepared guest with some heretofore unknown nugget of information. She was hoping Maria wouldn't disappoint.

Joe straggled into the conference room at 6:15am, Tully's double shot espresso in tow; Billy and Susan had been there since 5:30am, going over some of the new ads they were rolling out in the buildup to the Gaming Olympics.

"Damn, Billy, I'm not used to these early mornings. Their CEO can be such a bore, don't be surprised if he puts me back to sleep," the 55-year-old lawyer groused before taking a swig of his coffee. The two attorneys had some history, both being graduates of the University of Washington Law School and having served together on various state technology initiatives.

"I'm just hoping he got a frantic call from his lawyer like I did when I went on the show," Billy laughed, "and he's forgotten everything he's supposed to say!"

"Look gentlemen," Susan interjected into the banter, "Maria's a pro at this and she's not having the CEO of StormClouds on because of his good looks or charm. She has an angle that he doesn't know about. I've seen her in action enough times to know that when she goes after her prey," she cast a side glance at her boss, "she can be treacherous." A hint of a smile came to Billy's face as he remembered the event.

"Frankly, I'm surprised his lawyers are even letting him on the show," Joe added. "He's right in the middle of a lawsuit and he's acting like it's a media event. At least you going on that show made sense because of the IPO. Maybe you're right, Susan."

#

Beth walked into the lounge at two minutes before nine and flipped on the TV. She hoped Jeremy would be able to join her. She enjoyed his company and he didn't seem at all put off by her self-confidence or occasionally cutting remarks. She also found his willingness to ask for her thoughts on technology-related issues exhilarating.

"We are here this morning with Kyle Shepherd, the founder of Seattle-based StormClouds. His company has developed a state-of-the-art artificial intelligence logistics application that is wowing the tech community. But that's not the only thing the tech community is buzzing about, as StormClouds is locked in an increasingly bitter lawsuit with its cross-town rival, Cloud Gaming Co., over allegations that a portion of the code that makes CGC's Battle for Babylon *such a hit, was stolen. Sounds like fightin' words, Kyle, tell me about it..."*

Beth looked around and sighed. Jeremy wouldn't be coming again today.

#

Joe took another swig of his coffee as he and the CGC team watched Kyle Shepherd respond.

"Well, Maria, first of all, thanks for having me on the show. I never miss it back home."

"Ha ha, he's already BS'ing," Joe cackled. "I know he can't stand her and he's pissed because Billy got to go onto her show first!"

"The lawsuit will be played out in the courts, so I can't really comment on it, but when all is said and done, I think the merits of our case will stand on their own." The CEO smiled and replied calmly, sounding like the arrogant lawyer he was. Maria leaned towards him, crossing her legs in the process and shifting her weight to the edge of her chair. Though it was imperceptible, Susan watched Kyle Shepherd drop his gaze from her face to her chest and then briefly to her legs.

"Which are?"

The question was as blunt as it was brief. While Kyle Shepherd's canned reply to Maria's first question was completely expected, the terse follow-up was not.

"Which are what?" he replied in a flustered tone.

Maria had done her homework. Kyle Shepherd had a reputation as a playboy in the Seattle area and Maria figured she'd flaunt her assets and try to knock him off his line. She had already succeeded and there were still 25 minutes left in the interview.

"Oh my!" Susan's eyebrows arched as she envisioned what was likely about to unfold on the TV screen before her. Both men simultaneously looked at her puzzled. They were somewhat confused by the curious response of the normally unflappable CEO, but they had completely missed why it had happened.

"You didn't see it, did you?" Susan chuckled, shaking her head as she responded to their perplexed looks. "He checked her out from head to toe. That'll be all over Twitter before she asks the next question." Susan disgustedly remembered her own experience. She had met the CEO of StormClouds once and he had done the same thing to her, though he had been more obvious about it because he had been drinking. As she watched the body language between Maria and Kyle, it was clear to her that something was going on between the two and Susan felt sure that Maria was going to eviscerate him on national TV.

#

"The merits of your case against CGC, of course, Kyle. Everything I've heard from experts is that the two systems are nothing alike," Maria clinically pressed on. "Military applications and their security features are so far removed from video game architecture that it stretches the imagination to think one could be useful for the other, don't you think?"

Why Maria had a bee in her bonnet was unclear, but she was pulling no punches right from the gate and her guest was clearly uncomfortable. What most people didn't know was that for all her glitz and glamour, Maria Incandella had a solid computer science degree from Brooklyn College and had become a tech reporter only later. The question, whatever the reason for it, was a legitimate one.

#

Jeremy rushed in as Kyle Shepherd prepared to reply.

"Hi Beth, thanks for saving me a spot," he said as he slid into the open chair next to his colleague, offering her a Diet Pepsi in the process. "Did I miss anything?"

"The fireworks are about to start," Beth excitedly replied, "Maria just lit the fuse!" She looked down at the can of soda and then up at Jeremy, who was focused on the TV screen. "Hey, thanks," Beth softly said, taking the can from Jeremy's hand.

"You're welcome! Us rookies gotta stay together, yanno?" he replied, his gaze still locked onto the screen.

"Well Maria, as you know, much of what we do at StormClouds is classified, so while your question might be reasonable on the surface, we both know that I can't really engage in a full defense without compromising national security, but suffice it to say that if the case didn't have merit, it would have been thrown out," Kyle sharply replied.

"Wow," Jeremy whispered, "I did miss something. Didn't the show just start?" Beth cast a sideways glance and nodded, a faint smile on her lips. She was enjoying this.

#

"Of course, but the injunction to prohibit sales of *Battle for Babylon* was rejected, wasn't it?" Maria shrugged her shoulders and opened her hands for emphasis. "It would seem logical if the case were that strong, the judge would have granted the injunction."

"The judge said he didn't have enough information to grant the injunction, Maria, but that he would reconsider after reviewing further evidence," the CEO of StormClouds battled right back. "It's not just a commercial case, after all, so from a national security perspective, we have to be careful what we turn over. The world is a dangerous place and I'm proud that what we do at StormClouds is working to keep it safe for Americans here and abroad."

"That's a great point, Kyle," Maria deftly backed off, sensing her guest might just get up and walk off the set if she pressed. She'd already been surprised by one of the Seattle tech mavens; it wouldn't happen again. She'd made her point and it was time for a commercial break.

#

"What the hell just happened?" Billy looked at his two colleagues. "I hope I didn't come across like that in my interview."

"You were nothing like that, Billy," his lawyer flatly stated. "You were a total pro. Like I said then, it kind of surprised me how well you did. Not sure what is going on today, though." Both Joe and Billy looked at Susan, who seemed to have a better pulse on what might be happening back in New York than either of them did.

"As crass as it sounds," Susan started, "I'd venture to say their dinner was last night and it didn't go so well. This might just be payback."

"What? You're saying it's personal?" Billy jumped in.

"Might be," Susan replied. "Look, Maria Incandella is known for using every trick in the book to soften up her guests into saying or doing something stupid. Among the women in tech, Kyle's got a reputation for being a womanizer. I'm just putting two and two together. It's not like the bitch is a saint."

Both men laughed heartily at Susan's words.

#

Mikhail Yikovich topped off his nearly empty glass of sherry and settled back onto his sofa to watch the rest of *Tech Movers*. It had been extraordinarily entertaining so far, even if he had learned nothing helpful. Maria was back in all her sartorial splendor.

"So Kyle, can you tell us what are some of the particularly difficult things you have to consider in the modern warfare age where technology reigns supreme?"

General Yikovich's head jerked up—this was exactly the challenge vexing them.

"Well Maria," Kyle replied in a more professorial manner. Whatever beef they had had in the previous segment seemed to have been resolved. *"The biggest challenge is trying to prevent failure, because the cost can be so high. We want to make sure that our brave young soldiers relying on StormClouds make it back to their families. Programming is hard enough when things are stable, but when you are faced with a hostile environment in terms of terrain, weather, time, people shooting at you, and things breaking down, the obstacles can seem insurmountable. The goal is just to make sure it works all the time, not to make it work perfectly."*

General Yikovich pondered on that thought a few moments. It reflected an understanding of the battlefield in a manner he had almost forgotten. A good, usable weapon was far better than a perfect one that failed when you needed it most. He filed the thought away.

#

Billy also appreciated Kyle's practical wisdom and nodded at the application of its simple truth: things that didn't work when you needed them to were worse than useless, they were liabilities. He wondered how he could apply that idea to his own business.

"Interesting thoughts, Kyle," Maria's response was her cue that the conversation was headed in another direction. Susan watched Kyle shift in his seat, waiting for the next volley. Given the antagonism of the first segment, she thought he had handled himself remarkably well.

"I hope you don't mind me asking another question about the lawsuit," Maria started off on her next train of thought, not really caring if her guest had an issue with it or not, *"but wouldn't it make more sense for someone other than a video game maker to break into your system? Given what just happened in the Ukraine, it sounds like your software would be perfect for someone like the Russians, for example?"*

#

Mikhail Yikovich nearly aspirated the sherry in his mouth when he heard Maria's question. He could not conceive of any way someone could reach such a conclusion on pure speculation alone. Was it possible there was a mole in his own department? He shuddered at the thought, but couldn't reject it outright, either. The men in his department were all tech devotees and so it was possible they, too, were watching *Tech Movers* at this very moment and one of them might have provided the blonde bimbo in the tight sweaters this valuable piece of information. Who knows what he might have gotten in return?

#

Jeremy's mind revved into overdrive at the question. He hadn't thought of the Ukrainian battle from the perspective of artificial intelligence, but it made sense. He had wondered to his boss about how they could have achieved so much, so fast, with so little loss. Was it possible that they were just using old weapons in a smarter way? Or more worrisome: new weapons in new ways.

#

The CEO of StormClouds shifted nervously in his chair. He knew that Russian code had been left behind on his firm's server—perhaps on purpose, perhaps not—but very few other people knew it. Was this question from an internal leak or was it just an educated guess?

"Cyper-espionage occurs everywhere we look, Maria, but there is nothing that makes us think that happened to us. But as I have said before, the legal process is ongoing, so I'd rather not answer any more questions about it." Kyle's response had an "or else" feel to it. The set cut to another commercial.

#

"Beth, what do you think about that?" Jeremy asked his colleague.

"About what? Russian hackers?" she queried back.

"No, using AI to run a battlefield strategy," said Jeremy.

"Hmmm, not sure how you could pull it off. Too much uncertainty and insufficient consistency of inputs to really make it feasible," Beth replied. She had done research on AI at Stanford and had a good grasp of it.

"So why is the government paying StormClouds to use their system?" Jeremy retorted.

"StormClouds is just using their AI for logistics and most of the inputs are pre-programmed or are environmental—temperature, terrain—stuff like that. Their ability to deal with incoming ordnance on the fly is pretty limited I'd suppose. But it's not like the government doesn't waste money on all kinds of things, you know?" she said, before adding in a giggling voice, "of course, that doesn't include you and me!"

Jeremy smiled.

CHAPTER 27

While Mitchell had earned a scholarship to attend Queen's, part of the arrangement included at least an hour a day helping out Dr. Johnson. Mitchell originally wasn't keen on the idea of having to work while in school, but over time it turned out to be a perquisite instead of a hassle. Dr. Johnson rarely had him doing mundane things like filing papers or correcting tests, and usually turned him loose in the Computer Storage Room in the basement to work on equipment.

The room was full of old PCs, laptops, Apples, printers, and smart phones, and most of them had perfectly operational, if antiquated, technology. Given that Mitchell's skill at breathing new life into old equipment is what got him into Queen's in the first place, Dr. Johnson figured he might as well put that talent to good use and have him resurrect whatever he could from the "junk pile." Mitchell loved it and often ended up spending a lot more than his required hour tinkering with the hardware and software. He was also surprised at how good some of the discarded equipment actually was, and managed to get Queen's to donate some of it to the public school in his hometown. It was a win-win.

He had also discovered that in addition to the used equipment, the storage room was a treasure trove of old books, research publications, and articles on topics that Dr. Johnson found interesting. Mitchell had been working through a stack of articles on tech legends such as Bill Gates, Steve Jobs, Larry Ellison, Andy Grove, and of course, Billy Wilson; it was fascinating to see how these men had molded the companies they founded in their own image. The folder on Billy Wilson was particularly thick, and filled not only with articles from trade journals and third-party sources, but some of his personal student files, as well.

"Wow!" Mitchell exclaimed to himself, looking at one of Billy's senior year report cards with perfect scores in the four AP courses he had taken. "Man, no wonder he decided not to go to college—he probably would have been bored out of his skull!"

Mitchell shuffled to the bottom of the stack—past all the report cards that had nothing but A's on them—to see if there was anything else of interest. He found an old letter from Billy Wilson's aunt, who lived in North Seattle, inquiring about the availability of spots in the computer program. He put the rest of the papers down and started reading:

"My sister, Charlotte Wilson, has a very precocious 13-year-old son named Billy, who lost the father he idolized in a car accident last month, and she is worried because Billy has fallen into depression. I have heard wonderful things about the work you are doing at Queen's in computers and wonder if you could meet with Billy and her when they are out for Christmas. She is not only dealing with the death of her husband, but trying to save her young son. Computers are the only thing he seems to respond to and she is at wit's end. Sincerely, Karen Merrill"

Mitchell had heard a version of how Billy had ended up at Queen's from Dr. Johnson a few weeks before, but reading a letter from a relative hit so much harder; his eyes teared-up, trying to imagine how he would have dealt with something like this. *At least I have brothers*, he thought. A brief obituary from the *Washington Post* was attached to the letter:

"William Wilson Jr., a computer scientist who pioneered some of the earliest computer artificial intelligence research, passed away on November 12, a victim of an automobile accident; he was 52. He is survived by his wife, Charlotte, and his son, William, III. Memorial services will be held at Cross & Crown Church in Falls Church, Virginia on Saturday, November 20 at 2pm."

Mitchell looked at the calendar; the eleventh anniversary of the accident was in two days.

What an awful day that must be for the dude, Mitchell thought, wondering if one could erase something like that from memory. Then it hit him: November 12, 2002—111202—had to be XX12XX! It made sense, if there was one day Billy Wilson would likely never be able to forget, it was the day his father died.

It was also a clever disguise. The number sequence was not a list of the inaugural day of wars in which the US fought—it just appeared to be. Rather, it was a list of dates important to Billy Wilson, the apparent war angle only serving to throw people like Mitchell off the scent. Juxtaposed to a long sequence of numbers, the anniversary of the death of William Wilson Jr. would be the only one that didn't make any sense to someone who had cracked the rest of the code. For Billy, it would be the number etched on his brain forever. Mitchell was sure he had found a key to a backdoor.

132

"Mr. Wilson's line, Claire speaking, may I help you?"

"Hi Claire, Mikel Johnson here, is Billy in?"

"Oh hi, Dr. Johnson," Claire enthusiastically responded. "How have things been? I understand you have a crackerjack team for the Gaming Olympics this year. Can you win it all?"

"Ha-ha. We shall see. Every year the competition seems to get tougher and tougher and at the end of the day, unlike the pros out there, my kids still have to do more than play video games all day long. But, yes, we have a good group of kids."

"Well, good luck!" Claire amiably chirped. "Just a moment please."

#

Billy Wilson picked up the line behind his closed door.

"Dr. Johnson for you, sir," came Claire's voice, *"shall I put him through?"*

"Please do, Claire," Billy replied, as he watched her hang up the line at her desk. "Dr. J," Billy said cheerfully, "as expected." He looked down at his calendar; it was November 12, the anniversary of his dad's death. Dr. Johnson never forgot to call him.

"How is Forbes Mr. #99?" Dr. Johnson responded playfully. His own wealth had swelled as a result of CGC's IPO, too.

"Is it that high already?" Billy surprisingly queried back. He had more than enough, which was enough. How much he had compared to others mattered little to him.

"Just calling to see how you are doing. I remember what day this is," Dr. Johnson somberly intoned.

There was a momentary silence on the other line, before Billy said, "You know, things are truly better. There's so much going on with the lawsuit, the Olympics coming up, the IPO, the ad campaign—my head is spinning sometimes, so I haven't had time to dwell on the past. But I've got some good help, too."

"So I've heard. Joe says that you and your Marketing VP might be an item. Any truth to that?" Dr. Johnson was as close a thing he had to a father and Billy enjoyed the back-and-forth, even if it embarrassed him a bit.

"Well. I hope so, Dr. J. I really hope so," Billy sheepishly replied.

"I've seen some pictures of her. She's a pretty girl—"

"Smart, too." The conversation with Dr. Johnson made him realize how fond he had grown of Susan.

"Well, Billy, if anyone deserves someone like that, it's you," Dr. Johnson replied affectionately. Having no kids of his own, he felt a special bond with Billy Wilson, even though he was surrounded by teenagers in school. *"Just be careful. She does work for you after all."*

"Thanks, Dr. J. I'd like you to meet her—you coming to our Christmas party next month?" Billy asked hopefully, ignoring the words of caution.

"Wouldn't miss it for the world," Dr. Johnson replied, *"which reminds me, do you have our scholarship banquet on your calendar? It's December 15th."*

Billy quickly scrolled from November to December.

"Yep, Claire put this on the calendar long ago—you know Claire!" Billy replied.

"Yes, I do. Not sure what you'd do without her. And bring Susan, too," Dr. Johnson responded. *"There's one kid in particular that I'd like you to meet. A Native American kid from up north past Marysville. Super smart and thinks outside the box."*

"Oh? How so?" Billy was always on the lookout for good minds and if Dr. Johnson thought he was worth mentioning, he definitely wanted to meet him.

"Very creative thinker. He's written some rudimentary artificial intelligence code—but just for kicks. The kid doesn't recognize how unusual he is. A bit of a renegade, too. Just your type!" Dr. Johnson laughed the boisterous cackle that made Billy remember his days at Queen's.

"Love it, Dr. J! Keep 'em coming!" Billy rejoined. They shared a good laugh.

\#

Mitchell found himself spending more and more time in the Computer Storage Room reading through the old files and papers that Dr. Johnson had stored down there ever since coming to Queen's twenty years ago. It seemed strange to him that someone who taught computer science and was also a major player on the Seattle tech scene would have saved so many of his e-mails and papers in hard copy form. However, Mitchell also recognized that Dr. Johnson was very old school in some ways—all the textbooks and computers gave the storage room a bit of a museum feel. His Native American background gave him an appreciation for tangible things of real value that were not just tossed aside because there was something with a few more whistles and bells on it to take its place.

His phone pinged; it was a text from Marjorie: *"Where are you?"*

Mitchell looked at his watch, wondering if he had forgotten some appointment or homework assignment.

"I'm working in Dr. J's office…why?" It wasn't entirely true, but he hadn't told anyone about his secret sanctuary in the Computer Storage Room. It had become too valuable a source of information for his "hacking project" to let anyone know, even someone as seemingly disinterested in technology as Marjorie was.

"I have something I want to ask you…in person."

Mitchell gulped, his mind racing with possibilities—did she really think he was harassing her? Did her brother take her phone to play one of his nasty tricks? Did she just need help with math? He wanted to think pleasant thoughts, too, but he had been distant since his talk with Dr. Johnson. He knew how serious harassment charges were.

"Um, sure. When and where?" he tapped with his thumbs before touching the send icon. A few seconds passed by.

"How about in ninety minutes down at the gym? I have basketball practice now."

Mitchell looked at his watch; it was about 4:30.

"Sure. Can I ask you one thing? Can you send me a selfie of you right now so I can be sure this text is from you? I think you know why…"

Marjorie both smiled and winced. She couldn't imagine how hard it was for this boy from a different culture living away from home and going to school with a bunch of cliquish kids. She knew how mean her brother could be; she was also a bit embarrassed to be part of a lot of those cliques. She snapped a picture, tapped in *"it's me"* and hit SEND.

"See you at 6!" Mitchell tapped back. He stared at the photo for fifteen seconds. She was a very pretty girl, despite the slight look of sadness her smile betrayed.

He put the phone down and returned to the rows of filing cabinets stuffed with folders. He wasn't really sure if it was okay to be reading all the papers, e-mails and other documents the computer science teacher had left in the room, but he rationalized it as a perquisite of the scholarship. He was sure Dr. Johnson knew what was down here, and also that none of it was locked up. Mitchell just thought of it as hacking into some of Dr. Johnson's personal hard copy files and everyone in the computer industry knew the danger of being hacked if you didn't take security measures. He smiled at the analogy as he finished off another pile of research papers. He had learned a great deal already from perusing the thousands of pages that Dr. Johnson had stored over the years, and he had just finished going through his ninth filing cabinet.

He pulled at the top drawer of the last one. The tabs were organized alphabetically by the tech companies on which Dr. Johnson had consulted and were full of old e-mails and agreements. He pulled out the folder with the name, *Online Gaming, Co.,* the predecessor entity of what had become Billy Wilson's brainchild, *Cloud Gaming Co.*

"Whoa!" Mitchell exclaimed, pulling out the first folder, which was a stack three inches high of e-mails between Dr. Johnson and Billy. "This is pure gold!"

He put the folder down and went over to make sure the door was locked. Dr. Johnson had never come down when he was here, but it would just be his luck to have him walk in now, to find him snooping through the teacher's filing cabinets.

He came back and picked up the first e-mail, a back-and-forth from five years ago on the role of crowd psychology in video games. It was an interesting dialog between two sharp minds, but he stopped reading after one paragraph. He'd found another piece of information to the backdoor problem his mind had been working on the last few weeks.

CHAPTER 28

"You coming?" Mitchell was knocked from his deep reverie by a text from Marjorie. He looked at his watch; it was 6:10pm.

"Dammit!" he screamed at the walls. He was in one of his deep thought processing modes and he was now in danger of standing up the cutest girl in school.

"Almost there...give me 3 minutes...got hung up on some work for Dr. J" he furiously typed—at least part of the text was true. He rushed out of the room, forgetting to close the filing cabinet, and dashed up the stairs and out the door the moment he hit SEND. Fortunately, the gym was down the hill and he was fast. He made it in two minutes.

"I am really, really sorry, Marjorie," Mitchell exclaimed, breathlessly. He looked around, making sure his tormentors weren't lurking. They were alone.

"No problem," she sounded relieved. "I'm actually glad you're a bit late because all my girlfriends are gone and I wanted to ask you something...um...in private." She looked down as she stumbled over her last words.

Mitchell found the whole scene both charming and a bit confusing as well. He had been the one who was late, yet she was apologetic. Cute or not, these Queen's girls were a curious lot.

"Well, here I am!" Mitchell cocked his head and opened his arms with palms upraised. He was as charming as he was good looking. "Fire away!"

"Um...do you want to go to the 'Tolo' with me?" Marjorie's words came out haltingly. She was completely certain she wanted to go with him, but completely uncertain if he would say "yes." It was an uncomfortable position for her.

Mitchell's eyes opened wide, she had just asked him out on a date—she did like him! He wasn't imagining it!

"Yes, absolutely!" Mitchell blurted out, his emotions exploding, "I would love to go with you! What's a 'tolo'?"

Marjorie burst out laughing.

"It's a school dance where girls ask guys and I'm asking you," she smiled, thrilled at his acceptance, even if he didn't know to what he was agreeing.

"A school dance?" Mitchell replied hesitantly, realizing that much of the school would be there, including her brother and his posse.

"Yes, a 'dance', silly." Marjorie wondered if this had been such a good idea after all. She definitely liked this boy, but he was acting funny now.

After a few moments of awkward silence, Mitchell turned serious, looked at her and said, "Yes, Marjorie, I would love to go to the dance with you."

Marjorie melted. She reached up to his cheek and kissed it gently, before quickly turning to go.

"OK, I gotta run now, see you tomorrow!"

With that she was gone. Mitchell stood like a statue, alone in the parking lot, but flushed from head to toe. The girl he had had a crush on for the past year just asked *him* out on a date and kissed *him* on the cheek, and he had just stood there. He was thrilled Marjorie liked him, but slightly embarrassed at his reaction. His mind was a blur of confusion, but he felt good inside.

CHAPTER 29

Greg's discovery about what had happened to both his father and William Wilson, Jr. ten years ago had given him a new found purpose: he would avenge two murders that—at least in his own mind—had occurred on the same day. The first was the immediate death of Billy's dad and the second, the slow, torturous death of his own father that Greg believed had begun the moment the drug wore off and he was lucid enough to understand the gravity of what had happened.

He wrestled with the idea of contacting his old friend with this new information and trying to mend their relationship which abruptly ended when they were young teenagers, but decided he needed to take care of some business while still in the shadows. There was no telling how his life might change again if he were successful in contacting Billy Wilson and it just made more sense to wait until he had dealt with the two Russians.

The two Russians, he thought to himself. Greg did not know who they were, or if they were even alive, though he hoped they were. He wanted them to feel some of the pain and desperation he had experienced the past decade.

Greg was as adept as anyone when it came to hacking into secure systems—he made a living at it after all—and alive or dead, these two men would still be in the Russian military computer system. He had never tried to break into the Russian network because he never had a reason to—until now.

Yet because of the information his father had left behind, breaking into the Russian military computer system turned out to be quite simple. The papers he had taken home after his mother's death had seemed meaningless when he first looked at them, but after reading the second e-mail draft his father had left, he immediately recognized the cipher hidden in plain sight. He decoded the information and soon was in possession of his father's backdoor access into the network.

He marveled at his father's cleverness. He also chuckled at the irony: the two men who had been primarily responsible for his father's death, would likely end up ruined or worse because of the assistance of that same man, now dead for ten years. If there ever was a case of the old adage, "revenge is a dish best served cold," this was it.

Greg used facial recognition software to find the two men who had been involved in the death of William Wilson, Jr. and quickly found a match for both: General Oleg Petrov and Sergeant Sergey Kachinko, now had big, fat targets on their back. The latter was part of the technology team in the Russian military. *This ought to be fun,* Greg thought, knowing he would be matching wits with someone trained in the same system as his father had been. He quickly logged off, though not before his anonymous actions had been recorded in the activity register that followed every Russian soldier everywhere.

#

Class had ended for the day and Mitchell couldn't wait to get back to the Computer Storage Room. He wanted to look through more of the e-mails between Billy and Dr. Johnson for other tidbits of information and just liked hanging out there. But as he walked out of the classroom, Brad and his buddies were lurking, cornering him at the end of the hallway.

"I told you to stay away from my sister, jerk! She doesn't like you, so leave her alone!" Brad glared at him as his friends took a step closer.

"What's your problem dude?" Mitchell retorted, "Why don't you just leave me alone. From what I can see, you gotta whole lot of practice ahead of you if you want to even sniff the Games!" Mitchell wasn't afraid of Brad and after seeing his weak video game session, didn't think Queen's even had a chance to make the top 100.

The barb stung, and Brad jacked Mitchell, shoving him against the wall. Mitchell was a nanosecond from drilling him back, when Dr. Johnson walked out of the classroom.

"Boys, boys! Whatever it is, there is no need to fight," Dr. Johnson started. He then looked at Brad, "Mr. Jeffries, you are supposed to be my ace, but you are playing like a joker and acting like a clown. You and your pals," he stopped momentarily to glare at each one individually, "already lost a virtual three-against-one fight, I'd hate to see you how you'd do in a real one. Do I make myself clear? Pull it together son." Dr. Johnson's disgust was palpable.

"Stay away from her," Brad couldn't help one more jibe under his breath, "or you'll be sorry, trust me."

"Yeah, whatever dude." Mitchell was tiring of the constant bullying, but at least Dr. Johnson had finally seen it.

#

The plan Greg had devised to destroy the two Russian military officers who had ruined the life of his father, was designed to create an escalating sense of fear and panic over time. Both involved money, but his plan for Oleg Petrov would also be publicly humiliating. Greg had watched this man savagely attack and then berate his drugged father for fifty-minutes. He had seen him deliberately drive off the road and hit an innocent man, and then watched him clinically dispatch the injured, but clearly alive, William Wilson, Jr. with the violent twist of the defenseless man's neck. It made General Oleg Petrov a very marked man.

But tonight, Sergey Kachinko was the target. The Sergeant used the electronic payment system for virtually everything, though he always took out enough cash on Friday to get through the weekend. Because of the growing demands on his work time, this almost always occurred after the bank closed its doors for the day, but he had no issue using the ATM machines that were everywhere. He had big plans this weekend and needed more cash than usual, though he had plenty of money—or so he thought.

You have insufficient funds to withdraw this amount. The screen blinked back at him with a message he had never seen before.

"Huh?" He was as surprised as he was angry. He looked around; there were four people in line behind him, looking impatient. He tried his card again, but got the same message. Another three people had joined the queue. Now he was also embarrassed. He shuffled away mumbling, as the next person in line withdrew a few hundred rubles.

He walked across the street to where the US megabank, Citibank, had a branch and an ATM. Same card, same result.

"What the—," he mumbled under his breath. He knew he had money in this account. But the banks were closed for the weekend, so he couldn't deal with someone at a counter to get it resolved. He pulled out his phone and punched in the customer service number listed on the back of his card. Two rings later he was on the phone with a chirpy customer service agent.

"Hello, my name is Veronika, how may I help you?"

"I am having problems withdrawing money from my account. Can you please check it for me?" He exchanged account information with the agent and a few moments later she came back on the line.

"Yes Mr. Kachinko. According to our records you have 5,134,000 rubles in your account and available to be withdrawn."

The Sergeant was relieved. The amount was more or less what he thought, and had initially feared that it had been stolen. He was now just irritated that he couldn't access it.

"I have tried at two different machines and was unsuccessful in getting anything out. Is there a problem with your system?"

"Just a moment please," the customer service agent put Sergeant Kachinko back on hold for about twenty seconds. *"I do not see there being any record of system problems. I also do not see any record of you even accessing the system at all today. Perhaps you used another card—"* The agent was trying to be helpful, but the Sergeant wasn't interested. He hung up before she finished.

He walked down the block and tried one more place, with the same result. *Damn,* he thought to himself. He was more angry than worried, but he needed the money, and he was also concerned that if he tried to use the card for pleasure, it would be rejected and he would be humiliated.

He retraced his footsteps back to where the Swiss giant, UBS, had a branch and reluctantly pulled out a non-descript bank card, linked to his private Swiss bank account. He had just seen his statement so he knew he had money, but he hated using this account anywhere inside Russia, in case prying eyes started asking questions. He looked around to make sure there were none. It took him all of fifteen seconds to get the money out…

#

…and less than ten seconds for Greg to add another electronic data point to his collection for one Sergeant Sergey Victor Kachinko, Russian Army, #348692. The wheels were in motion. It was time to reach out to his old, childhood friend.

CHAPTER 30

Mitchell entered Ms. Jackson's Biology lab two minutes before class started; the teacher looked up.

"Mitchell," she icily greeted him. "I just got a call from Mr. Richardson and he wants to talk to you in his office, so you are excused from class."

Ms. Jackson was no one's favorite, and she didn't seem to particularly care for Mitchell, but he detected an extra chill in her voice that sounded ominous. He looked around to see if any of his classmates had heard their brief conversation; none had. As he hurried out the door, Marjorie was coming down the hall in the other direction. She cheerily smiled at him.

"Where are you going?" she asked.

"Um...I have to go see the Principal for something. I'm not sure why..." his voice trailed off in trepidation. Marjorie's countenance also changed, knowing that he had already been in trouble once.

"Oh? I'm sure it is nothing," she tried to sound reassuring, but they were both thinking the same thing, if for different reasons. She figured Mitchell was the fall guy for some mean-spirited prank her brother and his buddies had pulled, while he wondered if somehow the school had found out that he had been trying to hack into his classmates social media accounts. She touched him reassuringly. *At least I have someone in my camp,* he thought.

He slowly walked across campus. There was absolutely nothing he could think of that he had done to anyone that warranted a visit to the principal's office, except his hacking and if they had found out about that, he would surely be expelled, if not end up in jail. He poked his head into the Administrative Offices of the school and Mrs. Black, the school's longtime assistant, motioned him in.

"Good morning Mr. Patkanim. Mr. Richardson and Mr. Keane are expecting you." She was pleasant, but very business-like. Mitchell groaned at the news that the Dean of Discipline was also in the room; it was about as bad a sign as there could be.

"Thank you, ma'am," Mitchell respectfully replied, opening the door.

He quietly closed it behind him and sat down opposite the two men.

"Hi Mitchell," Mr. Richardson started somberly, "I'm sure you know why you are here." The principal shifted uncomfortably in his chair. He liked Mitchell and felt that the school's outreach to disadvantaged youth in Washington State was one of the best things it did for the community.

"No, sir," Mitchell replied, "I don't have any idea."

The two men looked at each other with knowing glances. This was going to be harder than they thought. Expelling a student was the worst thing a school had to do—in some ways it showed they had failed in their mission. When a student was in denial and fought, it was particularly hard. But with harassment charges, their hands were tied, particularly given that Mitchell had a prior offense.

"Now, now, Mitchell," Mr. Keane jumped in, a mix of arrogance and petulance in his voice. "I know that Dr. Johnson talked to you about harassing Marjorie Jeffries, but judging from this collection of text messages," he stopped to wave a stack of papers, "it doesn't appear that you learned anything from either his comments or your previous episode with the young lady."

Mitchell looked at the Dean of Discipline with a genuinely puzzled look on his face.

"I honestly have no idea what you are talking about," Mitchell forcefully retorted. "I acknowledge that Dr. Johnson talked to me about it, but I haven't ever said nor done anything to her that is harassing in any way at all."

Mitchell had been unprepared the first time he faced Mr. Keane, but not this time. He had come in ready to be expelled for trying to hack into a publicly-traded company's network, but now that he could see that wasn't the case, he was angry.

"Let's calm down a bit, shall we?" Mr. Richardson interjected, sensing it might quickly get out of hand. "Ed, please show Mitchell the texts you got from Mr. Jeffries. I think the young man might have a change of heart after seeing the evidence we have."

Mitchell's blood was boiling. He knew he had done nothing wrong to Marjorie—she had asked *him* out for Pete's sake.

"Well, Bob, I don't think we can show him all of them," he said, somewhat embarrassed, "some of them are pretty crude."

"No, Ed, he deserves the chance to defend himself," Mr. Richardson firmly replied, "particularly given the circumstances." Mitchell appreciated the Principal's fairness.

"OK, here's a sequence of a few messages between you and Miss Jeffries from last week." He pushed the paper forward to Mitchell; both he and the principal had copies.

Mitchell started reading the crude exchange, his emotions rising with each line. He turned red after reading the back-and-forth, but out of anger, not embarrassment.

"Well young man?" Mr. Keane haughtily demanded. "What do you have to say for yourself?"

"No disrespect intended Mr. Keane, but these are lies. Every single one of them. They didn't come from me or from her. I'd also guess your whole stack of 'em are lies, too. Someone is trying to make me look bad. I swear to you that I did not send these."

Principal Richardson was silent for a moment, looking at the two defiant males in his office; it was quickly escalating into a mess. The student before him was adamant about his innocence, but his Dean had shown him disgusting and vulgar evidence of what appeared to be text message exchanges that were worrisome to say the least.

"OK, Mitchell," Mr. Richardson started, "you say you are innocent. Can you prove it?" He was willing to give his young student the benefit of the doubt. He had seen enough students in his thirty years of teaching to know when someone was trying to lie his way out of discipline and when someone was truly innocent and he was beginning to wonder if he had the latter case on his hands.

"This is Marjorie's number, but it isn't the only one she has. I have a ton of texts from her, Mr. Richardson, and the number is different. Would you like to see them?" Both men's eyebrows arched upon hearing this.

"No, that won't be—," Mr. Keane nervously interjected.

"I'd like to see them, Ed," the Principal cut him off. "If the boy's lying we will know immediately. If he's telling the truth we have a different problem on our hands."

Mitchell took out his phone and pulled up the text message thread with Marjorie Jeffries and handed his phone to the Principal.

"You have her picture?" Mr. Keane said, peering over the Principal's shoulder with a look of growing anxiousness on his face.

"Yes sir. She sent it to me a while back. This is her private number," Mitchell said, a touch of pride in his voice.

"Private number?" the two men chimed in together.

"Yes sir. She told me her brother took her phone sometimes to embarrass her so she had her dad get her a private one," Mitchell was spilling the beans, but not in the way either man had expected.

"Wait, she asked you to the Tolo?" Mr. Richardson said, surprise in his voice.

"Yes sir," Mitchell replied with a huge grin, sounding more like a young boy with a crush, than a harassing menace, "but I'm really nervous, to be honest with you."

After a few moments, the Principal spoke again. "Mitchell, we might have a misunderstanding here. Give us some more time to look into it, OK?" Mr. Keane looked down glumly.

"Um, OK," Mitchell replied anxiously, "But I swear I haven't done anything."

"Just give us some more time Mitchell," Principal Richardson tersely replied. "You are free to go."

As the door closed and Mitchell was out of earshot, Bob Richardson looked at his Dean of Discipline. "Ed, we are damn lucky that boy's not some rich white kid or daddy's lawyers would be in here right now asking for your head—or worse. You better sort this thing out quickly or it could get ugly."

CHAPTER 31

Though Mikhail Yikovich and Sergey Kachinko were technology specialists, they were also military men and were mindful that the two fields weren't always compatible. So, while they were enamored with the seemingly limitless possibilities of how the integration of their two "acquired" programs could revolutionize warfare tactics, they also had to deal with the more mundane, but equally critical, physical elements of the battlefield: getting equipment from Point A to Point B, maintaining supply lines, dealing with balky or broken equipment far from home, and creating the element of surprise.

The plan, at least as much as had been revealed to Sergeant Kachinko, was clever, though it would be fraught with logistical difficulties. While most of the troops and materiel would be on the ground in Iran long before the attack itself, they still needed to move some of the troops and attack drones over the Zagros Mountain range that traversed Iran from its northwest corner to the Strait of Hormuz on the Persian Gulf. Both men knew the mountains had stymied many an invader, though Kachinko also conceded that because much of the attack would be carried out by drones, the military hardware and troops needed could be carried by relatively few of the large Russian transport planes. The Iranians used the same style of aircraft, so the radar signature would not likely draw undue attention flying through their airspace.

Operationally the plan was aided by the fact that Iran and Syria would both be allowing Russian access to their territories, and the use of airfields near their ultimate target, Israel. Iran was going so far as to allow Russian troops unfettered rail passage from the Caspian Sea. But this battle was not going to be about overwhelming military force on the ground, but rather the revolutionary use of drones and other military hardware guided by a sophisticated video game system and an integrated artificial intelligence program.

#

Though Sergeant Kachinko no longer had any problems withdrawing money from his Russian bank account, the episode at the bank had shaken him. He knew that Russian banks weren't known for their security, but very few Russian hackers were foolish enough to go after military officers, and hackers from elsewhere went after banks where the big money was. Though he was willing to concede that it could have been a simple electronic malfunction or a problem with his card, he also wondered if his involvement in developing the new military strategy had made him a target within the Russian military itself. He decided to keep those thoughts to himself, lest he unnecessarily alarm General Yikovich. Nevertheless, he checked his account almost every time he passed an ATM, momentarily reassured each time he received confirmation that his five million rubles were still in the account.

It was a false sense of security.

#

Greg boarded the non-stop flight to Seattle, as anxious as he could ever remember. He was going on a mission to try to rebuild a relationship he had had with someone who was once closer than a brother, but whom he hadn't seen or heard from in more than ten years. Yet he had no idea if the feeling was mutual. Greg wasn't even sure he had the courage to follow through with the visit, appointment or not, but at least he had had some time to think it through. As far as he knew, Billy didn't even know—maybe didn't even care—if he were alive. Yet Greg felt it would be much harder to be turned down if he just showed up, so an unannounced visit seemed like the only reasonable course of action.

The discovery of the video showing the death of Billy's dad coupled with the fact that he now had access to the Russian military network and was devising a plan of revenge, made Greg more cautious of everything he did. As he settled into his first-class seat, he made a mental note of those around him; no one seemed suspicious in the slightest. The flight attendant approached him.

"Good afternoon, Mr. Galkin, may I get you something to drink?"

He looked up from the *Washington Post*. "Sure, a glass of red wine would be great." He felt like he needed something to subdue his nervous edge. The flight attendant was back in one minute with a glass of cabernet and some cashews.

"Thank you," he murmured, before downing half the glass in one gulp. He hadn't eaten breakfast and the alcohol immediately had a calming effect. He scanned the Technology section of the paper, chuckling to himself at the increasingly vitriolic position of StormClouds in their suit against CGC. He'd have to ask Billy about that.

As the final boarding announcements were being made, he engaged in chitchat with the Georgetown student sitting next to him who was returning home to Seattle for winter break. Though they were probably only a year or two apart in age, Greg felt infinitely older, given the twists and turns his life had taken—particularly in the past few weeks.

"So what are you studying?" Greg dutifully asked, more out of politeness than curiosity.

"Political Science," the young woman responded, "I'm hoping to get into counter-terrorism with the government when I graduate. The world's a dangerous place, you know?"

Greg nodded, *if she only knew,* he thought to himself. "No doubt. Somebody's got to defend us from the crazies, that's for sure."

"You in the tech business?" she asked, noticing his newspaper was opened to the Technology page; he was impressed with the girl's attentiveness.

"Yeah, I'm a security consultant heading out to see some clients," he vaguely replied, hoping to steer the conversation in another direction.

"Oh yeah? Which ones?" the girl inquired innocently.

"Well," Greg responded, "my clients like to remain confidential and I respect their wishes, you know?"

"Cloak and dagger, stuff? Cool!" she volleyed back, having no idea how close she was to the truth. It made Greg slightly uncomfortable, but he played along. The banter was innocent and the girl was attractive.

"Naw, nothing like that," he chuckled, "sorry to disappoint!"

"Bummer!" she cheerfully replied, as the plane made its turn onto the active runway. The sharp increase in the whine of the engines signified they would soon be airborne. The newspaper in Greg's hands drooped as he drifted off to sleep; the conversation with the college student next to him, over.

CHAPTER 32

As Seb reviewed the diagnostic reports that his software tech had run, he thought about possible benign reasons for the perceived difference between the Threat Board and the management reports. Frankly, he wasn't even sure there was a divergence, as he was just relying on his intuition, experience, and recent memory. But he had a good feel for the technology and had spent enough time staring at the sea of lights to know what normal was and at least in his mind, this wasn't it.

His reports did show an uptick in Russian activity, but in the buildup to the Gaming Olympics, this was likely normal. There was a growing contingent of video gamers in Russia and after CGC went public, the firm saw a meaningful increase in subscribers all over the world. Russians were notorious hackers, so it was probably natural that CGC's Threat Board would be showing this. Maybe Billy was right that they did need more equipment, but Seb wasn't quite ready to concede that thought because more equipment just meant more complexity. Besides, he trusted what his eyes were telling him.

#

What Susan lacked in technology knowledge and experience, she more than made up for in her ability to sift through disparate and complex information to reach actionable conclusions involving people. It was why she was such a successful investment banker and made her an increasingly valuable member of the CGC management team. Her unique perspective as an outsider gave her an advantage in almost every interaction she had in a firm so heavily reliant on computer skills. Fortunately, she found the men in both the financial and technology industries to be remarkably similar: quick to either take credit for success or to cast blame for failure. She punched in Seb's number.

"Seb DiCarlo here."

"Hi Seb, this is Susan Green."

"Hello Susan, Billy told me to expect your call." He was terse, but polite. Susan felt his reluctance; whether it was the Wall Street—or the woman-in-tech—stereotype didn't matter, it was there. She plowed on, asking what would be the first of many questions.

She had a gift for drawing people out to reveal their inner thoughts, and she found she could get men to talk just by asking questions.

"Is now a good time?" she asked.

"Yeah, sure," Seb replied, softening his initial tone, *"I have a meeting in 45 minutes, but this is obviously pretty important."*

"Great, thanks for being accommodating. Billy just gave me the thumbnail: what you're seeing on the Threat Board doesn't seem to jibe with what your reports are saying and you wonder if maybe we've been breached. Does that sound about right?"

Seb chuckled. *"Well that's definitely the stripped down version, but yeah, that about sums it up."*

"Well, why don't you put some flesh on it for me—give me an overview of what you think is going on and what some possible scenarios are that might explain what you're seeing?" Susan replied. Attitude or no, she had a job to do, so she was not going to be deterred by some smug techie. "I don't profess to be an expert, so I will ask questions, if that's OK."

Seb knew no one from Wall Street and had formed his negative opinions based on what he had heard and read, but Susan was not fitting any of the stereotypes. She was polite, asked questions, and didn't pretend to know it all. *Maybe she isn't so bad after all,* he thought.

"OK, sounds good," he started, categorizing the thoughts in his head. *"First of all, as a guy who has been involved in computer security for ten years, I appreciate the real emphasis that Billy has always placed on it. I'd say 'he gets it' in a way that I'm not sure a lot of his peers in the industry do."*

"What do you mean by that?" Susan was genuinely curious.

"Well, I can't articulate it very well, but while he seems to recognize there are a lot of threats out there, he doesn't seem to take any of them personally. It's just a part of the business—a nasty part, maybe—but nothing specifically aimed at him."

"Hmmm. That's an interesting observation, Seb," she asserted, "I've seen it, too. He seems to lack the oversized ego some in the industry have and just wants to get it right."

"That's a good way to put it. Anyway, as we've built out the security system, he's been willing to listen to some novel ideas that we ultimately implemented, and I think everything has made the

overall system stronger and more robust." Susan felt Seb warming up to her.

"For example?" Susan interjected.

"Take our security system. The fully automated structure we have is more than sufficient, but the visual Threat Board structure creates an immediate and totally human element that looks at the user environment in a completely different way."

"And it's what you're seeing on the Threat Board that has you worried, that someone may be on the system illegally, right?" Susan was fascinated by the dialog. Most techies acted as though they preferred the machine to the human and yet the Security VP's intuition seemed to suggest that the machines were being fooled and he was willing to trust it enough to call the CEO of the company.

"Well, I can't quite put my finger on it," Seb cautiously countered, *"and while I'm not totally ready to concede someone has hacked into us, something does seem amiss."*

"So what isn't adding up in your mind?" Susan queried.

Seb pondered on it a bit. Susan was very systematic in how she asked questions. *She probably would have made a good programmer,* he thought. *"Well, the LogInReport suggests minor anomalies—the kind of stuff we normally see when the system is taxed—but the Threat Board suggests they are more than minor."*

"Based on what?" Susan asked.

"Based on ten years in the trenches. Based on being involved in a lot of the early development of the CGC security platform and the Threat Board. Based on an understanding of what the Threat Board is designed for. I do know what I am doing, Susan." Susan could feel his defensiveness growing, though she just let it slide.

"Of course. Well, maybe you could spend a bit of time explaining the Threat Board and what it is designed to reveal. Billy briefly showed me, but didn't provide a lot of detail," Susan was walking through her due diligence process, something she was very good at and which no doubt would have made her one of the youngest partners ever at McDonough if she had stayed. She was used to far more antagonism than she was getting from Seb.

"Well, in simplest terms," he couldn't help himself, the tech world was still mostly guys, after all, *"the Threat Board shows where the action is from a visual perspective. The floor is laid out*

geographically and the colors represent different levels of threats from—" Susan immediately interrupted.

"'Threats' defined as what?" she queried.

"Unusual stresses on the system," he didn't seemed annoyed by the interruption, *"either in the form of deliberate attacks by hackers or because of a significant increase in volume—for example, if everyone in Paris logged on at once, the Threat Board would interpret that as an unusual stress."*

"Got it."

"—so, the colors represent different levels of threats from the outside. Normally you see mostly green and blue," Seb continued almost exactly where he left off before the interruption, *"and if we're doing things correctly, hardly ever orange or red. Yellow, the midpoint color is the top of the fence, so to speak, and it seems we are seeing a lot of that lately."*

"Meaning?" Susan continued to draw him out with questions.

"Maybe that our system is being attacked more aggressively, but maybe nothing," Seb said philosophically, *"we've seen an uptick in activity since we went public, it could just be the new normal."*

"And the LogInReport?" Susan swatted it back like she was playing tennis.

"That report is showing nothing out of the ordinary really." Susan could tell that Seb was beginning to feel unsure about his concerns. She hadn't doubted anything he said or his worries, but to clinically defend what was just a gut feeling was difficult.

"Look Seb," Susan tried to allay the security chief's uncertainty. "Billy thinks you're the best. Based on this conversation and your willingness to honestly engage in this back-and-forth with me, I can see why. Frankly, I think it is stunning that given how much data flies around our servers, you don't spend all day putting out fires. We all trust your judgment—now we just have to figure out how to interpret it. I'm not questioning your conclusions, just trying to draw something out that maybe makes you see it in a different context."

Seb was silent for a moment, basking in the warmth of a genuine compliment, but also processing the depth of the questioning.

"Seb?" Fearing she had just insulted her colleague, Susan broke what was turning into a slightly awkward silence, "are you still there?"

"Yeah, yeah, still here. Just thinking," he replied distantly, his mind in overdrive. *"The LogInReport shows log on activity, while the Threat Board shows activity of those logged on—"*

Susan interrupted again. "Aren't those the same?"

"Practically, yes, though theoretically, not necessarily," Seb was clearly deep in thought. *"Think of it this way, the LogInReport only shows people unlocking the door and walking into the house, once they are in it doesn't track them until they leave. The Threat Board really only monitors what happens inside the house. There is only one door and it doesn't open or close without a key—a heavily encrypted one perhaps, but a key nonetheless."*

"Meaning?" Susan was formulating her own thoughts, but wanted Seb to solve this problem.

"Well, there shouldn't be anyone in the house unless they have come through the front door with a key. That's exactly what the LIR says, but I feel the Threat Board is suggesting that there are more people in the house than should be, but we don't have any backdoors as far as I know, and I probably know more about the code than anyone."

"Interesting," Susan replied, though she actually thought it terrifying to think that, in a sense, there just might be an intruder in *her* house. "How is that possible?"

As one question followed another, it was clear that Seb was a willing participant in this game of *Twenty Questions*. Susan was adept at getting people to relax so she could develop a thread and get them to tell her what they really thought, which is why the namesake of McDonough & Partners had grabbed her for his firm. By the end of her interview, she had completely turned the tables and was interviewing him. He had never been played like that by a college kid and figured if a seasoned vet could be disarmed by this young woman, prospective investment banking clients would be child's play. He was crushed when she left for Cloud Gaming Co.

"I'm not sure if it is possible—at least not without us knowing about it," Seb opined. *"That's what has me so perplexed. Usually hackers leave a trail, but there don't seem to be any here,"* Seb looked at the clock. It was two minutes before his next meeting.

"Look, I've gotta run, but I'll spend some time on everything you have identified and get back to you in the next few days, OK?" It was more of a statement than a question.

"That seems fair. Thanks for your time, Seb, I learned a great deal today," she warmly replied.

#

Seb hung up the phone. Susan hadn't attacked him in any way, but he hadn't felt this unsure of himself in a long time. She had asked some hard questions and not only wasn't he sure of the answers, the dialog with the Marketing VP had generated a lot more questions about the security of CGC's system than he had before.

#

An hour before the plane started its descent, Greg awoke with a jolt, startling his seat mate.

"Are you OK?" she wondered, genuinely concerned.

"Huh?" Greg replied, slowly emerging from the fog of his deep sleep. "Uh, yeah. Just a weird dream I guess." But it wasn't weird; the nightmare of the Russians chasing him was back, and this time there were faces to the attackers: those of Oleg Petrov, Sergey Kachinko, and the old man from the duck blind. It was terrifying.

"Phew, I couldn't understand what you were saying, but I thought you were having a heart attack!" she sympathetically replied.

Saying? Greg thought. He looked around again at the passengers in first class, no one but the girl next to him had seemed to notice.

"I'm sorry," Greg said, "it might have skipped a beat, but I'm fine. Didn't mean to startle you."

"It's OK, just glad I didn't have to administer CPR!" she replied, turning bright red when she realized how it sounded. "Oops! I am really sorry how that came out, I didn't mean for it to sound so...um...forward."

Greg laughed and then smiled, motioning at the 50-year-old businessmen and elderly women sitting with them in the front of the plane, "Just looking at our friends here in first class, you'd be the one I'd pick if I needed it!" The girl turned red again.

"My name is Greg, by the way," he continued, extending his hand.

"Mika," she said, grabbing his hand. "Mika Kobayashi." She had a firm handshake.

"Please to meet you, Mika." He paused for a moment, before continuing. "I'd love to get together with you when you are back in Washington. Would it be too 'forward' of me to ask for your phone number?" He winked as he said it.

The young Japanese woman looked down, embarrassed for the third time in less than a minute. Nevertheless, she quickly pulled out a personal business card from her wallet and handed it to Greg.

"I'd like that," she softly replied.

The conversation continued back-and-forth for the last twenty minutes of the flight and as the plane pulled in to the gate, his seatmate turned and said, "I really enjoyed talking with you, Greg…uh…"

"Galkin," Greg quickly replied. He dug out a blank card from his wallet and wrote down his name and cell phone number. "Sorry, I don't have any business cards with me," he said apologetically.

"OK, Greg. I look forward to hearing from you back in the other Washington," she shook his hand again. "How long are you going to be in Seattle, anyway?"

"Oh, it really depends on business. Just a few days I think, but it could be longer." Greg truly had no idea how long he would be in Seattle. In fact, the question made him realize that he still had no real plan for his trip, but if meeting the Georgetown student was the only success of the trip, that was probably OK, too.

CHAPTER 33

Greg hopped into a cab and headed downtown. He had a reservation at the Washington Athletic Club, right across the street from Two Union Square, where CGC's head office was located. He checked into his room, dropped off his bag and decided to go for a walk down to the waterfront. However, the moment he exited the building, he impulsively decided to head over to CGC's building instead. *No time like the present,* he thought.

He hustled across the street and walked into the building, surprised that security was so lax, though Seattle had not been hit by the terrorists like the East Coast had. He took the elevator up to the reception area three floors from the top and approached the receptionist. His heart was racing.

"May I help you?" a young woman in her early twenties inquired, eyeing him somewhat suspiciously. Greg was neatly dressed, wearing a sport coat over a button-down shirt and dress jeans, but there were no visitors expected at 4:45 in the afternoon and he wasn't much older than she.

"I don't have an appointment, but I am an old childhood friend of Billy Wilson in town for a few days. I'm staying across the street at the Washington Athletic Club and figured I'd just drop in to say 'hello'. Is he here?" It was slightly rehearsed, but the receptionist didn't seem to notice.

"Your name, please?"

"Greg," he took a deep breath, "Greg Galkin."

"Just a moment please," the receptionist replied, writing the name down and punching in a number, "Hi Claire, it's Anne at the front desk. There's a 'Greg Galkin' here who wishes to see Mr. Wilson."

Greg couldn't hear the other side of the conversation, but could guess.

"No, he doesn't have an appointment."

Greg walked over to the floor-to-ceiling windows overlooking Puget Sound, ostensibly to give the receptionist a little more space, though the view was magnificent. He could see why so many people liked the Pacific Northwest if this was indicative of the environment and scenery.

"He says he's a childhood friend who happens to be in town for a few days."

More discussion on the other end, then the receptionist hung up.

"Mr. Galkin? Mr. Wilson's assistant will be out here in just a moment."

"Thank you."

After a few moments, a woman in her late-40s appeared and approached Greg.

"Mr. Galkin? I'm Claire Rothberg, Billy's Executive Assistant." She extended her hand to shake and he reciprocated.

"Pleasure, ma'am. Greg Galkin," he replied.

"Mr. Wilson is not in the office now," it was a lie, but Claire was a pro at deflecting unscheduled visitors, "but if you give me a number where I can reach you, I will make sure he gets the message."

"Of course," Greg figured it was a long shot anyway, coming in unannounced at the end of a business day. "I left my business cards in my hotel room at the WAC, so I'll just write it down for you." He picked up the pen offered by the receptionist and wrote his name and number down. He was sure Billy had all kinds of crackpots seeking out his time, so he figured adding his secret nickname would identify him as a legitimate caller.

"Thank you, Mr. Galkin. I will make sure this gets to Mr. Wilson," she asserted.

"Thank you, ma'am. I am only in town till the end of the week at the latest, though my schedule is a bit up in the air right now." That part was definitely true. "Please tell him I'd like to catch up."

"I will make sure I tell him," Claire said, extending her hand once more.

She waited with Greg for the elevator and the two exchanged pleasantries as the doors shut. Greg exhaled a sigh of relief. He had taken the first step towards what he hoped would be a repaired relationship with the best friend he had ever had. He wasn't quite sure how he was going to be able to share the video evidence of an event that would probably be more gut wrenching to Billy than it had been to Greg. But he would let Billy decide where and when that happened. For now, he was in a beautiful city by himself with nothing on his schedule; he fingered the card in his pocket and thought about calling the girl he had met on the plane, but decided against it—he needed to have a focused mind on this trip. He headed down to Pike Place Market instead to see if the salmon were as delicious as everyone said.

#

Billy, Susan and Joe were finishing up a meeting on the StormClouds' lawsuit when Claire walked back to her desk. Joe had already left Billy's office and Susan was gathering her notes at the conference table in his corner office when Billy walked out to see if there was anything left on his schedule for the day.

"Mr. Wilson, I just spoke to a gentleman named 'Greg Galkin', who said he knew you," Claire stated.

"Greg? Greg Galkin?" Billy looked like he had seen a ghost. "Are you sure?"

Claire looked up at her shaken boss. "Quite sure. Here's his number, he's in town for a few days. Are you feeling OK, Mr. Wilson?" His face was completely white, the blood having drained from it in a single beat. He saw nothing on the piece of paper but the number "2" that Greg had jotted after his name. No doubt it was his old, childhood friend. Just then Susan walked out of Billy's office, noticing the tension in the air, then Billy's unsteady emotional state.

"Billy, what's wrong? Are you OK?" Susan looked at Claire quizzically.

Billy took a deep breath and the color started to return to his face.

"I'm fine. I just hadn't heard that name in…forever," the CEO said, a distant look coming over his face.

"What name?" Susan wondered out loud. Claire glared at her ever so subtly, wondering if it were any of the Marketing VP's business.

"Remember that friend from DC, Greg, that I talked to you about?" Billy asked. He had never shared much about his past to anyone, even Claire, who probably knew as much about him as anyone on his staff—except now, Susan.

Susan remembered the name from his cathartic outpouring during the ride back from the football game, but a lot of that conversation was a jumbled mess of emotions and it wasn't totally clear who was whom.

"*That* Greg?" Susan replied incredulously; she had assumed he was dead. "*Here?*"

A twinge of panic crept into her mind. Was it a coincidence that a long lost "friend" would be visiting Seattle right when they were dealing with a major lawsuit and a possible breach of their security system? She didn't think so.

"Did he say how long he was here?" Billy asked. "Where's he staying? Why is he here?"

The rapidity with which the questions tumbled out made it clear to Susan that he was rattled—or excited—she couldn't tell which. As sharp as her boss was, he was also overly naïve and trusting, and part of Susan's job was to protect him.

"He said end of the week at the latest and he's staying at the Washington Athletic Club. He didn't say why he was here. Shall I call him and set up an appointment?" Claire was efficient and always on duty.

Billy thought about it a few moments before replying, "I'm not sure." He looked at Susan with an, *I need your advice,* look.

#

Mitchell tethered one of his "hacking" computers to his android phone and logged onto the web using his private VPN, making sure he opened a private browsing window before doing so. There was no sense leaving any obvious traces behind and figured if he managed to get in to CGC's network, he at least wanted to make sure it wasn't a computer with an IP address linked to his own. He found the URL for CGC's secured website; the cursor blinked at the user name. He typed in www3@ogc.com and hit the TAB key, moving the cursor to the password box. He slowly typed in the long string of numbers, starting with 072814, the date World War I started, and ending with the day Billy's dad died. He took a long, deep breath and stared at the screen.

Do I really want to open Pandora's Box? he thought to himself, knowing that if he were successful and somehow was discovered, it was a criminal offense. He hesitated another fifteen seconds, but ultimately couldn't help himself: he hit ENTER. The screen went black. He hit the PAGE DOWN key to reveal a listing of directories. Mitchell gasped.

"Oh my…" his voice trailed off. He wasn't quite sure what to expect when he typed in the user name followed by the password, but it never occurred to him that he would be getting inside the gaming system of Cloud Gaming Co., itself. A chill came over his body when he realized the enormity of what he had just done. Dr. Johnson spoke reverently about the security system at CGC and—at least as far as he could tell—he had blown right past it and was now inside. Finding the passwords to one of his classmate's social media accounts paled in comparison to what he had just accomplished. This was way better; he was both giddy with excitement and terrified with fear.

He clicked on the first highlighted section and was immediately looking at code. It was very simple, yet complex at the same time. He had heard that Billy Wilson was a master coder and after reading dozens of articles on him and his business, he could see first-hand what people meant by that. But Mitchell was more interested in something else he figured would also be in this program: user names and passwords.

He went back to the directory, scrolling down and looking at all the sub-directories until he found the one he wanted. He highlighted and clicked on USERS, then typed in "BetterThanYou" into the search function. It was all there: Brad's user name, his password, his security questions, where he lived. It couldn't have gotten any better for Mitchell.

"Bingo, baby!" he exclaimed. "You are mine now sucker, I OWN you!"

He carefully wrote down the pertinent information in his notebook, using a cipher so as to disguise his find in the event one of his tormentors managed to get a hold of his notebook. He did likewise for Nate Brackman and Jerry Anderson's information. Mitchell wondered who else in the school was a *Battle for Babylon* player, but resisted the temptation to go on a fishing expedition. He already had enough on his plate, and there was no telling when his illicit activities might trigger CGC's security team into action and get him arrested.

After perusing a few other sections, he carefully logged out of the system. His conscience tugged at him, but he disregarded it.

He knew he had crossed over a line, but the chance to watch Brad Jeffries and his clowns publicly humiliated was too good to pass up. He wasn't exactly sure how he would do it, but he was certain he had discovered a mechanism to do so, and for now that was enough.

#

Though it was well after seven o'clock, Billy sat in his office and looked at the message Greg had left. The "2" written next to the name made him certain that it was his old childhood friend, but he also left open the possibility that it was someone much more dangerous. There was a soft knock on his door; it was Susan. He looked up and waved her in.

"Hey there," Susan started, concern in her voice. "Are you OK?"

Though Susan clearly was worried about the potential business ramifications of the stranger's name that had knocked her boss for a loop, she was also smart enough to go the soft, feminine route first.

"Um, I think so," Billy answered, but it wasn't very convincing. The look on his face also betrayed him, one Susan had never seen—a mix of fear, sadness, surprise, nostalgia and curiosity.

"Do you want to talk about it?" Her interest was genuine, but hoped she didn't have to put on her Marketing VP hat and insist. Billy wasted no time in responding.

"Should I meet him?" It was a question, but it had a rhetorical feel to it, as though he had already made up his mind.

"Well, as your Marketing VP, assuming he is who he says he is, I think there are a lot of questions that need to be answered first," she replied, doing her best to be professional and project the potential seriousness of the situation, before softening, "but as your friend, it would be hard to counsel you to do anything but meet him. It clearly has you pre-occupied."

"It's that obvious?" Billy replied, a bit deflated and somewhat surprised. The news had clearly left him shaken, but thought he had done a better job of hiding his feelings.

"Very much so, Billy," Susan smiled and shook her head in the affirmative. "Fortunately it is the end of the day and we don't have anything on the calendar for the next few days. I would probably advise you to cancel them if we did, at least until we can figure out why this person is here now."

Billy looked up, shaken back to reality. He had an inquisitive look on his face. "What do you mean?"

The question surprised Susan. Until now, her interactions with Billy had shown him to be a very thoughtful, insightful man, not the naïve twenty-something that Joe Williams had warned he could be. That her boss could not see all of the ugly downside given the lawsuit with StormClouds and the real possibility they had a major security issue right before the start of a worldwide event that would shine a very bright spotlight on his company worried her more than a little. She paused for a moment to collect her thoughts, but also to calm her nerves.

"Here's how I see it," she started, sounding very much like an investment banker making a pitch. "As a firm, we are currently faced with two potential threats—a lawsuit from a competitor and the very real possibility that we have been hacked." She had Billy's undivided attention. "Both of these by themselves could be devastating. The market only knows about the lawsuit, and it has affected the stock price." CGC was down 25% from its high and while it was still above the IPO price and revenues were strongly up, StormClouds' aggressive media campaign was putting pressure on the stock. Billy nodded his agreement as Susan continued, "If the market hears that we are under attack in another critical area, it will punish us ruthlessly."

Billy intuitively understood this, but to have it laid out in stark terms was sobering. His preoccupation with Greg had momentarily evaporated.

"How are your conversations with Seb coming on that score, by the way?" Billy once more sounded like the confident and demanding CEO of the fast growing tech company. Susan was momentarily knocked off her line, surprised at how quickly her boss had switched gears.

"Uh, Seb and I have talked and we're working on it, but let's leave that be for now," she replied. She didn't want to add one more thing to the list of worries her boss was now facing, particularly when they were no closer to solving the problem. She continued, "But let's focus on 'Greg'," Susan held up both her arms to form quotes as she emphasized his name.

Billy cocked his head, as another puzzled look came across his face. Susan sighed imperceptibly. *He doesn't get it,* she thought to herself.

CHAPTER 34

Mitchell unlocked his room and sat down at his desk. He hadn't realized how much the week's events had taken a toll on him. Though he was relieved that he hadn't been disciplined by Mr. Richardson, he knew he wasn't out of the woods yet. He was certain that Brad and his posse had used technology to get him in trouble the year before and assumed they were behind the latest episode, too. As he booted up one of the school's old computers and logged onto the CGC site using his newly discovered backdoor, he could barely contain his glee: it was payback time.

#

Brad's eyes were locked onto the screen, alone in the gaming room of his family's mansion. His avatar, a tall, ripped warrior with a long, blonde mane, engaged in heated battle with a number of other virtual warriors and it was clear Brad's groove was back. He and his troops methodically moved 600 miles across the Middle Eastern desert, striking down a dozen opposing warriors in the process. His two wing-men, *MVP* and *Slasher,* were close by, but it was Brad and his troops who were front and center. He had risen into the top ten on the *Battle for Babylon* leader board, which would seed his team in a good spot for the Gaming Olympics.

"Die sucker!" he cackled, as he dispatched another Master wannabe like it was a buzzing mosquito. He was on a roll. While most of the time the group practiced together, they split up at least once a week and combined forces over the web. Dr. Johnson felt it made them all better gamers, forcing them to anticipate what their colleagues were going to do, rather than just relying on them talking to each other while in the same room.

#

Mitchell was extremely careful as he navigated within the *Battle for Babylon* gaming system. He had spent enough time studying the code to know his way around, but he was still petrified that he would inadvertently do something foolish and be discovered.

"There it is," he said out loud, a feeling of supreme satisfaction in his voice, even though no one was around to hear it.

Mitchell had found the code that affected how Brad Jeffries' avatar behaved and after a few keystrokes, he was in control.

#

Nate grumbled to himself in his room as his avatar trudged through the desert. He liked his buddy, but it felt unfair to him that Brad got all the glory and he and Jerry had to do all the grunt work. He couldn't remember how many times he had saved Brad's butt, and yet here he was again, a few steps ahead of him, expected to be ready to take a bullet to protect the Queen Bee from attack. He understood the strategy, and it was one of the reasons they were so successful the prior year, but he was sick of Dr. Johnson playing favorites.

He was knocked from his pity party in an instant.

"WHAT THE—?!" Nate screamed at his computer screen. His avatar was staggering in a pool of blood, thrashing about as *BetterThanYou* towered above him. Nate was in a rage as he watched his avatar swallowed up by the black tunnel that signified relegation and soon it was two levels lower.

#

"Huh?!" Brad's reaction was similar to Nate's in its surprise, if not in its intensity. His avatar, *BetterThanYou,* had just stabbed *MVP,* driving his sword into the back of his friend's avatar, piercing the heart and killing him. Brad seemed to have momentarily lost control of his keyboard, but he wasn't entirely sure because things seemed to be working just fine now. What he was sure of, though, was that his virtual warrior had just killed one of his teammates. The other, *Slasher,* was also dead, savagely attacked by Brad's army, programmed to defend its Master General from all perceived threats by CGC's advanced gaming system. The moment *Slasher* assumed an aggressive, though defensive, posture after the bizarre attack on *MVP, BetterThanYou's* army engulfed him and he was soon fading from view, too.

#

Just before Mitchell logged off CGC's gaming system, a curious string of characters popped up, gone in an instant. He didn't recognize the language, but the symbols and nomenclature surrounding it identified it immediately—at least to him—as an artificial intelligence query. *Hmmm,* he mused, *that dude thinks of everything!*

Mitchell had been logged in less than a minute, but was delirious that he had not only taken control of Brad's avatar, but caused the death of his other two nemeses in the process. He tapped a quick text to Marjorie.

"How are things? Great day here! So glad it's the weekend, excited for Tolo, thanks for asking me!"

All of it was true, some of it for reasons Marjorie could never guess.

#

"I swear to God, Nate, I don't know what happened! It was like I lost control of my avatar and it had a mind of its own!"

Marjorie could hear her brother on the phone from the other room and she had never heard him so apologetic. She got up to see why the moment Mitchell's text message caused her phone to vibrate. She smiled when she read his kind words. *What a nice guy,* she thought to herself. *Cute, too.* She looked at his picture an extra few seconds.

"Brad's having a fit about something that happened on his video game," she tapped back, before hitting SEND. Brad was off the phone.

"What happened," Marjorie asked her brother innocently enough, before ending with a sarcastic, "'General'?"

"I killed Nate, sis," he replied with genuine remorse and alarm in his voice, "I don't know how, but I did!" Marjorie was immediately sympathetic. Jerk or not, he was her brother.

"What do you mean?" Brad's younger sister inquired, not even sure what her brother was talking about.

"I stabbed him in the back! It's like I didn't have control of my warrior! And then my guys killed Jerry, too! It was awful!" He was rambling, like a guilty man who had blacked out, only to awaken with blood-stained hands and wonder why his wife was dead. It was almost scary.

"It's just a video game, you know. Get a grip. It's not like it's real or anything," Marjorie was trying to calm her brother by getting him to see the ridiculousness of his incoherence, to little effect.

"He's my teammate! I killed my teammate!" he shrieked, holding his head with both hands as the doorbell rang. It was Nate and he was livid; Jerry wasn't far behind.

CHAPTER 35

Greg had spent two days in Seattle, hearing nothing from Billy. It was a beautiful city, but he hadn't come for the sights. Yet, he could understand if Billy hadn't wanted to meet him after all these years. The memories of that period of Greg's life were painful for him, most of them suppressed out of fear that his dad might just be a monster. Though he had recently been released of that fear, he wasn't sure the vivid knowledge he had gained as a result was all that comforting. He could only imagine how it had been for Billy, having his dad ripped from him in an instant and finding out his best friend's dad had been responsible.

Greg made a reservation to return the next day to Washington, DC, though felt colder and darker because of it. He had taken a chance and flown across the country to reach out to the best friend he had ever had and had gotten nothing in return. Old wounds were re-opened, and the anger and hurt he felt as a 13-year-old were back, though this time there were faces and names towards which they could be channeled. Oleg Petrov and Sergey Kachinko would rue the day they had killed William Wilson, Jr., regardless of whether Billy Wilson knew that justice—even of the vigilante kind—had finally been served.

#

While Sergey Kachinko knew how technology could be used to ruin people, he was not only shocked at the discovery he had been a target, but also that his attacker had been so successful. His reputation within the Russian military was of a tech-savvy, up-and-comer, probably as clever as anyone in the organization. He felt it unlikely the Russian mob would be willing to risk going after someone with Kachinko's growing influence and power, and anyone who knew him figured he could easily inflict retaliatory electronic mayhem anytime and anywhere. Sergeant Kachinko had also purposefully diversified his accounts among a mix of Russian and foreign banks, choosing to have his most important account in the country best known for secrecy and security, Switzerland. Yet it appeared it was all for naught.

All but $5,000 of the money the Russian had accumulated through privilege over the course of the last twenty years had vanished in a series of wire transfers. The amounts were small enough to not attract attention in the secret world of private banking, but large enough—$2 million in total—to ruin the cushy retirement life the Sergeant had been planning.

Worse though, was the indifference shown to his plight by the banks. Regardless of how he had managed to accumulate so much money, it was the bank's job to protect it and every one of them had failed miserably at it. He had complained forcefully and loudly, and while his position within society was causing the wheels to move, they weren't moving fast enough for him. He decided to take matters into his own hands.

His attacker had to be remarkably computer savvy, given that it appeared he had even escaped detection from the Swiss private banking system and its security. At least in the Sergeant's mind, this required someone with real technology credentials, a decidedly smaller universe of cyber criminals than Russian mobsters, though it didn't specifically point to anyone. He began to develop a counter-attack in his mind, nonetheless, though it would have to percolate on its own while the Russians pressed forward on their new military strategy and he competed in the Gaming Olympics.

#

Mitchell slid into his seat in Biology class right before the bell rang. He was good at the sciences, but the only thing he liked about the class was that he sat four rows behind Marjorie Jeffries and could stare at her all class.

"Mr. Patkanim, may I see you a moment?" the teacher said in a loud enough voice for everyone in the class to hear. All eyes turned to look at him, wondering what was going on. He had missed class the prior week and while it was rumored he had been expelled, he was still at school. He made eye contact with Marjorie, who had only sympathy for him. She knew that his previous meeting with the school administration had resulted in no disciplinary action, but still wondered what was going on.

Mitchell and the Biology teacher exchanged words and Marjorie could see him shake his head in resignation. He walked back to his desk, grabbed his backpack and walked out of class, heading back to the Administration Building.

What now? he thought. He wondered if he should leave Queen's and return to his local high school.

When he opened the door to Mr. Richardson's office, not only were the Principal and the Dean of Discipline there, but Brad Jeffries and his dad, Andy, as well. Mitchell froze in fear. He knew he hadn't done anything, but the room was thick with tension.

"Hi Mitchell," Principal Richardson solemnly began, "I'm sorry to pull you out of class again, but after some additional due diligence, we think we have gotten to the bottom of the alleged 'harassment' of Marjorie Jeffries you have been accused of."

Mitchell looked at the four other people in the room, totally confused.

"I thought we already dealt with all that stuff last week, Mr. Richardson," Mitchell was almost pleading, figuring the appearance of a parent—particularly Marjorie's father—doomed him. "I swear I didn't send her any of those texts, I can show you my phone records if you want!"

"No, no Mitchell. This isn't about you, it's about Brad. Apparently he sent those texts and made them appear to come from you to get you in trouble." The Principal looked at Brad Jeffries with daggers in his eyes. "Isn't that right, Bradley?"

The younger Jeffries lowered his head. "Yes, Mr. Richardson. Mitchell, I'm really sorry. It was really mean and stupid of me. I sent those texts last year, too, and I'm sorry you got suspended for three days. I embarrassed my family and you. Will you forgive me?"

Mitchell couldn't believe what he was hearing. He just figured that as an outsider, no one would ever believe him, and yet here he was being exonerated in front of both the perpetrator and his dad. He heard his great-grandfather speaking as he opened his own mouth.

"Yeah, it's cool man. We all do stupid things. Just don't do it anymore, OK?" Mitchell sounded like a man, not a 15-year-old kid. Before Brad could respond, Andy Jeffries spoke.

"He won't have the opportunity to do so, Mitchell. He's being suspended from school for three days, but more importantly, I'm banishing him from all electronics for the next three months. I am really sorry you had to go through this. I'm really embarrassed for my son's actions."

"Three months?!" Mitchell responded, his eyebrows rising at the same time. The penalty seemed incredibly harsh to Mitchell, whose life revolved around electronics, but it also meant Brad would miss the Gaming Olympics.

"I want to teach him a lesson. He could have ruined your life, son," Andy Jeffries replied. He seemed like a good father.

"Well, Mr. Jeffries, the Olympics' team really needs Brad— he's a light's out gamer." Mitchell didn't really believe that, but Brad was the lead dog on the team and his tormentor's face lit up at the compliment, nonetheless. "Don't ruin it for the rest of the team and the school just because your son's done something stupid. They have a real shot to win it this year, but not if Brad can't compete."

Mitchell didn't believe that either, but laid it on thick anyway. He wanted payback and now that he had Brad's account information for *Battle for Babylon,* he knew how to get it. He didn't want some do-gooder parent ruining it for him by banning him from the Games. It also didn't hurt that it made him look good in the eyes of the father of the girl with whom he was going to the dance.

#

After a spirited dialog and a number of meetings, Billy was finally coming to see Greg's appearance as potentially more than coincidental.

"What if *he's* the guy who has hacked into the system and is here to blackmail us? You said yourself you didn't know anyone like him in the business!" Susan was almost pleading to get Billy to see the gravity of the emergence of this stranger after more than a decade.

"Yeah, but that was ten years ago, Susan, stuff is way more advanced these days," Billy retorted, defending the memory of his friend. "Besides, he never did anything malicious—"

"—as far as you know," Susan interrupted.

"Yes, yes, as far as I know," Billy said resignedly. He sighed. "OK, here's what we'll do. Let's meet him here in the office, during normal business hours, and you come join me to protect me from myself." He smiled when he said it, the first bit of levity he had shown in the two days since Greg had shown up unannounced.

"That's a good idea, Billy," Susan replied.

"Even if it's exactly what you wanted me to do," he said, shaking his head and chuckling. "Damn girl, you are tough. I'm glad you're on my side!" Susan smiled.

"Me, too," she said softly, though her mind was still in work mode. It was almost 8pm. It was too late to call Greg now, but she was worried that he might leave town if they didn't communicate something soon. "Look, let's leave a message at the front desk of his hotel for him to call us at 9am. We've already waited two days and who knows, he might already be gone."

Billy hadn't thought of that; an anxious look came over his face.

"Can you do that for me?"

Susan wasted no time dialing the Washington Athletic Club's front desk from Billy's office.

"I'd like to leave a message for guest, 'Greg Galkin', please. Is he still staying there?"

Billy could only hear the buzzing sound of a faint conversation.

"Tomorrow?" Susan replied, a hint of concern in her voice, "OK, well just please make sure it gets delivered tonight." Susan hung up the phone.

Susan turned towards Billy. "He's scheduled to check out tomorrow, but he should get the message. Hopefully he can stay an extra day."

"Damn. I hope I'm not too late," Billy fretted.

#

Greg returned to his room at the WAC after a quick bite at one of the local restaurants. He wasn't much of a foodie, but he did enjoy the people-watching that going out afforded and the crisp, cool air made for an enjoyable walk back to the club. There was an envelope waiting for him as he opened his door:

Please call Claire Rothberg at 9am tomorrow. Billy would like to meet.

His heart raced, a flood of emotions rushing back as he wondered about the reception he'd receive. He'd have to change his flight.

CHAPTER 36

Billy was in the office an hour earlier than usual. He had tried to sleep, but was so anxious about meeting Greg that he was up pacing long before the sun and decided to drive in early. He sat at his desk, reviewing reports and occasionally glancing at the screen of his muted TV, but he was having trouble concentrating. Ostensibly it was morning, but at 4:30am in Seattle in November, it was pitch black outside. He watched the traffic snake down Interstate 5, the car lights symmetrically forming a river of red on one side of the road, and of white on the other. He picked up the phone and absentmindedly called Susan's line.

"Billy?" came the voice of his Marketing VP, as startled by the call as he was that it was answered.

"You're here, too?" came the surprised response. "Mind joining me for coffee down here?"

"Be right there," Susan responded, heading to the door before she could even hang up. She had come in early to try to deal with some of the backlog the unexpected events had caused in her normal workload, but she never missed an opportunity to spend time with her boss.

Billy could hear the approaching sound of her high heels rhythmically clacking against the wood floors, though they came to a stop before she was in view.

"Billy, are you in your office?" Susan asked, with a touch of uncertainty in her voice. She knew the call had come from his line, but it was dark on his side of the building, with only the hall lights softly illuminating the corridor that circled the floor.

"Yeah, I'm in here," he said, emerging from his office, "I like to keep the lights off in the morning, it helps me think better, though this is early even for me. I just couldn't sleep." Susan had never been in at this time, though there was a certain peace about it.

"Yeah, me neither," Susan replied. She had been worried about a lot of things lately—the ad campaign, the lawsuit, the possible security breach—and Greg's sudden appearance was the last straw. She received the mug Billy had poured for her, wrapping her fingers around its warmth.

"A splash of half-and-half, right?"

Susan was impressed he had remembered.

She took a sip. "It's perfect."

"So what brings Susan Green into the office at 4:30 in the morning? I hope it's not a regular occurrence for your sake." His face was partially illuminated by the pale glow of the TV monitor.

"Just trying to stay ahead of things, you know? The last few weeks have been pretty hectic." She wasn't normally this open, but the fact the two of them were alone in the dark office made her less guarded. "It's been a blast, though, it really has! I still can't believe I found my dream job so young. Thanks for hiring me."

"Thanks for saying 'yes'," Billy replied. "Sure glad Joe knew the Street. There's no way I would have found you on my own, but you fit right in. I couldn't be happier."

They both took a sip at the same time and looked at each other in silence. Susan broke the ice.

"Do you mind if I ask about Greg?" She was worried about a lot of things besides him, but thought that was probably what had kept Billy up and she figured it might calm him down before the possible meeting if he had a chance to talk about it. It would also help her understand if there was a motive Greg might have for showing up unannounced.

"Frankly, Susan," Billy started, "even though I have a million questions, I'm not even sure what I'm going to say to him. It's overwhelming to think we haven't so much as exchanged an e-mail in ten years. Hell, I don't even know anything about him but the past. It's kinda' scary."

Susan was a great sounding board and soon the first streaks of sunlight were coming up over the Cascade Mountains as Billy talked about his childhood friend. She hoped for their sake, he was still a friend.

#

Like clockwork, Claire was in the office at exactly 8am, listening to her messages when Billy came out. She immediately hung up and turned her attention to the CEO.

"Good morning Mr. Wilson," the Executive Assistant cheerfully said. "Good to see you feeling better."

"Thanks, Claire. Good morning to you, too," Billy responded before turning serious. "Hey, I left a message for that 'Greg Galkin' guy to call for an appointment. I think he may be flying out today, so if he can only meet at a certain time, do whatever you have to do to my calendar to make it happen. This is an important meeting."

"Yes sir," Claire replied, looking at the day's calendar to see if there were any other critical meetings. She spent a good chunk of the day shifting her boss' calendar around, so she was used to the drill.

"Susan's joining me in the meeting, so make sure she gets notified, too," he said, walking back to his office.

Billy was soon at his desk again, plowing through his e-mails, though preoccupied with the prospect of this unexpected visit. He was reading Joe Williams' notes about the status of the StormClouds' suit—it seemed they were making progress—when Claire knocked on the door. The CEO looked up.

"Excuse me, Mr. Wilson. Greg Galkin will be here at 10am. I have you in the Olympus Room," Claire said.

"Thank you. Make sure Susan knows," Billy said, a hint of anxiety in his voice.

"Yes sir. I will make sure Ms. Green is in attendance as well," she replied, ducking out of the room.

Billy took a deep breath. *One hour from now,* he thought. He returned to his e-mails, but struggled to focus, blankly looking at the computer screen while his mind raced to the meeting with his old friend.

#

Greg was the last to get into the crowded elevator; someone had already punched "53." He had no idea what to expect—or even what he was going to say—but he was committed to following through on what caused him to fly 3,000 miles without an appointment. He did his best to take slow, deep breaths as the elevator raced to the top of the building, his ears popping along the way. He closed his eyes and remembered what Billy looked like at thirteen, when they last were together. How would he have changed? The elevator slowed and stopped on the 53rd floor; he'd soon find out. He was led upstairs and into one of the conference rooms with sweeping views of the Seattle surroundings.

#

Billy and Susan were meeting when Claire knocked on the door, "Mr. Galkin is here, Mr. Wilson. He's in the Olympus Room."

"Thanks Claire, we'll be right out," Billy nervously replied. As the door closed, he looked at Susan, "Well, let's see what he's been up to the last ten years." He smirked and shook his head, wondering if this was such a good idea.

#

Greg was standing, looking out over Puget Sound and the Olympics Mountains, when Billy and Susan entered the room. He turned, seeing what was clearly the grown-up version of his 13-year-old friend, though much taller than he would have figured.

Billy walked over and extended his hand, cautiously.

"Hello Greg…" he started, not sure what was coming next before blurting out, "damn, it is really good to see you." He meant it. He hadn't realized how much he had missed his friend. Once upon a time, they had done everything together and while circumstances had suddenly torn them apart, Billy was old enough to realize none of the blame for that could rest on a teenage kid.

Greg was relieved. He grabbed Billy's hand and reached out with his other to touch his shoulder. "Man, it's good to see you, too, 3," Greg replied.

Billy chuckled. "I had forgotten all about those nicknames until your message." Both men seemed oblivious to the fact that there was someone else in the room, though Susan actually enjoyed seeing Billy connect with someone he had clearly missed. She subtly cleared her throat.

"Oh man, I'm sorry. Greg, this is Susan Green, our Marketing VP," Billy motioned to Susan, who emerged from behind Billy and extended her hand.

"Pleased to meet you, Greg," Susan responded professionally, firmly shaking his hand.

For the next twenty minutes, the two men caught up on the last decade. As Susan assessed the back-and-forth, she wasn't quite sure whether to put Greg in the friend category, but she didn't think he was a foe, either, and that was a relief. There was a brief lull in the conversation.

"So," Billy shifted uncomfortably in his seat, "what made you decide to contact me after all these years?" It was the 800-pound gorilla in the room. While Billy was clearly happy to have reconnected with his past, he figured something else had brought his old friend back into his life.

"Well, when I went back to Russia for my mom's funeral, I found something that my father had left for me," Greg's tone immediately turned somber. "It was something that would only have meaning to me, but once I stumbled on it, it led to a chain of discoveries that..." Greg was choking on emotion and paused for a moment.

Susan studied the man sitting across from her. She was intrigued by him. She immediately could tell why they had been such good friends growing up. They both had the same idiosyncratic quirkiness and as they shared their memories, there was a connection on a level that Susan could not comprehend; it was almost telepathic. She had always had a talent for seeing what wasn't there and her Wall Street experience, though brief, only refined that skill. She had a sixth-sense for understanding when occasionally reluctant counterparties were hiding something important and it was pinging non-stop in her brain now.

Yet, she never felt like Greg was deliberately withholding anything, it was just a slowly unfolding story. He was clearly cautious about what he said and how much detail he provided, but there was a genuine openness towards Billy that was endearing.

Billy was moved by his friend's emotion. "It's OK, man, take your time. You're among friends here." Susan wasn't quite willing to concede that yet, but she could sense Billy's empathy for his friend's pain.

Greg took a deep breath. He reached inside his coat pocket and pulled out a small thumb drive, holding it in his palm, "...that led to this." He suppressed tears a second time.

"What is it?" Billy queried. "I mean, I know it's a thumb drive, but what's on it?"

Greg struggled to compose himself, but managed to choke out, "It's a video...of the...accident."

Billy recoiled in his chair, a wave a nausea blasting him with the force of a tsunami. He lowered his head into his palms and fell silent. It seemed as though the oxygen had been completely sucked out of the room. Even Susan's heart was racing. After a few excruciating moments, Billy opened his mouth.

"What? How?" He was incredulous.

"Long story, but my dad was afraid he was being set up and hid a camera in his truck about two months before it happened. There's other stuff on it, too, but this is the only thing that matters today."

"I want to see it…" Billy's voice was full of emotion.

Greg looked at Billy. "It's gruesome man, in more ways than you know," he had gained control of his own emotions and delivered the kicker, "and, my Dad wasn't driving."

"What?!" Billy exclaimed, his mind reeling with the second of two totally unexpected pronouncements. "Then, who?" Billy had always heard that Greg's father had been driving the truck, so this was news, as well.

"Russian military. It was a hit," Greg replied in a cold rage.

CHAPTER 37

Though General Petrov was a relative neophyte when it came to sophisticated technology, he did know people who weren't, and plenty of them were in the banking community. The president of his main bank, a casual, but powerful acquaintance, had been apoplectic when he heard his bank's security had allowed someone to steal most of General Petrov's money. He immediately called his most feared client for a face-to-face meeting.

"Comrade General," the bank president nervously started, "I do not know how this happened, but I assure you, we—no, I—will get to the bottom of it."

"And what of the blunders that led to this criminal activity that happened right under your nose?" the General replied gruffly and threateningly. "Who will pay for these?" General Petrov was unpleasant even when he was in a good mood and today he was most decidedly not in a good mood.

The bank president shifted uncomfortably in his chair. "The bank of course will make you whole and we will bring the perpetrators to justice."

"How am I to believe such incompetence will not happen again?" the General demanded.

"Of course, I cannot guarantee such a breach will not occur again," the president cautiously responded. It was a courageous reply for someone facing Oleg Petrov in private, and the General faintly smiled. He had seen sterner men wither at his gaze and at least the bank president was showing some backbone. The president continued: "We live in a world where technology cuts both ways—I myself do not like how it has invaded into areas of life that used to be based on trust and relationships, but it is what it is. But one thing I can guarantee: you will never lose even one ruble at my bank!"

General Petrov looked at the man carefully. They were about the same age and sounded like they struggled with the same things, at least as far as technology went. It also took courage to speak his mind. He liked what he saw.

"Yuri," Petrov began, showing a flash of humanity by calling the president by his first name. "I, too, despise technology. I, like you, live in a world where we have forgotten the old ways that made this nation what it is. There is no accountability." The president nodded in agreement, not sure where the General was heading with this line of discussion.

"Someone must be held accountable for what happened to my money at your bank," Petrov somberly stated. The bank president squirmed in his seat, wondering if he could make it to the door before Petrov snapped his neck. "So here is my offer: give me whatever evidence you have regarding the perpetrator and I will handle it…"

General Petrov paused for effect, before continuing: "…but not with technology. I will use the old ways."

"Perhaps we can make a public example of such a person," the bank president quickly chimed in, surprising Petrov, though his face betrayed not the slightest twitch.

"Then we have an agreement," the General tersely said. "Comrade, I must say, I like your style." General Petrov's smile was genuine; he had found a useful, kindred spirit.

#

"Claire, this is Susan in the Olympus Room," the Marketing VP softly spoke into the telephone. "The meeting is going for at least another hour, so please clear Billy's calendar—mine, too, if you don't mind. And absolutely no interruptions, please."

After a brief set-up, Greg clicked on the video clip and it sprang to life. It was clear to everyone in the room that Greg's dad was immediately in danger, but the suddenness and brutality of the Russian attacker was nonetheless shocking—Susan audibly gasped. She had seen scenes like this in movies, but knowing this was a real event that involved the fathers of both men in the room caused her to shake.

"My God, Greg!" Billy exclaimed, "This must have hit you like sucker punch!" He glanced over at his guest. Greg's teethed were clenched.

He nodded. "It gets worse. Trust me," was all he said.

Susan had never seen anything like it and it made her extremely uncomfortable. She almost wished she hadn't been asked into the room, but as Billy's closest advisor—and perhaps more— she needed to be here, even if it gave her nightmares later.

About halfway through, Billy asked Greg to pause the clip.

"What the hell is he saying to your dad?" Billy queried.

Greg gave him a steely look. "Does it matter?"

Billy swallowed. "No, I guess not," he murmured almost inaudibly. "Sorry man, no offense meant."

Greg's countenance softened. "I know. It just gets more sickening every time I see it." He paused a few more moments, before continuing, "Look, we don't need to watch the next twenty minutes, it's just more of the same. I only wanted you to know the truth."

Billy sadly nodded in the affirmative. "I get it," he replied softly.

"Billy, the last bit is going to be tough to watch. You sure you want to see it?" Greg sympathetically said.

"Want to? No, I don't want to," Billy tersely replied, "but I have to, man, I have to." He looked over at Susan, who sat with a grim look on her face, both hands invisible but clenched under the table. "You don't need to see this Susan," he murmured gently, wanting to spare her what was no doubt a ghastly scene.

"Thanks, Billy, but I think I should stay," she replied, "unless you'd rather I not." He was her boss after all.

"I appreciate the support."

It was a heartfelt response and made her feel needed. But professionally, she also felt an extra set of eyes and ears in the room was important. Greg had seen this video and figured that he had some thoughts about what it all meant. As a member of the Management Committee for a publicly-traded company, she had to make sure that she protected her boss from something that could lead almost anywhere. Nonetheless, she was dreading the next few minutes.

"OK, here goes then," Greg stated as he hit play again. "Just let me know if I need to stop it, OK?"

Billy nodded, his eyes riveted to the screen. He could see his dad off in the distance, but was powerless to help. As the wheels screeched and the thud of a body getting hit by a car could be heard, Billy closed his eyes and quickly turned away. Susan sat there stunned, her eyes wide and her hands over her mouth.

"Oh my God!" she repeated half a dozen times, before catching herself, then screamed as Oleg Petrov snapped the neck of Billy's dad with a powerful twist.

Though the events had happened more than ten years ago, Billy looked on in horror at the scene as though it were live.

"You bastard!" was all he could say.

As understandable as the reaction was, it was nevertheless frightening in its intensity. Greg hit STOP.

"That's all there is, Billy," Greg was clinical in his words. "You needed to know…" he paused. "*That's* why I came out here."

CHAPTER 38

The Gaming Olympics began with the chaos one might expect of an on-line event where fifteen million players were simultaneously logging on. CGC's Threat Board was flashing Yellow and Orange in all the world's major internet hubs, though more because of the sheer volume of players than anything else. There was the occasional Red, likely more a result of probing from countries that were always looking over their citizens' shoulders, than true attempts to break through CGC's security system.

ESPN had a special multi-screen video feed directly from CGC's servers, with twenty-four screens showing different battlefields. Not surprisingly, Las Vegas, Atlantic City, Monaco, Macau and other venues were taking bets on virtually any kind of action, and while Cloud Gaming Co. had no direct connection to any of the gambling, they very much had a vested interest in the success of the next six months.

Not surprisingly, their servers were under extreme stress, but despite all of the activity, were holding up remarkably well. This was both a testament to the amount of infrastructure CGC had deployed for the event, as well as the complementary strengths of their strong gaming system and robust security.

#

Dr. Johnson's gaming varsity kicked off their Olympics a few hours later than the official start, so they could do it in class; it was one of Dr. Johnson's favorite days of the year. The buzz at the school was palpable and Queen's got off to a great start, methodically moving through two levels during the ninety-minute class; muffled cheers could be heard throughout the school as the team vanquished foe after foe. Even Mitchell felt proud.

#

The Security VP stood in his office above the rows and rows of servers that both ran CGC's gaming system and kept track of who was doing what to whom in the *Battle for Babylon* when his phone rang.

"How's it going, Seb?" Billy excitedly asked after the crush of the first few hours of the Gaming Olympics. *"It looks like we are off to a great start. Anything making you nervous?"*

Seb had watched the Threat Board ebb and flow between a comfortable Green and an uncomfortable Orange for the last few weeks, as gamers from around the world pushed the limits of their training, working on the hand-to-hand combat which would ultimately determine success or failure in the final chambers of the *Palace of Babylon.* He was sure not all the activity hitting his system was benign, but because the Olympics officially started today, hadn't expected anyone to have already tipped their hand yet as to their real motives.

"With so much data flying around, it all makes me nervous, Billy," Seb exclaimed, "but so far things are holding up as well as could be expected given the fact that we are in unchartered territory as far as internet volume goes."

"Anything new to report on the possible breach?"

"All the internal checks we have done suggest that our employees are not engaged in anything outside of the bounds of normal work and play," Seb replied carefully.

The company recognized that many of its employees also were avid gamers and on their own time, used the very system they were responsible for building and maintaining on company time. It resulted in fewer conflicts of interest than might be imagined because having the tech mettle to meet the high standards demanded at Cloud Gaming Co. was a badge of honor for those who worked there. Everyone knew abusing the company's trust in its employees was the cardinal sin, and it meant being immediately fired and losing all the stock options; many of the young employees were already millionaires—at least on paper.

"I'm glad to hear that," Billy said somewhat matter-of-factly, pausing for a moment to watch the Threat Board's flickering lights on his office screens that Seb was surveying in person 150 miles east of Seattle.

"But...?" Billy continued, noting the uncertainty in Seb's voice.

"But it still seems something isn't right. We get these intermittent sharp pulses from Russia, some here in the Pacific Northwest and elsewhere in the US, but there are no abnormal logins anywhere." Seb was frustrated at his inability to decipher the disconnect between what his reports were telling him—which was nothing—and what his intuition and experience were, which screamed: "INTRUDER ALERT!"

"And it's not just because of all the new users and the intensity of the Olympics?" Billy queried.

"It could be, I just don't know," Seb responded with resignation in his voice. "The only thing I can say is that despite my misgivings, there hasn't been any damage done to the gaming system...yet."

"Yet?" Billy interjected, a hint of worry in his voice.

"Look, the most logical reason for an intruder is to game the system for the Olympics," Seb replied, "and those just started."

#

Jeremy had been with the CIA for less than a year and already felt like a seasoned veteran. His boss was clearly relying not only on his technology skills, but his analysis and judgment as well; he felt lucky to be mentored by a person who didn't see him as a threat to his own job, but as an intelligence asset of the United States.

Jeremy also realized that he liked Beth Hopkins and it seemed the feeling might be mutual. But he wasn't sure if he wanted to start a relationship with a work colleague—even someone affiliated with a different desk—so soon in his career. For now, he would just enjoy her company at work and follow her closely on *Battle for Babylon,* except when he was playing, of course.

He put on his headphones and dialed up his gamer playlist. Though he was currently a Master 2-Star, Jeremy was also a *Samurai,* so it was unlikely that he would have any realistic chance to be a top finisher in the Gaming Olympics without a lot of luck and help. But that didn't matter to him. Part of the reason he was a *Samurai* was the freedom it allowed to be off-line as his work demanded and it was demanding a lot lately. However, tonight was his time and he was ready to go.

Jeremy immediately noticed the battlefield intensity. Not only were there a lot of competent competitors, Masters were everywhere, many choosing to start the Games later than the official opening to avoid the initial crush of activity. He engaged what appeared to be a team of solid competitors, but dispatched them quickly. Jeremy had great reflexes, partly genes and partly a result of playing video games most of his life. Coupled with his days as a computer scientist at MIT hammering out programs, he was as quick on a keyboard as anyone, the perfect skill set for a *Samurai.*

Without a supporting military, *Samurais* typically moved on the fringes of the battlefield, attacking unsuspecting foes or unprotected Generals engaged in full-scale battle with other Generals. It was the virtual equivalent of guerilla warfare and Jeremy was quite effective at it.

He saw his next victim. A Master 3-Star General, *Yin&Yang,* was engaged in an intense air and ground battle in Jordan. He couldn't tell who the opponent was, but they appeared to be equally matched and were inflicting heavy damage on each other. It was a perfect opportunity—or so he thought.

Drifting along the tree line, he quickly moved into position to dispatch part of the left flank of *Yin&Yang,* leaving a direct path to attack the Master 3-Star General. Suddenly, a shadowy figure emerged on the scene. *Thunderstruck* ducked behind a tree, unseen as the figure moved stealthily out into the field shielded by the sun coming up over the hills. It was clear he had the same idea that *Thunderstruck* had, just fifty feet ahead. As *Thunderstruck* crouched, the dark figure turned and momentarily looked his way revealing a grotesque face—half human, half animal, but more significantly, five stars on his epaulets.

"No way!!" Jeremy exclaimed out loud. *Ronin,* the Master 5-Star *Samurai,* was a few steps ahead of him, ready to pounce on *Yin&Yang,* yet totally oblivious to *Thunderstruck's* presence. Jeremy watched in fascination as *Ronin* raced through *Yin&Yang's* helpless army, soldier after soldier falling after no more than a quick wrist flick of the lightning fast *Samurai.*

Sensing the danger on his left flank, *Yin&Yang* wheeled around to see the onrushing *Ronin,* and quickly called back his ground forces to deal with the immediate threat. As *Yin&Yang's* front-line collapsed to create a momentary wall of ground forces five-men deep to protect their avatar, the unseen foe fighting *Yin&Yang* in the mountains, rushed in to fill the void left by *Yin&Yang's* retreating army. As the unknown army emerged from the valley to the plain where *Yin&Yang* and *Ronin* were poised to face off, Jeremy could see it was that of *Blunt Instrument's.*

It was the first spirited engagement of the Olympics, and *#EpicBattle* already had been blowing up social media even before the two *Samurais* emerged onto the scene. The crush on the ESPN on-line feed from the Jordanian battlefield was unlike anything ever experienced on the internet. Yet through it all, CGC's platform performed flawlessly as the chaos of war streamed across the globe in HD—twelve stars, four distinct battle styles, two Generals, and two *Samurais* were in close proximity, with blood flowing like a river.

Thunderstruck slowly moved forward from the shadows to the battlefield. Because *Yin&Yang* and his army were focused on simultaneously defending against *Ronin* and *Blunt Instrument,* *Thunderstruck's* advance met little resistance from *Yin&Yang's* army. The gap between *Thunderstruck* and the two avatars battling hand-to-hand was shrinking with each step. So was the distance between what would no doubt become the place of certain death for at least one of these Masters, and *Blunt Instrument,* who was thrashing *Yin&Yang's* army in an impressive display of tactics, herself.

As Jeremy's fingers flew across his keyboard, he was suddenly within one soldier from the intense one-on-one battle. *Yin&Yang* noticed him first, distracted for the split-second it took *Ronin* to stab him through the heart. As *Yin&Yang* and his army dissolved away, *Thunderstruck* was suddenly face-to-face with the cat-like *Ronin.*

Ronin had risen to the highest rank in *Battle for Babylon* by not only being a skilled warrior, but also by being smart in the face of unfavorable odds. Yet he suddenly was in the middle of an unpredictable situation. He was two steps from a 2-Star *Samurai* that he had not seen—who knows how long he had been stalking him? There was also a 2-Star General, *Blunt Instrument,* racing in to fill the vacuum left by the vanquished *Yin&Yang*. *Ronin's* master had seen her fight before and knew how dangerous she could be.

The nanosecond hesitation ending up being fatal. *Thunderstruck* feinted left before dropping his shoulder and rolling right just as a rocket from *Blunt Instrument's* air force came screaming in near where *Ronin* stood. As the Master 5-Star *Samurai* warded off the missile with a deft flick of the sword in his left hand, he took a swipe at the fast closing *Thunderstruck*, barely grazing his neck, but drawing a trickle of blood, nonetheless. The next instant, *Ronin* was staggering, the victim of a sharp swipe from *Thunderstruck's* trailing sword. Momentarily stunned, he collapsed to his knees, swinging one last violent time at *Thunderstruck,* taking a chunk out of his leg before the second of two missiles from *Blunt Instrument's* air force ripped through *Ronin's* torso and shredded him into a thousand pieces.

Blunt Instrument, now standing where *Ronin* had just faded from view, raised her sword above the defenseless *Thunderstruck* before recognizing him as the stranger who had rescued her in an earlier battle. She pointed to the trees, giving the limping *Thunderstruck* a free pass back into the shadows.

#

Ronin's master sat stunned in front of his computer. Despite the cheat codes he had as a Master 5-Star, his avatar, *Ronin,* had been defeated by two Master 2-Stars, albeit in the most chaotic battle in which he had ever engaged. As he watched the denouement of the battle just fought, he saw the warrior princess, *Blunt Instrument,* whom he had seen kill ruthlessly, allow the wounded *Thunderstruck* to slink back into the shadows of the forest and into the ether, rather than kill him. *Curious,* he thought.

#

As soon as *Thunderstruck* was back among the tree line, safe from danger and relegation, Jeremy hit EXIT and was out of the game, licking his wounds, but alive. He sat in front of his computer, drenched in sweat. *I knew it,* he thought to himself, *she knows who I am.*

CHAPTER 39

Sergeant Kachinko gently knocked on the door of Vladimir Buskin's office. As the political officer of *Operation Oblaka,* it was his responsibility to keep the Premier apprised of the true progress of the new strategy. It was a tricky position, given that the Premier and his own boss, General Yikovich, were old friends, but one he relished, nonetheless. He saw it as a no-lose situation for him: he would share in the accolades if the strategy worked, and would be seen as the cautionary voice to the Premier if it failed.

Although he was a true believer in technology, he was also a pragmatist. He saw the same danger that his old colleague, Oleg Petrov, did—over-reliance on technology could have devastating consequences if something went wrong in the execution of such a revolutionary strategy. As brilliant as the strategy was, there were plenty of things that could wrong.

"Comrade Kachinko, what is your report today?" Premier Buskin was blunt and to the point, though he thoroughly enjoyed these sessions with the Sergeant. The Premier was a technology enthusiast and relished the mental rigor that it demanded. He knew that General Yikovich was his superior intellectually, but in his sessions with Kachinko the last two years, Buskin had learned a great deal—much more than he let on with his boyhood comrade. Though he trusted Yikovich as much as any man in the Russian system, it just made sense to have an extra set of eyes and ears, given the stakes involved.

"We are truly making progress with the integration of the AI program and the data feed," Kachinko started. "The gaming system of that American company is remarkable in its efficiency."

"How so?" the Premier inquisitively replied.

"The amount of usable information in any line of code is a number of times greater than our own and according to our intelligence, easily twice as efficient as anything their own military has. It is remarkable that such a valuable company is allowed to thrive without the government as its partner."

"And they still don't know of our activities?" Buskin volleyed back.

"We have accessed their software on numerous occasions and am quite certain they would have shut us down by now if they knew," Kachinko replied matter-of-factly.

"Excellent."

#

Three days after his meeting at Sberbank, Oleg Petrov received a private letter from the bank president, Yuri Fedorov. He opened the envelope to find a number of faxes and electronic communications between Sberbank and the private Swiss Bank into which his money had disappeared. As he scanned the pages, his eyes froze on the name of the account holder.

What a fool, he thought.

#

Though Mikhail Yikovich was working late, he had his avatar, *Polar Bear,* on autoplay and was keeping a close eye on the Gaming Olympics. He had logged a lot of hours playing *Battle for Babylon* and so his autoplay was probably as robust as any in the field, but the strength of competition made it less effective than he had expected.

His technology team was at a critical testing phase and was putting in extra hours during the early stages of the Olympics. The increased activity and stress on the *Battle for Babylon* platform served two key purposes for the Russians: it would likely make General Yikovich's incursions through the backdoor less susceptible to detection, and it also allowed the Russians to ensure the data feed from CGC could withstand the intensity of millions of gamers playing at the same time as the Russians siphoned off the data for their AI feed.

CHAPTER 40

The stress on CGC's infrastructure and personnel was only matched by the surging fascination across the globe of its flagship product, *Battle for Babylon*. Interest was growing among all video game age groups, and even first time users outside the traditional demographics were on the rise, wanting to see what all the hype was about. The systems were functioning extraordinarily well given how many people were on line at any given time, yet the management team was no closer to resolving what still seemed like a clandestine breach of their system. As the demands on their time grew, nerves started to fray. Sebastiano DiCarlo's phone rang; it was Susan Green.

"Yeah," Seb was brief and blunt.

"Good afternoon to you too, Seb," the Marketing VP replied, with a slight edge in her voice, before recovering, *"do you have a few minutes?"*

The Security VP was being challenged every day in new ways and it was starting to wear on him. He hadn't gotten much sleep and though he had competent lieutenants, Seb still felt the burden of keeping the system safe. He had declined—foolishly it seemed now—Billy's offer for more equipment. His staff was working overtime and things were starting to slip through the cracks. And he still hadn't made any real progress on what was potentially the heart of the problem. After a few minutes of back-and-forth with the Marketing VP, Seb was clearly exasperated with his inability to lend credence to his fear about the system breach.

"I don't know, Susan. I'm at a loss," Seb sighed. "I really have nothing more than my gut at this point, so maybe we just drop it. I've got enough on my plate to keep me busy 24/7, as it is."

"Look, Billy trusts your gut and until it says 'all clear', we keep going, looking for something."

Seb sighed again.

#

The Queen's team spent the night at the Jeffries', before loading up in an SUV to head over to the school for a few hours of gaming. Though it was Thanksgiving, they wanted to make sure they kept up the momentum of their solid start in the Games. Brad and Nate had managed to sort out their differences after the virtual back stabbing incident, chalking it up to computer error. As they watched the replay, it did look like Brad had somehow lost control of his avatar, however briefly, but computers were strange things and so it was impossible to tell. Ultimately, despite their competitiveness, the two boys relied on their long standing friendship and moved on.

They were in the middle of the Saudi Arabian desert where a number of avatars—some with armies and air forces, some without—were battling. *MVP* and *Slasher's* main job during skirmishes in the open spaces like they were in now was to make sure that Brad was protected from wandering *Samurais* so he could focus on the forward strategy. *MVP* was engaged in battle with the other contending high school team, *The Jersey Boys,* from Princeton, New Jersey.

#

Mitchell was also up early, the campus quieter than normal, as all the maintenance and administrative staff were off, too. The solitude made it easy to focus. He knew with the Olympics in full swing, the Queen's team would already be competing since they were three hours behind the main contenders on the East Coast, and eleven hours or more behind much of Eastern Europe, Russia, and Asia.

Mitchell logged onto the ESPN feed and scrolled through the screens to where Queen's was competing. He figured that if he was going after them, he needed to at least get a sense for their strategy and tactics. He also believed that watching the ESPN feed rather than using the video feature of his own *Battle for Babylon* account would make it harder to track his actions. Since the Queen's team was already among the leaders, they were receiving a fair amount of air time and ESPN was given feeds not available in the game mode, so it made for interesting watching.

#

Though it was the start of the traditional four-day Thanksgiving weekend, it was also the inaugural week of the Gaming Olympics and Billy Wilson's company was front and center, so he wanted to make sure it went off without a hitch. The intense scrutiny on his company in its current role as the star of the gaming world had him energized and even though he was sleep deprived, the coder in him didn't seem to notice. It was 5:30am and he had already been in the office for an hour.

Billy was troubled that his Security VP still suspected there might be a hacker, and increasingly frustrated he hadn't been able to identify why, how—or more critically—who. He was paying Seb a lot of money, not only to make sure the gaming system held up in the face of the overwhelming stress on the system caused by the Games, but also to keep intruders from getting in and doing who knows what. Seb was acing his job on the former front, not so much on the latter. He wondered how Greg would deal with this problem.

The CEO was watching not only the Threat Board, but also the ESPN feed of the Queen's gaming varsity. Although he didn't know any of the kids, it was his *alma mater* and the team was managed by his mentor, Mikel Johnson. Dr. Johnson had expressed hope that this team, which was returning its three top players from the previous year, could make a legitimate run for the gold. The video game strategy and tactics he taught as part of his curriculum at Queen's, coupled with their systematic team approach, made them a formidable opponent.

Billy was focused on the *Samurai, MVP,* who was a quick and agile gamer. Dr. Johnson had told him how difficult it had been not to make him the lead General, but ultimately decided that his recklessness might compromise the team at a critical moment. Yet here he was battling a 3-Star General in the open, close enough to prevent that General's air force from engaging and preoccupying the army while the Queen's team marched through the desert.

After a slick move, *MVP* was poised to lance *Tiger,* the General of *The Jersey Boys,* through the heart. "Wow!" Billy exclaimed to himself, "that kid is good. I'll have to let Dr. J know he might have made the wrong decision!" He laughed out loud.

Out of the corner of his eye, Billy caught a red blip on the Threat Board close to home, as Nate dropped his weapon, kneeled on the ground and lowered his head, the universal sign of surrender. The 3-Star General took *MVP's* head off with a savage swing, relegating him two levels and leaving *BetterThanYou's* left flank exposed. *The Jersey Boys* and their army rushed in to attack.

#

Dr. Johnson couldn't believe what he had just seen. If any of his warriors had the killer instinct, it was Nate Brackman, yet he just stopped in mid-attack and offered himself to a defeated opponent.

"What the hell are you doing, Nate!?" Brad roared, while simultaneously sending his air force in to kill *Tiger,* who was suddenly exposed after mistakenly thinking *MVP* was the General, and not *BetterThanYou.* Brad's recovery brought a smile to the teacher's face, but he also wondered what his other star was doing. It was exactly the kind of reckless behavior the teacher used to rationalize his decision to put Brad over Nate.

"I didn't do anything, man!" Nate screamed. "My keyboard went dead! Now I'm two damn levels lower and have to fight my way back!" Nate was furious. Before Dr. Johnson had a chance to get an explanation, his phone buzzed; it was Billy Wilson.

"What in the world just happened, Dr. J?!" Billy shouted in his speakerphone.

"I'm not sure," Mikel Johnson replied, "the kid says he lost control of his keyboard for a few seconds. The same thing happened to another one of my guys a few weeks ago as well, and he ended up killing one of his teammates. Is everything OK over there?"

#

Billy had a hard time making out Dr. Johnson's explanation over the noise of the game and the yelling of the boys, but he heard the question and had seen the red blip on the Threat Board—it was gone now.

"Everything is fine here, Dr. J," Billy forcefully snapped back, though he knew it wasn't true. Susan had prepped him that no one outside the inner circle could know they were struggling with a potential hacker. As tempted as he was to ask his mentor's opinion, he knew he could have the SEC after him if he did that. "We've got over fifteen million gamers on the line right now, Dr. J, and the system is holding up pretty damn good!"

"I'm sure it is Billy," Dr. Johnson tersely replied, *"just something to think about. My guys don't just lay down and die!"* It was as intense a discussion as the two men had ever had.

Billy backed off, worried that his frustrations might make things worse.

"Noted, Dr. J. I'll have Seb take a look at it. I must admit it seemed pretty strange when I saw it."

#

"Who was that Dr. J?" Jerry Anderson asked.

"That was Billy Wilson," replied the seething teacher, "he called to ask what that…that…that—whatever *that* was—was all about." The room immediately went silent. The school's most famous alum had been watching *them*.

"I told him this was the second weird thing that had happened to us in the last month. He's going to look into it," Dr. Johnson coolly replied.

The gaming varsity was in awe. The guy responsible for designing the game they were playing with fifteen million other gamers had just called *their* teacher and now was going to check to see if something was wrong with the system because Dr. Johnson had asked him to.

"Ask for cheat codes next time," a steaming Nate Brackman hollered, as he clawed and scratched his way back to the rest of the team.

#

Mitchell pumped his fist. "Yep! I own you ALL!" He gleefully watched as Nate Brackman's avatar had his offered head lopped off. It was his second success at altering the outcome in *Battle for Babylon* in a way that humiliated his tormentors. He had been logged onto the CGC system all of fifteen seconds, and while the strange code he had noticed last time briefly re-emerged, Mitchell ignored it, already engrossed in the highlights being replayed on the ESPN feed. "Loser!" Mitchell shrieked with glee.

#

As the end of his work day approached, Mikhail Yikovich was increasingly distracted by *Polar Bear's* fierce battles. Though his avatar had managed to ward off any disasters with strong defensive play, his army was being painted into a corner on the Sinai Peninsula by a group of Master 1-Star Generals, one with air power, one with just an army. It was an effective tag team strategy, and he increasingly felt he needed to be fully engaged to avert disaster.

He walked over to his colleague, Sergeant Kachinko, who was working with the AI team. "Sergey, I think it is time to call it a day. We have been pushing the team hard these last few weeks and though we have made great progress, I am concerned we might overdo it. What do you think?"

The younger Russian was surreptitiously following his own *Battle for Babylon* action as well, though as a *Samurai,* he had no men or equipment to worry about so didn't need to be so close to the action. Still, he thought it a good idea. He knew that gamers tended to overdo it the first few days of a competition and he wanted to be ready to pounce when fatigue hit.

"*Da,* the men have done well, but I agree it is time for a break," replied the Sergeant, before continuing, "perhaps an extra day off would do everyone some good, as well." It was a surprising suggestion from such a workaholic, but it sounded appealing to the General, as well. Neither man could have guessed that his counterpart was just interested in playing video games.

#

Though it was Black Friday and most firms were off for the day, Cloud Gaming Co. was humming with activity. The Olympics had quickly become the most watched on-line competition in history and the firm took pride in making sure the competition was about the players and not the game or the system. Billy punched in Seb DiCarlo's cell phone on his speed dial. Two rings later, he heard the groggy voice of his Security VP on the line, who grabbed the phone without checking the caller ID.

"It's 6am, this better be good!"

"It is," Billy responded, "trust me."

"Oops, sorry man," came the now contrite voice of the Security VP.

"No worries." Billy chuckled. He was neither surprised at the comment, nor by the fact that Seb was already at his post. "Look, I was watching the Queen's varsity team yesterday and saw the strangest thing. A kid was about to kill an opponent and just laid down. I called the teacher, who was there with his students, and he said it's the second time he's seen something like that happen to one of his players."

"Humph," Seb replied, mostly to acknowledge he was paying attention.

"And," Billy paused for emphasis, "I also saw a red blip on the Threat Board almost at the same time and then go out about ten seconds later. Any ideas?"

"Interesting," Seb responded, almost casually, though his mind was in overdrive. *"I saw the blip, too, but wasn't watching the feed. What exactly happened and to whom?"* It was their first break.

CHAPTER 41

Jeremy Thomas was one of a new breed of analysts at the CIA, relying on computer science savvy to decipher usable information from electronic video and audio information. Integrating his program into the camera feeds had been a stroke of genius and it was being adopted agency-wide as an add-on to most video surveillance.

Yet there had been a curious lack of activity since Russia had routed the Ukrainians some months earlier. The Russians had continued to build up their ground forces and artillery along their western border, but other than the occasional flurry of activity following the random trading of shots, there had been little use for Jeremy's electronic wizardry that was focused on the Ukrainian front. *What are they waiting for?* he wondered.

A heavy snow was falling as Jeremy slogged into work, deep in thought. He was mesmerized by the multi-colored Christmas lights dancing through the falling snow adorning the homes off in the distance; they appeared to be moving through space as the train chugged along. *Looks like my electro-kinetic program,* he mused. A smile came across his face. "Of course!" he said to the nearly empty Metro car, "I'm looking in the wrong place!" In an instant the Christmas lights were gone, swallowed up by the darkness of the tunnel as the train went underground.

#

As Jeremy hung up his coat, his iPhone vibrated. His boss would be about an hour late because of the snow, giving Jeremy some time to test out his theory. He figured that if he was right, a Wi-Fi signal would lead him to where the action was, even if it was far from the front. After the Ukrainian battle, he had seen no material additional electro-kinetic activity on the front and yet such a revolutionary military strategy would require a lot of time and practice to perfect. It had to be going on somewhere.

Fortunately, the CIA had a number of overhead satellite cameras so he didn't need to touch the main feed on the Ukrainian border, something he wouldn't have done without Tony's permission, anyway. Besides, in a country twice the size of the United States, there were plenty of places to look—many of them remote and desolate. He decided to start where he had first discovered the Wi-Fi system: Northern Siberia.

Not surprisingly, it was still operating, though it was clear it was not active. Humorously, some of the older equipment that had been part of the staging ground for the early testing was exactly where it had been left, seemingly tethered to the ground by the already overgrown vegetation. There were regular pings from the towers, but it was obvious that nobody was home. *What a waste of perfectly good equipment,* Jeremy lamented as he continued his search.

He moved to regions that had known military bases and while they all had electronic pulses of one type or another, there was nothing extraordinary about any of them. The contrast between how antiquated much of the Russian technology seemed to be and the revolutionary drone strategy he had observed was shocking; it was clear who had the power in the halls of government in Russia.

Jeremy directed his video feed to head east towards the Urals, a mountain range traversing Russia from north to south. It divided the country between the main cities of the west, and the Great European Plain, a vast, but relatively flat area to the east. Fortunately, he wasn't looking for a single plane or vehicle—the proverbial needle in the haystack—but rather a Wi-Fi grid that he expected would immediately light up his electro-kinetic program. As the satellite camera automatically panned across the southern part of the West Siberian Plain, it suddenly came to life in the middle of nowhere, northwest of Novosibirsk.

"Whoa!" Jeremy exclaimed as he leapt to his feet to stop the satellite camera's movement. "What do we have here?" he excitedly said to himself as he zoomed into what was clearly an active Wi-Fi system. As he got close enough to make out the surface, he could see it was crawling with military vehicles, tanks and drones, and there was a crude runway. The video screen was alive with multi-colored lights. A simulated battle seemed to be going on, though it was hard to determine who the enemy was.

"Damn snow," Tony Smith growled. What was usually a twenty-five minute commute had taken two hours because of an accident on the Beltway Parkway. He was in a foul mood.

"What the hell is that, Thomas?" perturbed that despite what appeared to be a full-scale battle going on somewhere—he couldn't quite make out the geography—nobody had even bothered to call him about it. Jeremy patiently explained to his boss what he thought he had stumbled upon.

Tony shook his head in amazement and nodded his approval. "I like the thinking Thomas, stay on this and figure out what it is and why it is out in the middle of nowhere."

#

Mitchell's curiosity about CGC's gaming system extended beyond his ability to engage in mischief. He found its simplicity profound and was beginning to understand how brilliant the school's most famous alum was. While the software's clarity spurred him to focus on simplifying his own code writing, it was the strange artificial intelligence program that most intrigued him. It was radically different from the code that powered the video games, and as Mitchell analyzed it, he could see it was designed to mine data from the game itself.

The interface between the two programs was hard to spot as well, buried in the same code that allowed him to hack into the system. Yet most perplexing was that it seemed to have been constructed by two completely different thought processes. *Maybe this is what Dr. Johnson meant about the strengths of team software writing*, Mitchell thought. He had figured out that what had briefly danced across his screen were Russian characters, but why and for what purpose eluded him. It was also perplexing that Billy and his team would put such an unusual overlay onto such an elegant software program. As he analyzed it, he compared it to his own artificial intelligence code writing, surprised at how well he measured up; he even considered how he might enhance the code if given the opportunity.

#

Over the course of the next few days, Jeremy Thomas became convinced that whatever the Russians were planning, he had located their training site. He had been certain drones were an integral part of the plan. But the fact that he hadn't seen any at all on the Ukrainian front since the Russians had attacked so decisively months ago, made him begin to wonder if he had been wrong. Yet here they were in abundance, smoothly and seamlessly moving through the air. It was obvious that not only had the Russians figured out how to generate a robust Wi-Fi signal, they also figured out how to deliver it to a much bigger fleet of drones.

Worrying, too, was the fact that there did not appear to be any Wi-Fi towers anywhere, it was all being done with a mobile system—specially equipped tanks on the ground and AWACS-type planes in the sky. Whatever the Russians were planning, they had figured out how to take it on the road.

Yet despite all the things about which Jeremy was certain, it was what he didn't see that perplexed him. He wheeled his chair over to where Tony was watching the growing military buildup on both sides in Eastern Europe.

"Tony, I'm stumped," Jeremy said. His boss looked up, then over at the video screen that Jeremy's program had turned into a laser light show. "Take a look at this and tell me what's wrong."

The Director studied the screen a few moments and zoomed into a few places. "There doesn't appear to be an enemy—at least one we can see," his boss exclaimed.

"Exactly, yet it looks like they are engaged in a ferocious battle, from both a visual perspective and an electro-kinetic one as well."

"I admit it does seem strange," Tony replied, "but it could just be a training ground, though I don't remember seeing one like this on the map anywhere. What is your threat assessment?"

Jeremy thought about it for a few moments. "One, each drone seems to be engineered for a single purpose, some for communications, some for aerial attack, and some for ground attack; there are others as well, though I haven't figured out what they do. They are all simple, yet very effective, and there are a lot of them.

"Two, the herky-jerky, Wi-Fi freezes we saw in the Ukraine battle are gone and they have gone totally mobile to boot. Impressive technically for them, though definitely not good for us. But, frankly Tony, it's what I don't understand that worries me most."

"What do you mean?" Tony shot back, clearly engaged.

"Well, to begin with, this is pretty ground breaking stuff. Though drone technology isn't that sophisticated, using an army of them in battle is unprecedented. But because we can't see if there is a real opponent in these training sessions, we actually don't know what their capability is. I mean, how do we defend against this?"

CHAPTER 42

Queen's was among three leading teams that were engaged on the Syrian plateau. Despite Mitchell's antipathy for Brad and his friends, he did find their success to be a source of school pride as well and wished that he had taken Dr. Johnson up on his offer to join the gaming varsity earlier in the year. For his part, Brad had sincerely apologized to Mitchell for his mean-spiritedness, still bewildered that Mitchell had been willing to go to bat on his behalf with his dad. More importantly, he had even gotten his friends to lay off, as well.

But Mitchell was tired of seeing them strut around campus. The Queen's high school wizards had become the darlings of ESPN and seemed to be on almost every feed they had. He figured they needed another dose of humble pie.

Brad's air force was circling a team from China, *New Capitalist,* whom they had pushed into a precarious position near the Mediterranean. *New Capitalist* was a Master 3-Star General, but rather than having an army and an air force or navy, had opted to have a second army with extra artillery power instead. It was a clever strategy as most *Battle for Babylon* competitors were not used to fighting on such a congested battlefield, but the Queen's varsity was skilled at hand-to-hand combat and had managed to push *New Capitalist* to the edge of the sea.

#

A major winter snowstorm was blowing down the East Coast, paralyzing a vast area of greater Washington, DC; Jeremy decided it made more sense to stay at work and just sleep in the employee lounge. He was bummed he couldn't log in to *Battle for Babylon,* but as a *Samurai,* at least he didn't have to worry about losing hard earned territory like the Generals did. Beth had decided to make a run for it and managed to get home; she was probably on-line right now.

With no way to play video games, he figured he might as well spend some time with his team's colleagues on the day shift, many of whom he had never met.

"Hi, I'm Jeremy Thomas and I work the graveyard shift, but got stranded here this morning," Jeremy said as he stuck his hand out to Andrew McBurney, the day supervisor.

"Oh, hey, you're the guy who programmed these cool video feeds, aren't you?" Andrew excitedly replied, "I've wanted to pick your brain on that for some time. You free now?"

"Absolutely. What's on your mind?"

"Well, I think the idea of a heat map is brilliant, even if I haven't a clue on how you manage to pull it all together. But I haven't seen a lot of activity on the front and wonder if maybe I've got it programmed wrong. Can you can walk me through how it all works?"

"Sure, Andrew," Jeremy countered, "though you're probably using it correctly. There's just nothing happening on the front right now—at least electro-kinetically. But let me show you where there is some activity." The two men walked over to an open computer station.

Jeremy sat down and switched on the satellite feed to the coordinates of the training center in the West Siberian Plain he had discovered a few days earlier. A crowd of analysts started to form behind them.

#

"Prepare for engagement!" Brad yelled as he dialed in his air force that had been circling just off the coast of Syria. "I'm going to scream in low from the west and bomb the hell out their rear guard, then circle back and nail the front line!"

"Sounds good, *BTY,*" Nate replied emphatically, and as he looked over at Jerry and the other Queen's gamers who were keeping the left flank in check, called out, "prepare to disengage on my call!"

"Roger," yelled Jerry, and the rest of the Queen's team got ready to fall back.

#

As *BetterThanYou's* air force began to circle into attack formation, Mitchell could see what Brad was planning. He tapped into the backdoor, ready to take control of Brad's air force.

#

Fortunately for Jeremy and his growing entourage, the training site was active—in fact, very active.

"Whoa!" he exclaimed, as the camera feed slowly panned to his programmed coordinates revealing a pulsating spectrum of lights from yellow to purple. It was night in Russia and yet the screen looked like it was broadcasting a laser light show; the Russians were clearly active.

"What in the world is that?!" exclaimed Andrew, as all eyes in the room turned to focus on the video feed monitoring a desolate area of central Russia, "and more to the point, where?"

"It looks like our Russian friends are putting on a show for us tonight," Jeremy said, loudly enough for the room to hear. He zoomed out to show how far from Moscow the training site was, and then quickly zoomed back in, explaining in detail what each color meant and what it signified in terms of danger. Jeremy was amazed at the intensity of what was taking place under the surveillance of the satellite cameras, as perplexed as ever at the absence of a readily identifiable adversary. He was also surprised to see more than just the drone signature; there were fighter jets involved as well.

#

"Dammit, Dr. J! I can't control my planes!" Brad screamed at the top of his lungs as he furiously hammered his keyboard. His air force was diving, but too hard and too fast.

"Pull up, Brad! Pull up!! *Dammit PULL UP you moron!!*" Nate was livid. He had agreed to play wing man to his best friend, partly because Brad was the better aerial fighter and yet here he was, about to crash his entire air force into the Mediterranean.

#

Suddenly, Jeremy's screen flashed brightly once, then twice, then a third time. All the electro-kinetic colored tracer lines went dark.

"Holy Cow!" boomed Andrew. "What was that?!"

#

"WHAT THE HELL?!" Mitchell's eyes were as big as saucers. He hadn't touched the controls to Brad's air force and yet

one by one, the planes went crashing straight into the Mediterranean. He tried to log out of the CGC account, but couldn't and then his computer crashed. Mitchell's heart was pounding, *I crashed the freakin' gaming system! I am dead meat for sure!*

#

"NO!" screamed General Yikovich, as one of his assistants, tripped and bumped the computer that was running the CGC gaming system, knocking it off the desk in the process.

"YOU IMBECILE!!" he yelled at the twenty-something private. The soldier had managed to prevent the laptop from hitting the floor, but in grabbing the computer, inadvertently pressed a handful of keys, shutting down the system momentarily and causing the Threat Board to turn bright Red in Moscow. Brad's crashing planes were not the only casualty.

#

Jeremy zoomed in on the sites of the flashes of light. The wreckage of three Russian fighter planes appeared to be smoldering on the ground, pulverized by the force of impact after having crashed straight into the ground. There was nothing virtual about it.

CHAPTER 43

"Claire, get Seb on the line! And tell Joe and Susan to get up here NOW!" Billy yelled at his assistant in a way no one in the office had ever heard. But they were seeing it, too. CGC's gaming system had crashed, the first Code Red any of them had seen, and their boss was a blur of action. As his eyes raced from screen to screen, he processed every piece of information hitting him: he had seen that same red blip in the Seattle area, Russia was lighting up like a Christmas tree, the ESPN feed was being scrambled, and every alert system in his office was flashing. It was finally clear that someone had breached their system.

Susan Green rushed down to Billy's office. She could hear the commotion, and it was only a matter of time before she would have to deal with the calls from the press. She could see Billy with his cell phone to his ear, gesticulating wildly with his free hand, and hear Seb on the speakerphone. They locked eyes momentarily and he frantically waved her into the office. Joe Williams was right behind her, closing the door as he rushed in. The Security VP was on the phone.

"I see it, Billy, I see it!" Seb DiCarlo was nearly hyperventilating in the Security Center in Eastern Washington. *"We shut down the Russian main feed and went to back-up immediately. Whoever hacked into us—or whatever it was—seems controlled for now."*

"How is this still happening?" Billy was as intense as Susan had ever seen him, though given the stakes, it was perfectly understandable. "Haven't you been able to figure out what the effing problem is?!" Billy glared at Susan. She looked down uncomfortably. He had tasked her with this job and they had gotten nowhere. He had also been distant to her ever since the video.

"Look, we are contained for now," Seb replied. The ESPN feed was back and the *Battle for Babylon* game was continuing, but their technical help line was being inundated with phone calls. *"Not everyone got automatically transferred on backup though, so logins are spiking now, but there doesn't seem to be any lingering problems."*

Billy looked at his two senior advisers, before speaking. "OK, Seb. We just had our first—and hopefully last—Code Red. Figure out what went wrong and how we prevent it from happening again. Nothing is more important than that right now. Understood?" He sounded like a military general.

"Got it. I'm just making sure we are all back together first, but it'll be all hands on deck," Seb responded; he knew Billy was pissed.

"Just get it done," he barked, hanging up before Seb had a chance to say anything more.

Billy looked at the Threat Board. It had dropped back to mostly Green and Yellow, but more importantly, all the Red was gone. Whatever—or whoever—had crashed the system was gone, and despite what could have been a major disaster, the system was only down for a few seconds.

Billy looked at his Chief Counsel.

"What is our legal exposure?"

"I can't give you an answer until we know more, but if it's just a system interruption or something like that, probably nothing." The veteran attorney had seen his share of system breakdowns to know it wasn't out of the ordinary. "But if someone inside caused this to happen, it could be a problem." Susan and Billy shot a quick glance at each other.

"What if it's a hacker?" Billy inquired.

Joe looked at him, then at Susan, with a quizzical look. "Something I should know about?"

"Seb and Susan have been working on what appears to be a breach into our system," Billy reluctantly started, "Seb thinks he can rule out an inside job for now, but we don't really know what is causing these problems."

CGC's attorney rubbed his chin. "When were you going to tell me about it?"

Billy looked at Susan, who was ready to reply.

"When we had an answer, Joe," Susan confidently stated. "You have been up to your eyeballs in the StormClouds' lawsuit and at the time, this was a gut feeling that Seb had, nothing more."

"Still, as a public company—," Joe started, before being interrupted by the Marketing VP.

"—we are required to file an 8-K when there is a relevant material event," Susan jumped in, "which this doesn't qualify as."

"Correct, Susan, but we still should have talked about it," the lawyer retorted, feeling left out. It was particularly worrisome to him given their developing personal relationship.

"Sorry, Joe," Billy replied apologetically, "this one's on me. I put Susan in a tough spot. She made sure I knew not to sell any stock, but I didn't want to drag you in just yet. It won't happen again."

The Chief Counsel looked at the two professionals in their 20s, thinking about how naïve his own kids were at that age; at least Susan had hit the big one for insider trading. He held his tongue.

"So tell me about the breach," Joe stated unemotionally. For the next twenty minutes, the three of them had an animated dialog, ending without resolution.

#

After the adrenaline rush brought on by the training site incident subsided and Jeremy debriefed the supervisor on his interpretation of what they had just seen, Jeremy could feel his body starting to crash. He had only gotten three, restless hours of sleep in the employee lounge, and still had his own shift ahead of him. The only thing he needed more than sleep was food and so he headed to the cafeteria.

He grabbed a few slices of pizza and a Diet Pepsi, and shuffled over to where ESPN was replaying the day's proceedings from the Gaming Olympics. He had hoped to see *Blunt Instrument* figure in the highlights, but instead the main topic of conversation was the brief system crash that had occurred earlier in the day. The host was replaying a few of the more prominent battles affected by the outage and Jeremy was riveted by what had happened to the Queen's team over Syria. Three jets had plowed almost straight down into the Mediterranean moments before the system crashed. His heart skipped a beat. He could swear he had just seen the same thing in the middle of nowhere in Russia, thousands of miles from the Mediterranean. *What are the odds?* Jeremy thought, suddenly awake.

#

Vladimir Buskin was officiating a heated discussion between his two alpha dogs, General Yikovich and General Petrov, over the loss of three Russian air force jets. The planes were old and fortunately had been unmanned, but the crash made it clear that despite the Wi-Fi system's success at manipulating the attack drones, controlling the larger weapons was a more difficult task.

"This is exactly what I feared, Comrade Premier!" thundered General Petrov. "It is complete madness to turn over our weapons to computers. We must fight wars with men!" Premier Buskin slightly nodded his head, moving his eyes from Petrov to Yikovich.

"This event was not caused by a failure of computers, Oleg," retorted General Yikovich, "but by the very same men who fight our wars! Our system is designed to fight and win with as little human involvement as possible and our training numbers reflect significantly less failure than we see in our regular strategy."

"Rubbish!" an increasingly animated General Petrov roared. "We just lost millions of rubles because of your system. Millions! Do you not think that is enough to pull the plug on this stupid experiment?" General Petrov saw his opening.

"I agree with you Comrade," General Yikovich methodically countered, "the system has shown itself to need the skill of our highly trained pilots—we reached too far. We had to stress the system to know where we needed to stop."

"Comrade Premier, this is madness! If such a thing happens in a real battle and we lose air cover, we are doomed!" General Petrov was ready to explode.

Premier Buskin raised his hand, indicating a cessation of verbal hostilities.

"Gentlemen, what you fail to see is that you are both correct. Do you not know that I trust both of you because you have consistently put the safety of the Motherland ahead of everything?" Premier Buskin knew the competition between his two top officers was a healthy thing, but also feared events like this could make it spin out of control. He could not afford to lose the allegiance of either man.

"But do you not see the danger in this fully automatic strategy, Comrade Vladimir?" The question from General Petrov was more rhetorical than not.

"Of course, I do, Comrade General. It was never my intention of allowing it to be so," the Premier replied. Mikhail Yikovich winced. It was the first time he had heard anything but unrestrained enthusiasm for the technology strategy he had been working on for more than five years.

"Comrade Mikhail. What your team has accomplished is unequalled anywhere in the world." The Premier knew that his old friend would be stung by the perceived lack of support and wanted to stem any concern he might have about its importance. "Yet, we must remember the goal is success, not perfection. Your drones and their integration into our command structure are the cornerstones of our return to prominence as a nation. But our men, not computers, will fly our jets, and our army will follow Comrade Petrov's lead on the battlefield. Understood?" It was an order, not a question. Both men grudgingly nodded.

CHAPTER 44

Susan walked down to Billy's office for her regular weekly update. She was worried that the Security VP had too many day-to-day fires to put out to give the breach its due. She had also just seen Billy as angry as she ever had, and while she did not know computers like these two men did, she did understand they were in a crisis situation bigger than just their system crashing. She would have to be careful because Billy held Seb in high regard, but they had to do something.

Susan gently knocked and walked in, meeting Billy at the conference table in the center of the room. He was definitely burning the candles at both ends and hadn't shaved in a few days.

Billy jumped right in, rushing through his thoughts. "I've gotten two calls from Dr. Johnson up at Queen's and he says that right before the system crashed, his Master 3-Star lost control of his keyboard. I've also seen two local red blips on the Threat Board before each episode," Billy paused for emphasis. "I think that Dr. Johnson might be able to help us, what do you think?"

"Hmmm," Susan replied, "Dr. Johnson has a team in the Olympics and that's a conflict of interest. I was thinking more of Greg." She figured if Billy was going to raise the issue, she would jump in with both feet.

"Greg Galkin?" Billy was surprised at Susan's response. "I thought you didn't like him!" He smiled and chuckled at the same time. "But I like the idea."

"I am not sure what to make of him, but I don't dislike him," Susan retorted. "I just think that based on what you've told me about him, he's about as good as it gets when it comes to security and that's Problem #1 right now."

"Greg, huh?" Billy was obviously toying with the idea, but Susan wasn't sure how seriously.

"I'm just concerned about how Seb might react," Susan interjected before Billy could say any more, "security is his baby." Susan didn't think Seb had done the job as well as someone in his position should have, but she knew the two of them had a long standing relationship.

"Susan," Billy sternly replied, "it's *my* baby." The Marketing VP was momentarily caught off guard by the sharp rebuke. "But I like the idea. I will call him today."

#

As Beth Hopkins excelled in her favorite pastime, video gaming, her avatar was developing a following on social media as she climbed the ranks in the Gaming Olympics. Very few females ever made it to the top ten in video game rankings—girls were generally just too social to spend the long hours staring at a two-dimensional screen required to become an elite gamer. But *Blunt Instrument* not only attracted the hard core fanatics who loved the clinical and vicious way she fought and finished her foes. Her avatar seemed to be the epitome of Hollywood's version of the female super-heroine: beautiful in an understated way, and drawing in a whole different set of groupies—teenage boys and girls who followed her because of what she looked like.

Strangely, as skilled as Beth was at gaming, she was relatively oblivious to the buzz surrounding her; she just went about her business. That single-mindedness was one of the reasons that *Blunt Instrument,* along with the Queen's team and *Polar Bear,* had become the favorites in the competition. The three competitors were slowly being drawn together, as though they were all being sucked into a giant whirlpool and brought closer with each rotation around the edge of it.

#

"Greg, Billy Wilson here."

"Hey man, good to hear your voice. It was great seeing you." Greg animatedly replied. "What's up?"

Greg had been following Billy's company more closely since their meeting in Seattle. He had heard about the system crash that put a bit of a kerfuffle into the Gaming Olympics; nothing like a computer to gum up the works.

"I need your help," Billy's reply was as blunt as it was open, catching Greg off-guard.

"Me?" The surprise was palpable in Greg's voice. He was also flattered. Billy was one of the wealthiest men in the world and though he had no doubt he could help him, it still felt good to hear it.

"Yeah, man," Billy casually responded. *"I'm sure you heard about the crash. We think there may be a hacker."*

"Where?"

"Russia, maybe. We are getting a lot of noise from there. Possibly Seattle, as well, though that one's harder to tell."

Greg's conscience was immediately pricked. He knew he had hacked into CGC's gaming system a few years ago and sold access to it for $4 million. How it would be used, he did not know, but the idea that his friend was asking him to fix a problem he might have had a hand in creating made him feel very uncomfortable—in fact, guilty.

"Why me? I don't know the first thing about your system."

The response was an obvious lie, as Greg had taken a tour when he had hacked into it a few years ago. Yet, as curious and interested as he was in helping Billy, he also felt like he needed to play a little hard-to-get.

"Look man, you were always the best at getting in and figuring out how to keep slugs out. I'm guessing you're still at it," Billy paused, waiting for a reaction, though Greg didn't take the bait. *"Besides, you'll see a good chunk of the stuff I wrote myself, you'll probably recognize more than you think."*

Greg knew this, too. In fact it's what made it so easy to get into CGC's gaming system in the first place. If the buyer to whom he had sold access was the source of the problem, he could probably figure it out in a few minutes and be done with it. But the opportunity to begin trading ideas again with the best friend he had ever known, meant he was in no hurry to get in and out.

"It's tempting. What do you want me to do?" Greg had already made up his mind, but business was business.

"Just say 'yes'," Billy enthusiastically replied, *"we can figure out the details later. Can you get out here by Monday?"* Billy was thrilled at the possibility of working with his old buddy again and was acting like CGC was a start-up, rather than a publicly traded company.

"I'm not cheap, Billy," Greg cagily interjected.

"How much do you want?" Billy was suddenly snapped back into reality.

"How about half?"

A heavy silence hung in the air for a few moments, before Greg laughed at his friend's naiveté.

"Almost had you man! You haven't changed at all!"

"You dog, you," Billy cackled, though he had actually given it some thought.

"I'd love to come out and see if I can help. $500 an hour is my rate, but I'm sure your HR people will have a say." Greg was back to business.

"It'll all be fine, Greg. I run the place, yanno?" Billy sarcastically replied.

"Ha. I heard the lawyers run all those public companies, they just let you sit in the corner office," Greg snidely shot back, before turning serious again. "Let me sort out my schedule, but I'll see you early next week. It'll probably be Tuesday, though."

"Sounds good, 2," Billy joked.

"Ha-ha. Copy that, 3," Greg replied. "See you soon, buddy."

Greg hung up, feeling a mix of euphoria and trepidation. He figured it had to be his client who was hitting the system, though it sounded like there were other problems, as well. He also wondered if there might be a connection to the Russians that had killed—either directly or indirectly—their fathers. This might be his chance to find out.

But he first had a few loose ends to tie up before leaving for Seattle. He needed to finish wiring the money that was sitting in the dummy Cayman Island account he had set up to steal Sergey Kachinko's money, immediately making him a Russian pauper living paycheck to paycheck.

Likewise, the financial attack on Oleg Petrov was also almost done. Petrov had accounts scattered around a number of Russian banks and although emptying them was simple, it was time consuming because there were so many. Greg had routed them through Sergey Kachinko's private Swiss account and then to offshore shell companies set up to make it seem that Petrov had been betrayed by an early protégé.

Phase One was complete. Greg Galkin could only smile at his craftiness.

CHAPTER 45

Jeremy was burning the candle at both ends. In his "day" job, he had become an integral member of the Russian and European team, with his boss almost completely relying upon him for technology related issues. His analysis and programming skills had also identified a critical communications link in a new Russian weapons system, and while they weren't entirely sure of its total capabilities, it had proven quite effective in the recent Ukraine battle.

After hours, Jeremy's avatar, *Thunderstruck,* had made ESPN's *Top Ten* for his encounter with *Ronin* and he was now spending every free moment competing in the virtual world. The adrenaline rush from success in his work and private lives was keeping him sharp in both spheres, but his body was wearing down from an ever increasing lack of sleep.

He looked at his phone: 0915. He had been in the middle of a fairly complicated program and wanted to maintain his train of thought, but now he was done and hustled into the employee lounge, hoping to find Beth before she left for the day. He really wanted to ask her out, but wasn't exactly sure how to broach the subject—until now.

He had been spending hours poring over intelligence videos, analyzing every frame in an attempt to figure out how the Russians were able to react so quickly in their military tactics. It was truly revolutionary in its effectiveness, yet every time he finished analyzing a video, he had a gnawing feeling that he had seen it somewhere before. The fact that he had witnessed three Russian fighters crash moments after one of the top gaming teams had had the same thing happen to them was more than an eerie coincidence to him. Nevertheless, he was unwilling to entertain what he had been thinking with his boss because he was certain Tony would find his conclusions ridiculous—regardless of how compelling the evidence might be. He needed someone with whom to flesh out the idea, someone who would understand in the way he did. That someone was Beth Hopkins, but she wasn't here. *Damn,* he thought, dropping his shoulders in resignation, *too late.*

Jeremy wheeled to grab his things and head home just as Beth rushed into the lounge. They should have crashed into one another, but Beth quickly pirouetted away from the collision.

"Whoa, Beth!" Jeremy exclaimed in admiration, "sweet move!"

"Nine years of ballet finally comes in handy!" the blonde analyst laughed.

"Ballet?" Jeremy responded surprisingly, "well that explains a lot." Beth cocked her head and looked at him curiously.

"Huh?"

He was committed now, even if he wasn't totally ready.

"Um, you're *Blunt Instrument* right?" Jeremy blurted out.

Beth smiled, knowingly. She had always realized that her ballet lessons were part of her video game skill and now the colleague on whom she had a crush had just confirmed it.

"A virtual stalker?" she giggled as she winked at him, causing him to blush.

"Not really. Well...OK...maybe. I'm *Thunderstruck,* actually," Jeremy replied, fully expecting her to confirm what he figured she already knew. He was wrong.

"You?" Her surprise was evident, even a bit humbling.

"Is it that shocking?" Jeremy retorted, feigned outrage masking his true hurt.

Damn girl, Beth thought to herself, chagrined at her uncharitable response. *Do you have a death wish or something?* Her countenance immediately changed.

"I'm sorry, Jeremy," she softly and genuinely apologized. "That was mean of me. I dunno, sometimes it just sneaks out." She searched his face for forgiveness.

"Well, you are a 'blunt instrument' aren't you?" He smiled and winked. Beth laughed, though Jeremy didn't really notice, already framing in his mind what he would say next.

"Look, Beth. Ummm...I came in here looking for you because I have something I want to pick your brain about. And maybe I thought, uh, you know, maybe I could take you to breakfast to talk about it." He paused, wondering what else to say.

Beth put her index finger to her lips and smiled.

"You had me at 'Look'," she sweetly replied. "I'd love to. Oh, and by the way. That was one, sick battle with *Ronin.* Absolutely *filthy!"* She turned and sashayed out of the room, looking back at him: "where to?" she said invitingly.

Jeremy and Beth slid into a booth at the local pancake house and after ten minutes of chitchat, Beth turned serious. She was always good at compartmentalizing problems.

"So, what did you want to ask me?" she asked.

"Huh?" Jeremy was momentarily confused by the sudden change of gears. "Oh, yeah. It's kind of out there, but I figured that someone closer to my age and interests might be able to tell me if it's too crazy to believe."

"Our job as analysts is to ask questions, no matter how bizarre, and then figure out if there are answers to them." Beth sounded like a CIA recruiting video, as she continued: "So fire away." Crush or not, her colleague was wrestling with an intelligence problem and she loved the intellectual rigor it demanded.

"Remember when I asked you about whether you could use AI for military tactics?"

"Yeah. I don't think it's possible yet, but things are really changing fast, so who knows where we'll be in a few years," Beth replied, before ending with a question. "Why do you ask?"

Jeremy paused before responding. He wouldn't be surprised if Beth laughed at what he was thinking, but he had already received his share of her barbs—a few more wouldn't hurt.

"You know about the Russians' new drone strategy, right?" Jeremy started. He knew all the CIA desks got a briefing on hot spots around the world and Beth nodded as she took a bite of her pancakes. Jeremy continued, "I have analyzed the intel to the nth degree and I keep coming back to the same thought—it seems like they're mimicking a video game and are playing at a level above everyone else."

Jeremy stopped, watching for a negative reaction. There was none.

"A video game, huh?" Beth took a quick sip of her water before continuing, "I suppose it's possible, but if everyone isn't in on it, how could you tell what to do next?"

"Actually, I think it would be an incredible advantage if the other side didn't know what was going on," Jeremy replied, "because you would be basing decisions on two sets of data—what was going on in both the real and virtual battlefields."

"Perhaps," Beth nodded her head at the insightful remark, but countered, nonetheless, "but the battlefields and weapons would have to be more or less the same, don't you think? I mean mixing a baseball and football video game wouldn't be very much fun for anyone now would it?"

"True," Jeremy replied, "but in war, both sides are already playing the same game, so to speak."

Beth nodded. She enjoyed the back-and-forth as much as Jeremy did.

"Yeah, I could see that would give them an advantage, but how would you know ahead of time what battlefield to use?"

"What if it was already chosen for you?" Jeremy countered with a leading question. Beth was all over it.

"You mean like in *Battle for Babylon?*" Her eyes lit up as she connected the same dots that had been rattling around in Jeremy's head.

Jeremy grinned. "Exactly!"

Beth got right to the point: "Do you have any proof?"

For the next ten minutes, Jeremy walked through his theory, Beth excitedly nodding affirmation that he might have stumbled upon something important.

CHAPTER 46

CGC's stock opened 10% lower on rumors that despite the relatively problem-free Gaming Olympics, someone had broken through their security system. Billy, Susan and Joe were meeting to determine what—if any—statement to make. It had been the second hit to the stock since going public, and while there was some speculation that StormClouds was exacting revenge, they vehemently denied it in a press release. Maria Incandella had already called Susan Green three times wanting a statement. It was the start of what would be a crazy week.

"Joe, we don't know what happened, and until we do, the less said the better," Susan aggressively countered the Chief Counsel's take that they engage in public speculation as to what happened. "The worst thing we can do is leave the impression we don't know what we're doing."

"But we do know Susan. Our system crashed because of a hacker," Joe was equally as animated, wanting to err on the side of caution. "Maybe we don't know who or where, but we're supposed to be the best in the business and somebody managed to breach us."

"I think we should just say there was a spike in the system in Eastern Europe, our secondary systems quickly switched on, we are back to normal and working to make sure it doesn't happen again."

"But that doesn't say anything, Susan!" the lawyer forcefully countered.

Joe's friend at McDonough had said that Susan was as persuasive a junior banker as they had ever had, but he found himself frustrated by her unwillingness to compromise.

"It says enough, Joe, it says enough," Susan retorted. "Tell me what is untrue about it?"

Joe had no counter. The statement was vague, but it wasn't false, and what had happened certainly didn't require disclosure under securities laws. In fact, he begrudgingly acknowledged they weren't even sure what had happened.

Billy enjoyed the back-and-forth. He had always been a bull with Joe, but Susan was better equipped to match wits with him. It was good to see the lawyers lose from time to time.

"So, we're agreed?" Billy hoped it was a rhetorical question.

"OK, I can live with it," Joe curtly replied. "Just make sure all the normal disclosures are in it. And let me see it before it goes out."

The Chief Counsel shuffled out of the office. Billy grinned at his Marketing VP.

"Good work," he said. "Not sure I would have won that one."

#

Greg Galkin stood up to collect his things as the Alaska Airlines' flight docked at the gate in Seattle. It was on-time, but had seemed particularly long, though Greg just chalked it up to the anxiety he felt about renewing his relationship with Billy. Tomorrow would be the start of his consulting gig at Cloud Gaming Co., and though it was a grim reason that brought them together again after more than ten years, perhaps they would have another shot at collaborating on that "next, big thing" they had fantasized about as young teenagers.

"Washington Athletic Club, please." Greg figured it was as convenient a location as any and not staying in a regular hotel made him feel safer. Though he was certain he left no traces after emptying the bank accounts of both Oleg Petrov and Sergey Kachinko, he *had* stolen nearly $3 million from the men and if he were discovered, he could end up in prison—or dead.

It was almost Christmas and while only a few weeks had passed since his last visit, the holiday season was in full swing. Seattle was much milder than DC in the winter, though he felt the chill in the air as he gathered his suitcase from the taxicab.

"Welcome back, sir!" The doorman greeted him like he was family, another advantage of staying at a place with reciprocal rights to his own club back East. Greg was in his room in no time and generously tipped the bellboy. The view of Puget Sound from his room was the same one he had seen from Billy's office a few weeks earlier, though at least thirty floors lower. He fired up his laptop to see if the media had picked up on the next phase of his plan to exact revenge and smiled at the article in the *Financial Times;* it was perfect.

#

A few minutes before 9am, the elevators at Two Union Square deposited Greg Galkin on the 53rd floor. Unlike his first trip to CGC's main office, Billy Wilson was there to meet him.

"Hey Greg," Billy enthusiastically greeted his friend at the reception area, "thanks for coming out here on such short notice!"

"Anything for a friend," Greg replied back. The response was genuine.

"Can't wait to get to work," Billy said. "You remember Susan, of course." The two shook hands while exchanging pleasantries as Susan returned to her office. He wondered if she and Billy were dating; he sensed the same chemistry between them he had noticed on his first trip.

"My Security Chief, Sebastiano DiCarlo, will be in later," Billy stated as they climbed the stairs to the 55th floor where the local security team sat, "but we've already got you set up in one of the offices up here so you can get right to work. I think you know what I'm looking for, right?"

"Find out how the bad guys are getting in," Greg confidently said.

Billy nodded. "Who they are and what they are trying to do would help, too."

"Of course," Greg glibly replied, "just like old times."

"I'll be upstairs if you find anything," the CEO said, leaning into the office. "If you need something, just ask Rose out here, she knows where everything is."

"Got it," Greg replied. "I'll call you in ten minutes when I figure it out."

Billy laughed. "Ten minutes? Man, you're slowing down!" But he figured it would take him at least ten days, if not more. They had had a security consulting company test the system and its vulnerabilities, and it had achieved the highest rating they had ever given out.

Greg had already tuned him out as he logged into the company intranet and then the gaming system. It hadn't changed that much in two years. He knew where he would look for a backdoor and when he had hacked into it two years ago, he was not surprised to find it had been right where he expected. Two years later, it was still there, embedded in the compiler as cleverly disguised as before, but exactly as the two of them had coded it twelve years ago in one of their programs.

Billy had barely made it back to his office when his phone rang.

"Mr. Galkin for you on line two, Mr. Wilson," Claire called to Billy as he walked past her into his office.

#

"What?" Billy was incredulous. "That's impossible!"

Greg was laughing on the other end of the line. *"Dude, I can't believe you used the exact same code we thought up twelve years ago. It was right where I expected it would be!"*

Billy laughed himself, partly out of embarrassment. "I can't believe I forgot about that." He was shaking his head as he noticed Seb talking to Claire. Billy motioned for him to come in. "Hey, Greg. Seb just got in, I'll bring him right down. I think you guys will hit it off."

"Sorry I'm late," Seb apologized, "Snoqualmie Pass was a mess and I just crashed when I got to the hotel. Slept right through my alarm."

"No worries. You've probably gotten less sleep than anyone here these last few weeks."

"Well I'm ready to go now," Seb replied, "and if this guy is as good as you say, hopefully we can figure out who and how—"

"Greg already figured out 'how'." Billy interjected, sheepishly. "I forgot that I had put in a backdoor. He figured it out in five minutes."

"Five minutes!" Seb was blown away by how quickly Greg was able to find what he must have stumbled over a hundred times and never thought about twice. Regardless of whether he knew what to look for or not, he was incredibly impressed.

"Yep. I hadn't even gotten back to my desk yet."

"Wow! I can't wait to meet the guy." Seb's excitement was palpable. He had come into work today feeling slightly threatened, but if this guy had already figured out how to hack into CGC's gaming system, Seb had a million other questions for him. He had heard about certain guys operating in the shadows who could get into anything. He figured Greg must be one of those guys, though he doubted he went by "Greg" in cyberspace.

CHAPTER 47

Tony Smith occasionally wondered why he worked the graveyard shift, given how grueling the schedule was on his body. But as he drove his oldest son home from his first basketball game as a high school freshman, he was immediately reminded.

"Thanks for coming to my game, Dad," the lanky, 14-year-old said as he slid into the car and fist bumped his father. "They had absolutely no answer for that up-and-under move we worked on all summer. Total domination!" His son had just led his team to a nine-point victory in his first frosh game; the elder Smith beamed.

"Yep. That's what happens when you put in the work," Tony said. "They all won't be that easy, but you played one heckuva game!" The two of them jabbered back-and-forth as they pulled into the driveway.

Tony's wife was at the twins' game and so they flipped on ESPN to catch the latest football news; the Gaming Olympics' highlights were on instead.

"No wait, Dad, I want to watch this!" his son yelled as Tony reached for the clicker. The highlight of *Thunderstruck, Blunt Instrument* and *Ronin* was playing. "*Thunderstruck* is one nasty player—watch how he gets this 5-Star *Samurai* dude. Sick!" He quickly thumbed a text message to one of his buddies.

Tony never really paid much attention to his boys' video games, but he was blown away by the realism of the graphics and he also recognized the Middle Eastern territory on which they were fighting. "What is this?" he inquired, captivated by what was playing on the screen before him.

"It's the Gaming Olympics." His son was mesmerized by the action as a missile blew *Ronin* into a thousand little pieces. The mishap of the Queen's team was next, this time it was Tony who was riveted.

Damn, he thought to himself, *it seems real.* The clips almost looked like intelligence videos. He was reminded of Jeremy's references to video games and wondered if he played like his own boys did.

"That is so lame!" Tony's son howled as three of the airplanes from the Queen's air force crashed inexplicably into the Mediterranean.

Tony just shook his head and chuckled. *Well maybe not quite like intel videos,* he mused.

#

The Annual Scholarship Banquet was one of the highlights of the year for Dr. Johnson. He got to show off the current crop of the school's computer stars, help Queen's raise funds to buy the next generation of technology, and hob-knob with the local tech community.

This year was particularly special as it honored Billy Wilson and the recent IPO of Cloud Gaming Co. It was at this very dinner some years ago that one of Mikel Johnson's tech guests had met the young prodigy, Billy Wilson, and provided early start-up funding for what was now Cloud Gaming Co.

Dr. Johnson was hoping that Mitchell Patkanim might have a similar conversation about his artificial intelligence ideas with one of the tech titans. He was already an inspiration among local Native Americans and with a little help from the tech community, might emerge as a next generation tech leader.

Unlike most of the Queen's students, who were awestruck by the technology glitterati gracing the halls of the Administration Building, Mitchell seemed completely at ease. The articles he had read in the Computer Storage Room allowed him to converse at a high level with most of them about their fields and he was making quite an impression.

"I see what you mean about Mitchell," Billy said to Dr. Johnson. "He has that unusual mix of brilliance and common sense. Artificial intelligence seems like the perfect fit. I could use someone like him in the future." *Hell, I could probably use him now given the problems we're facing,* Billy thought, though he needed to keep that to himself now that they were a public company.

"Reminds me a lot of you in some ways," Dr. Johnson replied. "I've really had to think about some of the concepts he just casually explains."

"So why isn't he on your gaming varsity? I'd have thought a kid like that—particularly from a family of boys—would be totally into video games and just the kind of person you'd want on your team." Billy loved talking video games about as much as anything and had had a great conversation about *Battle for Babylon* with the team leaders. As impressed as he had been with Brad, Nate, and Jerry, he figured that Mitchell's uniqueness would have been a net addition to the personality of the team.

"Yeah, it's a shame really. I've seen the kid play and he's a whiz. He'd be one of my best players for sure and it doesn't even seem like he spends much time on it. Unfortunately, there is some bad blood between my top three kids and Mitchell," Dr. Johnson explained. "I'm not really sure why, but they have made that kid's life miserable from the day he got to Queen's. Mitchell has shown real resilience in dealing with it, though. In fact, he's the only reason Brad is even competing in the Olympics right now."

"Huh?" Billy interjected, losing his train of thought as he watched Susan Green work the crowd. She clearly had exquisite taste in her professional attire, so it shouldn't have come as a surprise to Billy that her eye for clothes extended beyond business suits. Still, he hadn't been prepared for how stunning she looked in semi-formal attire.

Dr. Johnson turned his head to see what was distracting Billy. He chuckled as he looked back at his young protégé. "You're hooked aren't you?"

"Yeah, I think so," Billy sheepishly replied. "What were we talking about again?"

Dr. Johnson laughed as he looked at his watch; it was time for Billy's keynote speech. For the next thirty minutes, the founder of Cloud Gaming Co. held his audience in rapt attention about his journey from Washington, DC to the *Forbes 400*. He talked about the death of his father, how the Queen's community had stabilized him as he struggled with it, how Dr. Johnson had been instrumental in much of his early work, the IPO, and the most current topic, the Gaming Olympics. He even spent twenty minutes answering questions; the crowd loved it. The speech touched just the right chords and the fundraiser hit a new record for the school.

Dr. Johnson was ecstatic. He could fund an additional scholarship and upgrade his entire computer lab. His charges had also met the school's most famous and wealthiest alum, though most of them seemed more interested in Billy's date than they were in him. *Boys will be boys,* Dr. Johnson chuckled to himself.

#

"Thomas!" Tony Smith barked in his Marine drill sergeant voice. Part of his daily routine as Director was reviewing the intelligence data gathered during the other shifts and he was hunched over his computer screen.

"Yes sir?"

"What is this?" he growled, while looking at the screen. A replay of the Russian fighter jets crashing was playing on the screen.

"I'm not sure I understand what you mean, sir." Jeremy deferentially replied. He could feel his colleagues staring.

Tony pointed to the screen as the Russian air force spread out for a dive bomb attack, then watched the three lead fighter planes plow straight into the ground.

"Last night, I swear I saw this same video clip on the ESPN highlights of some video game competition," the Director barked. "How is it possible that a damn video game company could create the graphics to simulate top secret Russian intel moments after it occurred?" Tony was more perplexed than angry.

"Sir," Jeremy started, wondering if he would regret what he was about to say, "maybe it's the other way around."

Jeremy carefully walked his boss through his logic, before springing the conclusion on him: the Russians were somehow tapped into CGC's gaming system and mining the video game data to run their military strategy.

"Jeremy," the Director replied in a calm, but pointed manner, "when you brought me the idea that the Russians were using a Wi-Fi system to run their military tactics, I thought you were crazy. Yet it turned out to be spot on. Your electro-kinetic program has given us a new level of intel and my hat's off to you..."

Jeremy nodded at each step of his boss' comments. He knew how lucky he was to work for someone not threatened by his technology skills, but he also knew that some things, no matter how sound they were logically, were just not tenable in the world of politics; he waited for the kicker.

"...but there is no way I am going to the White House and advocating that the Russians are mining data from a video game to run their military strategy—no matter how reasonable you make it all sound. Hell, based on what you've just shown me, it would be hard to argue against you. It just sounds all too—" Tony paused, searching for the right word.

"Implausible?" Jeremy finished his sentence.

"Exactly!" Tony exclaimed, "'Implausible' is exactly the right word."

"But Tony, thousands might be killed. Don't we have to do what we can to stop that from happening?" Jeremy countered his boss' perspective, almost pleading with him.

"That is ultimately up to others. Our job is to provide them enough information to make intelligent decisions and we've done that. I think your logic and your conclusions are sound, but what do we do about it? Ask them to shut down a public company on a hunch? Do you have any idea how many lawsuits that would spawn? What if we did it anyway and the Russians still succeeded?" Tony sounded like a professor. His pragmatism, borne of thirty years in the cauldron of politics and intelligence, was maddening to Jeremy, despite its perverse logic.

"I suppose you're right," Jeremy said. The resignation in his voice was painful.

"Look, son. You are one hell of an analyst. The things you have uncovered totally blow me away." Tony felt real sympathy for his young charge. "But just because you give good advice doesn't mean it is always going to be followed. There usually isn't one best answer, most of the time there are multiple competing good ones."

"Yeah, but—" Jeremy tried to interject, but Tony shut him down.

"No 'buts'. We do what we do and then the politicians do their thing," Tony rejoined. "We have a hard enough time just getting them to continue funding us, we don't need to spin our wheels trying to persuade them on something that is way out in right field, no matter how reasonable." Tony's phone vibrated and as he picked it up, it was clear the conversation was over.

#

"Hey, Jeremy. Why the long face?" Jeremy's pity-party was shattered by the sound of Beth's voice. He smiled.

"Aww. Tony just shot down my video game analysis. He said it sounded reasonable, but he was never going to tell the White House that a video game system was running the Russian military," he started, realizing how far-fetched it sounded himself. He started to laugh, and Beth joined in.

228

"At least you can watch me dominate…" Beth started, before immediately turning red at how it sounded. Jeremy laughed even harder as Beth stumbled over her words, "…um, I mean, on the video…um, video game, I mean."

"Wow! That's a classic, even from a 'blunt instrument'," Jeremy howled as he pushed the vending machine button for his Diet Pepsi, handing it over to his blushing, cute colleague.

"You know what I mean," Beth defensively retorted, her hands on her hips as she admonished her colleague.

"Do I?" Jeremy winked as he responded. They both shared a hearty laugh.

CHAPTER 48

Mitchell finished up in the Computer Storage Room and walked upstairs to Dr. Johnson's office, gently knocking on the door. His teacher was alone.

"Dr. Johnson?" Mitchell quietly asked, half hoping he wouldn't be heard.

"Yes? Oh, Mitchell, how are you doing?" the teacher enthusiastically responded. "What brings you up here today?" The sophomore had a hard time making eye contact and shifted his weight uncomfortably, wondering how best to raise the topic that had kept him awake since the Scholarship Banquet.

"Dr. J, I have a confession to make." Mitchell briefly made eye contact with his teacher to gauge his reaction. Dr. Johnson had been in the business of dealing with high school students and their problems for long enough to wonder if this was a "real confession" or just a young kid struggling with the typical ups-and-downs of teenage life. "I've read most of what you left downstairs in the Computer Room, even the stuff you had locked up."

"I see," Dr. Johnson clinically responded, neither angrily nor accusatorily. He had forgotten half of what was in the room and so wasn't quite sure where the conversation was leading. "And?..."

"And based on some information I read, stuff in some of those old textbooks down there and just some tinkering, I managed to figure out how to break into, uh…CGC's gaming system." Mitchell stumbled over the last words, understanding their gravity as he spoke them.

"The *gaming system?*" Dr. Johnson replied, unsure if he had heard his student correctly. He had not heard of anyone ever hacking into CGC's gaming system, much less a high school kid. And yet here was a precocious 15-year-old, not publicly bragging about it *incognito* on some message board like most hackers would do, but genuinely apologizing for it in private, knowing full well that it might result in expulsion from the school that had already dramatically altered his life for the positive.

"Um, yeah." Mitchell glumly responded, his gaze dropping to his now shuffling feet. "And that's not all. I messed with Brad and Nate's controls while they were playing to get back at them for all the hassling. That's why some of that weird stuff happened to them.

I'm sorry...well...sort of. They're still jerks, but I swear I didn't have anything to do with their planes crashing into the Mediterranean."

Dr. Johnson had to suppress a smile. He knew this kid was sharp, but he wasn't even sure Billy Wilson could have pulled off a stunt like this. Yet, Mitchell had just told him he had committed a crime, so he couldn't just look the other way.

"I'm sure you know that's a federal crime, Mitchell," Dr. Johnson sternly replied, even though he knew that even if charges were brought and Mitchell were convicted, the kid's status as a minor would likely result in little or no real criminal punishment. But it would become part of his record and might change his path forever. Dr. Johnson knew the allure of the dark side of computers and worked as hard as he could to keep his graduates out of that world. He particularly felt Mitchell needed the structure of Queen's to keep him from embarking down that road.

"Yeah, I do. And I wouldn't be surprised if you threw me out of school." Mitchell was truly contrite. "But after seeing what a cool dude Billy Wilson was, I felt really bad and figured I needed to say something...at least to you."

"I'm glad you did Mitchell, I'm glad you did," Dr. Johnson replied, wondering what course of action to take next.

#

"Kyle, Joe Williams here," CGC's Chief Counsel started his phone conversation with the sometimes friend, sometimes adversary, CEO of StormClouds.

"Joe Williams?" Kyle Shepherd mockingly started his side of the conversation, *"The Joe Williams?"*

"There is only one, Kyle, at least one rich one!" came the retort. Both men laughed heartily; lawyers were a strange breed.

The two men had known each other for twenty years, meeting when Kyle was in high school. The current dust-up over the alleged stolen code of StormClouds was just business for the two men, though Joe wondered what his counterpart's real angle was, because in an unguarded moment, both men knew there was no legitimate merit to the lawsuit.

"Look, Kyle," CGC's chief counsel said, as the call suddenly turned serious. "We need to have a conversation about something that has come up. Are you free this afternoon?"

"Oh?" Kyle responded, taken aback by the sudden seriousness of the conversation.

CGC's attorney paused a moment, wondering how much he should say over the phone. "Actually, Kyle, we have something that affects us both, but that's all I feel comfortable saying on the phone."

Kyle Shepherd paused himself. It was an unorthodox request in the middle of a lawsuit.

"Should I bring my lawyer?" Kyle responded. *"He'd kill me if I met with opposing counsel without his knowledge."*

"Kyle, I know this is going to come across wrong," CGC's lawyer responded, somewhat apologetically, "but Billy wanted me to talk to you one-on-one."

"Damn, Joe, you have me intrigued, that's for sure," Kyle replied. *"Let me check my calendar."* He tapped on his keyboard. *"The earliest I can meet is 2:30, but only for an hour max. Do you have a place in mind?"*

"How about the WAC?" Joe responded. They were both members of the downtown athletic club, and were known to lift weights there in the afternoon. Any interaction could be chalked up as a chance meeting between two workout junkies.

"OK, I'll see you there at 2:30," Kyle responded, typing in "workout" in the 2:30 time slot of his schedule.

"Great, I'll meet you in the lobby and then we can just 'bump' into each other on the way upstairs."

"Sounds kind of sneaky, but OK," replied the StormClouds' CEO, growing increasingly more curious with each statement. *"See you this afternoon."*

#

General Petrov's life was unraveling and he had no idea who was behind it. He was still one of the most feared men in the Russian military, but his inability to derail the technology strategy that General Yikovich had championed caused more than a few of his enemies to begin to whisper about the fall of the old guard. Yet that was a legitimate disagreement on military strategy, aired behind closed doors. He could live with that.

The disappearance of his money was more troubling, but also a private matter. As he looked through his bank statements, he could see that every account had been systematically looted, leaving no more than the few rubles necessary to keep the account active. While he had intimidated a few of the banks into making him whole so he could keep up the illusion of wealth, he had a fraction of what he once had.

But the front-page news in the *Financial Times* that his oldest daughter, Katarina, was being expelled from Cambridge in a cheating scandal was excruciatingly public. The article described how someone had broken into the computer system and altered the grades of a number of students, including the Russian grad student, and Scotland Yard had discovered an electronic trail leading back to her. Those who knew Katarina were certain she had nothing to do with the crime and that it was probably a malicious attack by an enemy of her father, but the damage was done. The once proud Petrov family name was in tatters.

General Petrov sat silently in his office, head in hands. No one within the Russian military was surprised that Petrov had enemies, but the viciousness of the attacks shocked even the most hardened of those skilled in the political arts; they all wondered who among them had such a bitter axe to grind. At least he still had his command.

#

Joe Williams and Kyle Shepherd hopped on the elevator together and headed for the 21st floor of the Washington Athletic Club. CGC had a private room there for out of town guests and it was set up as a functional office.

"Damn, Joe, what's with all this cloak-and-dagger stuff? It's giving me the creeps."

"Here's the deal, Kyle. The Russian military tried to hack into our gaming system," CGC's chief counsel stated bluntly, figuring the quicker he got to the point, the less chance their absence would be missed. "That's why our system crashed the other day."

"You guys?" Kyle was incredulous that CGC had been hacked, the fact that it was some foreign government was a side note, at least initially. CGC's reputation for being impenetrable was known throughout the technology world.

"I'm afraid so. We had been getting inklings that we were being probed, but couldn't figure out by whom—until this past event," Joe paused as he gauged his counterpart's reaction. "In some ways we were fortunate it was such an egregious breach—our guys think they must have had some kind of an accident and it immediately flagged us."

Kyle processed the information through his legal filter. It seemed reasonable and based on what he had heard, something clearly had happened to CGC. But he was also sure that Joe was putting as positive a spin on it as he could.

"So why do you think it was the Russians?" Kyle queried, still not sure how any of the conversation so far affected StormClouds, but as long as he had the Chief Counsel of Cloud Gaming talking, he wanted him to continue.

"Security was able to grab a part of what was attacking our system as it was crashing. We ended up with some code fragments of the attacker, some of our OS and," Joe paused again, this time for dramatic effect, "—some of yours."

"Ours?" The CEO of StormClouds was floored.

"Well, let me restate that," started CGC's lawyer, "at least we think it's yours. I brought the sequence we were able to capture to show you." He handed a printout of a mix of three types of code.

"This is ours," Joe stated, pointing to the fragments of Billy's clean code, "this is clearly Russian," he continued, pointing to the Cyrillic lettering, "and this we think is yours." He pointed to the last bit, circling it with his pen.

"Damn," Kyle said under his breath, though loud enough for his counterpart to hear. "Yeah, this is our stuff," he finished dejectedly. He knew it cast very reasonable doubt on the merits of his firm's case against CGC, but more importantly, confirmed what he already knew about his team's own findings of Russian code left behind when they had been breached themselves.

"Tell me, Kyle," Joe tried to steer the conversation into another direction. "What do you think the Russians are doing with video game code interfacing with logistics code?"

It was an intriguing question. As a defense contractor, StormClouds had access to intelligence and Kyle had heard bits and pieces of information about some new Russian military strategy involving technology. It seemed a stretch that some logistics program—even with artificial intelligence embedded in it like theirs—could be of any real use to it, but even more ridiculous to think video game software was part of the plan.

"Hell, Joe. I don't even know what they would do with my stuff, much less yours," Kyle said, thinking about the implications. "I mean, I guess it's flattering in a way, but anything I say now would just be speculation."

"Yeah, you're probably right," CGC's lawyer replied, "kind of far-fetched to think it has some kind of military application." Joe was fishing. His team had already identified more than he was letting on, but was trying to draw out his counterpart.

Kyle looked at his watch. "Look Joe, we probably better start our workouts. Let me think about this and get back to you."

Joe nodded. "OK. I appreciate you coming over on such short notice. Why don't you head out first and I'll follow in' a few minutes."

"Plausible deniability?" Kyle quipped, laughing.

"Yep," Joe replied, a twinkle in his eye. Their conversation had taken thirty minutes; both men could get in a brief workout and be back in their offices by 3:45.

CHAPTER 49

Though Sebastiano DiCarlo and Greg Galkin had both spent the better part of the last ten years dealing with the dark side of computing, they approached the field from diametrically opposite perspectives. Seb felt his job was to keep the bad guys out—period. He had never flirted with the temptation to hack into anyone else's system; he had too much respect for the programmers who toiled day and night to make computers run faster and better. He viewed hackers as the virtual equivalent of neighborhood drug dealers—scum in the shadows doing the bidding of some unknown master to prey on the unsuspecting and getting paid handsomely for it.

Nevertheless, Seb didn't believe that hackers had contributed nothing in the defense of computer systems. Indeed, many of the best security guys were reformed hackers who had grown up, gotten caught, or couldn't stand the stress of constantly being one mistake away from landing in jail. He had also filled more legal pads than he could remember with notes from conferences where hackers had been featured speakers. They were useful; he just didn't respect any of them.

Greg, on the other hand, had practically lived on the other side of the law, just not as a renegade. His father had taught him from an early age that if you were going to write code, you needed to protect it from those who sought to steal it, and the best way to do that was to learn to think and act like they did; anyone in security who didn't was a fool. None of this made him a criminal and the fact that people were willing to pay him for skills that many criminals had didn't make it wrong either, at least in his eyes. He was very good at what he did, but it was a job, not something to boast about like many hackers did. Yet very few people thought this way and so Greg was careful when sharing his thoughts about it.

"So how did you manage to find the backdoor so quickly?" Seb queried. "Man, I must have blown past it a thousand times and never thought anything of it!"

"Well, you have to remember Billy and I grew up together and we shared a lot of our ideas," Greg said guardedly. He knew nothing about Seb and wasn't sure how much he could trust him. "He spent a lot of time putting that code together and he was writing good stuff like that even way back then. My job was just to make sure nobody could break in and if they did, find a way to get it back. Billy was always the most trusting guy I ever knew, so the fact that he used the same stuff I wrote doesn't surprise me one bit. Frankly, there are a lot of concepts here that we worked on together. It's obviously a lot more sophisticated, but the ideas are the same."

Seb could certainly understand the value of having a programming partner and if what Greg was saying was true, it would explain how CGC's gaming system had always been so far ahead of its peers in terms of security. It also made him more than little nervous. After spending only a few moments with Greg, Seb recognized he was an extremely talented programmer, but the fact that he had never heard of him raised red flags. Many of the best programmers were hackers as well and they rarely went by their given names. Friend of Billy or not, he would do some sleuthing to see what he could find out about this mysterious Greg Galkin.

#

Sergeant Kachinko walked down the hallway towards General Petrov's office. When they had worked together a number of years ago, he had learned a great deal from the General about both the exercise of power and intimidation by fear. It had been a difficult decision when he was asked to join General Yikovich's technology team. Given the generational difference, he understood Oleg Petrov's reluctance to embrace technology, but Sergeant Kachinko also recognized how much easier it was to defeat an opponent by stealth and deception, rather than just by having a better battering ram.

The Sergeant knocked gently.

"*Enter*," came General Petrov's muffled reply behind the solid oak door, meeting him as he walked in. The General closed it behind them, locking it in the process.

Petrov wasted no time. Before Kachinko could even sense danger, Petrov had his arm twisted behind his back and his head firmly slammed against the General's desk. The Sergeant feared he was to become another victim that had "slipped" in General Petrov's presence, suffering a fatal blow to the head.

"Did you not think I would find out?!" the General demanded, slamming Kachinko's head against the desk another time for good measure. "You and your technology *prima donnas*. What has happened to you, Sergey?"

"What do you mean Comrade General?" came the anguished reply. Kachinko was no match for the burly Russian.

Another slam, this time drawing a trickle of blood out of Sergeant Kachinko's left temple.

"Do you think me a fool?!" the General was in a rage—a controlled one lest his colleagues hear, but a rage nonetheless. "I may not understand computers, but I do understand betrayal and how many do you think have betrayed me and lived to tell?"

"None, General. But you speak of 'betrayal'? I have done nothing of the sort!" the Sergeant's body tensed, expecting a further, perhaps final, blow.

"Oh come now, Sergey. The bank statement has your name on it! I have friends in high places! Did you really think I would not find out?"

"Bank statement?" the Sergeant anxiously queried. "All my money has been stolen from me, Comrade General!" Sergeant Kachinko blurted out, "I don't have even have my money, much less yours. I swear it!"

A drop of blood splattered onto the copy of the letter provided to the General by the president of Sberbank.

"Explain this, then!" Petrov growled, stabbing the letter with his thick index finger.

As the junior officer read the letter, he saw the same hallmarks of the pilfering of his own account. The extra money that had flowed through his Swiss account now made sense: it was Petrov's. It was plain to him that both of them were targets, narrowing down the universe of perpetrators significantly. The two men had not worked together for five years.

Twenty minutes of desperate explanation later, General Petrov was furious once more, but no longer at Sergeant Kachinko. And despite the rough treatment to which he had just subjected his once protégé, he had another ally in his search for the criminal that had stolen his money.

#

Maria Incandella was surprised to hear the lawsuit brought by StormClouds was withdrawn. She had serious doubts about their chances for success to begin with, but Kyle Shepherd had seemed adamant about carrying it through to a court date. Perhaps cooler heads had prevailed, though she wanted to get to the bottom of it.

"Susan, Maria Incandella here."

"Maria, great to hear from you," Susan replied in an upbeat manner. *"That was some interview with Kyle Shepherd. I must admit I enjoyed watching you make the man squirm."*

Maria laughed. After her interview with Billy Wilson, she had done some homework on Susan Green and what she uncovered had impressed her. She could see her being a worthy interview sometime in the future.

"We do what we have to do," Maria replied, "but thank you. It is always gratifying to hear that people are getting something out of the interviews." She quickly shifted gears. "That's partly why I am calling," Maria continued. "What in the world caused Shepherd to agree to drop the suit? Did you settle?"

"We are not totally sure, perhaps they just decided to move forward. They take their national security role seriously. Kyle made that very clear during the interview." Susan played to Maria's vanity.

Maria volleyed right back, reading between the lines: "Then the government asked them to drop the suit?"

"I have no idea about that, Maria," Susan responded coolly, *"nor have we been told as much by anyone. I am purely speculating, but the world is becoming a more dangerous place."*

Maria conceded that much was true, as both the Russians and the Western Allies were posturing over the Ukraine and its future. She jotted down *"military application?"* on her notepad.

"Indeed," Maria replied, pausing a moment. "Nothing off the record then?" Maria continued to probe.

"You know what I know, I'm sorry I can't be more help."

"I see. Perhaps some insights on the system crash, then. Any truth to the rumor that you've been hacked by the Russians?" Maria had heard through her contacts in government that the Russian military was hard at work on some new project.

#

Susan stiffened. *Damn, how does she do it?* she thought to herself. Maria seemed to have her pulse on every situation. "As we stated before, the system crashed due to a server malfunction in

Russia," Susan had allowed her eyes to wander to an e-mail she had just received from Billy about Greg's findings on the Russian connection and hoped the careless reply would go unnoticed. It did not.

"Russia?" Maria pounced. *"I believe your statement said 'Eastern Europe' did it not?"*

"I'm sorry, Maria, I have to hop. I hope you understand." Susan was unwilling to deny her mistake and hoped that Maria meant it when she said "off the record."

"Of course, Susan. Thanks for your time. I'd still love to get Billy on my show again. Just say when."

"I'll see what I can do, Maria. We've got a lot going on as you know." Susan smiled, figuring Maria Incandella would be insanely jealous if she knew Susan's words had a double meaning.

"Just say when," Maria repeated.

"We'll be in touch. Thanks for the call."

#

As Maria hung up the phone she finished her notes. *OTR: Russia, not Eastern Europe.*

CHAPTER 50

Dr. Johnson and Mitchell pulled out of the Queen's parking lot, and headed downtown for a one-on-one meeting with Billy Wilson, a perquisite of scholarship recipients. As they drove into the city, Mitchell peppered Dr. Johnson with questions about life, technology, girls, college, and a host of other topics, and despite the traffic, it seemed they were downtown in seconds. Dr. Johnson believed an apology for hacking into the company's gaming system was due to the man who wrote most of the code, but he wasn't sure how he would raise the topic. Mitchell spared him the trouble.

"Dr. J?" Mitchell hesitated briefly before blurting out: "do you think I'll be arrested if I apologize to Mr. Wilson?" It elicited a genuine laugh from the teacher.

"No, I do not, Mitchell," Dr. Johnson responded, amazed at the kid's maturity. "But I do think an apology would be well received—might even start an interesting dialog. It's not like you're the first person to ever hack into someone's system, if you know what I mean."

Mitchell chuckled, as much in relief as anything.

"OK," he bluntly replied.

#

As the two visitors from Queen's were ushered into the conference room on the 56th floor, Mitchell stood at the windows and marveled at the view. It was breathtaking to a kid who had never been in a building taller than the three-story Administration Building at Queen's.

"Wow," he murmured to himself as a pair of seagulls floated by below them. Just then Billy Wilson gently knocked and walked in the room.

"Some view, isn't it Mitchell," he said as he walked over to the young student. "I love it—it helps me think knowing I might be higher than the eagles."

Mitchell smiled as they shook hands. "I was thinking about the birds, too, Mr. Wilson." Billy laughed.

"I'm not 'Mr. Wilson' to anyone these days, but my assistant. You can call me 'Billy'."

"Thanks, Mr. Wilson, but my mom would kill me if I spoke to one of my elders by their first name," Mitchell replied. Billy was immediately taken by the young man's humility.

"OK, then," Billy said, slightly nodding his head. "Why don't we go on a little tour?"

As they walked through each department and Billy introduced him as a scholarship kid from Queen's, Mitchell was struck by how respectful they all were of his interest in computers; he was in a brand new world and it made him excited about the future. In short order the three of them were in Billy's office, sitting at the conference table.

"So what do you think?" Billy started with an open-ended question.

"Well, Mr. Wilson," Mitchell started nervously, "I'd like to say 'thanks' for sponsoring my scholarship. I've learned a ton already."

"You're welcome!" Billy enthusiastically responded, "Queen's has meant so much to me that I'm glad to be able to give something back."

After a slightly awkward silence, Mitchell opened his mouth again. "Um…" he started to stammer, before spitting out in a torrent: "I also wanna apologize for hacking into your system."

Billy looked at Mitchell, then Dr. Johnson quizzically.

"Excuse me?" he interjected. He had no idea what Mitchell was talking about. Dr. Johnson had said the boy had something he wanted to say, but this he wasn't expecting.

"Yes sir, I found some notes of yours in an old textbook, then pieced the rest of it together." Mitchell proceeded to walk through the whole story, as Billy shook his head at what he was hearing.

After five minutes of discussion, CGC's founder got up and walked over to his computer.

"Show me," he tersely said. Mitchell nervously glanced at Dr. Johnson, who affirmatively nodded his head. Mitchell joined Billy at the computer, and after a few clicks was at the user interface.

"OK, what user name are you using?" Billy queried.

"www3@ogc.com," Mitchell replied.

Billy chuckled and shook his head. "I forgot that one," he said to no one in particular. "But how did you figure out the password, Mitchell?" As chagrined as he was at his own foolishness, Billy was clearly impressed with this kid.

"I spent hours reading through stuff Dr. Johnson left in storage and your doodles in an old textbook and just kinda' figured it out." He tapped in the long password and they were soon inside the gaming system.

"Wow!" Billy responded with a whistle. "You're even deeper than most of my guys are allowed." In the last few years, the team had built in some additional protocols to protect the system, but this backdoor had not been superseded.

"Uh, thanks, I guess, but I'm still really sorry," Mitchell said morosely. Billy felt the genuineness of the apology.

"Well, I'll have to clean that one up for sure," Billy wrote himself a note, though he doubted he would forget.

"Can I ask you another question?" Mitchell asked hopefully.

"Sure, do I need to check my bank account, too?" Billy mused.

"Huh?" Mitchell looked perplexed, before realizing it was a joke. "Oh, I get it. Duh."

Billy turned serious again: "So, what's the question Mitchell?"

"What does the AI program do?" Mitchell asked, genuinely curious.

"What AI program?" the look on Billy's face betrayed his surprise, and though Mitchell didn't notice, Dr. Johnson did.

"This one," Mitchell grabbed the mouse again and rolled through a few screens before highlighting his find.

#

Sberbank, the bank that Yuri Fedorov headed, was not only General Petrov's main bank, it was that of the Russian government's, as well. As such, it processed the lion's share of financial transactions involving the government and third parties. Russian privacy laws were not nearly as strict as those in the West, but only the bank president had unlimited access to customer accounts and transactions. While Fedorov was careful about not abusing his position as head of the country's largest bank, he knew whom to fear; Oleg Petrov was such a man.

"Yuri," General Petrov greeted the bank's president as though they were best of friends, raising his open arms to the heavens before pulling the man close in the typical Russian greeting.

"Comrade Oleg," Yuri reciprocated. Whether they were truly friends mattered little to the bank president in front of his staff, but everyone knew who General Oleg Petrov was and if their boss was a friend of such a dangerous and powerful man, then perhaps they should also fear the president. They were soon in Fedorov's office.

"What have you found for me?" General Petrov wasted no time.

The bank president discreetly slid an envelope across his desk to the General. "My head of security says that this information should be extremely helpful to your technology people."

"Excellent!" The General was genuinely pleased. They spent a few more minutes engaged in chitchat before the General stood and extended his hand. "It is a shame we did not meet sooner, Comrade Yuri. I have the feeling we are cut from the same cloth."

"Indeed," the bank president simply replied, before continuing, "please keep me posted on how things go and should you need anything else, do not hesitate to contact me directly."

#

Mitchell's discovery of the embedded artificial intelligence code troubled Billy to the core. The CEO struggled to believe anyone on his staff could betray him like this, though it was clear someone had provided the Russians more or less unfettered access to his baby. That his Security VP had not flagged it, made him either incompetent or suspect number one.

The moment Dr. Johnson and Mitchell left, Billy punched in Greg's number on his phone and his old friend was there in a flash. Greg had known about the common backdoor code that he and Billy had devised when they were young, but was surprised that there had been another one, as well.

"Geez, how many backdoors did you put in there, man?" Greg asked incredulously.

"I know, I know," Billy replied defensively. "We're going to clean it up, but for now we are going to leave them alone until we figure out who's sneaking around."

"I can help with that if you need me to," Greg offered. Each day he was at Cloud Gaming, he felt more and more convicted about why they were currently in this situation; he wanted to do whatever he could to rectify it.

"I appreciate that, but there's actually something more worrisome that I want to pick your brain on. The kid at Queen's found a parasite AI program tacked onto the gaming system and I want you to figure out what it's there for. I doubt one of my guys put it in there, but before we go shut it down, I want to make sure."

"What?!" Greg could not believe what he was hearing. "Another problem? I guess you can't believe everything you read. I thought you guys were impenetrable."

"Very funny," Billy said in mock seriousness. "So did I, but obviously that's not the case. My guess is that someone is trying to cheat in the Gaming Olympics, but why the Russians are involved is perplexing."

Greg bit his lip. Although he also didn't know why, he did know that the Russians were involved, and wondered if maybe they had inserted the parasite as well. *Damn,* he thought, *what a mess I created.*

"OK. I'll get right on it," Greg replied. "Should I ask Seb for help?"

Billy paused momentarily before replying, "No. Let's keep him out of this for now. I want to make sure it isn't an inside job and right now, only you and I know. I'd like to keep it that way until we have more facts."

"Got it."

Greg was in his element once more. He had worked on more than a few consulting jobs where he had to uncover hackers, but they never had the same purpose he felt now. He was back with his boyhood chum and while the stakes might be higher, Greg's role was exactly the same as it had been many years ago: figure out how to protect Billy's code.

He logged into the system using Mitchell's backdoor access rather than his own, figuring that the system would not allow multiple logins of the same user and didn't want to alert the hacker that they had been made.

"There it is," Greg murmured to himself, as he navigated deep into the CGC gaming system. The AI software portal was hidden, though not as cleverly as the backdoor that Billy had put into the system. If a high school kid had found it and Seb had not, it made him wonder if the Security VP was really as good as Billy thought. With a few clicks, he copied the whole program onto his desktop.

As he went to close out of the gaming system, the AI program went active, and Greg watched in fascination as the mix of Russian and StormClouds' codes reached into CGC's gaming system to pull out data. Though he was not an artificial intelligence expert, Greg knew enough to tell that the data being accessed was shadowing something that was happening live.

He dialed Billy's line.

"Get down here right now! The AI program is engaged." Greg excitedly said.

#

Blunt Instrument was steadily moving up the leader board. Her aggressive attacking style was so consistent in its execution, and created such a favorable virtual military signature, that her army and air force were almost clones of their avatar. By the time competitors realized what they were up against, it was usually too late. *Blunt Instrument* had already managed to defeat two of the three main Asian favorites, overwhelming them with a mix of hand-to-hand combat, ground forces, artillery, and air power.

Beth's fingers danced across her keyboard as the major South Korean power, *Viper,* arrayed his forces on the high ground of the hills of the Zagros Mountains north of Babylon. *Blunt Instrument* was at a geographical disadvantage, but her air force was superior to that of *Viper's,* who, like many of the Asian players, relied on hand-to-hand combat in close quarters to overwhelm an opponent's army. She figured she could draw *Viper's* army from the hills and down into the plain, and then use air power to attack the stronghold in the hills.

Yet, ever since Beth had defeated *Ronin* with *Thunderstruck's* help, she had been wary of another sudden appearance of the mysterious *samurai* while her forces were on attack. Still, she knew *Viper* was a foe she would meet at some point on her way to Babylon and decided it better to fight on an open battlefield where it would be easy to spot interlopers. As the two top-ten teams engaged in a *pas de deux* in an attempt to draw first blood, the ESPN logins started to edge higher, then went parabolic when Maria Incandella tweeted: *"blonde babe fixin' to strike down snake in the desert!"*

#

Greg and Billy watched as the embedded artificial intelligence software continued to interface with the CGC gaming system. They had determined it was drawing data from the battle between *Blunt Instrument* and *Viper,* but where the data was going, or how it was being used, was a mystery—at least to Billy.

Greg, however, knew the Russians had been hacking into *Battle for Babylon* for some time. That it was now coming so close to home, made him realize he had to let his friend know somehow. He just couldn't bear to come clean about his own involvement, particularly after finally connecting with Billy after ten long years. He was very careful with his words.

"Billy," Greg paused, as his friend looked up from the screen. "Part of what I discovered from my dad's notes was that there's a special group of technology experts within the Russian military called Department T. My dad used to be the head of it, though I didn't know it at the time." Billy nodded, absorbing this new information. "Part of their mandate is to hack into secure systems and steal software they can use in their own military applications. I believe they are the ones that caused the Code Red."

"Our Threat Board suggested it likely occurred in Russia, so that makes sense," Billy volleyed back. "But why would they want a video game?"

"I'm sure they are after the on-line gaming system. I think you underestimate how powerful it is, Billy. And based on what we have just learned from the parasitic AI program, I'd venture to say they are up to something nefarious—and I'm not talking about cheating in the Gaming Olympics."

"But how did they get in? And how could we not know?" Billy plaintively asked.

Greg paused. Billy had given him an opportunity to confess.

"Look man, there are a lot of untrustworthy people out there in the cyber community, and for the right price, they'd sell their grandmothers down the road. But frankly, at this point, 'who' or 'how' is of secondary importance," Greg cagily replied, deflecting the spotlight away from himself and onto the problem. "We just have to clean up this mess, and judging from what we've seen, as soon as possible."

Billy shook his head in disgust. "Well, at least you have my back again, buddy," Billy looked back at the screen they had been watching, not noticing Greg's obvious discomfort.

"I do now, 3. I do now," Greg replied, feeling like Judas Iscariot. "Look, there's something else." Greg continued, wanting to redirect the conversation. "One of the senior guys in Department T, Sergey Kachinko, was in the getaway car when your dad was murdered."

Billy's head snapped back to Greg. "WHAT?!" Billy growled, "How do we get back at the bastard?"

"One thing at a time, Billy, one thing at a time," Greg calmly rejoined. "We need to deal with the current problem and not get too far ahead of ourselves." It was an accurate statement, even if Greg held all the cards. Both men looked at each other knowingly; their work had just taken on a very different, more sinister aspect.

#

Artillery fire from *Viper's* army suddenly started raining down on *Blunt Instrument's* position on the plain, while a volley of surface-to-air missiles was directed at her air force circling over the Mediterranean. *Viper's* army rushed from the plateau in an attempt to overwhelm *Blunt Instrument's* main force. But Beth had formed three columns and when the bulk of her opponent's forces swept down off the mountain plateau, *Blunt Instrument's* left flank emerged from behind and began to mow down *Viper's* army.

Viper was immediately on the defensive. Its surface-to-air batteries had been momentarily exhausted to buy the army time to rush down the mountain, but they now found themselves surrounded and outflanked. Half of *Blunt Instrument's* air force swooped down to attack the now defenseless *Viper* army, the other half racing to engage in dog-fighting with *Viper's* air force. *Blunt Instrument's* execution was almost flawless, destroying one jet after another.

The battle appeared to be coming to a surprisingly rapid end, when the Master 5-Star, *Ronin,* suddenly emerged from *Viper's* army and shed his camouflage. Beth saw it immediately, jettisoning her air focus and hoping her army and air force could finish off *Viper*.

#

"Ha-ha," Mikel Johnson growled ghoulishly, "we'll see how you fare this time, Blondie!" His avatar, *Ronin*, was still the highest rated Master and Dr. Johnson used one of his cheat codes to hide within *Viper's* advancing army. It was payback time.

#

Jeremy had been watching the battle for the last five minutes, logging off from his own engagement when his twitter account had broadcast what was going on in the desert. The emergence of the camouflaged *Ronin* enraged him.

"YOU SCUM!" he shrieked, logging back in as rapidly as he could. He would not leave his work colleague without some kind of support; fortunately he wasn't far away. As he closed along the margins of the battlefield, he could see that *Blunt Instrument* was holding her own against the Master 5-Star. "Go girl, GO!" he shouted in his empty apartment.

But while *Blunt Instrument* was matching *Ronin* blow for blow, the rest of her forces weren't faring so well. *Viper's* air force had managed to neutralize Beth's air advantage, and her ground forces were starting to crumble when *Thunderstruck* swooped in.

Viper was completely unprepared for the attack, and only the quickness honed from years of martial arts enabled him to parry *Thunderstruck's* first blow. But Jeremy was a man on a mission—he would do whatever necessary to help Beth in her battle against two strong foes. *Viper* had gotten used to *Blunt Instrument's* methodical style of play, but he was totally unprepared for the raging bull that *Thunderstruck* had become. Jeremy's avatar carved up *Viper's* bodyguards with a few quick, savage strokes and *Viper* himself was now in his sights. The South Korean's army was rapidly withdrawing in an attempt to come to the aid of its Master 3-Star General, under siege by a feral animal.

#

"Damn!" Dr. Johnson screamed. He could see *Viper* running from *Thunderstruck,* and as the South Korean's army hastily retreated, his advantage against *Blunt Instrument* evaporated. Suddenly, it was just two avatars toe-to-toe, the blonde warrior princess spinning away from danger and attacking *Ronin* in a rhythm that suggested an oft rehearsed choreography.

#

"YES!" Beth screamed primordially, as she noticed *Thunderstruck* on the plateau, "kill that damn snake. *KILL IT!"* Beth's whole body shook with a surge of adrenaline when she saw Jeremy covering her back. Her avatar gracefully jumped, corkscrewing like a figure skater to avoid the swipe of the sword of the now over-committed *Ronin,* and sweeping her sword violently across *Ronin's* neck. His head exploded like a pumpkin dropped from a ten-story building.

#

Dr. Johnson sat in front of his computer, speechless and stunned into paralysis by the events that had just unfolded in front of him, scarcely noticing that CGC's servers were asking if he wanted to continue.

#

"That was FRICKIN' AWESOME, Beth!" Jeremy's yelled, his jaw dropping in amazement. Mesmerized by the acrobatic move and *Blunt Instrument's* fatal blow to *Ronin,* Jeremy momentarily forgot that he himself was in a battle as well. He recovered his senses a split second too late, staggering forward as *Viper* withdrew the sword he had just used to lance *Thunderstruck* in the heart.

#

"NNNNOOOO!" Beth's scream was blood-curdling. She had just seen Jeremy's avatar disappear into the ether, dying while defending her back. She raced up the hill, outrunning her army and slicing up every straggler from *Viper's* army. In a moment she was standing toe-to-toe with the South Korean video gamer's avatar.

Beth had forgotten everything she had learned about warfare in one irrational move to defend the honor of her friend. Fortunately, her target wanted no part of her, desperately trying to exit out of the game, but acting too slowly. *Blunt Instrument* was upon him like an enraged hornet, stabbing him in the heart at the edge of the cliff, twisting the blade enough to send him backward off it, blood spurting out of his virtual heart as he fell to the rocks below.

Beth was emotionally and physically exhausted. As her avatar stood on the cliffs above the Tigris and Euphrates Rivers, she clicked on the EXIT icon.

Are you sure you wish to EXIT? came the auto prompt. Beth covered YES with her cursor and clicked. She logged out of the system, crushed that Jeremy had been a casualty of her military battles. She wondered if he would forgive her.

#

Within seconds, CGC's servers had calculated the action of the key players in the battle that had just occurred. *Ronin* had been knocked all the way down to 3-Star. Not only had he been defeated by a lower-ranked player, it had happened after using one of *Battle for Babylon's* normally most effective cheat codes. *Blunt Instrument* ascended to the top of the leaderboard in the Gaming Olympics, becoming a Master 4-Star General in the process, and putting a big, fat target on her back.

CHAPTER 51

"What do think we should do, Greg," Billy started, wishing Susan's cool-headedness was there instead of just the two of them, "contact the Feds?"

Greg leaned on his elbow, his hand over his mouth.

"Hmmm," he replied, letting Billy know he had been heard, though his mind was on a totally different track. "I'm purely speculating, but the only logical explanation of what I see is that the Russians are somehow integrating information from the video game feed to help them with military tactics. Nothing else makes sense."

Billy put his hands together on top of his head and looked out the window. "How so?" he queried, his mind deep in thought.

"At my mom's wake, I heard people talking about the Ukrainian battle as though they had used some kind of drone weapon," Greg started a line of reasoning.

"Go on," Billy replied, wrestling with the implications, though Greg had obviously thought it through.

Greg continued. "Drones are piloted by ground based operators looking at battlefield screens—not much different from a video game. If you can figure out how to use it with an artificial intelligence system, it could be lethal. The only thing that makes sense is they are preparing for a real war. I know it sounds far-fetched, but can you think of any other reason?"

"It sounds compelling," Billy replied.

"The news makes it sound like they are gearing up in the Ukraine for war," Greg opined. The two friends were clearly riffing off each other.

"Naw, the only thing that makes sense is the Middle East. It's called *Battle for Babylon* for a reason and with the Olympics going on, it's where all the best gamers are going to be, at least virtually." Billy paused, distilling the significance of what he had just said. "Damn. We're talking World War III, Greg."

"Or maybe a great way to get back at the bastards who killed our dads," Greg volleyed back.

Billy listened to Greg's idea about payback. Although it wasn't just an ordinary management decision, Billy analyzed it as such. He felt the government would hurt the momentum being generated by the Gaming Olympics, and what he decided as CEO wasn't any of their business anyway.

But it was personal, too. Once Billy discovered that the Russian military had murdered his father, he wanted some kind of revenge. If he could avenge the death of his father using what he had learned from the man, there was a sense of poetic justice about it. And if it didn't work, they would just close the backdoor on the Russians.

"Let's give it a shot," Billy said. "I'll call Dr. Johnson later today."

#

Billy looked out the window. A late February snowfall had ceased and the sun created a picturesque, though blinding, visual from his office. Greg's recommendation to allow the Russians continued access to the gaming system made him nervous, but once it became clear that Russia's goal was not to influence the outcome of the Olympics, but develop a war strategy, Billy's biggest fear had been allayed. In a strange way, both CGC and the Russians had the same wish—see the Gaming Olympics be a smashing success—though for radically different reasons. Claire popped her head in his office.

"Dr. Johnson on line one for you, Mr. Wilson." Billy had called him earlier and though didn't expect a call back until after classes, he had been pleasantly surprised.

"Dr. J," Billy said, "thanks for returning my call."

"Anytime."

"Looks like your boys have a fighting chance this year," Billy wasn't sure how to ask the question, but figured a bit of chit-chat might result in an easy segue.

"Yep," Dr. Johnson proudly responded, *"they have been pretty steady the last six weeks and it looks like a dogfight among the leaders."*

"Yeah. I've been watching the highlights. You will have your hands full with *Blunt Instrument,* but hopefully your team strategy will carry the day."

"We'll see, but I like our chances. What's up? I don't think you just called to ask about the team, did you?" Dr. Johnson was

still licking his wounds from *Blunt Instrument's* humiliation; the fact that Billy mentioned the victor made it sting even more.

"No, I didn't," Billy replied, pausing to choose his words. "Say, we've been working on an artificial intelligence project down here and wonder if your boy, Mitchell, might be interested in an internship for a few weeks."

"Really?" Dr. Johnson could barely contain his excitement. This was exactly the kind of opportunity for which he had been hoping for Mitchell. *"Let me check with Bob, but I think we can swing it—assuming Mitchell's game, of course."* Dr. Johnson was sure he could convince the school's Principal—Billy Wilson was their biggest benefactor after all—and had no doubt where Mitchell's heart lay.

"Please do," Billy replied, relaxing as he exhaled. Based on what he had learned about Mitchell's AI programming, Billy thought he had the perfect skill set for *Project Restore,* as they had named their Russian military project.

"When are you thinking?" Dr. Johnson volleyed back.

"Yesterday?" Billy chuckled as he replied. They were struggling with some of the final pieces and were concerned the Russians might move before they were ready.

Dr. Johnson laughed heartily. *"Just like you! OK, let me set the wheels in motion—probably Tuesday at the earliest."*

"As soon as you can, Dr. J, as soon as you can."

#

Dr. Johnson's Advanced Programming class had just ended, though most of the students barely noticed, engrossed as they were in the Olympics. Dr. Johnson's classroom had the best equipment and since it was the last class of the day, the gaming varsity just kept at it. The Queen's team had consistently remained among the leaders and they were now in the top three, though they had all nervously watched the highlights of *Blunt Instrument's* recent battles. Dr. Johnson smiled at the atmosphere he had created.

"Mitchell, can I see you a moment?" Dr. Johnson walked over to where the sophomore was pulling his books together. None of his classmates noticed.

"What's up, Dr. J?" Mitchell replied as the two moved away from the engaged gaming varsity.

"I spoke to Billy Wilson a short time ago and they are working on an AI project and asked if you wanted to help. Interested?"

Mitchell's eyes grew as big as saucers.

"Really?!" His reply was loud enough to elicit an annoyed glance from the gaming team.

"Yep. He wants you as soon as possible. I have to run it past the Principal, but I think he'll be good with it."

"That's awesome, Dr. J!" Mitchell was over the moon. "Do I need to bring anything?"

"Just your brain, son, that's what he wants to tap into," Dr. Johnson smiled. Seeing his students get this kind of opportunity was his favorite part of the job.

CHAPTER 52

Sergey Kachinko gingerly opened General Petrov's office door. After surviving a "slip" in Oleg Petrov's office, he would be more guarded each time he met the man behind closed doors—even if they had a common goal like they did now.

"Well, Sergey?" General Petrov was single-minded when on a mission and this one was intensely personal. Fortunately, Sergeant Kachinko had made progress tracking the criminal who had robbed both men, identifying the full account number at two of the three banks to which their money had been wired.

"That's it?" Oleg Petrov plaintively asked. He had expected at least a name and possibly an address, though it was clear he did not understand the global financial system.

"'It' is significant General," Sergeant Kachinko patiently replied. "These two accounts are outside the Swiss banking system and those countries are more willing to be 'flexible' in terms of providing information. I have already initiated a dialog with contacts in the Cayman Islands and we should have more detailed information shortly."

"Excellent, Sergey, excellent."

#

Mitchell got off the bus and made his way to Two Union Square. Dr. Johnson had offered him a ride, but Mitchell figured he could manage and arrived with plenty of time to spare. Though he was dressed nicely, he was easily the youngest to get on the express elevator headed to the 53rd floor, resulting in a few double-takes from his fellow riders. He was the last to get off and headed to the Receptionist's desk.

"Hi, my name is Mitchell Patkanim and I'm supposed to ask for Mr. Wilson. I have an internship starting today."

"Nice to meet you, Mr. Patkanim," the receptionist politely responded. Mitchell flushed slightly from embarrassment, wondering if maybe his dad was behind him.

"Thank you," Mitchell replied, before drifting over to the floor-to-ceiling windows, mesmerized by the early morning view. He was shaken from his reverie by Billy Wilson's voice.

"Mitchell, thanks for coming down so early," he cheerfully said.

"Thank you for having me, Mr. Wilson." Billy chuckled and shook his head at the boy's politeness.

"Come on, you're going to be working with a long-time friend of mine and I want to introduce you to him." The two headed upstairs.

#

It didn't take Greg long to figure out why Billy's mentor was so high on Mitchell. After only an hour together, Greg almost forgot he was dealing with a 15-year-old. While Greg was clearly a more advanced programmer, Mitchell was light-years ahead of him in the artificial intelligence department; the two of them hit it off right away.

"Wait a minute," Greg jumped in to stop Mitchell before he hit the execute key. They were working on some code parameters that, based on certain conditions, would allow them to gain control of the software Greg had downloaded from the Russian site. "Show me what you just did." Mitchell worked through an example as Greg nodded his head.

"The programming goal isn't to string a ton of baby steps together," Mitchell explained, "but to use what's already known about the system to make a few big assumptions based on the environment, then execute and check the results. It doesn't have to be perfect, just accurate. Then you take it to the next level."

After a bit more back-and-forth between the two programmers, Greg finally understood, nodding his approval at the simple elegance of Mitchell's thought process. They were close to being finished and at each step along the way, Greg shared some of his insights and experience. Mitchell ate it up, though he was sure that Dr. Johnson would not approve.

#

Sergeant Kachinko walked into the headquarters of the large Russian bank to speak with its president, Yuri Fedorov. General Petrov had directed his military colleague to act on his behalf to not only recover his stolen wealth, but to identify the perpetrator as well.

If the Sergeant could piggy-back on the findings to recover his own wealth, all the better.

"Sergeant Kachinko, welcome," the bank president met him in the lobby. Compared to the rough and bombastic figure cut by the patriarch of the old guard, Oleg Petrov, Sergey Kachinko was clearly part of the new military—polished and disciplined. Yet to the eyes of the president's staff, Sergeant Kachinko could also easily pass for a member of the secret police, so few stared as the president entertained his second senior military officer in the past two weeks.

"My pleasure, President Fedorov," Sergeant Kachinko firmly shook his hand, taking stock of the banker that Oleg Petrov said would "play ball." The two men engaged in simple banter as they walked back to the president's private office, Fedorov assessing that any colleague of Oleg Petrov worthy of the General's trust, was a potential ally to Fedorov as well.

"Your assistance in this matter is appreciated," Sergey Kachinko stated. "With the intelligence you provided, we have identified the account owner as being a resident of the United States, though I need a few more pieces of information from your records, Comrade Yuri." He showed the bank president a printout of all the research he had done and the foundation of his conclusions; the banker was impressed. He could use a man like this on his staff. The president pulled up the info and printed it out for Kachinko.

CHAPTER 53

Vladimir Buskin sat at the head of the table, eyeing each of the senior officials gathered. He had been in this room many times, in front of these men, discussing his grand vision for restoring the greatness of the Russian nation and its people. Though he knew the real reason for the alliance he had secretly negotiated with Iran, he had publicly justified it and the increasing sales of nuclear supplies and material as being in the national interest. That the alliance had also paved the way for unfettered use of Syrian airfields and the Iranian rail system was known only to him and a handful of his trusted lieutenants.

"Comrades," the Premier solemnly began, "our oil wealth has allowed us to begin a totally new chapter in the history of our great nation. Today our military will once again be feared across the globe."

The men nervously looked at each other as Buskin slowly became increasingly animated. He was known to be theatrical, but he seemed particularly so this afternoon. They had all seen the new technology-based attack strategy used to great effect in the Ukraine, but none of them realized the extent to which it had become so integral to the military.

"Today we will use our alliance with Iran as a platform to destroy the nation of Israel with totally revolutionary weapons and tactics. It will be a first—but critical—step in controlling the entire Middle East..." The Premier stopped to momentarily search the faces of those in the room, drawing out his last words for emphasis: "...and the oil...and the power...and the influence."

General Yikovich, one of the few fully briefed on the strategy, struggled to maintain a stoic face. He was churning inside, excited that his dream of ten years was coming true almost exactly as he had hoped. He had always found Premier Buskin's contrarian thinking to be one of his greatest strengths, but the plan to control the Middle Eastern oil fields by attacking the only nation in the region without one—Israel—was particularly brilliant. Deprived of the enemy that had been their main, unifying force, the surrounding Arab countries would likely turn on each other in a religious civil war between Shia and Sunni factions, leaving the Russians to pick up the pieces and control the oil. Buskin fully believed that even if the United States didn't steer clear of the region because of the Cahill Doctrine, their eviscerated military would be in no condition to fight the new Russian military juggernaut.

"As I speak, three companies led by General Petrov, as well as more than five thousand battle drones, have travelled by a special train from the Caspian Sea to a secret area near the border of Iraq. They are waiting for my signal to commence the attack, poised to begin racing towards Jerusalem.

"In addition, once we are in position, four of our Illyushin military transport planes will carry another thousand drones and three elite battalions over the Zagros Mountains of Iran to Syria's main military runway outside of Damascus, just miles from the Israeli border. Finally, three squadrons of our Sukhoi T-50 fighter planes will be joining them as we attack from both the north and the east. The key to victory will be the integration of the new artificial intelligence system and weaponry, with our best ground and air troops. Any questions?"

The monologue was brief, well thought out, and to all but General Yikovich, reflected an extraordinarily high stakes' plan, though none of the men dared challenge the Premier. Everyone believed it rash to rely on a strategy that had never been used in any military battle, but each man was more worried about being on the wrong side of Vladimir Buskin. They had also seen the strategy and weapons work in the Ukrainian battle and were astonished by its overwhelming success. No one was willing to go on record as a naysayer.

#

The Russian military was in an extraordinary position to commence their eastern attack on Israel. The secret agreement the Premier had executed with the Iranian leadership allowed the Russian soldiers and materiel to travel across Iran by rail in the middle of the night. The heavily guarded train ride from the Caspian Sea port of Amir Abad went undetected. The thick cloud cover continued just long enough to allow the Russians to offload their weapons in virtual isolation just north of the Persian Gulf at Ahvaz.

They were ready to roll. The best troops the Russians had were deployed under General Oleg Petrov and despite misgivings at trusting the Iranians for safe passage, the Russians were already much closer to their target than any of the troops had believed possible when they were loaded onto the Russian cargo ships at Lagan a few days before. More importantly, they had arrived near the Iraqi border—a relatively short 800 miles from their ultimate destination—virtually undetected, a luxury that would no doubt be gone now that they had revved up their war machines.

As they initiated their push across the desert into Iraq, the unusually high humidity kept the dust normally kicked up by the tanks, artillery and armored troop carriers rushing across the desert, to a minimum, allaying one of their biggest fears: the gritty, desert sand clogging the engine air filters.

#

The reports of an almost perfect eastern attack environment reached Premier Buskin and General Yikovich in the Strategy Room, and they could barely contain their excitement. The plan they had so carefully and secretly constructed had started in ideal conditions and was now being orchestrated to perfection. They had a direct, HD-feed from the communications' drones that would be videoing the entire proceedings. From a distance, the now moving Russian army and the thousands of drones flying less than a hundred feet above it was a fearsome sight, with the humming of the whirring drone engines barely overwhelmed by the thunder of the Russian vehicles. The wall of sound was music to their ears.

"General Yikovich, you are to be commended for getting us ready in such a short period of time," Premier Buskin told the room full of senior military and intelligence officials. The General beamed, though was careful not to bask in the glow of the compliment for too long. He also knew they had a long way to go before success could be declared.

"Premier Buskin, none of this would have been possible without the support of everyone in this room and the clever agreement you negotiated with the Iranians. The vision you showed to proceed will put you in the pantheon of military greats across the ages." Yikovich knew he has going overboard, but so far everything had proceeded remarkably according to plan. The fact that the weather was helping them as well made it feel like it was somehow divinely ordained.

"*Spasibo,* Comrade," the Premier replied, but then continued cautiously, "yet there is much that must happen before the world trembles at the resurrected Russian machine from the North." The two leaders were brimming with confidence, but everyone in the room also knew that wars rarely went according to plan. Striking early and hard, before the enemy was prepared, was often the key to success. It seemed they had that advantage and more, as the intelligence chatter right up to the moment they started their race across the Iraqi border suggested the West was more worried about the buildup on the Ukrainian front.

"Moses to Polar Bear, come in." The intercom crackled to life, it was General Petrov in the command vehicle near the front of the advancing Russian ground forces. General Yikovich smiled to himself, knowing the call sign for headquarters in this operation was that of his own gaming avatar. It was no coincidence. At the very moment the real army was on course to destroy Israel and take control of the entire Middle East, his gaming avatar, *Polar Bear,* was on autoplay prosecuting a similar strategy in the Gaming Olympics.

"This is Polar Bear," bellowed General Yikovich, the senior military official in the Strategy Room.

"Operation Oblaka, is so far meeting with no difficulties or resistance. The rail trip was without incident and after offloading, the desert conditions have presented no problems to our advancing forces." The commanding and confident voice of General Petrov rang clearly through the HD system. His command vehicle filled the screen, followed by numerous vehicles and a phalanx of drones, looking like a swarm of desert locusts. The men in the Strategy Room looked on in awe at the scene in front of them. It seemed like a war movie with an unlimited budget for special effects. But it was very real.

"*Da,* Comrade Oleg," Mikhail Yikovich replied. Although these men were adversaries in the political realm, when they were fighting on the battlefield, they put aside their differences. "We are experiencing no communications difficulties with our mobile Wi-Fi system. Planes are flying in cloud cover, visually undetectable, none of the communications tanks have failed and our back-up systems are on standby if needed. So far, all according to plan," General Yikovich communicated as he exchanged glances with Premier Buskin.

But Jeremy's electro-kinetic mapping program had detected them. In fact, his system picked up all the mobile Wi-Fi stations racing at full speed through the Iraqi desert towards Israel, with more powerful signals flying overheard. As he adjusted the bandwidth on his system, Tony and the senior intelligence officials stood glued to their spots as Jeremy's programming wizardry showed a dense web of white lines pulsating and fluctuating just north of the Persian Gulf.

"What the hell is going on down there, Smith?!" bellowed Defense Secretary Bryan Jacobson, one of the senior government officials gathered.

"It appears the rumors of some secret joint military operations with the Iranians are true, though right now only the Russians are taking part. It is possible they are headed to Israel and at this pace, could be there in another twelve hours or so," Tony responded in his no-nonsense Marine voice.

"Israel?" the President's Chief of Staff's disbelief was almost palpable. Bill James had been the architect of President Cahill's domestic green, social agenda and while he held the military in low regard, he understood what he had just heard. "What about the buildup on the Eastern Front? I thought that's where all the action was supposed to be!"

The United States had played right into Russia's hands. President Cahill had promised that materially reducing military expenditures would be one of his signature accomplishments and halfway through his second term, he had almost achieved it; the Russians were ecstatic. Premier Buskin knew that the US could no longer effectively fight on more than one front and the two sides were now standing off in Europe, just as he had hoped. Buskin had seen the systematic emasculation of the United States' military forces as an unbelievable gift in the pursuit of his goal of establishing Russia as the preeminent world power and now he was ready to pounce in the Middle East, his real objective from the start.

"We are still monitoring the threat there, sir, but it appears it might have been partly subterfuge," Tony cringed slightly as the words came out, but it was the truth. Jeremy had flagged the unusual number of Russian cargo ships heading to Iran as possible cause for alarm, but Tony had discounted it. Russia had been very public in its desire to build trade relations with Iran and the lifting of economic sanctions by the West had accelerated the process, so the influx of cargo ships seemed reasonable to him; he was wrong.

#

"Apprise of the existence of enemy forces General Petrov," General Yikovich barked into the microphone. After a slight delay, Petrov's voice filled the room again.

"There has been no sign of any hostile military," General Petrov barked back, *"apprise of anything you are seeing."*

Premier Buskin smiled knowingly before speaking into the microphone, "Comrade Oleg," he confidently started, "there are no adversaries, nor will there be. At least until it is too late. They are all waiting for us to attack Eastern Europe, as we predicted they would when we used our forces to test *Operation Oblaka*. Gentlemen, our plan is working and even the weather has been favorable. There is no way the Western forces can mobilize in sufficient time to prevent us from total victory once Phase Two is implemented. It is ordained!"

CHAPTER 54

"How the hell could we be in the dark about the whole damn Russian military being on the western border of Iran?!" The Chief of Staff couldn't believe what he was hearing. To not know the chief historical adversary of the United States was halfway to Israel in full attack mode was a shocking development.

The Defense Secretary stepped in, "Bill, there is no time to point fingers here, we have an urgent military situation on our hands. At least we know now." He turned to Tony, "what *is* that down there, and how do we counteract it?"

Tony took a deep breath and looked at Jeremy. "It's a mobile Wi-Fi system that appears to be running their military operation."

"Wi-Fi? You mean the internet?" The Chief of Staff was incredulous at what he was hearing. "They are running their military operation using the internet?! What kind of CIA BS is *that,* Mr. Smith?" The Chief of Staff wondered to himself if they had cut enough of the budget if this was the kind of crap they would get for intelligence.

"Not exactly the internet..." Jeremy blurted out, *you idiot,* he thought. He had heard enough of the politician's inane drivel and couldn't hold his tongue any longer. All eyes turned to the young analyst manning the controls of the video feed.

"Who the hell are you?" The Chief of Staff's agitation was growing by the second.

Tony piped up, defending his young charge. "This is Jeremy Thomas, one of our analysts from MIT. He's the guy who programmed the Electromagnetic and Kinetic Mapping software that we are looking at right now."

"Huh?" It was the Defense Secretary's turn to chime in. "What exactly does that mean?"

"Jeremy, it might be best if you explained." Tony wasn't exactly thrilled at his analyst's outburst, but he didn't understand the program well enough to be able to describe it; he had no choice but to turn his young protégé loose.

#

Darkness was falling in the Middle East, as the Russian military machine continued its headlong rush across Iraq. The drones were flying close enough to the ground that they did not show up on the ground-based radar tracking the night sky. The four Russian planes providing the airborne Wi-Fi umbrella to the drones below were the same as the Iranians used, so their existence hadn't set off any alarm bells among Western allies until they strayed into Iraq. The urgent intelligence chatter had not only confirmed that that had now happened, but that they were also escorting a major movement of the Russian military. Israel was going on full alert as darkness fell. In a few minutes the Russians would turn on the lights.

#

Jeremy cleared his throat as all eyes of the senior political, intelligence and military leaders looked his way.

"Gentlemen, what Director Smith is referring to is a means of tracking movement using electronic signatures," Jeremy was nervous, but his voice was steady and confident. He knew this stuff better than all the men combined in this room, of that he was sure. "The bandwidth we all use in our Wi-Fi and radio communications is composed of different wavelengths that our system has been programmed to show up as different colors."

Jeremy split the screen to show the video clip of the Ukraine battle. "Please turn your attention to the left-half of the video screen if you will." Jeremy was obviously in his element. It made Tony proud that he had such an asset on his team, even if he was a bit worried that one of these men might try to make him look foolish.

The screen came to life with an array of multi-colored lines, like a laser light show. "Here is the program capturing the Russian attack in the Ukraine," Jeremy started. "Each color shows a different element of electronic warfare. The red lines are outgoing pulses locking onto targets. The return color is graded from yellow to orange, depending on how fast and in what direction the target is moving. The green lines are counter-signals, using the laser lock to attempt to send a deadly payload back to the attacker. The blue is the drone's response to being lit up on the counter-signal return message, changing hue as it takes evasive maneuvers. The explosions are what they are."

Chief of Staff Bill James was the first to speak.

"Damn, it looks like one of my kid's video games. But you're saying this was the real battle?"

Jeremy looked at Tony. The Director spoke.

"Yes it was. My reaction when I first saw it was the same as yours, sir."

The Chief of Staff seemed mesmerized by what he saw on the screen, but the Defense Secretary quickly interjected.

"Gentlemen, we have what appears to be an angry Russian army screaming across the desert, heading towards our closest ally in the Middle East, and while this video game stuff might be interesting to you, we have to give the President some options. And frankly, what I see on the right side of the screen doesn't look anything like the one on the other!"

Jeremy quickly fast-forwarded a few seconds to the segment showing the white lines that Tony had been first to notice. "Please bear with us a few more moments, sir." He glanced at Tony, who discretely gave him the thumbs up.

"As you can see in this clip above the Ukraine, there are white lines connecting all the drones to a number of central communications' drones, and the 'spider web' if you will, connecting all the drones, fluctuates as the they move." Jeremy quickly highlighted the live screen of what they were seeing in the Iranian desert, a web of drones connected by pulsating faint white lines to communications' hubs both on the ground and in the air. "In my estimation, that is exactly what we have here."

As the men looked at the screen, the communications umbrella suddenly took on a dark, burnt orange hue, as though the Iraqi desert floor had just caught fire.

"WHAT THE *HELL!!...*" The Chief of Staff's voice was quivering at the thought that the battle had already started on the Iranian-Iraqi border and he hadn't even spoken to President Cahill yet.

Jeremy looked down at his monitors, which had more detail than the screen above. The electronic signature indicated the infrared wavelength, as though all of the equipment in the desert went to night vision at the same time. Tony looked at Jeremy questioningly. What had just happened on the screen was out of his league.

"Fascinating," Jeremy whispered to himself, before formulating a response to the question.

"The change in hue reflects nothing more than that they appear to have turned on their navigational infrared lights," Jeremy announced as matter-of-factly as he could, "though they have increased their speed."

The electronic filter on the screen Jeremy programmed looked like a giant cloud of molten lava being dragged through the desert. Viewed through an electronic lens, Jeremy imagined it was what the "Pillar of Fire" mentioned in Exodus must have looked like.

"Can you go to the normal satellite link?" the Defense Secretary queried. It sounded more like an order.

"Yes sir." Jeremy deferentially replied, pulling up the normal feed from the birds in geosynchronous orbit over Iran. The lights of the cities in the area showed through the clouds, but where the "pillar of fire" had been, there was nothing.

"Put the infrared up next to it," the Defense Secretary barked. Jeremy did as he was told. The two visuals showed the same thing, but only Jeremy's souped up feed had the "pillar of fire."

"Damn, Bill. If what this boy is saying is true, we've gotta helluva mess on our hands. Buskin's fixin' to start World War III and we can't even see their damn military speeding free as a bird through the land of one of our sworn enemies. It doesn't get any messier than this."

#

The moment the Russian military command flipped the switch to turn on the infrared lights of every piece of equipment they had cruising across the Iraqi desert, the screens in the Strategy Room in Moscow went to a reddish-orange hue, reflecting the change in wavelength. But to the men in the desert riding in the transport carriers, the only thing they noticed was that the desert was very dark and thankfully, cool.

#

The United States' brain trust remained in the Strategy Room, discussing possible options. The Russian military was speeding towards Israel and as far as they knew, no one there knew how serious it had become. Everyone was fixated on the presumed threat in the Ukraine and it was all a ruse. The meeting was coming to a close.

"Hey boy, what did you say your name was again?" The President's Chief of Staff called out, his Southern twang more pronounced for effect. Jeremy tried not to be offended.

"Thomas, sir. Jeremy Thomas," he replied, somewhat crestfallen, though he remembered he was still a rookie; just being in the same room with these men of power was a significant moment in his short career.

"Thomas, huh? That's some real good sleuthing boy," the President's Chief of Staff said before surreptitiously handing him his business card. "Lemme know if you got any other ideas, ya' hear?"

"Yes sir," was all Jeremy could answer as he shoved the card into his pocket before Tony could see it.

The Chief of Staff turned to the Director, who was finishing up a conversation with the Defense Secretary. "You've got a real good 'un there, Tony."

#

Tony and Jeremy were left alone in the room, and Tony both scolded and congratulated Jeremy for his performance.

"I know that Bill James can be a pompous ass, but you need to pick your battles, son. I have seen him rake more senior people than you over the coals and I don't want to be scraping you off the floor."

Jeremy nodded apologetically.

Tony's tone softened. "Still, that was some quick thinking when they switched those infrared lights on, well done. Now go home and get some sleep and be back here in six hours. No telling what might happen in the next few days and I need you—particularly now that Bill James has you on his radar. Hell, you'll probably rue this day for that reason alone!" Tony laughed out loud, putting his arm around Jeremy as though he were his son.

CHAPTER 55

The President's military advisors were called into an emergency session to discuss what steps to take in the face of the rapidly escalating situation in the Middle East. They knew they did not have the strength to provide Israel with much in the way of military support, but there were some Delta Force units available. They would be sent to go after what had been identified as the weakness in the Russian plan, the communication links. Unfortunately, the American force had had fewer than twelve hours to prepare for a battle with mostly unknowns and they were already airborne.

#

"Delta 1 to MedCom," the Delta Force's commander barked into the com-link of his fighter plane as he led the team towards what they were told was a strange collection of attack vehicles of unknown strength and capability. "No visual of enemy yet, but radar signature suggests moderate threat." They were halfway across the desert.

"Roger, Delta 1," came the return call of the Mediterranean-based forces. *"Be careful. Intel says we aren't sure what's ahead, but be on lookout for drones."*

The Russian attack drones were flying in stealth mode and while the Delta Force capability was significant, they had no idea into what they were heading.

#

"Polar Bear to Moses," General Yikovich hailed his colleague with a sense of urgency. "Looks like we have company, Oleg, my friend. American fighter planes and jammers on the way."

"Roger, Mikhail. Nothing visual, but radar is picking them up. We are in 'stealth mode' no?" came the reply of the lead of the Russian forces racing across Iraq.

"Roger. 'Stealth mode' engaged and operational; the drones will protect you my friend," General Yikovich countered. "They are close, Moses. Happy hunting."

#

Oleg Petrov grunted. He was still unsure the Russian strategy was sound, but they would soon know if it could handle a real opponent and not just the virtual ones on which they had been practicing the last few months.

"All forces on alert. Bogies gathering for aerial attack." No sooner were the words out of General Petrov's mouth when a group of American jets emerged from the clouds near the horizon, screaming for the deck and looking for what appeared on the radar screens as a small contingent of hostile military vehicles. Almost simultaneously, the first wave of General Yikovich's stealth and attack drones merged like a flying wedge and departed from the rolling Russian military. General Petrov watched them go.

#

"Holy shit!!" yelled the American commander, looking out across the desert at what appeared to be a flying shield headed straight for them. His radar was showing nothing and yet he could not only see the dust cloud being kicked up by the Russian army steaming through the desert, but more menacingly, something flying directly at his group of attack fighters. "MedCom, do you see what I see?" His forward cameras were beaming a high speed video signal back to the aircraft carrier in the Mediterranean, which clearly showed they faced a much larger foe than they had anticipated.

"Roger, Delta 1," came the reply. *"Attack at your discretion, but prepared to get the hell out!"*

"Delta 1 engage NOW, but be ready to take counter measures as necessary. Attack force of unknown strength and capability!" the squad leader commanded, with only a trace of anxiousness in his voice. His fighter team peeled off two-by-two into attack position.

#

Queen's gaming varsity had maintained their dominance in the Middle Eastern theaters and they were about to engage against a Russian foe, *Polar Bear,* whose army and air force were heading east near the northern tip of the Persian Gulf.

"Here they come, boys!" Brad yelled. "Engaging air force!"

#

"They're in," Greg anxiously murmured as he monitored the Russian back door log-in; the artificial intelligence program kicked in as well.

"I see it," Billy calmly replied. Their visuals showed an impending aerial battle between the Queen's team and a Master 3-Star General, *Polar Bear*. Based on the success of each team so far in the Games, it had the makings of an epic battle.

Billy punched in Seb's number and his Security Chief picked up on the first ring.

"Seb, I want you to monitor the Queen's team for the next fifteen minutes or so," Billy cautiously said, trying not to sound overly concerned. "Dr. Johnson has noticed some unusual stuff lately and I told him I'd check it."

"Roger," Seb replied.

#

General Yikovich's mind was in overdrive. He knew his avatar, *Polar Bear,* was on autoplay and its aerial forces were in attack mode in the Gaming Olympics, facing one of the top three teams, Queen's. But unlike in the real battle for which he was currently commanding, Yikovich's air force was heading east, just as the American *Delta Force* was, poised to engage with General Petrov's forces. It was the first real test of the integration of StormClouds' AI system and the CGC gaming system.

#

The US Delta Force team was one of the best the military had for tactical warfare. Whatever it was they were facing, its commander had confidence they would prevail, though he always hated dealing with an opponent of unknown strength. His enemy was coming out of Iran and was clearly Russian, while he was flying over Iraqi territory and defending Israel. Geopolitics was a crazy game.

Suddenly the drones were upon him.

"What the—" he yelled into his cockpit, surprised how quickly it had occurred; he immediately engaged in evasive maneuvers, but he couldn't shake them long enough to get a bead on the advancing Russian forces.

"Master 3-Star, my ass!" Brad roared as he picked off *Polar Bear's* air force one-by-one. No matter how good CGC's virtual military signature system was, the autoplay feature was no match for Brad Jeffries' live aerial skills. *BetterThanYou's* air force and artillery fighters were dominating this battle of Master 3-Stars, though Dr. Johnson was not there to see it.

#

"I can't shake 'em either!...they're like locusts...I'm hit! I'm hit!...I've lost my wingman!" the com-link was a chaotic opera of voices, as the group of elite fighter pilots were being overwhelmed by *Operation Oblaka's* aerial attack drones.

"Retreat! Retreat! Get the hell out of here NOW!" screamed the squad leader, words he had never uttered in any battle before. But whatever it was that he was facing, he had never seen such a quick acting or evasive aerial force and he knew he needed to save as many of his men as he could. Five more planes went down as they tried to disengage, including his own. While they had managed to take out two of the Russians' mobile Wi-Fi tanks, their own ranks had been decimated, with only three of the original twenty-four fighter planes able to limp back to the carrier in the Mediterranean. It was a devastating defeat.

#

As Greg and Billy watched both the virtual battle and the computer program screen, it was still unclear how the two systems worked together, but if it was somehow recording a battle for playback, they were getting their money's worth. Queen's varsity had decimated the better part of *Polar Bear's* air force, which had decided to retreat rather than die.

The battle had taken about ten minutes. Both men had been so engrossed in what they were seeing, they almost forgot the Security VP was even on the line. Billy hit the un-mute button.

"Thanks Seb," Billy replied. "Did you notice anything unusual?" At Greg's suggestion, Billy was still keeping Seb in the dark about the AI program, though he wondered if Seb's insights might help them solve the puzzle of what the two programs were attempting to accomplish working together.

"No, maybe a bit more stress on the system in Russia, so I'll check that," Seb replied, before adding as an afterthought: *"but your boys at Queen's totally annihilated that Russian. Boy, what a butt kickin'! It's like they almost knew what was coming."*

Billy took note of his security chief's observation. It had been innocent enough, but Billy had been preoccupied with the system breach and was beginning to wonder if somehow Queen's was tied into it. Maybe they *did* know what was coming. He and Greg shared knowing glances.

"I was watching them, too," Billy cautiously said. Seb's comment, the one-sided nature of the battle and the fact that the AI program seemed to focus on the Queen's battle was pointing to something Billy didn't wish to countenance—Dr. Mikel Johnson just might be involved. His mom had been Russian after all, and while it had never occurred to him before that perhaps his mentor had ulterior motives for his interest in Cloud Gaming Co., it did now.

"Do you need me anymore?" Seb asked expectantly, *"if not, Susan is holding for me on the other line."*

"No, Seb. We're good. Thanks for your help and insights. Keep up the good work." Billy knew his Security VP had been stung by the Code Red and was also more than a little nervous about the emergence of Greg. He wanted to make sure he still knew he was a trusted part of the team. Billy punched the button to hang up.

"That was interesting," Greg said.

"Seb's comments?" Billy queried.

"No, the whole battle," Greg countered, "though Seb's comments about Queen's crystallized something for me." Greg was unsure how far to go with his thought, he knew how close Billy was to Dr. Johnson.

"What?" Billy dreaded the response. It was clear they both were thinking along the same lines.

"Maybe someone at Queen's is your problem. I don't think that Native American kid is it, but if he figured out how to get in, maybe someone else did, too."

"You mean like Dr. Johnson?" Billy voiced what they both were thinking.

CHAPTER 56

The American attack and recon team had been routed and though the Russians had lost a few communications tanks, their mobile network remained uncompromised. As General Petrov's force continued its headlong rush across the Iraqi desert, their video cameras focused on the smoldering wreckage of twenty-one American fighter planes.

"Polar Bear to Moses," Premier Buskin's voice boomed throughout the room as he hailed General Petrov's command vehicle. Buskin had been the one to choose the call sign of "Moses," feeling the notion the Russians had "wandered in the desert" as a second-rate nation for far too long as more than apt. He would be the one to take his country to the Promised Land.

"Moses here," came General Petrov's gruff reply.

"Damage assessment?" Premier Buskin tersely said, a smirk on his face.

"Us or them?!" roared Oleg Petrov, cackling as loudly as he had in months. He had had a front row seat to the next generation of battle tactics; he had to admit Yikovich's drones had been astonishing in their effectiveness.

#

Tony Smith watched the replay of the video screen in front of him for the tenth time, attempting to get his head around what he had just witnessed. He knew the fighters that had gone in were some of the best the United States had and they had been annihilated. They had been successful in destroying a handful of the communication's hubs, but at an enormous cost in life and equipment. There had to be another way.

#

Jeremy Thomas had been to the White House once before, as an eighth-grader on a field trip. He had been awestruck then by its grandeur, but as he walked through the halls of it now, it was its gravitas he felt. He had analyzed the electro-kinetic signal of the most recent battle, briefing his boss on what he felt would be the best course of action, and whether his advice would be considered or not, he knew it was sound.

His heart skipped as Bill James made eye contact and nodded as Jeremy walked into the room behind his boss and sat down. Moments later the President walked in and took a seat.

"What the hell happened out there in the desert, Bill?" the President wasted no time as he pointedly looked at his Chief of Staff. "I'm the one who has to tell those parents their boys are dead." The room suddenly had an urgency to it that Jeremy had never experienced.

"The Russians have a revolutionary drone attack system, sir. We knew they were working on it, but not how far they had gone with it," Bill James somberly spoke as he shot a quick glance at Tony Smith. The Director swallowed hard. "We've heard rumors they might be using some high-powered, wireless system to run their drones, though we don't have confirmation. We tried to take it out, but it is much more advanced than we thought."

"Director Smith, thoughts?" The President quickly shifted his glare to Jeremy's boss.

"Based on what we can assess, the drones are all single-purpose vehicles and some have stealth capabilities." Jeremy clicked through pictures they had taken with their surveillance cameras, followed by a few brief video clips of the just concluded engagement with the American force; the advisors in the room digested the one-sided battle being replayed on the screen.

"Damn," the President somberly intoned, "these are our best guys, right?" he continued rhetorically. "Does Israel know what's headed their way?"

"We have shared our intel with them," Director Smith replied.

"Thoughts on how to counter?" The President was wasting no time.

"Their actual attack force is skeleton in nature," Tony began, "the drones seem to be doing all the work, sir. As we have seen, their elusiveness makes them a formidable foe in a dogfight. I think our best option is to do whatever necessary to destroy the mobile Wi-Fi communication system, a series of tanks and airplanes."

"If we can't dogfight them, what do you suggest?" the President asked.

"We have identified the communication hubs that connect them together. We think the drones have an upper speed limit slower than our missiles. If we use our fastest and most evasive missiles to outrun them, we believe we can take out the communication hubs and render the drones ineffective."

The President pondered the plan for a moment. "How much time before they reach Israel?"

"As fast as the Russians are moving," Tony stated, "maybe six hours."

The President looked at his Defense Secretary. "Options, Bryan?" Jeremy had seen the Commander in Chief in the media and the methodical, calculating man in front of him was nothing like he remembered.

"Mr. President, we have seen the Russian capabilities and the plan seems like our best option at this point. Frankly, there isn't much time for anything else. We just need to keep the Israelis apprised of everything that is happening. This is potentially their Armageddon scenario."

"Do it," the President was as emphatic as he was brief. "Gentlemen, keep me abreast and good luck." And with that, the President was out of the room.

The Secretary of Defense walked over to Tony Smith and said, "We'll need your guy," he nodded ever so slightly at Jeremy, "to give us the coordinates of what we're going after and we'll take it from there."

#

Within ten minutes of the close of the meeting, a wave of fighter planes armed with HARM missiles were off the deck of the aircraft carrier, USS George H.W. Bush. The electronic signature of the communication tanks and planes had been loaded into the missile guidance system; all the pilots had to do was fire and then high-tail it back to the carrier. A second wave of jets would be right behind them, on a different vector; they were taking no chances. They had heard what happened to the Delta Force and so they would also keep their distance.

#

The Navy F-18s spread out, each team with multiple targets. The HARM missile was as close to a sure thing as the Navy had, fast and accurate to within a foot and given the exactness of the coordinates they had received from the CIA, maybe even an inch.

They could see the swarm of drones headed their way, but each team had loosed their missiles in short order and were already headed back to the carrier, hitting the afterburners and leaving Russia's new weapons in the dust. Nearly a hundred missiles were using the com-link signals as homing pigeons.

#

"Missiles are away," crackled the radio link. Jeremy was manning the controls of the electro-kinetic feed monitoring the attack. The missiles were pulsating in the ultraviolet scale— reflecting a speed faster than they hoped the drones would be able to match. The drones were reacting to the incoming threat, some attempting to form a shield of stealth above the tanks and others trying to determine an appropriate intercept vector. It was clear to Jeremy they were having trouble with both tasks.

#

"Incoming!" yelled a Russian soldier manning the controls of the first Wi-Fi tank under attack. He could see that his defense drones were being overwhelmed by the speed and nimbleness of the HARMs. There wasn't time to say anything else before his tank exploded in a ball of flames. A similar result was happening across the plain as one missile after another evaded the drone defenses to strike the targets.

#

"Yes!" Jeremy whispered to himself as he discretely pumped his fist; his recommendation they go after the Russians with speed was paying dividends. As he watched the tanks explode one by one, he could see that the drones were affected as well, some of them wobbling and others gliding towards the desert floor, effectively rudderless. While Jeremy was disappointed the drones weren't crashing, without the Wi-Fi network to guide them, they were virtually useless and as tank after tank was left in flames, the communication web was shrinking.

"Looks good, Thomas," Tony walked over and put his hand on Jeremy's shoulder. "As sorry as I feel for the men down there about to be slaughtered, what they were trying was madness. Let's just hope they don't have some kind of back-up."

Jeremy's heart skipped; he hadn't thought of that. He hadn't seen any back-up communications' system other than that on the planes, and they were being taken care of as well. Yet, as bold as the strategy was and as aggressive as their attack had already shown itself to be, perhaps there was another.

#

General Yikovich could see what was happening on the monitors and his momentary euphoria had turned into concern.

"Engage the satellite link," he ordered Sergeant Kachinko. In a few moments, the links between the drones and the military command came back to life, the downed drones lifting off to join their mechanical brethren in the sky and protect the men riding in the other vehicles.

#

"Uh oh," Jeremy mumbled to himself. While most of his team had been watching the main feed showing the destruction of the Russian tanks, he had been focused on the electro-kinetic screen and the system of communication links was coming back to life. "Tony, we have a problem."

The Director could see it, too. The multiple communication webs they had watched fade away with each successful tank hit, were coming back, linking to each other like mobile hot spots, but all powered by a strong signal from Russian satellites above.

"Damn," the Director exclaimed. He knew there was no way they were prepared to take down a Russian satellite; he hit the speed dial button for the SecDef. The conversation was short and while Jeremy could not make out what had been said, he knew it must have been glum.

#

Billy and Greg were trying to make sense of what they had seen. The Queen's team had overpowered a solid foe and the AI program had been engaged during the battle. Billy had wondered out loud if his mentor, Dr. Johnson, had anything to do with it because they had just seen his team trounce a solid foe. Billy's attention was momentarily distracted by the muted TV. The Fox anchor had just come on with a "Breaking News" story. He quickly hit the sound button.

"...the Defense Department has denied it, but eyewitnesses are reporting that US and Russian military forces engaged in an aerial battle in Iraq, just north of the Persian Gulf, with the Americans losing multiple aircraft to a revolutionary Russian weapons system..."

Billy and Greg looked at each other, their mouths agape, but not because they had been correct in presuming the Russians were working to implement *Battle for Babylon* into their military command structure in the future. They were stunned because the Russians seemed to already be using it. They hoped Mitchell Patkanim was as good a programmer as Dr. Johnson indicated he was and that his artificial intelligence program was ready to go.

CHAPTER 57

Surrounded by foes, Israel and its defense forces were as fast as any military in the world at getting to full readiness, and given the rapidity of the Russians approaching from the east, they would need every second. The intelligence received from the United States about the effectiveness of the foe was worrying, but they were defending their very existence, and would fight more desperately than any hired gun might. Their air force was rotating shifts, protecting their borders but not venturing into Iraqi air space until knowing for sure the intentions of their foe inching ever closer.

#

As the Russian armored vehicles and attack drones stood ready to begin their long descent towards Jerusalem from Mount Nebo, General Petrov was mesmerized by the sunlight shimmering off the Dead Sea. Though he had little time for fools who believed in a higher being, he was keenly aware of the history of the Middle East and knew how powerful a motivator religion could be for those inclined. He had read how the Jewish people had come to this very spot after wandering forty years in the desert, seeing the land promised by their God for the first time. Given the turmoil of the last few thousand years, he wondered if it had been worth it. It brought the faintest of smiles to his face as he kicked the dust off his boots and returned to his armored vehicle.

The Russian army was poised to achieve a breathtaking victory, and though he was one of those who had initially believed attacking the Middle East was an incredibly reckless gamble, General Petrov was pragmatic enough to recognize the visionary genius of Mikhail Yikovich. They had come this far almost exactly as his technology colleagues had predicted, though it did require his men to properly carry out the mission. Execution of the strategy of others was what Oleg Petrov excelled at, regardless of whether it was with an iron fist or deceptive guile. *There will always be the need of those to execute,* he thought, *perhaps that is the path of the old guard.*

On their march from Iran, his Russian soldiers and Yikovich's drones had obliterated all who had tried to stop them. The Americans had been first, and while their second wave had destroyed most of Russia's ground-based communications links, forcing them to rely on their satellite feeds, that, too, had gone off without a hitch. The Jordanians, nominal allies of the US, had put up token resistance, but weren't willing to be the last line of defense between the Russians and Israel. The Russians had not lost a single piece of equipment since the American missiles had blown up most of their communications' tanks. Their military force was in remarkably good shape for as close as they were to achieving victory.

Yet, General Petrov expected a stiffer fight from the Israelis—they were defending their homeland, after all—and their reputation for fighting was legendary. Nevertheless, as good as the Israelis might be tactically, he knew their equipment was essentially the same as that of the Americans, which had already proven ineffective against the advancing Russian army. They had also not needed to use their ground attack drones since the brief Ukrainian battle and felt the element of surprise was on their side.

General Yikovich's strategy of mimicking the best video gamers had performed remarkably well and he had ridden one of the leaders, Queen's, right to Israel's doorstep. His attack drones had worked almost to perfection both offensively and defensively, and now they were about to systematically destroy one of the best militaries in the world. They waited for the last piece of the attack force to take its place.

As General Petrov stood moments away from swooping down Mount Nebo, past the Dead Sea and on to Jerusalem, he wondered what the namesake of his attack's call sign, Moses, felt on surveying the very same land General Petrov and his army would soon take over.

#

Three massive Russian transport planes hit the ground with wheels smoking in southern Syria, the already retracted back ramps spraying a rooster tail of sparks as they dragged on the ground. Each plane slowed just enough to allow the boxes carrying the battle drones to be yanked out of the cargo bay one-by-one as the rush of the outside air hit each box's trailing parachute like a high-powered rocket. As the boxes slid to a stop, small explosives blew off the tops, activating the self-mobilizing Russian battle drones. In remarkably short order, a thousand of the armed aerial and ground attack drones were hovering, awaiting commands from the mobile Wi-Fi signal now being generated by a series of Russian satellites. The Russian troop carriers rolled off the planes last, barely touching ground before the pilot punched the throttle and banked left to avoid Israel's deadly surface-to-air missiles.

Timing was critical as the Russian fighter jets were closing fast on their target, and as the last cargo box lid skittered away, the aerial drones suddenly turned skyward and were soon two thousand feet in the air. The Israeli air force was already prepared for battle, having been scrambled as their radar system picked up the approaching Russian warplanes. The sudden appearance of a wall of drones preceding the fighters activated the surface-to-air missiles; Israel was now on full alert on its northern border as well.

#

"Russians planes just landed *where?*" the President's Chief of Staff was about to explode. He saw the President's legacy going up in flames right before his eyes, and he was the one driving the bus.

"Syria, sir," Tony Smith calmly replied via the com-link. *"They touched down only for a few moments to drop off drone weapons and men."*

"Dammit Smith!" he screamed, "I thought you and your boy managed to derail those damn things!"

"We took out the tanks and planes running the system, but didn't get permission to go after the satellites that are now running it," Director Smith continued to maintain his composure. He was not going to be drawn into a pissing match with President Cahill's Chief of Staff. The facts spoke for themselves. Though he had begrudging respect for all the Chief of Staff had managed to help the President accomplish, Tony hated what the politicians had done to both the intelligence service and the military.

"Any more good news?" Bill James hammered out each word as he spoke it.

"Negative, sir," Tony replied, all business. *"Sukhoi T-50s have also just showed up on radar—they are five minutes out. Israeli planes are already on the way."*

"I see," the Chief of Staff seemed finally over his tantrum and the brain trust was now trying to figure out what to do next. "Where are they vulnerable, Smith?"

"Their drones have proven virtually unassailable. We think the only way to stop them is to disconnect their communications. Thomas' program has them directly linked into three Russian satellites over the Middle East. Not sure there is time to take them out, though."

It was the Secretary of Defense turn to speak. "Director Smith, you know we will never get the President to authorize the destruction of a Russian satellite," he said definitively. "Is that the best you can do, Tony?"

"I'm afraid so, sir. I know we are talking about a dramatic step in terms of escalation. But if they are successful here, it is only a matter of time before those drones are descending on Washington, DC." The Director was remarkably calm on the outside, but raging on the inside. He knew half the senior Israeli intelligence corps and was sickened by the thought that they were all likely to be dead—or worse—in the next few hours.

Jeremy was also in turmoil. He strongly believed the Russians were mirroring the combatants in *Battle for Babylon* and though he had argued with Tony about how to use that idea, he had failed to persuade him.

#

For a war junkie like Billy Wilson, the Russian military command feed that Greg had hacked into was both riveting and terrifying. They had access to feeds of both Russia's northern and eastern approaches, and while the parasitic AI program was constantly activated, it would be easy for Greg to insert Mitchell's override code. It was just a matter of when.

Billy and Greg were astounded at how much the Russian military command seemed to have integrated *Battle for Babylon* and the ongoing Gaming Olympics into the overall strategy. The StormClouds' AI program was also more effective than they expected, but the fact that the Russians had to blend their own code into it made it less efficient and easier for Mitchell to create his hidden override command. Billy felt badly that Mitchell wouldn't get to watch his artificial intelligence in action; perhaps they could show him a redacted clip when the dust settled.

#

The Russians were ready to swoop down from Mount Nebo to the east and the Golan Heights to the north. The aerial attack drones hovered a few hundred feet above them, waiting for General Petrov's order to proceed.

"Mikhail," General Petrov began, "I have doubted your strategy from the beginning, but I now see you are right. You have shown yourself to be a visionary and a patriot, and I bow before you and your colleagues in Department T. We stand on the precipice of an era-changing victory, and I salute you."

#

Both General Yikovich and Premier Buskin were moved. They had seen the humiliations that General Petrov had endured from unknown foes, and yet he was humble enough to acknowledge the changing of the guard.

"Oleg, my friend," now it was General Yikovich's turn to laud his colleague. "I would never have been able to accomplish such a Herculean task without you constantly challenging me every step of the way. Together we will drink to our great victory on your return." And with a theatrical twist as he received confirmation that the fighter jets to the north were racing over the aerial drones climbing to accompany them, he turned his colleague loose: "Comrade, you are free to attack."

#

General Petrov revved up his troops and started his descent towards Jerusalem. He anticipated it would take his fighter jets at most five minutes to join him. He watched the video screens focused on the north, with the stealth drones flying below the Russian fighters, confusing the Israeli SAMs. The attack drones were positioned to support the fighter pilots as they had done against the Americans. A squadron of Israeli fighters coming out to meet General Petrov's desert group were quickly redirected north with the appearance of Russian fighters, though the Russian Sukhoi T-50 jet fighters had already begun their descent for a bombing run of Jerusalem. Soon, they would be providing air cover for General Petrov's troops.

#

The first Israeli counterattack to meet General Petrov's war machine was chopped up as easily as the Americans had been. The second and third ones fared little better; General Petrov was totally in his element as his ground attack drones and artillery moved through the best that Israel had to offer with little resistance. He could see a squadron of the Russian fighters headed his way after having strafed Jerusalem; it was all coming together.

CHAPTER 58

The efficiency of the new Russian attack machine was chilling even to a war buff like Billy. The Russians were clearly ahead of anything the rest of the world had to offer. He shuddered to think that his creation had the potential to be the impetus for such a one-sided World War III.

"It's time, Greg," Billy anxiously said as smoke billowed from Jerusalem. "Let's hope it works."

"Indeed," Greg worriedly volleyed back. He could hardly think straight. The conscience that had barely whispered to him in years was now screaming at him in a full-throated roar. Greg was sickened to think how his betrayal of Billy years ago had already killed hundreds—maybe thousands—of innocent people and unless they were successful in rewiring the Russian AI code, perhaps millions.

He could only wonder how Billy felt. The Russians had killed his father ten years ago and now were using his brainchild to start World War III to kill so many more. Greg's heart pounded as his fingers raced across the keyboard to gain entrance to the backdoor of the Russian artificial intelligence software and download Mitchell's code. It was elegant in its simplicity and reminded him of Billy's code so many years ago, but neither he nor Billy had any idea if it would work as hoped in real time.

Billy and Greg watched the video feed intently. They weren't exactly sure what they were looking for, but they noticed an almost imperceptible change. The drones had been surgically effective in their tactics against the US fighters, but their aggressiveness had now softened. The Israeli fighters no longer seemed to be sitting ducks for the drones, but they still had the Russian air force and a fierce ground force with which to contend.

#

Jeremy noticed the change in tactics, as well. The Israelis seemed to be doing better on the ground and in the air, though Jeremy couldn't tell if it was the fact that the Russians' drones no longer seemed to be in all-out attack mode, or that the Israelis had figured out how to fight the Russians.

"Tony, the Israelis seem to be getting the hang of it," Jeremy stated.

"Yeah, I see it, too," the Director said.

#

"Hmm," Billy murmured. "The Israelis seem to be putting up a better fight. Did we do that?"

"Hard to say," Greg shot back, "but it's not what I was expecting. Those things still seem to be damn effective." The stealth drones were a more than capable shield for the sophisticated Russian T-50s. Though the Russian kill rate had fallen, the Israelis were struggling against the Russian air force and were still losing more planes than they could sustain for long.

"Did we miss something?" Billy wondered anxiously. The Russian advance had clearly slowed, but they were still on offense.

Greg quickly countered. "I don't know, man, it's not my strength. What do you say we get Mitchell on the horn? I'm pretty sure I did what he said we should do, but we never got a chance to try it real time, so we might have missed something." Greg stomach was tied into knots and he had a splitting headache; he knew when he was out of his depth.

"Is that such a good idea dragging a kid into this mess?" Billy worriedly queried.

"Do you have a better idea?" Greg shot back.

"Not really," Billy replied. "I dunno, maybe we should just pull the plug on the game and see if that has any impact." They were getting desperate. They knew what was going on, they just didn't know what to do to stop it.

#

The Gaming Olympics were shaping up to be a final battle between *Blunt Instrument* and the Queen's team. They were fighting from different directions, but as each vanquished foe left the battlefield, the two leading combatants edged not only closer to each other, but to the halls of the *Palace of Babylon* itself. On paper, the Queen's team had the advantage, fighting with three Masters, each with their own idiosyncratic style. Brad's methodical approach made fighting him like running against the wind—it wasn't clear why it was such hard work, yet progress was modest and time consuming.

Nate's style was almost diametrically opposed—aggressive, occasionally reckless, always unpredictable. Engaging his avatar, *MVP,* after dealing with Brad was like being a batter in a baseball game and facing a flame-thrower after a knuckle-baller—the change of pace caught most opponents unprepared and few survived.

However, *Blunt Instrument* had already vanquished the Queen's team once. Her aggressive tactics made her more than an even match with Nate, but it was her discipline honed from years of ballet that had pushed her to the top as much as anything. Beth was also the only known player to have ever beaten *Ronin.*

Ronin. He was a dangerous wild-card, suddenly showing up in the heat of the most intense battles of the Games, and while he had no known allegiance, the Queen's team often seemed to benefit from his actions. Whether that was by design or sheer coincidence was not clear, but one thing that did seem to be the case was that after his two defeats, *Ronin* seemed bent on revenge as much as anything.

Dr. Johnson's class had lost all pretext of being a teaching forum, having become command central of the Queen's team's drive for the gold. Mitchell actually enjoyed the high level of fighting, even if he was ambivalent about his classmates' success. The team had just overwhelmed *Polar Bear* in a methodical, but entertaining, battle. Mitchell knew Brad was predictable, but his disciplined approach made him a formidable opponent, nonetheless.

Amid the noise, the cheering and the visual chaos of Dr. Johnson's high-tech classroom, Mitchell almost didn't notice his phone lighting up.

"Hello, Mr. Galkin!" Mitchell was thrilled that his internship mentor was calling, though surprised it was during the middle of the day when he had to have known he was in class. Dr. Johnson's ears perked up. Billy had told him about Mitchell's prowess at CGC, but established protocol was that all calls to students during school hours were supposed to go through Dr. Johnson.

As Dr. Johnson watched his prodigy's face, it was clear there was a serious conversation going on, Mitchell nodding in understanding as Greg walked him through their problem. After about a minute, Mitchell handed the phone to his teacher, whispering that Mr. Wilson wanted to talk. It was now Dr. Johnson's turn to be part of a serious conversation, though how serious he would not know.

"Absolutely," was all Mitchell heard the teacher say, before Dr. Johnson handed him back the phone. "You're free to go back to your dorm and work on an emergency project Billy has for you. It sounds like it's really important, so don't dally." Mitchell grabbed his backpack and was out of the room, almost before Dr. Johnson could finish.

CHAPTER 59

Sergeant Kachinko's undivided attention was critical to the actual battle escalating in the Middle East, but because he was also distracted by his avatar's fight in the Gaming Olympics, he missed the brief lull in the AI program that occurred when Mitchell's initial code was activated and started to entrench itself. In a matter of moments, whatever window of opportunity Kachinko might have had to counteract its growing control was gone.

Both Yikovich and Kachinko noticed the lessening of the aggressiveness of the drones. The Israelis still didn't seem to be making much progress against them, but they also weren't being decimated as had been the case prior to insertion of the new parasitic program. General Yikovich viewed the change in tenor of the battle with concern, though Sergeant Kachinko saw it merely as a function of the artificial intelligence, itself.

"Comrade General," Kachinko started, "what we are seeing is normal. As AI programs absorb data, they learn and often find ways that are more optimal than conventional thinking would allow. I agree it seems counterintuitive to see a lessening of aggressiveness as a positive, but perhaps it is leading the Israelis into a false sense of security."

Moments later their screens once again became a blur of explosions and smoke. The Israeli air force had decided to go into attack mode against the Russian aerial force. The attack drones suddenly resumed their aggressive attack on the opponent, with three more Israeli planes exploding in midair. The Israeli air force immediately disengaged.

"There, it is just as I presumed." A slight smirk emerged on Sergeant Kachinko's face. "The moment the Zionist attackers assumed an aggressive stance, our drones attacked when they were exposed. Perhaps we would have lost a few planes fighting things more conventionally." The Sergeant shot a quick glance the Premier's way. Though Buskin stayed focused on the screen, he had heard every word his political officer had uttered.

#

As soon as Mitchell booted up his fastest school computer, he called Greg back. He was immediately put on speaker phone.

After a brief review of the previous conversation, Mitchell logged into the CGC gaming system using his hacked credentials.

"So this program is going into that Russian code, right?"

"Yes, it is." Greg's unemotional response belied the cold fear he felt watching what was transpiring in the Middle East.

Mitchell had been fascinated by the Russian program's existence in the Cloud Gaming system and now that he specifically knew what he was trying to counteract, it was an easy fix. Billy and Greg could hear Mitchell tapping away on his keyboard, and after a few short moments, Mitchell announced he was ready to implement. The two friends looked at each other; they had found a kindred spirit.

"Let 'er rip, Mitchell!" Greg stated forcefully. Mitchell hit RUN and exited out of the program.

#

The impact was immediate. As the two men in Billy's office watched the video feed from the east focusing on the advanced Russian jet fighters racing in to provide General Petrov cover, the trailing T-50 exploded in mid-air, a direct hit from an unidentified missile. Moments later there was a second explosion, then a third.

"Whoa!" Billy and Greg said in unison, forgetting that Mitchell was still on the line.

"What?!" Mitchell anxiously interjected.

Billy shot Greg a worried glance. "Your program's just working like a champ, Mitchell," Greg casually replied. "Nice work."

#

"WHAT THE HELL IS GOING ON MIKHAIL?!" General Petrov shrieked as flaming pieces of Russian fighter planes rained from the sky. Though he was a seasoned military man and expected things to go wrong in battle, what Petrov was now witnessing indicated a catastrophic shift in advantage. The T-50 was a daunting dogfighter even without the drones, and though it had not appeared the Israeli jets had compromised the Russian line of defense, his eyes were seeing a radical change in the aerial battle.

As each T-50 dropped from the sky, it geometrically decreased the air cover that was supposed to protect General Petrov's small, but elite unit as it invaded Jerusalem. The Russian pilots suddenly were fighting two opponents—one flying the Star of David on its wings, the other their own attack drones. A fourth, then a fifth Russian plane was in flames, crashing into the Dead Sea like fire and brimstone.

#

"I do not know, Oleg!" General Yikovich yelled back, glaring at Sergeant Kachinko, who had been responsible for the artificial intelligence interface. Kachinko was furiously typing on his keyboard in a desperate attempt to shut off both the satellite link and the AI to let Petrov escape. Everything Kachinko tried worked momentarily, before being overridden by the subtle, but dramatic, macro change in the program that Mitchell had downloaded.

#

As the Russian troops dodged pieces of falling debris, the ground attack drones programmed to target the Israelis, began shooting at Russians instead, and then at each other. General Petrov could not believe his eyes. His best men were being gunned down in cold blood, not by Israelis, but by machines that his own colleagues had programmed. It was beyond comprehension. He had assumed the worst that could happen was that the drones failed to perform as expected. He could not imagine they would be turned against his own men and their weapons. He was powerless to do anything, the drones and his men being so close to each other that destroying one would mean killing the other. He was enraged.

#

"Vladimir!" General Petrov desperately screamed. *"I trusted you! And yet you sent me out to get slaughtered by Mikhail's damn machines!"* His screams echoed throughout the room, as the horrified country's military leaders began to cover their ears. *"You knew! You knew this would happen!"*

General Yikovich could feel the blood draining from his face as every video feed vividly showed how badly the Russian military was being trounced. As it became clear the system was malfunctioning, he and Sergeant Kachinko tried every possible tactic to shut it down. Yet every disengagement sequence they had integrated into the code was quickly overridden as the AI system recognized an outside force was seeking to kill it and fought back.

The two Russians had no inkling their program had been compromised, thinking the sheer audacity of their plan was sufficient to protect it. As a result, virtually all their time and energy had been spent on crafting an offensive strategy, and hardly any on building a defensive one.

Premier Buskin sat paralyzed. He had bet the farm on this new strategy and had believed the experts who said it would work. And it *had* worked—he had seen it—but the plan was going horribly awry and its crafters seemed powerless to stop it. He doubted even he would be able to politically survive such a debacle.

#

While the Israeli fighter jets did not know what was happening, it was clear that the Russian fighter planes—at least those still flying—were just trying to survive. The Israeli planes fired at anything that wasn't theirs. It was difficult to tell how successful they were, but one thing was certain: the Russian air force was being routed. In an attempt to salvage what he could, General Yikovich ordered his planes to disengage, leaving General Petrov and his men without air cover on the Jordanian desert floor.

#

General Petrov watched helplessly, with Israel in sight, as the drones he hated destroyed nearly every Russian plane on the mission, leaving his tank battalion and infantry vehicles completely defenseless from air attack. The drones designed to protect General Petrov's tank, only served to provide him with a front row seat of his helpless battalion getting machine gunned down by General Yikovich's drones. Petrov screamed at Buskin, he screamed at Yikovich, he screamed at everyone and anyone he could as he watched thousands of his men being slaughtered by drones painted with the Russian flag he fought to defend.

"TURN OFF THE SOUND DAMMIT!" Premier Buskin roared to nobody in particular, before the technician running the video monitor cut the sound. In an instant it was quiet—deathly quiet. But the intensity of General Petrov's rage filling the screen could still be felt, even through the silence. When the drones finally turned on General Petrov, the tank in which he was riding was destroyed last. It was a slaughter of Biblical proportions, with General Oleg Petrov, call sign *Moses,* dying just outside the Promised Land.

The toll was unimaginable: virtually all of the Russian air force that was supposed to provide air cover for General Petrov's ground invasion of Jerusalem had been destroyed, none by the enemy. The T-50s had been sitting ducks for their own attack drones, most of which fired their rockets simultaneously from point blank range. Every other piece of materiel had been destroyed or captured; the only soldiers to survive were the few in the T-50s that had managed to escape. It was ghastly.

#

The Russian high command weren't the only ones that had watched the slaughter. Greg and Billy had also seen it, as well, watching in stunned silence. While they felt no remorse at Petrov's death, it made both men feel less than human to know they had played a role in the death of thousands of others. In some sense, they had become just like the Russian monsters they hated. Greg quietly turned off the video feed and shut down his computer. They had seen enough. Not a word was shared between the two men.

CHAPTER 60

Yuri Fedorov sat alone in his office and looked at his watch. It was 7pm, two hours past the time his employees left for the day, the only sign they had been there being the flickering computer screen savers scrolling through random pictures. He checked his schedule again, wondering if perhaps he had miswritten the appointed meeting time with Sergeant Kachinko. The two of them were tantalizingly close to identifying who had looted the two Russian military men of their wealth, and the Sergeant wanted to personally share the final piece of information that he was certain would unlock the mystery. The bank president felt it prudent to meet after everyone had left for the day so they could work in private, but the usually punctual military officer was already thirty minutes late and his phone calls immediately went to voice mail.

#

Although Sergeant Kachinko had not returned to his flat in three days, his gaming computer was still on. His avatar, *Pinball,* was desperately trying to keep it together on autoplay, but with each passing hour, the increasing degradation of its tactics without Kachinko's direct input became evident. He had always relied on guerilla tactics and opportunism, a style that lacked the consistency necessary for CGC's autoplay feature to perform at its best. *Pinball* had already been relegated to Master 1-Star *Samurai* when the avatar's autoplay sensed an "opportunity" to re-engage a previously vanquished foe. This time he was no match for *Blunt Instrument's* well-oiled army. *Pinball* was quickly wounded by ground forces, before *Blunt Instrument,* herself, finished him off. Beth had no way of knowing that her real opponent, Sergey Kachinko, was undergoing a similar fate.

#

"I hope you are having a pleasant afternoon, sir!" came the baritone voice of the doorman. *If you only knew what I just witnessed,* Greg thought to himself, nodding as he walked through the entrance of the WAC. He shuffled to the elevator and was in his room in short order, switching on the TV to CNN. There was still no mention of the battle he and Greg had witnessed, making him wonder if the public would be kept in the dark about what could have easily been the start of World War III if they hadn't intervened. The burden Greg now felt given the death and destruction he had in some way set in motion years ago by betraying Billy and his creation was suffocating.

He hit the mute button and logged into the Cayman bank account he used for his consulting business. The balance was in the millions, much of it stolen from Sergey Kachinko, the tech savvy, single playboy of the Russian military. Greg stared at the screen and gently rocked back-and-forth, his left hand over his mouth. As he reflected on the last decade of his life and remembered the crushing pain of losing his best friend and then his own father, he impulsively tapped in a sequence of numbers and hit ENTER.

#

It was late at night when the unmarked utility truck stopped on Moscow's Bolshoy Kammeny Bridge, ostensibly to fix a burned out street light. While the driver placed a number of bright orange cones around the truck to warn the few passing drivers that work was being done, his colleagues began unloading their tools and setting up for the night. As the cherry-picker slowly lifted its occupant up to the flickering bulb, two of the other workers discretely pulled a tightly wrapped plastic bag from the side of the truck and unceremoniously dumped it over the side of the bridge. The muffled splash in the Moskva River almost thirty feet below began a journey that would ultimately end with the decomposed body of a Russian soldier washing up on the Iranian shore of the Caspian Sea. There was nothing to identify it as that of Sergey Kachinko's.

CHAPTER 61

The Queen's team had reached the final stage of the Gaming Olympics and the Jeffries' house was overflowing with friends and family, all seated in the fifty-seat, home theater in their basement. Mitchell was also there, staggered by the fact that he was sitting in a private theater as big as the movie theater in his home town, but thrilled to be sitting in the dark next to Marjorie.

Queen's and *Blunt Instrument* had reached the *Palace of Babylon* almost simultaneously, but on opposite sides. Brad and his team were at the west entrance, arriving via the longer, but less difficult Euphrates' route, while *Blunt Instrument* had navigated the more treacherous mountain route that led to the east entrance. Although there was no guarantee either team would leave victorious, the discipline both teams had shown throughout the Games made it a strong bet that the gold medal would be decided today inside the walls of the opulent, but dangerous, palace.

#

Yuri Fedorov looked at the envelope that had arrived by regular mail. It bore no marks of the sender, and both the address and the notation "PRIVATE", were handwritten. He opened it to find a piece of paper with a sequence of numbers on it. Though nothing else was enclosed, he knew exactly what he possessed: information he had expected to receive from Sergeant Kachinko the day he never showed for their scheduled meeting. He logged into the system and typed in the numbers.

"Hmmm, that's odd," the bank president absent-mindedly said to himself. He recognized the name that popped up from his query, though he thought he had been dead for over a decade. He would do some more checking.

#

Once in the *Palace*, Brad entered the *Chamber of Mirrors* with a mixture of boldness and fear. Although he had been eliminated in a similar spot the previous year, he had spent hours analyzing this year's final stage to prevent a repeat performance. He was confident in his approach, and as he slowly maneuvered inside the *Chamber*, it was paying dividends. Brad carefully counted his steps, avoiding the trap door sequence that had just claimed his teammate, *Slasher*. As *BetterThanYou* emerged from the corridor, he got a glimpse of *Blunt Instrument's* long blonde hair.

"There she is Brad!" Nate Brackman excitedly exclaimed, "lemme go after her!" *MVP* pushed his way past Brad's avatar, jostling him slightly and knocking him off balance, just as the mirrors rotated revealing not only the Queen's team, but *Ronin* and *Blunt Instrument* as well.

"Dammit, Nate," Brad growled, "you knocked me off my count and I missed the rotation sequence!"

"Sorry man," Nate said, though he wasn't really. He wanted the glory for himself and was much better than Brad in the close quarters of the *Palace*. He also had an innate feel for mazes and had already left Brad in the dust.

"Whoa, there's that *Ronin* dude," Brad said quizzically. "How did he get in here?"

#

Ping! Yuri Fedorov's computer alerted him to an incoming wire transfer to an account he had been monitoring; he clicked on the message.

"Oh my!" he exclaimed out loud. The president recognized the sender, as well: Sergey Kachinko. "Huh?" He was now totally confused. He had heard nothing from Sergeant Kachinko in two weeks and presumed him dead, and yet someone controlling the Sergeant's account had just wired $3 million to Oleg Petrov, someone he knew was dead.

CHAPTER 62

Dr. Johnson was alone in his classroom. He had been gaming non-stop for more than twelve hours and though exhausted, had managed to pull even with the leaders. He had positioned himself to help his protégés at Queen's win the gold, but if he could also exact some revenge in the process, all the better.

He had seen *Blunt Instrument* as well and despite the never ending reflections of the *Chamber of Mirrors,* felt he had a bead on her. As the mirrors rotated once more, he saw the warrior princess coming into view and *Ronin* crouched, poised to kill her as she emerged on his level.

"YAAAAWWW," Dr. Johnson snarled, as *Ronin* thrust his sword in a feral rage of vengeance into the back of his blonde nemesis. The avatar collapsed forward as *Ronin* stood over its body. Dr. Johnson's primordial scream of catharsis would have been heard by the whole school if it hadn't been the weekend.

#

"NO!!" Everyone at the Jeffries' home theater simultaneously erupted in anguish as *BetterThanYou* collapsed to the floor, face first. Brad Jeffries had been eliminated once again. The mood in the room considerably darkened. And while there had been whispers that *Ronin* was, in fact, Dr. Johnson, after watching him stab Brad Jeffries' avatar in the back, no one believed that now.

#

Hands on head, Dr. Johnson watched in stunned horror as *Blunt Instrument* came into view, mortified at the realization that it was not her blonde hair, but that of his prized student, he had just acted upon. He sat in shock, motionless, as *Blunt Instrument* twisted her dagger into *Ronin's* heart. Dr. Johnson's avatar soon joined *BetterThanYou* in a heap on the floor.

#

Despite the gloom at the Jeffries' house, Queen's still had a chance to win the gold. Cagey Nate Brackman's avatar, *MVP,* was quick and resourceful, but he had to beat *Blunt Instrument,* as talented a fighter as any he had faced. The two avatars simultaneously reached the *Invisible Bridge* that passed over the moat to the *Throne Room*. Their swords sparked as they clashed on the narrow strip of real estate, with Beth reaching the bridge first, backing out onto it with Nate in cautious pursuit. *Blunt Instrument* wobbled ever-so-slightly.

MVP saw the opening and lunged, extending his sword with his right arm for balance in the process. *Blunt Instrument* leaned back at the waist, just out of reach of *MVP's* dagger thrust, and kicked his plant foot just enough to send him tumbling face first towards her. She quickly skipped two ballet steps back, as the thrashing and screaming *MVP* fell into the abyss below. The Jeffries' fifty guests sat in stunned silence as the home theater fell deathly quiet.

#

Blunt Instrument was finally alone, but sensing danger, she quickly pirouetted. The *Throne Room* door was closing and the *Bridge* was crumbling. She immediately dropped her weapons and summoned all her energy and ballet experience, exploding in a leap.

#

Jeremy held his breath as *Blunt Instrument* floated over the chasm that separated his colleague from the gold medal and a million bucks. He thrust his arms out and screamed as she touched down and scurried into the *Throne Room* just before the doors closed. Beth had done it!

He pulled out his phone and punched in her number. A breathless Beth answered.

"Way to go, girl!" Jeremy screamed into the phone.

"I did it Jeremy!" Beth was both exhausted and elated; she had one more question: *"Um, Jeremy?"*

"Yeah?" he replied curiously.

"I've had enough 'virtual reality' for a while," she responded. *"I could sure use something 'real', if you know what I mean."*

"I think I do," Jeremy replied, grinning from ear-to-ear, "I'll be right over."

CHAPTER 63

While a week had passed since Elena Petrov had been told of her husband's death, he had confided in her of the attack on their finances and so the call from Yuri Fedorov wasn't totally unexpected. Nevertheless, she was still nervous walking into the headquarters of the country's biggest bank.

"Mrs. Petrov?" inquired a well-dressed man in his 50s.

"Yes," the woman answered, somewhat uneasily.

"I'm Yuri Fedorov," the bank president said, extending his hand. "I am so sorry for your loss. I liked your husband."

Elena Petrov nodded as the two of them walked to his private conference room, the click-clack of her high heels drawing the attention of the bank's staff. They were surprised at how pretty she was, given the notoriety of her husband.

"As you know, I was working with your husband on retrieving the money that had been stolen from you," Fedorov stated, as he leaned over her shoulder, glancing down as he placed a cup of tea in front of her. She was stunning.

"Yes, thank you," Elena replied somberly. "I am hopeful you have good news for me."

The bank president smiled.

"I do. In fact, I have very good news." Elena also smiled, the first time in months. "After a lot of investigation, we finally received a wire from the Swiss banking authorities earlier this week." Part of the statement was true, though President Fedorov had played no role in it. He was just trying to impress the now widowed beauty sitting in front of him.

"And?" Elena Petrov hopefully asked, leaning forward, while gently placing her hand on Yuri's forearm and squeezing; she felt liberated by the death of her husband.

"And I was able to recover $2 million of it." It was also a lie, but she didn't have to know the money had mysteriously showed up in the Petrov's account the day before, or that he had pilfered $1 million of the original amount.

Elena gasped as she put her hands over her mouth. "$2 million?!" It was significantly more than her husband had told her it would be.

"Yes, Mrs. Petrov—" the president started before she cut him off with another squeeze of his forearm.

"Call me 'Elena'," she softly purred. He could feel the blood rushing to his head.

"Only if you'll have dinner with me," he calculatingly volleyed back. "Of course, you understand to help the grieving widow of a patriot to manage such a sum would be my honor." He paused to assess her reaction; she squeezed his forearm again.

"Of course," the Russian beauty replied with a faint smile. "What time shall I expect you?"

Yuri Fedorov could not believe his good fortune. Not only had his acquaintance with Oleg Petrov provided him an opportunity to pocket an extra $1 million, but had also just resulted in a date with his beautiful widow. *Spasibo, Comrade Oleg, spasibo,* he thought to himself.

EPILOGUE

The last two weeks had been a whirlwind for Billy Wilson and his company. A winner of the Gaming Olympics had finally been crowned and the stock price was soaring because of it, quite possibly a major war had been avoided, and the murderer of his father was now dead. That he had been killed right before his eyes made him more than a bit uncomfortable—he realized it had changed him forever.

Billy's insides churned as he wondered how Susan would react if he told her what he had just witnessed, and that he had unwittingly helped orchestrate the killing of thousands—even if it included his father's murderer. His life had gotten a lot more complicated in the weeks since his childhood friend had unexpectedly resurfaced. Billy stared at Susan's picture as it lit up his phone on his speed dial; it rang twice before going to voice mail: *"Please leave a message for Susan Green of Cloud Gaming, where we're deadly serious about war games."*

Billy cringed. *Deadly indeed,* he thought. His heart sank.

\#

Greg logged into the backdoor of the Russian military system one last time. He not only wanted to see if either General Petrov or Sergeant Kachinko's e-mail account had been active since the final battle, but also to pay his last respects to his father. His heart stopped; there was a new e-mail in Kachinko's account from Yuri Fedorov: *I have traced the stolen money. Call me.*

THE END

Made in the USA
Monee, IL
22 January 2021